Steel Rose

By
Barbara Custer

Night to Dawn Magazine & Books LLC
P. O. Box 643
Abington, PA 19001
www.bloodredshadow.com

Print ISBN: 978-1-937769-51-2
Digital ISBN: 978-1-937769-52-9

Copyright 2016 by Barbara Custer

Front cover Illustrator: Dawné Dominique
Back Cover Illustrator: Teresa Jay
Editor: Carolyn Crow
Printed in the United States of America

Worldwide Electronic & Digital Rights
1st North American, Australian and UK Print Rights

Dedicated to Michael, as always, with love.

I would like to thank my editor, Maura Anderson, for helping me with the changes needed to ready Steel Rose for submission. My thanks go out to my fellow scribes at the Bucks County Pennsylvania Writers Group and the Writer's Coffeehouse for their support, encouragement, and critiques.

Finally, to Carolyn Crow and Dawné Dominique of Eternal Press / Damnation Books, thank you for your work in preparing Steel Rose for publication.

Chapter One: Deadly Toxins

Jackson Hospital's Intensive Care Unit, March 3, 2010, 11:00 a.m.

Shrill beeps blasted from Myles Stanwood's heart monitor. His oxygen saturation had plummeted again, testifying to the pneumonia ravaging his lungs. With pain stabbing through her gnarled, splint-clad hands, Alexis Carofalo grabbed a resuscitator bag and turned his head to feed oxygen into his breathing tube. She grimaced with each squeeze of the bag. Pain twisted through her joints like an old rusty nail. The frosty early March temperatures outside had made her whole day worse from the moment she walked out her door. She gagged at the fetid smell rising from the weeping gashes on his arms. The sight of the oily black pus trickling down his arms and elbows gnawed at her nerves. Most shifts in the intensive care unit left her too exhausted to feel any reaction.

No one said how Stanwood got those sores. Doctor Hoffman hated giving details and Stanwood's chart didn't offer any clues when she checked. Maybe she could ask another doctor. She couldn't remember when she last saw gashes like his. They looked like bites and the black, filmy drainage was getting worse by the day. Despite specialized medication, a formula devised by a Kryszka doctor, toxins from the gashes spread to his lungs, causing necrotizing pneumonia. His labile vital signs and dwindling urine output pointed to multi-organ failure.

The door opened moments later. A blonde nurse, Cindy, ran in, waving a slip of paper. "Stanwood's latest blood gas results," she said. "His oxygen readings are better. Doctor Hoffman said you can put him back on the ventilator."

"Thanks." Alexis edged her gloves off over her hand splints.

Indeed, she had to be gentle. Her joints stung with the slightest movement, and a four-workday stretch did not improve her symptoms. Ten years before, when she heard the words "rheumatoid arthritis," she'd convinced herself that a cure would come along before she had to consider Social Security disability. Now, looking at her crooked fingers, her bloated hands swollen against the white spica splints encasing them, she had to wonder. If only she'd chosen a desk job instead of respiratory therapy. At least with a desk job, she could use voice-activated software and other tools to accommodate her condition.

She rooted through her pillbox for a Percocet but found none. She must have used up her supply during yesterday's snowstorm. Wincing with every movement, she wriggled her fingers through the contents of her fanny pack. Surely, the wadded-up tissues and empty Reese's wrappers concealed a spare. She usually kept an extra pill wrapped in foil the way someone might stow a spare twenty. That was gone too. With a deep sigh, she called her doctor.

Another chorus of alarms tolled from Stanwood's room. Alexis raced back to his bedside and saw that his heart rhythm had ceased. She was giving him oxygen with the resuscitator by the time Doctor Hoffman led the code team, including the Kryszka doctor, into the room. A resident doctor began chest compressions.

"What happened here?" Hoffman demanded, looking at Alexis.

"He went into asystole." Alexis kept her eyes on Stanwood, trying hard to ignore Hoffman's reddening face. A renowned doctor in Philadelphia, Doctor Hoffman headed up Jackson Hospital's research floor with a temper that matched his rumored salary.

"I know." His voice grated with anger. "What happened before that?"

"Doctor Stanwood went into V-fib." Cindy referred to the monitor.

Morris, the nurse manager, cast a withering glance Alexis's

way. More than once, she'd overheard him saying he didn't want invalids working on his floor and he'd looked her way when he said it. She winced and dropped the resuscitator. After retrieving it, she squeezed it with her elbows. Better, but not great.

"The CA200 should have ..." Hoffman's silvery eyes darted from person to person. "Morris, set up the defibrillator. Now!"

"Right away." Morris reached for the paddles. "Alexis, get someone who can bag."

Alexis turned toward Hoffman. He was angrier than she'd ever seen him. His tanned face, features sharp like a rat's, had turned purple. He and Morris both had explosive tempers.

"I am bagging." She mustered defiance into her voice.

"No, I mean, I want someone who can *bag*."

Alexis scanned the room. Cindy and the code cart blocked the exit to her right. The resident continued his chest compressions at her left. Her coworker, Johnny, gestured at her from the doorway but the code team prevented him from entering the room.

"Johnny, I'm okay," she shouted over the alarms. "Morris has his problems."

Morris shook his head. "This is total..."

"I've got a pulse," the resident said. "Alexis, put him back on the ventilator."

After doing so, Alexis glanced at the monitor. His heartbeat was thready, but Stanwood had squeaked by with his life. So far. She turned to follow the others out of the room.

"Alexis." Hoffman's sharp voice cracked like a whip. "Not so fast."

Alexis whirled around, facing the head of the research department and his Kryszka partner. "What's the matter?"

Hoffman gave her another censuring glare. "You may not work on this floor wearing those splints. My patients don't need you tracking germs between patient rooms."

Alexis glanced down at her splints. They were great joint stabilizers, but unsightly ones. "I didn't track anything. I was wearing gloves, and besides, I wipe my splints with alcohol between every patient contact."

"Alcohol doesn't kill all pathogens, especially the kind Doctor Stanwood has. He's a VIP, and there's more to his condition than you know. I suspect we'll get more patients with a condition like his. I don't care what you do on other floors, but you may not wear them here."

Alexis felt her face flush. The Kryszka doctor, an anemic-looking male, listened with intent fascination. He wore a green isolation mask and tinted goggles that concealed his alien features. Maybe he knew how Doctor Stanwood got those gashes and he thought her splints might worsen the infection. Whatever. She'd taken enough grief about an illness no one could seem to cure.

"You don't have to yell at me in front of an audience. You're not my doctor, so go blow it out your ear!"

"Can you blow from your ear, Joe?" The Kryszka doctor spoke in a thick accent through his mask.

"Of course not." Hoffman frowned, and then looked back toward Alexis. "I may not be your doctor, but this is my floor. You do what I tell you."

"I'm talking to Human Resources about this." Alexis hoped she projected more confidence than she felt. "You don't know squat about the ADA laws."

"Maybe you are being too harsh, Joe," the anemic Kryszka doctor said in his thick voice. "She can wear special gloves over her splints when she cares for our patients."

"The gloves won't work, Yeron." Hoffman's frown deepened.

Yeron? Alexis stared at the pale man. Now she remembered when she'd last seen gashes with black pus. Jackson Hospital had received a rash of casualties with similar wounds before the underground Kryszka city exploded three years ago. Yeron had come to Jackson Hospital with a formula to treat them. She remembered attending the welcome reception the hospital had held for him. Maybe he wasn't so bad. At least he offered a solution that would allow her to work. She turned his way, ready to ask him about the ...

"I'm speaking with Dee about this. You may go now."

Alexis stared. "Doctor Hoffman, I ..."

"I said you may go."

Oh, how she hated his accusatory voice.

Chapter Two: Laurel's Error Causes a Death

Jackson Hospital, March 3, 12:00 p.m.

"Doctor Rat Face's an asshole," Johnny said in the hallway. "Don't let him get to you."

Alexis glanced at her watch. She was due to take her medicine. She had all her pills except the one she needed most. Her splints cut into her swollen thumbs and wrists. She shifted her assignment sheets to her left hand. Stinging flashed through her joints and made her drop her papers. If anyone asked her level of pain, with ten being the worst, she'd rate hers a twenty right now.

"Hey, are you okay?" Johnny retrieved her sheets and touched her shoulder. His blue eyes widened.

She shook her head. "Dee asked me to babysit Laurel. I forgot."

"Laurel can go to hell. Tell you what..." Before he could continue, his cell phone rang. He said something she couldn't hear into the phone and hung up. "I gotta go. Feel better."

* * * *

Between bites of tuna salad, Alexis massaged the joints in each hand. She glowered at the pages of charting yet to be done, all of it by keyboard. The pain had receded to a level three, but the relief she felt wouldn't last without Percocet.

Rustling startled her to attention. It came from a copy of the *Weekly World Reporter* in the hands of someone leaning against the doorway. Johnny Murkowski's wire-rimmed eyes peeped at Alexis above the tabloid. He folded the paper and walked toward her. He plopped down at the table beside her and burst into gales of laughter.

"The Kryszka think they can raise the dead." He shoved his newspaper toward her. "Get a whiff of this."

"I don't want to hear about it." Alexis continued massaging her hands. *Stop the pity party,* she scolded herself. *It's not Johnny's fault that your hands hurt.*

"How did Doctor Stanwood got those weird cuts? Does the article mention that?"

"They're not cuts. They're bites." He nudged his paper closer. "Read for yourself."

Alexis peeked at the headline. The words "Kryszka Revive the Dead" leaped up at her. Above the title, a full-color photo showed a scene that could have come from *Dawn of the Dead* with gaunt corpses marching down the street. The sight of those corpses sickened her. Gashes peppered their faces. Black liquid oozed down their cheeks and necks in ribbon-like strands.

"Holy shit!" She arched her eyebrows. "Their wounds look like Stanwood's. Do you think the people who made these creatures are trying to turn him into a zombie?"

Johnny shrugged. "Hell if I know."

"I thought all the Kryszka, other than Yeron, died when their underground city went up in flames. Steve told me about that place. It was gross, Johnny. The Kryszka strung dead people up on spider webs." She shook her head, frowning. "The newscasters assured us that we were safe. They said Yeron was the only survivor."

"The newscasters love to bullshit." Johnny leaned back in his chair. "If those zombies turn up at my doorstep, my Remington will send them to hell."

"You're lucky you can handle a gun." Alexis cast a baleful gaze at her puffy fingers. "I suppose I could poke out their eyes with my screwdriver and run."

"Shoot enough bullets, and that will take anything for a long dirt nap." Johnny raised his sand-colored brows. "What about your dad's gun?"

Alexis shook her head. "I can't handle it now. Too heavy." She took another sad look at her swollen hands. "Now if I had one of those plasma guns Steve told me about..."

The door banged open, rattling the empty chairs. A slow-moving moose of a woman, Laurel Grant lumbered into the room. She slapped her assignment sheets down onto the table where Alexis and Johnny sat.

Oh Lord, here it comes! Alexis regarded her half-eaten sandwich. If only her medicine didn't require the intake of food. The queasiness in her gut warned that her lunch might come up soon.

Laurel's husky body exuded the stink of stale oil and sweat. Her braided chestnut hair, blue-print scrubs, hazel eyes, and high cheekbones offered the potential for beauty. Instead, the oily streaks in her hair had turned her braids mud brown. Her dirt-crusted fingernails and hollow cheeks showed a poverty of both sleep and hygiene.

"Well, well, well." Her eyes glowered like muddy citrine. "Look who's sitting here."

"Whatsamatter?" Johnny grinned. "Got your panties in a twist?"

He followed his question with a bray of laughter. Alexis giggled until she glanced directly into Laurel's eyes. Cold, glittering marbles with birdshot pupils, they betrayed a dark crevasse, a woman disconnected from the familiar landmarks of her life.

Alexis touched her back pocket, felt her screwdriver, and breathed a sigh of relief. "What's wrong?"

"You!" Laurel stepped close to Alexis and bumped a hip against her shoulder. She leaned in close to Alexis's face. "You're the sorriest person I met."

Her breath reeked of spoiled meat.

Dammit, I should have called in sick. "Sorry about what? Never mind, I don't want to hear anything. Just go."

Another bray of laughter escaped Johnny.

"What's so funny?" Laurel demanded, her eyebrows lowered.

"Nothing." Alexis glared at Johnny, wishing he'd quit provoking Laurel. "Johnny's laughing over his tabloid."

"That's a load of bull. Dee dumped seven ventilators on me and gave you four. Then you sit here and laugh behind my back. Wait until I tell Abaddon."

"What are you doing here, Laurel?" Dee Hobson poked her

head to the doorway. "I got three calls from the nurses in your unit."

Any moment, her tears will start. Alexis tried flexing her fingers. Razor blades of agony cut swaths through her hands. That and the smell of soap-deprived therapist wafting from Laurel brought on another wave of nausea.

"I came here to ask for help." Laurel's dull eyes never wavered.

"You should have asked me to send someone instead of harassing people during lunch," Dee said.

"I'm sorry, but ... but..." The stony coldness in Laurel's voice shattered. Tears trickled down her cheeks. "I haven't charted, I haven't..."

Way to go, shithead. Alexis massaged her temples.

"Stop it." Dee edged toward the hall. "Go to your floor. Now!"

The tears stopped. Laurel stared with glittering, hate-filled eyes at Dee's back. Without answering, she scurried toward the elevator.

"That went well." Alexis managed a weak smile.

"Real well." Johnny cackled. "Who the hell's Abaddon?"

"Probably one of her imaginary friends. I'm surprised management hasn't noticed the way she talks to herself and the equipment."

Johnny shrugged. "They know, but they're afraid to do anything about it because she caught one of them doing nose-candy."

"Are you serious? Who?" Pain forgotten, at least for the moment, Alexis leaned toward Johnny. "Come on, give it up."

"All right." Johnny giggled and put his lips up close to Alexis's ear. "Doctor Tynan."

"Shit!" Alexis gasped. "You're talking about Dee's boss. Where did you ..."

"Shhh!" Johnny leaned back and waved toward the door. "I saw them around Christmas when I cut through the courtyard. Laurel's back was toward me. Tynan looked flustered."

Alexis chuckled. "I bet he was."

"Sooo ..." Johnny leaned back and looked at her. "What's

this about a plasma gun?"

"Steve said the Kryszka used them. They're like laser guns, much lighter than your typical gun, but just as deadly." Alexis sipped her water and remembered the haunted look on Steve's face when he'd described his foray into the Kryszka underground city. He was telling her "we all go through shit," but he'd needed to unload, too. "The police stockpiled an armory of those guns after the explosion. If I can get one, I'll roast any zombie that comes near my sister or me."

Johnny sighed. "Good luck. By now, the government's probably locked the guns away." He got up and started toward the hall. "I'd better get back to my floor."

* * * *

Alexis's cell phone rang five minutes later.

"Alexis." Laurel sounded like she was weeping. "I'm in room 415. Something's wrong with Bernice Mayes. She's choking."

"Shit!" Alexis jogged to the Surgical Trauma unit, grateful that she could still run. What'd happened now? During shift report earlier, someone declared Bernice Mayes stable enough for transfer to a routine care floor.

In room 415, Alexis squeezed past a crowd of nurses and peeked over Laurel's shoulder. Mayes's eyes rolled like those of a fear-maddened horse. Deltas of wrinkles converged on her gasping lips. Her mouth sought air and found none. The heart monitor tolled long, mournful notes, and each sound shuddered through Alexis's heart.

A purple cap closed off Mayes's trach tube, and Alexis knew immediately what the problem was. "Laurel, get rid of that cap. She can't breathe because you didn't deflate her cuff."

"What cuff?" Laurel hovered over the hapless patient, blocking Alexis's access to the bed. "What did I do wrong?"

"The balloon on her trach tube." Alexis nudged her shoulder. "Get out of the way."

"Huh?" Laurel gazed at Alexis with vacuous eyes.

"Move, damn you!" Teeth gritted, Alexis elbowed Laurel aside and yanked off the purple cap. Green mucus spewed from the trach, streaking her splints.

Too late. The line on Mayes's cardiac monitor went flat.

Alexis reached for the resuscitator bag for the second time today. This time she used the elbow and palm technique straight away.

"What happened?" Laurel wailed. "What did I do?"

Two interns rushed in, followed by nurse manager Morris. He glared at Alexis with eyes of deepest frost. "What are you ... never mind. Laurel, take over and bag."

"Huh?" Laurel's vacant eyes turned toward the ceiling. "What did I do?"

"Morris, something's up with Laurel," Alexis said. "If you have a problem, call Dee."

The senior intern started chest compressions. Even with the resuscitator wedged between her palm and elbow, Alexis paid for her efforts with white agony in both hands.

The cardiac line remained flat.

"What happened?" Laurel wrung her hands. "Oh, goodness, what did I do?"

You know what you did, shithead. Alexis winced with each breath she forced into Mayes. Someone hollered for the defibrillator. Morris wheeled the code cart toward the bed. Steve Leicht came in behind him. Laurel's rank smell wafted over Alexis, and she gagged.

Steve tapped her shoulder. "Here, let me do that. You don't look well. Go sit."

Alexis breathed a sigh of relief. "Thank you."

Alexis took one last look at Mayes, then Laurel. Johnny stepped in beside Steve and took over the bagging. Morris whispered something to Steve. The incident report would come next, but no report could save Mayes. If only she'd gotten here seconds sooner. She decided to muddle through the afternoon and let Laurel deal with the fallout.

* * * *

"Alexis, I need to see you."

Dee's summons impinged on Alexis's concentration. *Won't this day ever end?* She blotted the sweat from her forehead.

Inside Dee's office, hanging plants formed a maze, and room deodorizer oozed a vanilla fragrance. Alexis's hand started toward a ceramic dish of Reese's Peanut Butter Cups and Hershey

Kisses on the file cabinet. At the sight of the grim expression on her manager's mocha-complexioned face, she withdrew her hand. Anger bled through in Dee's dark eyes. Morris's report must have cited Alexis as the culprit, not that it surprised her. Those splints made everything her fault.

"I saw what happened before Mayes passed," she plunged ahead, taking a seat before Dee. "Laurel didn't put the tracheostomy valve on properly."

"I know." The anger left Dee's eyes, replaced by the resignation of a woman who'd received a dreaded diagnosis. "Doctor Leicht showed me the closed-circuit recording. The camera caught Laurel misusing the valve and you attempting resuscitation with your elbows. Worse, Laurel walked around a trance, mumbling, 'What did I do?' The Mayes family hired a lawyer." Her voice softened. "Laurel's dismissal process will get ugly."

Alexis jerked her chin. "Dismissal ... what?"

"Don't play dumb with me." Dee's features darkened again. "I heard you and Johnny talking about Doctor Tynan and Laurel."

Oops! Alexis covered her mouth. "I'm sorry."

"Doctor Tynan's going into rehab, so watch what you say." Dee sighed. "He asked me to handle Laurel's firing. I want Security present when I let her go. She's got the eyes of a person who'd kill just as soon as look at someone. Ask an officer to escort you to your car tonight. Better yet, take tomorrow off, too."

No kidding! Alexis touched the metal screwdriver in her pocket again. It came with a Good Grips handle and long, metal tip. She'd carried it since the explosion. Its solid, cushioned handle did more to ease her panic than any lame reassurances.

"I can take care of myself."

"I'm not sure about that." Dee's eyes widened with concern. "Doctor Leicht and Johnny said you looked ready to collapse. Does bagging hurt so much that you have to use your elbows?"

Uh, oh, here comes the Serious Discussion, the one leading to SSDI country. Alexis looked down at her bloated hands. "I made sure Mayes got good volumes of air."

"I'm sure you did." Dee leaned forward, eyes fixed on Alexis. "Are you taking narcotics?"

Alexis did not answer. Instead, she thought about the bottle of Percocets waiting for her at the pharmacy. Shudders crept up her spine. Before her death, her aunt, a board-certified junkie, had taken to Percocet like a frog takes to flies. On Auntie's good days, she slept. On her bad days, she added liquor to the mix and screamed with the slightest provocation. Perhaps Robin played her CD's too loud. Perhaps dinner was late. Alexis rubbed her shoulders, shivering.

"I didn't expect you to answer that one."

"You want me to go to Employee Health." Alexis dragged her trembling fingers through her hair, then stopped when her splint got caught in her thick curls. "This can't be happening. I promised my father I'd look after my mother and sister. Robin is mentally challenged. She's got severe asthma, worse than yours. I'll be useless to them now."

"Whoa, there." Dolores touched her arm. "Your health isn't a report card. Sickness happens."

"Some people don't understand that. The pain got brutal because I ran out of medicine. I heard Yeron—the Kryszka doctor—can work miracles. Doctor Leicht put me on the waiting list for Yeron's clinical trial, but it's taking forever for me to get my turn."

"Yeron's intelligent, Alexis, but he doesn't walk on water. The FDA has to approve all his treatments. You'll have to be patient."

"I can't afford patience."

"Can you afford trust?" Dee's tone of authority was gone, leaving behind the voice of a caring friend. "I never said anything about Employee Health. Morris and Doctor Hoffman complained because you stood up to them. They had it coming." She gave a sad smile. "Doctor Leicht and Johnny are worried about you."

"No Employee Health? No dismissal?" Better so far, but Alexis continued worrying her hair. "What options do I have?"

"Doctor Leicht recommended that you work routine floor care until your treatment options improve and I agree. I'd hate to see you hurt yourself so badly that you couldn't work at all. You've got to be honest with me when you need help."

"I appreciate that." Alexis let go of her hair and smiled. She was lucky to have friends. "Who will cover me today?"

"Johnny's taking your assignment. Give him your report and finish charting. Then go home and rest."

"Thank you." Alex got up and strolled to the candy dish. "Mind if I help myself?"

"Go ahead." Dee laughed. "You always do."

* * * *

Alexis quit her floor at two thirty. After picking up her medicine, she left the hospital through the back alley and headed to Bucella's for takeout.

Though she appreciated Dee's concern, no security person was going to babysit her. She avoided Security ever since her bout with pneumonia when a guard reamed her out for illegal parking. The officer's eyes had bulged when her cough shot a wad of bloody mucus onto his navy suit. He'd looked ready to piss his pants. She'd never trust her safety with such gutless wonders.

Outside, the biting wind whipped her face. Her breath came out in foggy puffs. Icy patches on the pavement threatened a back-breaking spill, but Alexis's mouth watered in anticipation of Bucella's garlic bread and stuffed manicotti. She paused a moment at the crunching sounds. Were those footsteps? The alley appeared deserted. With a shrug, she continued toward the restaurant.

A rancid odor hit her nostrils, sickly sweet and decayed sour. The stink worsened around an open dumpster near the back steps. "Ugh!" She gagged at the renewed onslaught of nausea. "Get me away from here."

Instead, her legs developed inquisitive minds of their own and stepped around the ice patches to the dumpster. Trash bags piled inside, but higher than the sides of the dumpster. A white towel with red poppies fluttered in the wind and slapped against the bags. Something rattled inside the dumpster.

Alexis crept up the four steps to the back stoop beside the dumpster and leaned over the railing to look inside. The stink of flyblown meat crawled down her throat, but she forced herself to look. Black, oily fluid leaked from a bag on top. Slabs of raw beef protruded through the tears in the plastic. Under it, someone had spread a huge towel across the bags. She realized the poppy designs were bloodstains.

So much for sanitation, she thought. *I'll be damned if I eat here now.*

Another gust of wind blew the towel, lifting it away from a headless skeleton sprawled on the bags below. Gristle and strips of blackened flesh coated the deformed xylophone of the rib cage and arm bones. Its skull rattled against the side of the dumpster. Beside the skeleton, a swollen green corpse in bloodstained dungarees grinned at Alexis with horrible chumminess, but with only half a face. More of the dark, filmy pus, like she'd seen on ...

"Oh, my God!" Alexis stumbled. The world swam around her in waves. Hand clutched against her stomach, she let loose a hot stream of vomit over the railing into the storm drain. Her hands throbbed, worse now with the cold. That no longer mattered. Someone had left two decomposing bodies in the dumpster near her favorite restaurant.

Her lips quivered. If only her father were still alive. With forty years of underworld connections, he'd known the answer to every problem. He'd have told her that someone had sent a warning.

Warning about what? Was Laurel involved? Doubtful, given her stupidity. Most likely a drug deal involving someone from Jackson Hospital had gone sour. She'd better stay out of it, especially if cops came sniffing around. According to her father, cops always caused complications.

A harrowing thought surfaced. Underground Kryszka who fed on humans left wounds with the black pus. Like the kind Stanwood had. The pus came from the toxic poison left by their bites. A hostile Kryszka must have survived the explosion and was killing now.

If her father were here, he'd talk to the "right people" in his organization. As a bodyguard, he'd dodged bullets and walked away from shoot-outs with minor wounds. He'd squirreled away enough money so her mother wouldn't have to work. Her mother spent sleepless nights, dreading the phone call, the one reporting him dead. Instead, a vicious growth in his lung felled him before

Alexis started college.

Aunt Susan had overdosed a few months later. Alexis ran into her health problems and a stormy marriage that nearly destroyed her. Now, this. Her father's death had opened Hell's gate.

Ice be damned, Alexis tore through the alley, clawing through her purse for a tissue. By the time she reached the cyclone fence surrounding the garage, her tears had come fast and hard.

"Oh, Daddy," she wept. "Why did you leave me?"

Chapter Three: Laurel Charts and Makes Plans

Jackson Hospital, March 3, 1:00 p.m.

After the doctors pronounced Bernice Mayes dead, Laurel stormed into the conference room adjoining Intensive Care. She plopped down before a computer, entered her password for charting and hesitated. Her head throbbed, a harsh, stabbing pain that aspirin wouldn't relieve. She'd taken a Steven Leicht reaming over Mayes and his shouts still boomed through her mind.

"Do you realize what you've done? Why were you staring into space?"

"Steve, I..."

"Did I give you permission to call me by my first name?"

"Alexis calls you anything she wants."

"That's between Alexis and me. You don't deserve a license."

"Neither does Alexis. I begged her to help me, but she was giggling over some magazine."

"Is that so? She seemed upset to me."

"Upset, my ass," Laurel said aloud. "I was just trying to relieve the poor lady's suffering." Was she? She remembered Alexis hollering about the patient's trach cap. The next instant, fifty people spilled into the room with a red cart.

"I'll never get any charting done unless I take something strong."

Massaging her temples, she darted a glance through the hall. Empty. After she logged off the computer, she crept out to the elevator and headed down one floor to the respiratory offices.

She stopped inside the coat room. After digging a bottle of Motrin from her purse, she swallowed four capsules with water from the bathroom. On the way out, she bumped against Alexis's locker. She recognized it by the photographs of her mother and sister taped to the front. "Damn bitch," she said to the locker. "If you'd kept your mouth shut about the trach valve, none of this would've happened."

Right now, she'd bet Alexis and Doctor Leicht were holding a meeting of the Laurel Grant Hate Club in Dee's office.

It was time Alexis got punished.

After another glance through the hall, Laurel crept into the equipment room. Most people avoided its cramped quarters, but no one bothered her there. The pain ebbed enough that she could chart while listening for her phone to ring. Silence. She smirked.

Dee could stew and posture all she wanted. Laurel's job was secure. She had taken out insurance the day she'd caught Vice President Tynan snorting nose-candy. She'd taken the photographs quickly. Her camera came in handy for photographing both dead people and miscreant executives. Tynan looked ready to faint when the negotiations began.

"You bad boy." She made a shame-shame motion with her fingers. "Go straight to jail. Do not pass go, do not collect two hundred dollars."

"Don't do this, Laurel. You must have children to put through college, medical expenses..." He went down the list, ready to give away his savings.

"I don't want your money," she said after Tynan sweated for a good half hour. "Keep me on your payroll and Dee Hobson off my back."

Laurel's smile widened. Charting complete, she headed to the break room where the other therapists congregated for shift report.

"Hey, shit drawers, what's up?" Johnny called from the window. Titters erupted amongst the recitation of vital signs and assessments.

"Johnny, stop." Yvonne, the slim woman beside him, slapped his shoulder. "I have to get a report from her."

The smile dropped from Laurel's face. Her heart hammered at the dark tumors of rage mushrooming inside her. The pounding in her head increased and thwarted the tenuous control medicine had over her pain. She plopped into an empty chair next to Yvonne. Yvonne wrinkled her nose.

"That's right, I'm here for report." She edged her chair close to Yvonne. "Where's Alexis?"

"Alexis left," Yvonne replied. "What's it to you? Just give me your report."

The headache grated like glass fragments against the inside of Laurel's skull. Her fist quivered with the urge to belt Yvonne one.

We'll see how much you mouth off after I get my hands around your neck.

* * * *

Dressed in her faded blue overcoat, Laurel stopped at a supermarket kiosk to buy cigarettes, then browsed the aisles for tomato soup and other supplies. After choosing a box of biscuits for her dog, Pluto, she meandered to the hardware section for duct tape and rope.

One her way to the cashier, she stopped at the bakery. Her helper, Sandra, had a birthday today. Her blue eyes and jet hair reminded Laurel of her older sister, Violet, and Laurel wanted to make her birthday special.

At the sight of a cake frosted with red roses and whipped cream, memories of her childhood tugged at Laurel, memories of a time when her sister Violet bought her a cake and treated her to the movies. Reminiscing over Violet's gentle laughter and hugs enabled Laurel to forget for a moment that her sister was gone. When they were growing up, *E.T.: The Extra-Terrestrial* offered a welcome escape from mommies and daddies who drank too much.

The sweet aroma filled Laurel's nostrils, waking the child within her, the forgotten one buried by beatings and diaper discipline. She remembered wearing dungarees and waiting at the bakery while Violet paid for the cake. Back then, Laurel didn't need to hurt people. She'd laughed all the way home, gazing at the azure sky, her golden-brown hair blowing in the breeze. She'd tried not to notice the pee-stained sheets flapping from her mother's clothesline, but the contempt on her parents' dark features did not allow room for denial. They stood waiting in the kitchen.

Her mother's bloodshot eyes and shaky hands spelled trouble. With one hand on Laurel's shoulder, she sang, "Happy birthday to you, happy birthday to you, happy birthday dear you-pissed-the-bed. Happy birthday to you-u-u-u!"

Amidst tearful protests, her mother and father had stripped off Laurel's clothes and pinned a diaper on her. "Since you act like a baby, we're going to treat you like one," her father said with good cheer. "Your mother's tired of washing your sheets every day."

"Mom ... Dad, I don't ..." *Slap!*

Laurel stumbled sideways. "That's enough," her mother said. "We're putting you to bed. Go upstairs. March. Now."

Laurel pleaded with tearful eyes for her sister to intervene. Violet looked back at her, lips quivering, eyes wide as soup plates. The cost of intervention ran high in the Grant home. The brutal beatings their mother delivered left her and Violet peeing blood for weeks.

On numb feet, Laurel had waddled up the stairs. The thick cloth diaper bunched between her legs and made rustling sounds. In the hallway, the odor of urine wafted from her bedroom. She turned toward the linen closet.

"Oh, no, you don't." Her mother yanked her by the hair, marched her into the room, and thrust her onto the mattress. Her mother knelt by her legs and her father by her head. They duct-taped her limbs to the bed.

"Mom, please! I haven't had my supper." Laurel's tears fell on the mattress. How could she eat anything at all? How could she go to school?

Without answering, her parents left, closing the bedroom door. Hours passed. She could tell by the darkening sky outside her window that night was approaching. Her stomach cramped, and pressure built up in her rectum. Laurel squeezed her muscles tight and wriggled her arms, hoping to loosen her ties. Instead, the tape ripped into her skin.

Moments later, the door creaked open. Violet's tentative face peeked inside. At the sound of bellowing in the background, she scampered off like a frightened rabbit.

"Get away from there, Violet." The clarity of her father's

voice meant he was nearby. "That girl made deals with the devil. Your mother wants her locked up until she straightens out."

Laurel slept in a soiled diaper that night, her pleas for changes and bathroom time unheeded. The diaper rash came next, accompanied by bleeding blisters. After a week, she went back to school with a note for her teacher and a warning not to discuss her "illness." Things were quiet until the next transgression started the cycle again.

Violet never complained, but the depth of her feelings came out when Laurel found her dead, bloodstains on her bed sheets, an empty bottle of Valium beside her, and a note about Daddy Dearest. That night Laurel dreamt about the devil. She woke up to pee and, in the dark, the radiator gave off an eerie orange glow. A strange voice chanted in a foreign tongue somewhere in her mind.

Days later, after another brutal beating, Laurel went another go-round with the duct tape. The tape tore at her wounds with the slightest movement. Every time she closed her eyes, she saw Violet's pale, cold body and the empty pill bottle.

You're not alone, a voice spoke up inside her. *You have me. Abaddon.*

Laurel's head jerked as if someone had shouted in her ear instead of inside her mind. It did not sound like her voice. It was cold and gravelly as if pebbles had lodged inside the windpipe of the speaker.

Laurel turned her head to look at her clock. It was one in the morning.

I shall bestow you with the power of Life over Death.

Laurel gasped. She turned her head until her eyes faced the radiator. The pipes inside went from black to glowing orange. Charcoal smoke wafted out and the speaker took the form of a male—a vampire, Laurel noted with horror—with fanged incisors and red eyes. Abaddon stood seven feet tall, with skeletal arms that ended in blood-scarlet talons. One claw pointed to the door leading to the hallway.

I am going to set everything right for you. I want them all punished, so listen to me, Laurel, and heed me.

Laurel listened. The deathlike specter's eyes burned into hers like heated coals. Their redness brightened until it consumed her entire being. Then the darkness waded in ...

When Laurel woke fantasies of tearing flesh danced through her mind, ideas she'd never entertained before. Her welts hurt but that no longer mattered. She stretched and found she could raise her arms. Someone—or something—had cut away the duct tape. A pair of scissors glittered by the bed. She burst into noiseless laughter.

That's right, Laurel, we're one now. You and I shall teach Mommy and Daddy a lesson. Daddy's not home, so let's start with Mom.

With a low snicker, Laurel changed her clothes, leaving strands of tape dangling from her arms. She sauntered toward her parents' bedroom, cradling her scissors, humming to herself. This night was going to end in fun.

The door banged open. Laurel's mother stormed into the hall, her eyes bloodshot, and her fists clenched.

"Who let you out?" she rasped in the voice of a long time, bottle-a-day, gin drinker.

Laurel grinned. "That's for me to know and you to find out."

Her mother lunged forward, and Laurel thrust her scissors. The blades sliced her mother's cheek. Blood poured from the open wound. A splash of it landed in Laurel's open mouth. It left a sweet taste, better than any birthday cake. Her mother screamed but that only excited her more. A red haze swirled around her. She slashed and drank ...

* * * *

"Moo..." A voice behind her jarred her back to the present.

Laurel spun around and stared at the angry face of her elderly neighbor, Alma Parker.

"I said, move!" The older woman's eyes flashed with fury. "I asked you four times."

"Sorry." Laurel moved her cart, allowing Alma to pass.

"Clean up your yard, too." Alma gave her the parting shot on her way to the register. "It smells like something crawled there and died. Next time, I'm calling the police."

"You'd better watch where you poke your nose." Laurel's lips curled into a smirk. "It might get browned."

You should brown all of her, Abaddon whispered inside her. *Imagine dining on her with barbecue sauce, enough meat to last a month.* Laurel licked her lips. The whipped cream cake went into her basket. She planned to teach Sandra Abaddon's Power.

* * * *

Mud peeped underneath the mounds of snow surrounding Laurel's two-story duplex. Four children, a German shepherd, and a full-time job left no time for shoveling and besides, the sun would melt it. With grocery bags slung on both arms, she hop-scotched over the icy patches to her door. Sandra met her in the kitchen, her face drawn, solemn and quiet.

"Help me put these away." Laurel shoved past Sandra, not taking notice. "What a lousy day. I work with bitchy people. You're lucky you can stay home."

Sandra peered at the groceries with swollen eyes. "Deborah's dead."

"What?"

"I tried to feed her, but she's not eating or moving. Her skin's cold and funny."

"That's a load of horse-feathers." Laurel slammed the bags down onto the kitchen table. She grabbed Sandra by the shoulder. "She's putting on an act. Come with me. I'll show you how to handle her."

Hand gripping Sandra's emaciated arm, Laurel marched her to the basement where she kept her other three children. Two of them huddled inside a six-foot dirt pit, their faces covered with mud. Laurel duct-taped each girl to metal rings by the shoulders, waist, and ankles. She made them all wear diapers, the way her parents had with her. The plywood board stretching across the top of the pit added extra security. The room reeked of feces and urine.

Her heart froze at the sight of their wasted faces. What was she doing? Hadn't she been trained to help the sick? Those poor girls were suffering. She started toward the pit, ready to loosen the board.

NO! Abaddon's voice screamed in her head. *You must not, will not let them go. The Power carries responsibilities, and unpleasant odors come with the territory.*

At his command, Laurel paused in midstep. Something with the grip of iron turned her head sideways. Deborah hung off a ceiling joist by a single handcuff attached to her wrist. How did she get there? This was terrible, so terrible, and ... sharp pain knifed through her skull. Her head became a hive, and the pain stung like bees as they flew through every chamber.

Don't you remember? It was Deborah's punishment for trying to move the plywood.

"I remember," Laurel whispered, and the bees stung with each look she took at Deborah. With her thick-lipped pout, whiny voice, and chiseled features, she reminded Laurel of Alexis, right down to the dark curls and olive skin.

You should hang Alexis by her most deformed wrist, Abaddon told her. *It's time these women learned real suffering. Forget the hospital and concentrate on the business here.*

Laurel burst into laughter that sounded like rattling bones. She laughed harder when she groped for Deborah's pulse and found none. Later, she'd take pictures and harvest the corpse for meat. That would make her headache go away. First, she had to deal with her frightened girls.

"Children, I think I'll have a cigarette." Laurel looked at her girls and smiled. "Don't worry about Deborah. I'll take care of her."

The two girls gazed back at Laurel with vacuous eyes and said nothing. Months of missed meals, veiled threats, and cigarette burns had schooled them into silence.

Laurel took a deep drag on her cigarette while eyeballing her charges, hoping they would provoke her. Smoking was a nasty habit, but a cigarette felt good before exercising her Power. The cigarette made a great disciplinary tool, too.

After she ground out the butt, she climbed up on a chair and unlocked the handcuff. Deborah dropped to the cement floor with a dull thud. Laurel's head throbbed with each movement: *ka-boom, ka-thud-ka-boom!* The pain drove her into a blind fury. Grabbing Deborah by the waist with one hand, and by her tangled hair with the other, Laurel threw her against the wall. Deborah slammed against the plaster and dropped, leaving spider cracks. Laurel followed up with three sharp kicks to her spine and ribs. Bone crunched underneath her foot. Her headache receded with each hit. She stepped back to inspect the body. No movement.

She turned toward her girls and nodded. "I'm sorry this happened. Deborah didn't know when to keep quiet. Learn from her mistakes, and you will live."

Their faces scrunched up, but they did not cry or comment. Laurel's eyes moistened at the sight of their pinched features. Things weren't supposed to get so ugly. Originally, Laurel had used the hole as a sump pit to drain water when her basement flooded. She'd longed to start a family but couldn't find a suitable partner willing to impregnate her. Instead, she began hunting the streets around Kensington and Somerset. Abaddon talked her through the process, pointing out runaway girls with limited intelligence.

At first, she'd allowed her charges to go and come as they please. Then small amounts of cash began to go missing. Six months after she brought the first girl home, one of them stole her debit card. Seven hundred dollars disappeared from her bank account. The headaches came next, punctuated by Abaddon's orders to discipline her children. He gave her instructions on how to prepare the sump pit and she listened. Abaddon knew best.

When the girls weren't looking, she dumped barbiturate powder into their iced tea. Oh, how they screamed when they woke up and found themselves duct-taped to the walls of the pit. Tears came to her eyes at the memory. She loved these girls, but when Abaddon gave the orders, she obeyed. School was in session for her and these young people.

"I hope we can avoid future tragedies." She blotted her eyes with a hanky. "Today is Sandra's birthday, so I've bought a whipped cream cake for dessert. She will help me look after Deborah. Sandra, you don't mind helping, do you?" She gave Sandra a cunning smirk that dared her to defy.

"Not at all," Sandra said in a faint voice. "I'll wash her."

Sandra hauled Deborah up the steps by the armpits. Her

feet made sickening thumps against the cement. Faint groans escaped the others, but their frightened eyes said, "We'd better not say anything."

How right you are, my dear children. Laurel nodded, smiling. She doled out generous slices of cake. By the time that she went up to the kitchen, Sandra had bathed Deborah and laid her on the table. A pot of water simmered on the stove. Deborah's head dangled over the side of the table, and Sandra placed two buckets underneath it.

At the table, her German shepherd, Pluto, was sniffing around the body. "Good doggy." Laurel smiled and scratched his head. She tossed him a couple of biscuits. "When I finish, we'll go for a walk."

Pluto scarfed down his treats and trotted to the living room. Cooking and cleaning up was going to get messy, even with Pluto out of the way.

"Where's my saw?" she asked Sandra.

"Right here." Sandra pointed to the chainsaw on the countertop by the sink. After slipping on rubber gloves, she cradled Deborah's head in her hands.

"Well done." Laurel gave her assistant an indulgent smile. "Tonight I will begin training you on the Power. That is my gift to you for your hard work. Happy birthday, Sandra."

Laurel gloved her hands and hefted her saw. She gazed raptly at the serrated blade and shivered at the energy rushing through her. After giving Deborah a final look-over, she pulled the starter rope and began her work.

Chapter Four: Laurel's Dismissal

Jackson Hospital, March 4, 7:00 a.m.

The next morning, every bone in Laurel's body ached. Last night's activity woke muscles she didn't know existed, but her headache was gone. She put on fresh scrubs and dragged her feet on the way to the car. She'd start by apologizing to Dee and paying attention to her patients.

Alexis was out. Someone penciled the word "sick" over her name on the assignment sheet. Her name wasn't on the list. The night-shift therapists left handwritten reports on the table. Three of the day-shift crew barreled past Laurel, toward their assigned floors, without a smile or a nod.

Screw them. She proceeded to Dee's office.

The door was open, and the scent of vanilla drifted from inside. Dee sat at her desk, chatting with two security officers.

"Dee." She mustered her sweetest voice. "You forgot to assign me."

"I know." Dee's almond eyes held the glint of deepest frost. "Please sit."

"Sure." She glanced at the officers and shrugged. "Dolores, I owe you..."

"Save it." Dee folded her beefy arms and rested them on her blotter, eyes on Laurel. "I'll keep this simple. Several people from ICU informed me you capped Mayes's trach improperly. The resulting asphyxia precipitated her cardiac arrest. I let things go ... forgotten treatments, spotty charting, but this..." She shook her head in disgust. "I won't allow."

There it was, the Let's-Get-Laurel-Club in action. Laurel

imagined running her chainsaw through Dee's fat chest. It would wipe the smug look off her face. Instead, she manufactured contriteness into her voice. A tear rolled down her left cheek. "I made some terrible mistakes, but not with the valve. Ms. Mayes had a mucus plug, and I panicked."

"That may be, but I saw everything you did on closed-circuit TV. You wandered around in a trance, asking, 'What did I do?'"

Laurel pushed away the hair falling into her eyes and gasped. "I said that?"

"According to the cameras, yes. Doctor Leicht caught everything on video for me."

Damn those headaches. They were coming with greater frequency, along with lost periods of time. *If you want your headaches to stay gone, don't make me tell you twice,* Abaddon's voice whispered. *I know what's best for you.*

"You're fired, Laurel, but I'm not stopping there. By law, I'm required to report you to the state licensing board; so you may lose a lot more than your job. Don't bother to clean out your locker. I'll mail your belongings and what pay you have coming."

The fury was building, and Dee's thick neck looked oh, so inviting. How she'd love to slide her hands around that neck and squeeze …

Not now, not with those officers watching, Abaddon cautioned. *Make up a hit list. Write Alexis's name on top and Dee's underneath.* "You can't fire me," she told her boss. "Only Doctor Tynan has that authority."

"Doctor Tynan told me about your attempt to blackmail him. He's informed his colleagues he has an addiction and is seeking treatment for it. You have nothing on him now."

Damned prick! His name goes on the list, too.

"Doctor Tynan authorized me to handle your dismissal. These officers shall escort you to your car."

The two men moved her way. The closer one wore a name tag that said "Tyrone Hobson." Dee's husband, Laurel supposed.

"Let's go." Tyrone prodded her to her feet. The officers stood by the door while she gathered her purse and overcoat. They walked her to the ground floor and then across the street to the garage where she parked her car.

Her battered Ford, caked with rust and debris, sat close to a silver Chevy van. Backing out of such tight quarters required careful maneuvering. As it was, new dents and scratches turned up every other week, especially after a blackout. The two men stood to the side, watching her as she plopped behind the wheel.

"Boy, do I have plans for you, girl," Laura whispered. She jarred the engine into an angry roar. "When I finish, you won't be able to talk. I'll cut out your tongue and strip your hands of flesh, one joint at a time. That's a promise."

She glanced at the Chevy, noticed her proximity to its fender, and shrugged. The two guards remained where they were, watching her. *The hell with them,* she thought. Only dimly aware of the sounds of metal scraping metal and shouting behind her, she tore out of her parking space and sped through the gate in a cloud of blue smoke.

At each traffic light, she rehearsed Alexis's address: Briarwood Condominium 12B, 800 Maple Street in Bernersville. She lived alone, without pets or security. The entrances to each building were locked, but such inconveniences didn't discourage Laurel. With fifty pounds and three inches on Alexis, the punishment would come hard.

She had plenty of chloroform, duct tape, and rope in her trunk. At a traffic jam further down Jonasville Road, she retrieved a slip of paper from her purse and began composing a hit list of people she planned to kill. Alexis first, then Dee, Morris, Doctor Tynan, and Miss Nosy Parker, her bitch of a neighbor. Tyrone was next, then Mark Adams, her boss from a previous job. No sweat. Most of them had few relatives, and sickly ones at that. Doctor Leicht might pose serious complications though. A rash of disappearances caused raised brows. He'd waste no time pointing the police in Laurel's direction.

I might have to kill the good doctor, too.

Doctor Leicht was going to be tough, considering his military experience with Kryszka weapons. He'd led vigilantes into the underground compound three years ago. His skills and a passel of relatives made eliminating him difficult, but Laurel had the Power over life and death. After she consumed her parents, she worked her chainsaw every other month or so. She could handle Steve Leicht if she stayed focused. With a smile, she tucked the list into her coat pocket.

Laurel was a can-do type of woman.

* * * *

Further up Jonasville Road, she cut right onto Church Street, a snow-covered thoroughfare that snaked through woods. Her headache exploded into a dull roar. Her surroundings blurred. Her car skidded, but Abaddon's voice egged her on. *Come on, you little pissant, kill her, kill her!*

The road curved left, and Laurel slammed on the brakes. Too late. Her tires skidded on an icy patch. The car nudged over the guardrail and hovered a few seconds before tottering down into a ravine.

"Oh, no!" she cried.

A thick oak loomed ahead. Laurel wrenched her wheel sideways. The tires whipped toward the right, but the car continued rattling past shrubs and trees. Seconds later, the driver's side T-boned an oak tree. The sounds of crunching metal and tinkling glass followed. Stabbing agony from the steering wheel flared through her chest only moments before grayness swallowed her. The deploying airbag added further insult.

* * * *

When Laurel woke, she lay sandwiched between her steering wheel and the seat. Smoke from the airbag drifted through the car. She was hurt. Badly hurt. Enough to require a 9-1-1 call. She groped through her pockets for her cell phone. Her phone was a battered piece of metal, but it worked. Not this time. Laurel couldn't remember when last she'd charged it.

She got to thinking about Pluto. More than anything, Laurel worried about her dog. If she died, Sandra would feed the other children, but ignore the dog. Most people shied from Pluto. No one loved him the way she did.

Voices jarred her to attention. They came from a dark sphere hanging in the early morning sky. These voices belonged to the people who had gotten her fired.

"You can't even make it to the bathroom," Johnny's voice jeered. *"Dee gave you the boot, shit drawers. Ha, ha!"*

"Administration listened plenty when I complained," Alexis's voice shouted with glee. *"Now I've got special accommodations, and you get nothing. Tee, hee, hee!"*

"Shut up," Laurel whispered, wishing Pluto was nearby.

Steve Leicht next: *"You thought you got away with stuff, but I caught everything on camera. How about I send your ass to jail?"*

"You couldn't even blackmail an addict like me, could you?" Tynan's voice piped up. *"I'm going into rehab, and you can rot in hell."*

Laurel's scream came out fast and hard. The voices swarmed through her mind like fire ants. She leaned on her horn.

The voices continued their babble, calling her shit drawers, asking how it felt to fall down a ravine, asking and laughing. Laurel screamed again in fury, and then the sphere itself changed to become Abaddon's face, pallid and cadaverous, eyes like red rubies. His thin-lipped grin parted to reveal his teeth. Two of them, pointed, dripped blood.

Laurel screamed again, not from fear or anger, but from abject terror. Abaddon's voice spoke. *"You must go to the hospital, Laurel. Go back to Jackson Hospital and destroy them. Kill them all, for my sake, and..."*

The seat shifted, and a blaring sheet of agony speared through her sternum. Laurel slid into darkness with Abaddon's voice chasing her: *"Get them, Laurel. Kill them all..."*

Laurel struggled to open her eyes.

The pain was brutal, but the sphere was gone. No voices, just the murmur of passing cars from the street. So far, so good. Maybe someone would stop. What was this? Crunching footsteps. The stranger looked like a woman. Closer now, and Laurel smelled blood. Her own perhaps. Its acrid smell was strong enough to overpower the airbag's smoke.

The T-bone had gifted the driver's door with a bent-in jam and molding. A few inches more and the dented door would have T-boned Laurel. Her chest felt like one big sore. The passenger door opened with a grating squeal and a woman with ash-pale skin and tangled, fiery red hair leaned in toward Laurel. She looked like a Kryszka, but Laurel didn't think any of the aliens, other than the Jackson Hospital doctor, had survived the explosion.

"Hello," she whispered. "Please help me... I'm hurt."

The woman stared at the mangled door and Laurel, her ruby eyes wide. Her lips parted, revealing a mouthful of needle-sharp, bloodstained teeth.

The haziness fell away, swapped for a stunned shock. The woman was Kryszka all right. "Will you help me?" Laurel begged, desperate to relieve her pain. "Please?"

"Fresh meat. You will do nicely." The eyes were red, no mistake about that, or the saliva dripping from her mouth. "Of course, I will help you."

The airbag had deflated, but the steering wheel pinned Laurel to her seat. This didn't discourage her visitor. With a cylinder-shaped device, she fired a red ray, shearing the wheel off its column.

Sliding her left arm behind Laurel's back, the woman yanked her over the passenger seat, then dumped her into the snow-crusted mud behind two nearby bushes. Laurel doubted that this slight woman could lift her, but the Kryszka used their minds to lift things. No doubt, this one was using her mind to assist with her physical strength. Mind-power or not, the stranger was rough. She left Laurel curled up on the ground, doubled over in pain. Her head hurt like hell; her chest worse. A coppery taste filled her mouth. Abaddon's voice was gone.

The Kryszka ripped open her coat.

Laurel licked her lips and swallowed blood. She must have broken several ribs, judging by how much her chest hurt each time she breathed.

Her car's engine was humming. It was an old car, battered more by the trees, but the engine still ran. Her list remained inside her coat pocket. At the moment, the names on it were the least of her concerns.

"I shall tear out your throat." The Kryszka smiled. "I am thirsty."

At the close-up view of her visitor, Laurel's eyes bulged like soup plates. Her mouth became a widened 'O' of terror. The stranger's teeth looked way sharper than Abaddon's. She wore a blue tunic of woven metal plates. Her eyes glowed like a demon's. Could she reason with this creature?

"Don't hurt me," she tried, babbling at once. "I can find you all the meat you want."

"Human meat?" The Kryszka woman laughed. "You bore me, animal."

"I mean it. I have a hit list in my pocket."

"Hit list? What is that supposed to mean?"

"It's got the names of people I plan to eliminate, people no one will miss. Please send me to a hospital."

More laughter. "Do you think I am stupid? If I send you to a hospital, you will tell your authorities about me. I doubt if you ever killed anyone, but anything is possible." She leaned closer, cupped Laurel's cheeks in her hands, and grinned. Her breath reeked of flyblown meat. "How will your list help me?"

"I'll tell you where these people live," Laurel whimpered, close to tears now. "You could have them for supper."

"Of course, you will," the Kryszka woman said. "You are leading me into a trap. Like most humans, you will do and say anything to stay alive. You are in big trouble, animal."

Laurel could stay her tears no longer. She bawled. "I told you, the list is in my pocket. Right coat pocket."

"You have a lot of muscle on you." The woman gave no sign of hearing Laurel. "Enough to feed me and two of my guards. Yours will not be an easy death."

Laurel bawled louder.

"First, I shall look at this list." The Kryszka woman two-fingered the folded paper from Laurel's right pocket and studied it. "Are any of these people soldiers?"

"Good grief, no! Half of them are sickly, and most of them never used a gun."

"I find it hard to believe you would betray your people, but anything is possible. I am training new soldiers, and they can use these people for practice and nourishment. If I find you sent them into a trap, I will fry you with my disintegrator."

Laurel bobbed her head, sniveling. The pain was getting worse. Her breath came out in pants.

"Do these people live near here?" the woman asked, studying the paper.

"Most of them do. Where I come from, people who hurt you get punished. These people hurt me in a big way, so they deserve to die." Laurel grimaced. "The meat tastes best if you barbecue it."

"I prefer my meat raw. Our former leader, Eigil, introduced me to human meat. His recklessness got him killed. Humans slaughtered my closest friends, so you could call my actions punishment." She gave a harsh laugh. "You and I think alike, Laurel."

Laurel gasped. "How did you know my name?"

"Your identification tag states your name."

"So will you send me to a hospital?"

The Kryszka stood silent, eyes on Laurel. Laurel could feel the woman's mind ticking a mile a moment. "No, because everyone here thinks I am dead. It would be dangerous for me if they found out differently."

Laurel swallowed hard and tasted more blood. She attempted a deep breath. Spasms tore through her chest. "Wait ... are you Woehar, Yeron's sister?"

"Yes."

That's nice, Laurel thought. *Meantime, I'm about to suffocate.* "What will happen to me? I don't think I can walk."

"If I leave you here, you will die of your injuries. I shall bring you to my clinic. A healer there will treat you. Most people sympathize with humans, but my assistants appreciate fresh human meat and people who help them obtain it."

"Clinic? I thought..."

"I am taking you to a second compound like Eigil's, near Royerstown. My assistants need practice and nourishment, especially humans who no one will miss. Give me all the information you have on these people. Cooperate, and you will thrive. Lie to me, and you will die."

Laurel struggled to a sitting position, one hand on her chest. This woman made Abaddon seem like Santa Claus. Her father's scolding about deals with the devil came to mind.

"I will give you all the people you want. Hell, I'd give you my mother, except..." Laurel lowered her eyes. "I already barbecued her."

"I eliminated my mother, too. Slow learners do not survive in my world." Woehar gave her a knowing smile. "I shall take you to the compound now."

Laurel braced herself, expecting Woehar to manhandle her again. Instead, her body rose off the ground and floated.

"Would you like to know what amuses me?" Woehar went on. "People think I died in the explosion."

Laurel nodded. "I heard about your so-called death in the news."

"I am remaining hidden while I make my plans for Earth." Woehar spoke without looking at Laurel. She was concentrating. "Our technology developed a drug that will make humans like the walking dead. We shall set them loose to attack and kill, starting with the Philadelphia area. One day, we shall rule the Earth. Its inhabitants will become our slaves and cattle.

"Right now, concentrate on breathing. I assure you the people on your list will die within twenty-four hours."

Laurel allowed herself to relax. She attempted slow, easy breaths. A creepy feeling filled the hollow places inside her. She looked up at Woehar and thought again about deals with the devil.

Chapter Five: Gruesome Discovery

Kryszka Underground Colony, March 4, 11:00 p.m.

Bloodcurdling screams startled Governor Quyeba out of a sound sleep. She jumped to her feet and threw on a navy tunic made of titanium, matching boots, gun belt, and a helmet. She slipped two plasma guns into their respective holsters.

The shouting reverberated from the lower level, which held a greenhouse, breeding farm, and Woehar's laboratory. Quyeba had to thank Woehar, a weapons and chemical warfare specialist, for running vitriolic gas into pipes that surrounded the passageways to the compound. When a mechanical eye sensed an intruder, it released the lethal gas. The mechanism didn't seem to have worked this time, though, and Quyeba wanted to know why.

Another shriek cut through the air. Female and decidedly human, it burned into her brain like plasma fire. Quyeba scanned her surveillance view screens. The laboratories, warehouse, dining rooms, and main floors showed no signs of suspicious activity. She changed her surveillance monitors to view the overhead circular steel door and the grounds above it. No sign of tampering. The plant life and dirt camouflaging the door appeared undisturbed.

The visitor needed a healer and her son, Zoltar, treated most injuries. He'd trained well under Teodon, who captained a clinic and medical laboratories at the former compound before dictator Eigil destroyed the building. Most residents greeted Zoltar with a smile, but the smile never touched their eyes. Their true feelings showed in the disparaging comments about him on the networks. Zoltar was part human, and most Kryszka citizens considered half-breeds inferior.

She dared not involve Zoltar, given the hostility toward him. Her tented fingers hovered over the intercom before punching in a call to Draekh. Draekh treated most injuries, but the careless way he disposed of dressings and needles sickened her. He wore blood and gristle on his teeth and reeked like spoiled animal meat. Quyeba could withstand his odor if it meant shielding Zoltar from people who might harass him.

When Quyeba emerged from her cubicle, Draekh greeted her with a frown. Blood oozed from the corners of his mouth. Another sign of abominable hygiene. "Why did you disturb me in the middle of supper?" he demanded.

Quyeba looked at her intercom again and grimaced. "Your meal can wait. I want to know who is screaming and why."

"Why does this shout concern you? Let the gas kill the intruder."

"It did not. The intruder managed to get past our mechanical eye. I want to know how." With Draekh close behind her, she rushed down the corridor. At the exit, a lift beamed them to the lower level.

The landing branched into two passageways, the greenhouses on the left, and the breeding laboratories and Woehar's quarters on the right. Quyeba paced from side to side, considering the best way to go.

"We have to split," she said after a pause. "I shall search the laboratories."

"All right." Draekh hurried toward the greenhouses.

So far, no trespasser, but she shuddered at the cacophony of wails. At the breeding laboratory, she slid open a paneled door with her mind. An overwhelming yeasty odor hit her.

Inside, she walked equidistant between two rows of caged animals. Their gargoyle faces snarled. Tongues hung, dripping saliva from maws filled with jagged teeth. At great risk, a technician or android harvested skin and meat from the grown ones. Quyeba proceeded without flinching. She would walk over smoking stones to find the source of those pained cries.

A panel at the wall facing her led to Woehar's laboratory. Quyeba pulled down her face shield and mentally shoved the entrance panel open. In the next instant, she gagged on the stink of things long dead and exploding with the gases of their decay. The face shield protected her from the effects of noxious gases but allowed odors to penetrate.

An overhead light threw pink shadows on human bodies in cubicles along the south and west sides of the room. Fifty of them at least. The live beings shrieked and writhed with agony. The dead ones reposed in various stages of putrefaction. Something had torn chunks from the faces and limbs, leaving behind raw fascia and muscle. Blood and black pus from their gashes dripped to the grid floor. Buzzing insects formed black clouds over their open sores. The foul odor intensified with each step through the laboratory.

The live specimens continued screaming. Their bulging eyes rolled in their sockets. Bloody spittle leaked through their gnashing teeth and ran down their chins. Frightened and angry, they would bite or attack anyone trying to help.

Her lips trembled. Such barbarism reminded her of the atrocities dictator Eigil committed when she lived at his compound. She and three trusted friends, along with a team of androids, had constructed this refuge so they could escape Eigil. Animal feces and plants dug from a vegetable field camouflaged the gate. Foraging for food and maximizing resources left scarce time for rest, but her compound provided asylum for hundreds of people.

Then Woehar came, and now these bodies were in her laboratory. These people needed help. Where was Woehar?

She should have brought Zoltar with her. He had experience treating injured humans. She rooted through the pockets inside her tunic for the basic tools needed to do a cursory examination. *Are any of these people salvageable?* She scanned the cubicles. *Bad as they look, I must try.*

On legs that wobbled with each step, Quyeba approached a cubicle occupied by a male. According to Zoltar, she could find the human's strongest pulse in the throat. She exchanged her thick gloves for thin, transparent ones that enabled her to palpate. The man's dried skin stretched like cracked leather over his bones, his smell rancid and overpowering. Gleaming white bone peeped through the tears. When her fingers trailed below the chin, his hand grabbed her right wrist and squeezed. Hard enough to grind her bones, making Quyeba, builder of compounds, do something she had not done since her mate Lyrus died. She screamed.

The instant of panic passed, and Quyeba withdrew her plasma gun. The man's other hand leaped out and caught her other wrist.

Another scream.

The grip was too strong for any man, let alone one near death. Lips quivering, she mentally pried his fingers from her wrists, digit by digit. She tiptoed toward the exit, ready to bolt when movement from the cubicle startled her to attention.

The man who grabbed her licked spittle off his chin and grinned. His arms rested by his sides. His wide-open eyes watched her. They were closed when Quyeba first saw him.

Quyeba bolted to the breeding laboratory. Only dimly aware of the snarling animals, she glanced about, wondering if Draekh decided to come this way. He did not.

With a sigh of relief, she headed to the lift and ascended to the main floor.

She intended to question Woehar after Zoltar examined her hands. She flexed her fingers without discomfort but winced when she tried to bend her wrists. What if the creature had broken...? *Get control of yourself,* she chided herself. *Zoltar will ask how the injury happened. You had better smile and lie well. Otherwise, you will upset him. Besides, certain reflexes linger in humans after death. Remember that when you see the bruises on your arms. So the man smelled like a corpse ... forget it. That was how you survived Eigil's tyranny ... by keeping silent.*

The mental scolding did no good when she glimpsed the greenish slime on her sleeve. Someone living in her compound was plotting something evil. Woehar was involved. Perhaps Draekh, too, since the two worked together. Silence was not the answer this time. The casualties demanded Zoltar's expertise, and he deserved the truth.

At Zoltar's laboratory, Quyeba hesitated. She anticipated a deluge of emotions. Perhaps Zoltar's human genes predisposed him to emotional outbursts. Whatever the cause, the truth required tact. With bated breath, she entered.

Zoltar was sitting before his electron microscope, studying its readout screen when she approached him. He looked up at Quyeba and started. A slide clattered to the floor.

"Mother!" he cried. "What happened to your hands?"

"Zoltar, lower your voice." Quyeba drew in a sharp breath. "I found over fifty badly injured humans in Woehar's laboratory."

"What?" He gasped.

"Some of them appeared dead ... almost like skeletons, but they are alive. When I tried to examine one of them, he grabbed my wrists and squeezed. He was so strong, Zoltar. I think he broke something." Another deep breath. "Please examine these beings ... they look tortured."

"So, Woehar is torturing humans. Like Eigil. I knew it!" His tanned complexion bleached paler than a purebred Kryszka. "I shall examine you first. Before I do, take a shower and get your clothing decontaminated."

"I would appreciate a clean tunic." Quyeba's lips trembled. She saw no easy way to tell him. "Otherwise, I am not infected. The skin is not broken."

"You do not know that, Mother. Do as I say." His voice notched louder with each word. "I do not want anything to happen to you."

Her face shield, gloves, tunic, and underclothes went into separate bags, earmarked for decontamination. Quyeba stood under the shower head and scrubbed hard, trying to clean every cell on her skin. The rancid odor lingered in her nostrils. She stood before a mirror while a dryer sprayed jets of perfumed air on her. Already, her bruises formed thick purple rings around her wrists. Each wrist had swelled to twice its original size. She donned clean undergarments and a uniform before proceeding to the examination room.

"Your bones are intact," Zoltar said after scanning her wrists. "So is the skin. Wear these tonight." He wrapped ice pads around each wrist. "Cold therapy will ease the swelling."

His professional demeanor faded, and his worried look returned. "What were you doing in Woehar's laboratory?"

"I heard screaming. I thought someone broke into the compound, so Draekh and I went to check. We must speak with Woehar about this."

"I suppose we do." Zoltar donned his uniform and helped Quyeba put on her gun holster. They started down the corridor to the lift. "Why do you let Woehar and Draekh stay here? Woehar has an evil look. As for Draekh, I will not touch anything that pig handles."

"You and Draekh are the only healers on this compound. Woehar is Teodon's daughter. I owe him her safety because he opened his home to us after Lyrus died. He made you his son and tutored you in medicine."

"I remember that, Mother. He and Yeron treated me like family, but they did not get along with Woehar either."

"That is true, but she is still a blood relation. Teodon taught me everything I needed to know to build this compound. He listened to my problems. I told him I could not thank him enough for what he did. He said, 'There is no need to thank me. I turned away someone else in a similar plight, and their eyes follow me everywhere I go. I do not want another set of eyes following me. Besides, my children will need a refuge if anything happens to me.'

"Children, Zoltar ... Yeron and Woehar. Do you understand his implied condition?"

Zoltar nodded. "That means we allow Woehar to do as she pleases."

"Family loyalty does not exempt Woehar from the rules." Quyeba led him through the breeding laboratory to the entrance to Woehar's laboratory. "We are here."

The panel quivered, and then slid open, silent as death. No sign of Woehar. The cubicles skirted around them, imprisoning the hapless victims. Their gnashing teeth, guttural sounds, and wild eyes intimated madness.

"Zoltar," she said.

"What?" Zoltar retrieved his plasma gun, his voice stoic.

Quyeba watched him, but the cacophony of cries cut to her inner being. Some of the specimens had lost toes, fingers, and limbs. The jagged edges of the stumps told her someone had amputated with a serrated blade.

"What?" Zoltar asked again, his face grim and white. "I am neutralizing the force-field around the live ones. Then I can examine them. Do you object?"

Quyeba shook her head. "We should have brought a team of androids."

"Yes, we should have. Since we did not, we can bring the healthier specimens to my laboratory. You were a laboratory assistant before you became governor. I know you are hurting, but I need your help."

Quyeba sighed. Zoltar was desperate to prove himself. He refused to believe that his peers would consider him inferior, even if he saved an entire race. But Quyeba had to consider her conscience. Dangerous or not, these beings did not deserve this torture.

"All right, son. Choose the most salvageable ones."

Quyeba grimaced at the sickening stink around the victims. None of them looked capable of being saved. Zoltar withdrew a syringe from his gun belt and jabbed the needle into a squirming victim. Another deafening scream.

"Zoltar, if the wrong people catch you—"

The laboratory remained deserted. That did not mean anything, considering the surveillance monitors in the compound. The human Zoltar injected went slack, but thick, shiny strands bound him inside his cubicle. Unfastening the strands required robotic machinery or androids. Zoltar let loose a stream of curses.

Footsteps. The panel whispered open. Woehar stood looking at Quyeba and gasped.

"Woehar!" Quyeba mustered her most authoritative voice. "What are you doing to those humans? This is barbaric."

"That is not your concern." Woehar's eyes, flashing with fury, met Quyeba's. She advanced, her finger jabbing toward Zoltar. "What are you doing? Neither of you has any right invading my privacy."

"It becomes my concern when I hear screaming." Quyeba stayed where she was without flinching. "Those humans have families who miss them. Eigil lost his empire due to his bloodlust. I will not allow such crimes here. Your lack of isolation protocol may introduce deadly bacteria to the other residents."

"I am working far away from your precious citizens..." Woehar hesitated. The anger left her voice, but her eyes smoked with fury. "We use negative pressure ventilation. Most people do not have access to this laboratory. Eigil ingested a toxic poison that made him violent. I do not consume humans the way he did. I would not have destroyed him if I wanted to continue his activities."

"You have not told me why these humans are here."

"The specimens were dead when Draekh and I harvested them. We are experimenting with their DNA to create a superior army." Woehar's voice oozed the sweetness of nectar. "My, Governor, you do not look well."

"I am fine," Quyeba snapped, exasperated. "You must consult with Zoltar or me on any experiments." She cast a baleful gaze over her shoulder toward the specimens. "This I will not allow. These humans have serious injuries."

Zoltar turned toward Woehar. "They look like someone tortured them. Did you?"

Woehar laughed. "Of course not. All of them are dead."

Quyeba gave the cubicle by the opposite exit another look. The man inside lay still, grin tucked into place. She stiffened. "Not all of them. Some are screaming and thrashing in their cubicles."

Woehar's jaw tightened. Any instant, she would lash out in a spate of anger. Instead, she gave Quyeba another smile.

"Why are you doing this?" Quyeba kept after her. "If you want to continue living here, you will answer me."

"All right. The live specimens are androids. I programmed them to scream in a way that would frighten intruders. Draekh applied layers off putrescine, blood, and other chemicals from the dead to make them look frightening."

Zoltar shook his head. "Do not believe her, Mother."

"We implanted a microchip to make them scream and attack. Most intruders would run if they survived the encounter." Another grin, and the glint of blood and pink flesh glittered between Woehar's parted lips. Her breath exuded the stink of carrion. Her eyes darted toward the rear panel of the lab as if she expected someone. A guard, perhaps, someone who might attack unwelcome visitors.

"Governor, you look terrified," Woehar said in a dry voice.

These bodies—this whole experiment is wrong, Quyeba longed to tell her. *If I try to evict you, you will destroy me.*

The words swayed on her tongue, waiting for her to say them, but Quyeba did not need psychic abilities to predict the outcome. Woehar might offer false reassurances this time and next. Eventually, she would dispose of her the way Eigil had with his illicit kills. Perhaps fry her with a disintegrator. It was easy since every resident in the underground city owned one.

"You did manage to frighten me." Quyeba forced a smile, humoring Woehar. "Your creations will terrify any human intruder. Most humans see monsters when they look in their mirrors. None of them forgot Eigil."

Neither will I, she thought. *I will not forget the way that creature grabbed me.* Her wrists throbbed but, in the dawning horror of Woehar's cold, empty eyes, and the way they focused on her son, the pain seemed trivial. Woehar was not going to harm her. She would go after Zoltar. Quyeba would do well to practice leniency with Woehar until she came up with a plan.

"I admire your genius." The biggest lie came with ease. "Where did you find these bodies?"

"Does it matter?" Woehar frowned. "Many humans designate plots of land to bury their dead. They do not cremate. That was where we harvested these bodies."

Quyeba gasped, stunned to silence.

"Why do they bury people?" Zoltar asked. "They could cause a pandemic."

"They do not know the danger of primitive burials. These specimens died of natural causes. Their loved ones have returned to their everyday affairs, so Draekh and I excavated the bodies from the soil."

"If humans designate land for their dead, they may plant surveillance devices."

"Only the most rudimentary kind. Most families visit the deceased's plot and later forget about the person. I can dismantle any security device at these places."

Her voice tightened, and she averted Quyeba's gaze. "I am trying to help you find a better and safer way to get food."

Quyeba nodded. "I appreciate your concerns for our safety, but do not use human specimens. Their bodies harbor toxic organisms. Too much history happened between the Earth people and us. Quarantine these bodies. Now."

"Understood." This time Woehar shot Quyeba a direct look of pure, uncontaminated hate.

"Let us go, Zoltar." Quyeba waved her son toward the door. Woehar closed the panel behind them.

* * * *

While Zoltar applied another ice treatment to her wrists, Quyeba contemplated the day Woehar arrived at her compound. Clad in a tattered tunic, face and hair coated with blood, Woehar oozed fear when she described the gruesome deaths of her father and brother and the way Eigil butchered both Kryszka and humans. She had recorded the last battle, including her talks with Teodon, Yeron, and the human prisoners. Quyeba could not understand the humans, but she appreciated Woehar protecting her family. Someone who hated this despot enough to destroy him would not continue his crusade.

"I do not believe Woehar," Zoltar said, interrupting her thoughts.

"Neither do I, son." Quyeba heaved a sigh. "She does not interact with any resident, except Draekh and a few officers. Her work with poisonous gas shows merit, but reports on her other projects are slow in coming. What reports I get omit vital data."

"What excuses does she give?"

Another sigh. "She gets defensive. I thought the explosion affected her mind. Draekh offered to counsel her. I agreed."

Of course, he counseled her, the phantom voice jeered inside her. *In time, you will believe that lie, just like you believe the one about the dead man's hands.*

What *was* Woehar doing with the bodies in the laboratory? Out of Quyeba's subconscious, more questions slithered like desert snakes. How many people were helping her? Where were the isolation suits? Woehar did not seem to provide any isolation suits or quarantine the specimens. Quyeba's face shield, gloves, and tunic afforded adequate protection, but an unsuspecting person might—*would,* no might about it—contract a fatal infection. Decaying bodies and Earth insects made prolific vectors for bacteria.

While Quyeba contemplated these questions, Zoltar paced back and forth, his lips tight, his eyes narrowed. Then he faced her, his lips trembling. He wanted to help those tortured beings and could not free them.

"When we came here, Yeron and Teodon ceased contact," he said. "Why?"

"Teodon and I kept contact for a while." She regarded her son. "He stopped because Eigil was spying. He would not allow Yeron to risk Eigil's notice."

"Did he say anything about Woehar?"

Quyeba nodded. "He told me Woehar shot his mate, but he refused to give details. Maybe Iska caught Woehar feeding on a human and tried to evict her from home. Perhaps the argument started over a minor infraction. He will never forgive her. 'Woehar is dead,' he told me. 'She sleeps with the enemy.'"

"Sleeping, indeed." Zoltar scowled. "Woehar was plotting with the enemy. I tried to warn you about her."

"I know, son." Quyeba cocked her head. His pained look shot arrows through her heart. "I regret allowing Woehar to stay at my compound. Teodon would never disown his child without a good reason.

"I know you want to help the victims, but we cannot do this without a plan. Let me think about this."

Another scowl. "Do not take too long. Innocents will die."

How well I know it. Quyeba dimmed the lights on her way to her suite. Somewhere in the deep recesses of her mind, she knew Woehar or Draekh might have her and Zoltar under surveillance.

Governor Quyeba, what have you done? she asked herself. *Woehar belittles Zoltar every chance she gets, but Yeron made him his brother. If only Yeron had survived and not Woehar. Sometimes the wrong people die.*

At her suite, she turned up her surveillance speakers and directed the mechanical eyes toward Woehar's laboratory. Woehar was speaking with Draekh and a soldier in the humans' English language. More than once, Teodon had encouraged her to learn English. It was not difficult, but after months of enduring names like "beast" and "monster" from the humans in Teodon's laboratory, Quyeba resisted any attempt he made to teach her. Now she regretted her stubbornness.

No matter how she adjusted the surveillance devices, the language barrier posed a challenge. A mechanical translator would not help because many humans spoke different languages and dialects.

There would be no more sleep for her tonight. She sat at her computer and reviewed the inventory. A spreadsheet came up on the screen, detailing supplies of foodstuffs, clothing, and other things people in the compound might need. Her eyes were not seeing the figures. With each stroke of the key, bands of fiery pain blazed around her wrists. She kept glancing at her bruised skin and thinking about people who slept with the enemy.

Chapter Six: Alexis's Visit Goes Sour

The Carofalos' Royerstown Home, March 4, 9:00 a.m.

Alexis woke the next morning, punk sore at the world and aching like hell. She flexed her fingers. Each movement sent bolts of pain through her joints. She dipped her hands into a paraffin bath. It didn't help. Her hands continued throbbing like a pair of old, splintered pilings under the gusts of a howling wind. Additional sleep was not an option. Every time she closed her eyes, she saw the decomposing bodies, the flies buzzing around them, their putrescent gristle.

Her stomach churned when she contemplated breakfast, but she had to eat. Without food, her medicine might erode her stomach. She cooked a cheese omelet without bacon or sausage. Red meat reminded her of the raw fascia on the victims. Damned if she could ever touch it again.

The clock played "Beauty and the Beast." Its dancers moved in rhythm to the lilting melody, but the music did nothing for Alexis's nerves. It was nine o'clock. By now, Laurel was unemployed and revving up to share her misery. Alexis would become the first recipient. Her heart thudded at the thought. It would be so easy for Laurel to find her address, so easy—

"I can take care of myself," she'd told her boss.

"I'm not sure about that," Dee replied.

"Maybe I can use that gun after all." Alexis's heartbeat slowed. She donned her wrist splints, a pink sweatshirt, and matching slacks, and waited for her medicine to take effect.

She then withdrew her Beretta from the safe. It was a gift

from her late father. She hefted the gun in her right palm. The weapon weighed about seven pounds, more weight than her fragile joints could wield, especially with the recoil when firing it. She might squeak by with it in a pinch. Standing by her safe, she contemplated the first time she'd fired a gun ...

* * * *

She reminisced about a photo album with her mother and Robin, and listened to Eric Clapton. Her father went out on a special job, but a guard was watching the house. Robin and her mother sang along with Eric. Alexis went to the kitchen for a soda. That was when footsteps outside caught her attention.

The front door flew open, banging against the wall. Alexis started and peeked toward the living room. A tall, bearded man and a short fellow with scarred cheeks strolled through the door as if they lived there. They stared at her mother and Robin with their beady eyes.

"Well, lookee here," the bearded one said with a crooked leer. "We get two for the price of one."

His partner cackled.

Robin scrambled toward the sofa. Not fast enough. Scarface grabbed her by the shirt collar. "Where're you going, little miss?" he asked. "We're here to teach your daddy a lesson."

"Don't hurt her," her mother pleaded. "She's only a child."

Alexis gazed at the wall phone, ready to dial Charlie's number. Charlie handled most emergencies, but he couldn't get there in time. She tiptoed to the study, where her father kept his spare Beretta. In those days, she glided like a cat. Her father had shown her how to fire a gun, and he'd taught her well. She'd never counted on applying her lessons so soon and not with an intruder pointing a gun at her mother's head.

"Why are you here?" Her mother's voice sounded like glass scratching against her throat. "What do you want with us?"

"Your old man has been naughty." Shuffling of feet followed and Robin screamed.

"Whatever happened between you and Louis ... has nothing to do with Robin. Do what you want with me, but let her go."

In the kitchen again, Alexis shoved the curtain aside and peeked outside. No guard. Perhaps their visitors had quieted him. The feel of cold metal in her hand took the edge off her shivering … but oh, how Robin screamed! Her cries sounded like a squealing pig in a slaughterhouse.

Her father said he'd made a lot of enemies, as most people did in his line of work. In Alexis's mind, the scene flashed forward to the men beating up her mother and Robin, using blunt instruments. Perhaps violating them in ways she couldn't imagine.

On sneaker-clad feet, she crept toward the living room in time to hear the ripping of fabric. The bearded fellow had torn open her mother's dress. Scarface was going for Robin's throat. Alexis leveled her firing arm and pulled the trigger. A splash of blood sprayed from the wound in Scarface's face, streaking the walls. He let Robin go and she scrambled underneath the sofa. The wounded man slapped his hand against the dangling flap of his cheek, trying to stop the gushing blood.

"Ow, you bitch!" he screamed. "This was supposed to be easy."

Tall-and-bearded shoved her mother sideways. She ricocheted against the couch before falling, and he burst out laughing. "Don't worry. I can handle that spitfire."

"Bastard!" Alexis fired at the big guy. This bullet ripped a hole in his chest. A coppery smell filled the room, followed by a thud as he collapsed.

Her mother dove behind the couch, hugging Robin against her, and weeping anguished sobs. Alexis was moving on automatic. A third bullet felled Scarface, his blood dripping on the sofa and hardwood floor. She headed back to the kitchen, stepping over the bodies as if they were tree limbs. Chills went down her spine, causing her to shiver as she dialed Charlie's number.

"Charlie, two thugs tried to hurt my mom and sister. They got past the guard, so I shot them. I had to because they would have killed all of us."

The average person might mistake her monotone for calmness. Charlie, who considered bloodshed an everyday occurrence, knew different. "I will send someone over for the bodies," he told her. "You did a brave thing."

"I guess so."

"You will get through this, but you must do as I tell you."

Charlie talked. Alexis listened. Alexis followed instructions.

* * * *

The weight of the gun woke the pain from its doze, nudging Alexis back to the present. Her fingers loosened, sending the weapon clattering to the floor. She looked down at her crooked thumbs and wrists. She knew full well how to handle any firearm, but the gun was too heavy for her. So much for taking care of herself.

"Damn it. *Damn it!*" Blinking back tears, she retrieved the gun and returned it to the safe. She packed a change of clothes before heading to her mother's. The Good Grips screwdriver went back into her pocket. It was a worthless piece of shit, but all she could handle.

* * * *

The Carofalos' Royerstown home was a brick rancher fifteen miles north of Alexis's condominium. When she opened the front door, the aroma of garlic and tomato sauce teased at her nostrils. Her mother sat in the kitchen, dressed in her nurse's uniform. She was talking in a muted voice on her phone. Her fingers knotted around the cord, the knuckles white. Alexis stood watching her mother and waited for her to finish.

Matilda Carofalo was a stout woman with graying hair and a grim expression. Her lined face told the world she had witnessed a terrible war and didn't expect the bloodshed to end anytime soon. Her skin went parchment pale as she spoke. She turned toward Alexis and dropped the receiver.

"Oh, my God!" she cried.

"Mom." Alexis went up to her mother. "What's wrong?"

"It could have been you or Robin!" she continued as if she didn't hear. "Robin trusts everyone who acts nice. I worry so much about both of you. If only Louis were alive."

"I miss Dad, too." Alexis kept her voice low and gentle. "What happened, Mom?"

"Fenimore called." Her mother's features darkened. "The police found two dead—decomposed—bodies in a dumpster in back of your favorite restaurant. Bucella's."

"What?" Alexis bit her lip to keep from screaming.

"You heard me." Her mother panted with each breath. "Fenimore went to Bucella's for dinner, but he couldn't get in because the police put up roadblocks. So far, they're keeping it out of the papers and ... hey! You're whiter than a sheet! Did you know anything about this?"

Go ahead, Alexis, tell Momsy how the Angel of Death killed another patient. You ratted on her, and now she's looking for payback. As for the bodies, fill her in on all the gory details. The Angel of Death might have left them there. Perhaps a Kryszka guerrilla survived the explosion, and he's out for blood. So get it off your chest, as Stevarino would say.

"Of course not," she said between clenched teeth. "I haven't gone near Bucella's. After what you told me, I won't eat there again."

"Smart thinking." Her mother nodded with a sigh. "You looked peaked."

"I'm all right." Alexis kissed her mother on the cheek. "My hands are bothering me. Steve ... Doctor Leicht wants me to spend a couple of days with you. I hate to put you out, but..."

"You can stay anytime." Her mother hugged her. "I have to work tonight. I won't be home until midnight, but I've frozen enough ravioli and meatballs for two meals."

"Robin can have my share of the meatballs." Alexis averted her eyes. "Did you tell her about the bodies?"

"I should say not. She's too sensitive. Watch her, Alexis. Alma called and said she's wheezing again. When Robin gets home, give her a treatment."

"I'll do that. Maybe both of us need rest."

"Maybe so. I hope you're not taking Percocet," her mother warned. "That's how your aunt died. Don't go near that stuff, no matter how bad the pain gets."

"I won't." Alexis lowered her eyes. "Don't worry about anything. I'll look after Robin."

* * * *

Hours later, Alexis and Robin sat on the couch before her mother's DVD player on the coffee table, watching *Dawn of the Dead*. Alexis propped her splint-clad hands on soft pillows. The swelling and pain had gone down, but it wouldn't last. At one time, she used to beat up playground kids who harassed Robin. She couldn't imagine doing that now.

Robin's sibilant wheezing speared her to attention.

Shit. "Robin, are you okay?"

No answer. Robin sat, rocking on the sofa, eyes on nurse Ana of the screen, whose husband was bitten. The death toll was rising from a mysterious plague that bred flesh-eating creatures. Nurse Ana was running for her life. Robin watched it all, intent on Ana's escapade, hardly aware of her pursed-lip breathing and hunched shoulders. Her wheezing drowned out the sound of the dialogue, but her eyes stayed locked onto the screen.

"Okay, kid, show time's over." Alexis reached for the DVD remote. She set the movie on pause. "I'm taking you to the hospital."

"No!" Robin whirled around, facing her. Though she had the figure of an adult, she spoke in the voice of a petulant child. "I'm not going to any hospital."

Alexis stared, saddened, at her sister. "Robin, you're not breathing right. I have to take you to the hospital."

"My briefing is okay," Robin said in a stubborn voice. "Lemme watch the movie."

Alexis shook her head. A queasy feeling filled her stomach when Robin made grunting noises. "You can watch it and take a breathing treatment. Then we're bringing the DVD to the hospital and finish watching the movie there."

Robin coughed and patted her chest. "Okay, I'll take one."

Alexis restarted the DVD. While Ana and the other survivors sought refuge at the Crossroads Mall, she slapped the mask for a nebulizer filled with Albuterol on Robin's face. In the next instant, images played in her mind: Laurel breaking into the hospital with a shotgun, Laurel blasting at the staff while the security guards stood around with their thumbs up their asses. Laurel moved in on Robin as Robin progressed from audible wheezing to respiratory failure. Liquid fear rushed through Alexis's veins, sending shudders up her back.

"Alexis!" Robin cried, fear in her widened eyes. "You're shaking."

Alexis threw a blanket over her hands to conceal her tremors. "Only a little."

"You look bad. Maybe Mister Fenimore should take me to the hospital."

Alexis rubbed her arms, trying to soothe her goosebumps. The chills spread through her body. How much should she tell Robin? Could she make Robin understand? The truth worked best with Robin, but where did honesty end and Too Much Information begin? "That won't be necessary," she plunged ahead, praying for Robin's attention. "I'm shaking because I'm scared."

She set the movie on pause again. Robin sat listening while sucking in her Albuterol. "Laurel ... someone I work with ... did a bad thing yesterday, and I reported her. Our boss fired her, and she's angry. She may come to the hospital and try to pick a fight with me."

"Uh, oh." Robin's eyes bulged. "Like the boys did with me at the playground."

"Exactly. So-o-o ... I'm going to ask the doctors to give you a fake name."

"That's lying."

"No, it isn't, because they use false names to protect people in trouble. They will know who we are, but visitors won't."

"A fake name." Robin gazed toward the DVD, her eyes brightening. "Can I be 'Ana'?"

"I think so, but you'll have to use 'Doe' for your last name."

Alexis slipped another vial of Albuterol into the nebulizer. The laboring breaths eased, but the wheezing persisted, audible without a stethoscope. Jackson Hospital was an hour away, given the Jonasville Road traffic. Forget the car. She was calling 9-1-1.

Robin accepted the second treatment without comment. She returned to watching the movie again. Alexis started toward the kitchen phone. At the sound of overhead footsteps, loudest toward the back of the house, she froze. Her heart thudded. She bolted to the living room, ready to run out the door. Then her gaze settled on Robin, who was watching her, lips quivering. Running was not an option.

"Take your treatment," Alexis said. "I'll find out who it is."

The footsteps switched to the living room and back to the

bedrooms again. Robin dropped her nebulizer. She stared with dark, fearful eyes at Alexis.

"It's da monsters." She shivered.

"What monsters?" Alexis humored her, trying for a calm approach.

"The people with da teef. I'm getting out of here."

"Robin, those people are gone..." *I hope,* she thought, fighting the panic edging into her voice. "I'm sure it's Laurel. She's a mean person trying to play a game. She can't hurt us."

"Those monsters can. They eat people."

"Robin, settle down and finish your treatment!" Alexis shot her sister a fierce look. "No one can get in here. Both doors are locked, and Laurel's too clumsy to climb through a window. If she does, we'll run."

"Maybe Laurel's a monster."

"No, Robin, she's a bad person who somehow found Mom's address. She's only trying to scare us. If we ignore her, she'll give up and leave."

"What if she doesn't?"

Alexis threw her hands up in the air. "Then we'll call Fenimore. To make you feel better, I'll check the back rooms. If I start screaming, you run."

You're making a mistake, leaving Robin by herself, a voice whispered from her subconscious. Right or wrong, Alexis poked through the kitchen drawers for a flashlight. She exhaled a sigh of relief when she happened on a paring knife with an ergonomic handle. Much better than the screwdriver. She tiptoed back to the hallway.

The footsteps were loudest near her mother's bedroom. *What do you think you're doing,* she imagined her doctors asking. *Your hands are useless. Better hope you can outrun whoever's trying to break into your house.*

Her hands might be useless, but she'd be damned if she let that pig intimidate her family. With knife and flashlight in hand, she crept to her mother's bedroom. She whispered an Our Father as she nudged the door ajar.

Chapter Seven: Kryszka Break into Mother's Bedroom

The Carofalos' Royerstown Home, March 4, 9:30 p.m.

Silence. Her splints flashed white against the gloom. The footsteps started again, outside the window. Kneeling beside her mother's bed, she shone her light toward the window. A tunic-clad woman stood outside, silhouetted against the moonlit night. The flashlight kicked too much reflection off the windows to see her face, but the intruder was too short and thin to be Laurel.

The footsteps stopped. The glass shivered. Alexis could hear so much now: the quivering window, the house creaking the way her joints did in the early morning, Robin's soft weeping from the living room.

She gazed into the ominous night, and then the window shattered inward, showering the bed and Alexis with glass slivers. A look up close and personal revealed the intruder's fiery red eyes, needle-sharp teeth, and crooked snarl of hate. No, not hate ... *hunger*.

"Oh, my God!" she hollered, and her cry betrayed her. Her ankle buckled when she tried to stand and run. She dropped her knife. The Kryszka grabbed her arm and flung her onto the bed.

She groped for the screwdriver and cried out at the glass slicing her right hand. Her back and neck hurt worse. The Kryszka withdrew a cylindrical device with her free hand. It looked like a plasma gun, the weapon that Steve had described. Its power would dwarf Alexis's piece-of-shit weapon.

Hot stabbing ripped through Alexis's spine. Something—an invisible force perhaps—rubbed her against the broken glass on the bed. This monster was dragging out the torture before killing her. Her right hand closed around her screwdriver. Despite the razor blades of agony slashing through her wrist, she pointed its tapered bit toward the Kryszka's face. The creature was too busy drooling over her shoulder and neck to notice. Eyes rolled back and teeth gaping, the Kryszka angled for her right shoulder. Alexis sank the screwdriver into the creature's left eye, slick as goose shit.

The plasma gun fell onto the mattress. Her attacker recoiled, shrieking. Her hands batted at the piece-of-shit weapon planted in her eye. Alexis rolled off the bed, screams tearing from her throat, snatched up the gun, and bolted.

Her right hand leaked blood down the hallway. She wiped it on her pants. In the living room, she snapped on a light and inspected the gun. It looked like the one Steve described, absurdly light, with curved grooves along its thick, round handle.

The Kryszka believed in the Good Grips concept.

Robin sat before the DVD player, sobbing, wheezing, and rocking herself. The nebulizer fizzed on the table beside her. She couldn't string five words together, let alone run and hide. Alexis's heart pounded. Her mouth went dry. Sweat poured down the back of her head and shoulders. How did these weapons work? Steve never said, and these guns didn't come with user manuals. This one had three buttons: blue, red, and green.

Plodding footsteps from the bedroom. The Kryszka wasn't done with her yet. *The hell with it. I'm pushing all the buttons.*

She whirled around in time to catch the Kryszka staggering down the hallway. One hand clutched at the screwdriver still buried in her eye. Alexis curled her fingers around her weapon. Stabbing pain corkscrewed through her joints and muscles, bringing tears to her eyes. Teeth gritted, she aimed the gun and squeezed all the buttons. Red fire streaked through the hallway, charring the walls black. The flames licked the Kryszka's cheeks. They spread down her chin and neck and around her head, giving off the stink of cooked flesh. The Kryszka let out deep-throated howls and hisses. Her remaining eye rolled like that of a lunatic on a rampage. She collapsed, thrashing on the floor, hands beating the flames

Alexis tensed, ready to dodge flying silverware or other dangerous objects. According to Steve, the Kryszka fought dirty with their mental powers. The light fixture overhead quivered. The light bulb cracked but did not shatter. Moments later, the Kryszka's feet drummed to a stop.

Alexis let out a dry breath. Her worries had only begun. She'd bet all the pasta in the house that the intruder wasn't alone. According to the *Weekly World Reporter,* Kryszka traveled in pairs. Most likely, the companion served as a backup. Maybe the Kryszka hated working alone. In any case, she and Robin had to scram while they could.

By the way, where was Robin? A deathly silence pervaded the house, except the smoldering fire.

"Robin?" she called. "Are you okay?"

No answer. Left hand clutching the gun, she crept back to the living room. Her father had shot his way through gangs of killers without blinking an eye, but Charlie and his organization stood behind him. She was fighting alone and with an alien enemy. Her health and her injuries posed capital obstacles. The glass cut into her back with each draw of her breath. Her right hand dripped blood, but she'd made a deathbed promise to her father to protect her sister.

"Robin," she called again.

Soft weeping came from behind the sofa, along with the smell of fresh pee. Robin cowered against the wall in a puddle of urine, her jeans dark around the crotch. Her breathing filled with high-pitched wheezes.

A light went on at Fenimore's house next door. An older widower, Fenimore had befriended her mother, helping her with the garden and driving Robin to doctors' appointments. Alexis guessed he heard the commotion and wanted to help. She tried to figure out a way to communicate this to Robin but, before she could talk, Robin bawled.

"I wish Daddy were here," Robin wept. "Why did he have to die?"

"I don't know." Alexis kept her eyes on their neighbor's house. The window gave her a view of his kitchen. Fenimore was talking on his phone. The sight of his face eased her shivering. No doubt, he was calling the police. "Robin, listen up. When I say go, we're leaving through the side door. Then we'll make a run through the garden to Fenimore's house. He'll take us to the hospital."

"He can't." Robin's cry grew shrill. "The monsters will get us."

"Robin!" Alexis covered her eyes with her uninjured arm and shook her head. "The bushes out back will hide us. If another of those monsters comes after us, I have the gun."

That's my brave girl, her father would have said, but her teeth chattered.

"You can't shoot ... you're bleeding." High pitched wheezes chorused each word, her voice squeaky. "Lemme out of here."

"Wait a minute." Alexis cracked the window and waved her light toward the garden. So far, it appeared deserted.

"Hurry up!"

"I said, wait!" She mustered authority into her voice.

"Why can't you call the cops?"

Alexis sighed between her clenched teeth. The nearest police station was fifteen minutes away. The newspapers had declared all the Kryszka renegades dead, and the cops associated her surname with Charlie, a Mob kingpin. They might interpret any call she made a prank. Fenimore, a trusted citizen, would get their attention. Could Robin process this information? She doubted it.

"It's safer if I call from Fenimore's." She tried for a simple approach. "The garden—"

"I can't breef!" Robin's harsh squeal cut into her voice. "I'm going outside."

Robin gasped in shallow pants. The escape plan did not allow time for extra breathing treatments. "Wait." Alexis groped through the side table drawers. Sometimes her mother hid extra medicine there. Her heart burst with gratitude when her fingers closed around a Proventil inhaler. "Take this. Four puffs instead of two."

Her sister complied but she was a continent away from being okay. Two treatments wouldn't dent a full-blown asthma attack. It was like trying to kill a ferocious tiger with a peashooter.

"Here." She draped a blanket around Robin's shoulders. "We're crawling through the backyard. Stay behind me."

* * * *

Outside, a thin coating of snow layered the garden, enough to cushion their footsteps. At Alexis's direction, Robin scurried and dropped on her knees behind an oak. Only dimly aware of her chattering teeth, Alexis knelt beside her, grimacing with each movement. The frigid air numbed her to the bone. She squeaked by with two sweaters since her heavy coat added enough weight to aggravate her pain. The glass shards in her back and scalp twisted with each movement. She tucked the gun into her waistband.

"Did that monster bite you?" Robin asked.

"No." Alexis kept her voice low. "I got cut on some glass. Fenimore's got his light on in his kitchen. I think he knows we're in trouble."

"You can't fight…" Robin coughed hard, expelling a wad of phlegm. "Not with your hands."

"I may have to, so be quiet." Alexis shrugged, not expecting much cooperation. "If I see any monsters, I'll blast them."

"How can you see out here? It's so dark."

Alexis did not answer. Her eyes followed a pink light that washed over the trees near where she and Robin knelt. Another Kryszka materialized from the shadows, his lips moving, brandishing a plasma weapon. Closer up, past Alexis's car, he made audible chittering sounds. Fenimore's house beckoned to her right, close enough to hear his voice but too far to reach safely.

Alexis shimmied further behind the bushes and nudged Robin along with her. She kept watching the Kryszka while she reached for the plasma gun. She listed to the right to avoid irritating her back and neck lacerations. Movement cost her nasty stinging, especially when she bent her fingers. *Please, God, give me a break,* she prayed without moving her lips.

The assailant paced to one side, shining his light. He wore a tunic of woven metal plates and a helmet. His red eyes flashed back and forth and settled on the tree where Alexis and her sister knelt.

He opened fire. The branches above Alexis and Robin burst into flames. Alexis skittered to the left, nudging Robin to follow. There she was, Alexis of the Percocets, Alexis of the hand splints, exchanging fire with this monster. The flames heated the spica, burning into her skin. She shed one splint and then the other.

"Fuck it." Nothing mattered now except staying alive.

Her first shot went wide and ignited her mother's azaleas. Another sprayed the assailant's chest but bounced off the metal tunic. The Kryszka's return fire burned a tree to ashes, the ray inches from Alexis. Another shot from Alexis seared his cheeks. Her assailant let out a shriek of surprised terror, but his blasts kept coming. Alexis fired back, praying her next shot would fell him. Robin huddled at her feet, coughing and gasping.

Sirens wailed in the distance.

The Kryszka soldier ceased fire and shambled off in the opposite direction.

Chapter Eight: Gunfire Exacerbates Robin's Asthma

Alexis's Mother's Garden, March 4, 10:30 p.m.

Robin straightened up, turned her back to the conflagration, and bolted.

"Robin, go over to Fenimore's." Alexis sprinted after her.

Robin ran in the opposite direction. Alexis raised her gun again, thinking she spotted the Kryszka, but he was gone. The flames from their weapons lapped through her mother's bushes and worked their way up the trees. The scorching smoke crawled down her lungs, burning her throat. Despite the 20 degree temperatures, heat broiled her skin.

The chorus of sirens built into a crescendo of harsh wails.

Screaming, Alexis jogged on wobbly limbs after her sister. Robin ran into the house with her arms stiff and straight against her legs. She slid over the ice patches near the steps and sagged against the door, her body wracking with coughing spasms. Clumps of bloody mucus trickled down her chin and plopped onto her sweatshirt. She must have dropped her blanket during the shooting. Alexis tapped Robin's shoulder. "The police are coming. Let's go to Fenimore's and wait. It's safer there."

Robin stared back at her with glazed eyes, her skin pale, her mouth panting. With a dull, aching moan, she jerked away from Alexis and trotted into the house. A ratchety gasp crept in with each breath. The lights revealed a bluish tinge on her lips. Alexis kept two steps behind, her hands throbbing and her back much worse. The stench of broiled flesh baked in with a smoky smell. The hallway walls charred. Fresh tears stood in her eyes.

This had to be more dangerous than any job Charlie had ever given her father. His line of work did not involve alien assassins.

Robin stumbled when her foot snagged on a coffee table leg. She fell into the sofa, back toward the DVD player that was now playing the closing credits for *Dawn of the Dead*. Tears rolled down her face, but wheezing and high-pitched crowing overrode the sound of her sobs. She flipped sideways, curled her knees against her stomach, wrapped her arms around her legs, and rocked back and forth. Outside, sirens wailed in chorus with the rumbling of tires on her street.

Alexis dragged the compressor to the sofa and fished out another Albuterol ampule. She bit the cap off the vial. After wedging the vial between her teeth, she squeezed its contents into the nebulizer chamber and hit the "on" switch with her foot. It was unsanitary, but she dared not trust her lacerated hands with this delicate operation. She palmed the mask over Robin's face. "Take this." Her voice cracked. Tears came to her eyes. "Come on, work with me. Nice easy breaths."

Robin rocked hard, eyes closed, oblivious to the treatment. Her body shook.

After the nebulizer fizzed out, Alexis stood. The room spun. She sidestepped the table, took two shambling steps, and then sank to the floor. She glanced at her watch. Over an hour had passed since the break-in. Given her injuries, she could expect over a month of sick time, with a warrant for disability. A dead monster was stinking up her mother's house, and her partner had run off on a rampage. Worse, Robin had slipped into a dark hole with incipient respiratory arrest.

Alexis's mouth went dry as if someone had stuffed it with cotton balls. She gagged on the fetid odors. She struggled to her feet and loped to the kitchen. Thumping sounded at the door.

"Hold on." Head spinning, she shuffled back to the living room, but the door was opening.

"Police." A tall husky officer flashed his badge. "Jim Hazlett. May I come in?"

Alexis nodded. "Please do."

Hazlett stepped in, darted a glance, and slapped on an isolation mask. He waved his hand toward two others, who were also donning masks. "My partners, Officer Mike Hammond, and Detective Julia McMullen."

Behind them, the houses across the street disappeared, the view obliterated by fire trucks and ambulance vans. Their blue and red lights cut swords across the lawn, reflecting off the flames in the garden. Alexis huddled against the wall, shivering, and staring at the officers with unbelieving eyes.

"What..." the one called Hammond began.

"Kryszka soldiers." Alexis licked her lips. "Two of them tried to kill Robin and me but I stopped them. One of them is dead. The other got away. Garden. That's where the second one surprised us. I hurt him but he ran when you guys came. He's hiding in the garden."

"I doubt it," said Hazlett. "Nothing can survive that fire."

"That monster can. He's tough. The woman cut me bad but take care ... Robin. The smoke set off her asthma, and she can't breathe." She waved her hand toward the sofa, where Robin lay unconscious, chest heaving.

"What..." Hammond began again.

"Can't you see?" Hazlett shot him a hard look. "Her sister's choking. Where are the medics?"

"They're unloading something from their truck," McMullen spoke up.

"I'm glad you guys are here, but ... be careful. The other one is alive and angry. Deadly." Grimacing at the pain, Alexis turned and hiked up her sweatshirt, exposing her wounds to the officers. "The fire started because of all the shooting."

The three officers stared at the lattice of bleeding gashes on her back for long seconds.

"Good Lord," the female detective whispered.

"I tried to tell you." Alexis's voice grew quiet. "He's out for blood."

"Let's go outside," Hazlett said. "Your sister too. The tree behind your property is about to fall."

"Okay. I'll get my purse." Alexis turned, and pain exploded in a gigantic bolt up her back. Her head swam. She took two steps and pitched forward, her knees crumbling.

Hazlett grabbed her shoulders, quick as a cat. "Hammond, get the medics in here. Now! Julia, call for backup and find the bastard who did this."

"I'm on that right now." McMullen raced out the door.

Alexis tried to stand. Each movement sent jolts of pain through her back. She let out dry sobs. "I can't do this."

"Easy, Alexis ... that is your first name isn't it?"

"Yes. Did Mister Fenimore call you?"

"Yes, he did. He heard the commotion here." Hazlett sighed. "Apparently, several rogue Kryszka managed to survive the explosion, because we've gotten other calls like Fenimore's. The medics will take you and your sister to Jackson Hospital. Royerstown Hospital is closer, but we send all Kryszka casualties to Jackson."

Was that what she and Robin had become? "Listen ... that other Kryszka is still alive, and she can kill someone by just thinking about it. Does your officer know that?"

"She knows what she's up against. Now let these guys help you."

The rattling of wheels followed. The medics moved a stretcher beside her.

"Easy." Alexis grimaced as Hazlett lowered her onto to the cot. "Everything hurts."

She lifted one leg onto the stretcher, and then the other, peddling with her feet. She lay on her left side, eyes toward the sofa where her sister remained. Two medics swung over to Robin with another gurney loaded with equipment. They closed in over Robin, one man breaking open a package of IV tubing, another with a box of resuscitator supplies. It wouldn't be the first time she'd needed a ventilator.

"May I have this?" Hazlett's voice intruded on Alexis's observation.

Without waiting for an answer, he withdrew the plasma gun with his gloved hand and dropped it into a plastic bag. She guessed it no longer mattered. "Be careful with Robin ... please," she called to the men ministering to Robin. "She's delicate."

She winced as the medic put on the cervical collar, then strapped her onto the stretcher. The straps pulled taut, rubbing against her lacerated side. Stabbing pain in her neck followed as he turned her face to slip on an oxygen cannula and again when he wrapped a blood pressure cuff around her arm. Her hand stung when he clipped a pulse oximeter probe to her finger. The arthritis was bad, but this was brutal.

"Hazlett." Hammond came to the door. "Get a whiff of this."

"Later," Hazlett said.

Outside, Fenimore and three other neighbors gathered around the ambulance and fire trucks. The flames were dwindling, but the fire personnel had gotten there too late to save the garden. The smoke irritated Alexis's throat again. She forced back a cough, not daring to agitate the gashes in her back.

Two medics brought out Robin's stretcher. Too many people were crowding around Robin for Alexis to see what the medics were doing to her. The neighbors backed away at Hazlett's sharp orders. The medics loaded her into the rig. Her stretcher went inside a tent-like cubicle made of clear plastic. Hazlett hopped in to sit beside the tent. Fenimore called out his concerns, but the driver slammed the doors shut before Alexis could answer. He went around, hopped into the front seat and hit a switch. Red lights flickered across the street and bounced off the nearby houses. He started the engine and pulled out. The other vehicles followed.

Alexis hurt too badly to give a damn about lights and gadgets. Her father would have made witty jokes with the medics. He'd never lost his humor despite his cancer. Alexis wanted to lay there and die.

"I'm putting in an IV." The second medic lifted a tent flap. "Are you allergic to any medicines?"

Alexis nodded. "My hands are cut, so go easy on them ... please." She gazed at the two men's widening eyes. The tissue-thin plastic surrounding her gave her a clear view of their faces. "Officer, my hands were messed up to begin with. I'm supposed to wear wrist splints. The heat from the fire melted them." She turned her gaze toward the medic. "I've got a list of my medicines and my allergies with my insurance cards in my purse. Feel free to look."

"All right ... if you don't mind."

"I don't." Alexis gritted her teeth at the sharp prick in her arm. IV's were tough, no matter the circumstances. "After what went down tonight, that's nothing."

Hazlett nodded. "I can only imagine the emotions you're feeling. Want to tell me what happened?"

Alexis gazed at Hazlett's muddy brown sympathetic eyes. "Okay." Her thoughts came slower than she wanted. "Shit ... I don't know where to begin."

"Who gave you the plasma gun?"

"Plasma ... what?"

"The silver gadget you used to shoot the Kryszka. It's a classified weapon."

"Oh, that. I grabbed the gun from the first assailant after I blinded her with my screwdriver."

"What were you doing with a screwdriver?"

"I've been carrying a Good Grips screwdriver since the Kryszka attacks three years ago. I thought I could use it to protect my younger sister."

"Apparently, you did," Hazlett said with admiration.

"I made a deathbed promise to my dad that I'd protect Robin and our mother. Robin and I were alone when we heard footsteps on the roof and outside our mother's bedroom tonight.

"I went into the bedroom to check, and the Kryszka woman broke in through the windows. I knew she was Kryszka because she had red eyes...and teeth. She threw me on the bed and was about to...to bite me on the right shoulder. I stabbed her in the eye with my screwdriver before she got the chance. Then I grabbed her gun and ran. She came after me, so I shot her. Her backup was waiting for me outside, and we went at it in the garden."

At that, she did smile. The pain was awful, the nightmares worse, but underneath it all lay a sense of pride. She had fended off two alien attackers.

"Adrenaline enables people to do amazing things," the officer said.

"So did the Good Grips the Kryszka use on their weapons. The plasma gun was easy to use." Alexis eased her head sideways, facing the cardiac monitor. Her vital signs danced drunkenly across its screen. She closed her eyes.

"Stay with me." Hazlett nudged her shoulder. "Where was Robin in all this?"

"Robin and I ran outside. We were trying to get to Fenimore's house. Since the other soldier was lying in wait, I made her hide. He and I battled it out, and I wounded him. He took off when you guys got here."

"So you came through for your sister." Hazlett offered a smile.

"No, I didn't." Alexis's voice broke. "Robin stopped breathing. I know because I saw the medics getting out resuscitator supplies."

"Sometimes we get them as a precaution," the medic told her.

"Don't sugarcoat it. I'm a respiratory therapist, and I know when such supplies are needed. My father must be spinning in his grave. He taught me to shoot so I could protect my mother and sister. Setting our home on fire wasn't what he had in mind. Steve told me about the plasma guns, but he never said how they worked."

"Who's Steve?" Hazlett and the medic exchanged looks.

"Steve Leicht. He's a lung doctor at Jackson Hospital, but he's my internist. He takes care of Robin, too."

"Any other doctors?" questioned the medic.

"I see an orthopod ... Jack Levy. My mother ... Matilda Carofalo ... is an RN. She works evenings at Jackson Hospital." She gave the paramedic her mother's number and then yawned. "She can tell you about Robin's medicines and allergies. Now, let me go to sleep."

"Not yet." The medic held up his left hand and splayed out his thumb and first two fingers. "How many fingers?"

"Three fingers, plus two men who love to talk."

Hazlett laughed. "Given your unique circumstances, you'll meet many people who will want to talk. That's a good thing. Do you have any other relatives? Significant other?"

At the words "significant other," Alexis reflected on another cold March evening ten years ago, when she'd ridden on an ambulance with her then-husband Mark Adams. Robin was having a killer asthma attack. Mark had been oh, so gentle when the breathing tube went in. He promised he'd look after Robin ... until the van pulled into Jackson Hospital's lot. The sight of Jackson's spotless tiles and antiseptic smell promised great care, a sharp contrast to Meadowood's shit-stained floors and foul odors. Not a spot marred the doctors' lab coats. A few recognized Alexis from day shift. Her mother was on duty. She and Alexis conferred with the doctors, never noticing that Mark had lapsed into stony silence.

His silence persisted during the cab ride home. Alexis was too exhausted to care. After he paid the fare, he followed her into their rancher. Without saying a word, he closed the door behind them. Alexis ignored Mark and flopped into a chair with Stephen King's *Rose Madder*.

"So you think Jackson Hospital is great." Mark placed his left hand on her shoulder.

"Uh-huh." Alexis kept her nose stuck in her novel. "They used a new ventilator. I was impressed by their bedside manners and the cleanliness of the hospital."

"Don't you think Meadowood is good enough for Robin?"

Alexis jumped, grimacing at the thought of Meadowood's threadbare sheets and broken toilets. The truth would get her into deep shit since Mark captained the respiratory therapy department there. He wanted to fight, but she wasn't accepting this invitation, not with Robin being so sick.

"Meadowood is a decent hospital," she lied. "Jackson Hospital happened to be closer."

"Don't you think I'm capable of caring for your sister?" Mark edged closer, yanked the book out of her hands and tossed it across the room. "Look at me."

Alexis looked up at Mark, wincing. He kept his grip on her shoulder while, with his right hand, he waved a splintered baseball bat at his side. Her purse and car keys hung over the doorknob, calling to her to run to safety.

"Mark, let it go," she begged. "I just want Robin to get better."

With that, she broke free of his grip and hurried to the door. Too late. Mark yanked her by the forearms and shoved her against the wall. Something else happened, but there was a gap somewhere. The next thing she remembered was lying on the couch in her bathrobe.

"You're not going anywhere until you tell me what's wrong with Meadowood."

"Nothing." Alexis winced at his grasp. He did not let go. "All right, Jackson has newer equipment ..."

Smack! Stinging pain flared through her left cheek.

"You were chatting up Leicht and the other doctors, telling them about the dirty floors at my hospital. They know me, and you made me look bad."

"I never mentioned you."

"You didn't have to. They looked at me like something that crawled from a rock."

Another slap, this time on the right cheek. Alexis's head reeled. "Mark, stop!"

"I'm not done with you yet." He punched her in the gut, igniting a ball of fire inside her. An inch or two higher and he might have cracked her ribs.

Alexis lurched off the couch, stumbled, and socked her hip on the floor. She rolled onto her buttocks and peddled away from Mark, panting. Home correction was nothing new. He'd belted her for farting at his mother's table or coming home late without calling. Tonight, he was angrier than she'd ever seen him. His neck veins stood out like corded ropes under his reddened skin. He shifted the bat back to his dominant hand as if he were at baseball practice.

Only he had other things on his mind besides baseball. The splinters, on second glimpse, were nails.

Alexis scooted back another inch; then he grabbed her right leg.

"Get over here!" He dragged her toward him, swinging his bat, and whacked her across the leg. The shock traveled all the way up to her hip.

At the right angle and with better technique, he would have busted her kneecap. As it was, the skin on her calf split open in a lengthwise tear. Blood poured from the wound, drizzling on the laminate floor in a ghastly crimson trail. Alexis screamed and screamed. He raised the bat again and, in that instant, her rational mind seized control.

If I don't fight back, I'm going to die.

Mustering as much force as she could with her free leg, she kicked him in the groin. Her slipper-clad foot plowed into his balls, the sound like striking a carpet. That was enough. All the steam went out of Mark Adams.

He let out a high-pitched squeal and sank to his knees. His hands gripped his crotch. His head went back, lips in a tight grimace. His left knee came down on the studded side of his bat. Another squeal issued from his throat. He rolled onto his side, one hand gripping the knee that was now squirting blood.

"Oh, shit," Alexis whispered, "he needs a doctor."

Then her rational voice kicked in again, the one coming from her instinct for self-preservation. *Run, girl, before he decides to have another go at you!*

Alexis scrambled to her feet, trying hard to ignore the blood soaking her bedroom slippers. No pain so far, but that wouldn't last. She limped toward the door, snatched up her purse and keys, and lurched to her car in a sidestroke motion, all the while glancing over her shoulder. Her breath came out in foggy puffs. The cold air cut through her robe to the bone. Her injured leg dribbled huge drops of blood onto the sidewalk.

In the car, she wrapped a scarf around her leg. She took one last look at the rancher house. Mark and she had bought it hoping to raise a family until an infection in her fallopian tubes shit-canned their plans. The fighting started afterward. Alexis tried to find a way to suggest adoption, but Mark's sharp tongue discouraged suggestions. A look at her leg told her what she needed to know about children and Mark's temperament.

Alexis pulled out of the driveway, her breath coming out in gasping sobs. Deep down, she'd loved Mark and loved him still, but his brand of love made her feel oh, so dirty. No amount of showering would make her clean again. Her heart was freezing to ice. She'd be damned if she ever let another man touch her.

She drove through the streets, trying to decide where to go. Her mother kept a spare bedroom, but Jackson Hospital was the wiser choice. It was closer and she needed someone to stitch her calf. Besides, Mark wouldn't dare try his gorilla routine on the staff.

Closer to Jonasville Road, Alexis stopped, her body wrecked with chills. The cuts and bruises forming on her cheeks screamed domestic abuse. The Jackson staff considered it their duty to report such injuries to the police. The necessity for stitches was obvious, but her mother as a nurse knew how to suture. She pulled into the lot, limped in through a back entrance and filched a wheelchair in the hallway. She wheeled herself to Intensive Care, where her mother was holding a vigil over Robin. Alexis stared into Robin's room for several minutes before her mother gave any sign of noticing her.

Her mother gasped. "*Mio Dios*. Alexis, what happened to you?"

"Mark beat me up." Alexis's shoulders shook as she held out her cut leg like a burnt offering. "I got away, but I got a nasty cut."

"You're not even dressed. Where's your coat?"

Alexis hugged her robe across her chest. "I didn't have time to get my coat."

"You should go to the Emergency Room. At least call the police."

"No Emergency. No police. You know my feelings about cops."

"Then make an exception." Her mother's voice trembled. "Doctor Leicht's here. He can stitch your cut and prescribe antibiotics. You should press charges. That animal might come after you again."

"I doubt it. I hurt him real good. I want to come home ... but I need help getting my clothes and stuff."

"I'll ask Fenimore to help you pick up your things." Her mother rushed from Robin's bedside and folded Alexis in her arms. "We can get a restraining order against Mark. Come home and take time to get your thoughts together. When the weather breaks, you can look for a condo. One day a man will come along who appreciates you."

Alexis did not want to hear about house hunting, men, or anything else. As far as love was concerned, winter would last forever.

* * * *

The paramedic's hand on her shoulder nudged her to the present. "You're fading again. Do you have a significant other?"

"No, but someone should notify my boss. I'm a respiratory therapist at Jackson. Dee Hobson is my boss and a friend." Alexis shook her head and yawned. "Why are you preoccupied with keeping me awake?"

"You've lost a lot of blood. You've got Kryszka saliva on your cuts, the kind that's highly toxic to humans."

"Toxic?" This was getting worse by the second. "Wait ... you've got that part wrong. The creature didn't bite me."

"The Kryszka's saliva contains the poison, which makes drool as bad as a bite," the medic's voice droned on. "I'm watching your level of consciousness in case you go into shock."

Any bad injury could cause shock. It started with dropping blood pressure, followed by respiratory problems, and ended with multiple organ failure. From what Steve had told her, Kryszka poisoning was the worst way to suffer. "Am I going to die?"

"Not if you stay strong and focused."

"My mother's sixty. She's caring for my special-needs sister. Now she'll have to care for me. She can't handle two needy daughters."

"You don't know that." Hazlett leaned closer. "Besides, if you die, your attackers' friends will gloat. Do you want to give them the satisfaction?"

Alexis shook her head. "I thought the explosion killed all the bad guys."

"So did we, but we were wrong. Partially eaten human remains are turning up in back alleys again. Some calling card, yes?"

Alexis nodded with a sigh. "I can't do anything about it."

"You can't, but any information you give me may lead to the capture of these rogues." Hazlett kept at her like a dog after a bone. "You don't think they would stop at one try, do you?"

Alexis gritted her teeth against the pain. She didn't like where this was going. Not one bit. "Okay, you win. Do everything you need to do to save me. What will happen after Robin and I get to the trauma bay?"

"After the doctors stabilize you and Robin, they will move you to the seventh floor," the paramedic told her.

"The seventh floor?" Alexis shook her head. "Uh, oh. I'm not exactly welcome up there."

"That will change when Doctor Hoffman finds out you killed those aliens," Hazlett said. "Heroes like you get treated like royalty on his floor."

"I don't feel so heroic."

"Tonight's shooting made you a hero. Whatever you and Robin have wrong, Doctor Hoffman and his partner, Yeron, will find a way to fix it."

Alexis tried to imagine Hoffman treating her with kindness the day after reaming her out over her splints. It wouldn't fly. Still, the prospect of a cure stirred embers of hope within her. "Will they find a better treatment for my hands and be able to save Robin?"

"They'll try," Hazlett said, but his voice sounded unsure.

Eyes on the two men, she tried shifting her legs and paid for her efforts with another stab of pain.

"I've wanted a cure forever," she said. "Doctor Leicht said the waiting list was long."

"That's true." The medic nodded in agreement. "Fighting those killers and living to tell about it may have bumped you and your sister to the top."

"I know they put Robin on a ventilator. You think they got to her in time?"

"I hope so." The medic lowered his eyes. "They'll have to treat your injuries before they can work on the chronic problems."

"I figured that, but I'm hoping for the best," Alexis panted, excited over the prospect of a cure. She turned her head toward her monitor. Her blood pressure was cruising at 90/50, her heart rate 120 and oxygen saturation 95 percent. "I used to take Robin fishing. Maybe I can do that again."

"I've seen Jackson's research team work miracles for people." Hazlett smiled. "I know one survivor who married and started a new career."

"I will never marry again in this lifetime," Alexis said to her cardiac monitor. "Robin and I talked about taking a trip with our mother. Florida sounds great this time of year." She gasped. Her chest tightened, and her sudden air hunger set off alarms in her head. "Right now, I'm having trouble breathing."

"We're almost there." The medic switched her nasal cannula for an oxygen mask. "Go easy on the talking. Conserve your oxygen."

Alexis nodded. Her injuries may be life-threatening, but she would walk through fire for a cure. What most people took for granted—buttoning coats, zipping jackets, cooking—ushered in a world of pain. She longed to join her coworkers after work for a drink or two, to hear who got hired and who quit, but her flagging energy precluded after-work outings. All of that would change, but right now she was starving for air. Something as heavy as an elephant's foot squeezed her chest. Despite her symptoms, her saturation remained in the nineties.

Suppose Kryszka technology could save Robin and augment her intellect? Would that make her self-sufficient? Fantasies of manicures, fishing trips, and shopping sprees waltzed through Alexis's mind, but they seemed impossible, given her breathlessness and chest pain.

Perhaps she was heading toward shock with respiratory symptoms. She'd seen it happen to her patients many times. The medic gave her epinephrine and cranked the oxygen flow. The attacker had left a saliva trail on her right shoulder, she remembered now. Of course, the poison had gotten into her system. *Oh, God, Robin and I are in so much trouble. We should have gone to the movies or something.*

The flickering numbers on the monitor mocked her. The medic reached for a red box, the one labeled "respiratory supplies."

Yes, Alexis could expect a better quality of life. If Robin didn't survive, she would stand by her mother. Later on, she might help Officer Hazlett figure out why the attack happened.

First, she had to stay alive.

Chapter Nine: Casualties Arrive

Jackson Hospital's Emergency Room, March 4, 11:30 p.m.

Over a solitary snack of a raw egg and a banana, Yeron reviewed the autopsy report for Myles Stanwood. The results had come in quickly since Myles had been a surgeon at Jackson Hospital. Yeron read and reread each paragraph. His mind kept straying to the other day, when Joe Hoffman scolded the respiratory therapist with the deformed hands. The woman directed her widened, frightened eyes toward Joe. Her pale face creased with raw pain.

Moved by her plight, Yeron decided to approach her privately and ask what the matter was with her hands. Perhaps she had a treatable condition. A quick glance at her ID badge gave her name—Alexis Carofalo, Respiratory Care Practitioner. When she left the unit, he followed at a short distance.

At the respiratory therapy offices, he waited inside a utility room while she spoke with her superior and finished charting. She stepped into a locker room and came back out with her overcoat and purse. To Yeron's relief, she took the stairs to the ground floor. He followed, keeping out of sight as she exited the hospital and headed down a rear alley. He opened his mouth to call her name, and then he noticed the bloodstained towel in the dumpster. What words he was going to use left him. The air reeked of fish that had lain in the sun for hours.

The young woman stood many minutes, gazing inside the dumpster. She turned and vomited. She then ran in Yeron's direction, screaming, "Oh, Daddy, why did you leave me?"

Yeron ducked out of sight behind a parked car, close to tears himself. He knew how awful it felt to lose a daddy.

He longed to tell Alexis how much he missed his father, but

he couldn't. In a world where people classified his kind as monsters, she wouldn't listen, for something in that dumpster frightened her badly. She'd run screaming to her superior. It wouldn't be the first time someone complained about him.

Yeron returned to his floor, the mantle of despair weighing heavily on his shoulders. That was when Myles went into cardiac arrest for the last time. He contemplated offering sympathy to Myles's wife but memories of previous altercations bludgeoned through his mind.

"Doctor Hoffman, I don't want this man near my wife. You can teach him English and put a fancy suit on him, but he's still a man-eater."

"Get that creep away from me!"

"Brrrrr." Yeron shivered at the memories. He never considered joining the other staff after work for beers. His digestive enzymes prohibited tolerance to most processed foods and beverages, including liquor. That, and the sparse invitations, except an occasional outing with Becky and Steve. The white plaster walls of his suite surrounded him, with a cot, refrigerator, chest of drawers, TV, desk, and a computer for furnishings. Tentacles of loneliness clutched his heart when he sighted the lone photograph on his bureau. It was of Becky, Steve, and their child Chloe. He would have given his six-million-dollar retainer for a family of his own.

Every so often, Steve and Becky invited him to go to the movies, but the pity in their voices was not lost on him. Besides, they enjoyed frightening shows about the living dead, people who were somehow dead and yet not alive. None of these shows made sense. Yeron had no time for foolishness when his own life was agony.

His life centered around his laboratory, the one adjoining his suite. He could do worse than chase cures for humanity's ailments, but no one thanked him or asked him how his day went.

A knock at the door interrupted his observations. The door opened and Steve, a muscular man, marched in without formality.

"Yeron, they called three Level 1 Traumas." He tossed a yellow folder onto Yeron's desk. "We've got fifteen minutes. Gown up. Wear your goggles and mask. I'm talking strict isolation."

Yeron let out a tired groan. The staff's hushed comments

and pointed fingers shadowed him everywhere he went. Most conversations never went beyond "yes" and "no."

"I think not," he told Steve. "My presence will distract the staff when they should concentrate on their work."

"That's true." Steve nodded with the stoicism of a referee used to handling temperamental workers. "However, these injuries involve Kryszka toxins, and only you and Joe know how to treat them. Joe's in Emergency now, getting a report." A dark shadow crossed his freckled face. "These injuries sound like the kind we found with Myles. Some of Eigil's troops must have survived the blast. I thought you should hear it from me."

Steve's words fell on Yeron's ears like rocks dipped in acid. That some troopers from Eigil's regime might survive was not surprising. For casualties to turn up after three years ...

"Are you sure?" Yeron slipped into a blue gown and tucked a face shield, cap, and gloves into his pocket.

"I'm one hundred percent sure. The police anticipate more casualties." Steve indicated the yellow folder. "Their names, injuries, and medical histories are in there. You've got a few minutes to take a look. You might know these people."

"I doubt it, but I should have expected this. Eigil had a lot of dedicated followers."

"Yeron." Steve arched his eyelids. "If you know anything specific, say so."

Yeron dragged his fingers through his thick, coarse curls. Steve's information brought back memories of Alexis's terror-stricken screams and the bloody towel that, no doubt, concealed a body. The news channels hadn't reported any crimes. He hadn't notified the police and, apparently, neither had Alexis.

Yeron, the self-pity must stop. You are a healer, and these people need your attention. "I do not know anything definite. Who tested positive for the toxin?"

"Shively Bogart and Alexis Carofalo did. Mark Adams did not. Joe recommended the CX249 antidote for all of them. The interesting thing is, the victims know each other. Shively and Alexis are neighbors."

"I met Alexis when Joe reprimanded her for wearing the

splints." Yeron grimaced. "I cannot understand that man."

"Not many people can." Steve heaved a weary sigh. "Mark and Alexis used to be married. It ended badly. So..." He turned toward Yeron, head tilted toward one side. "Do you have enough CX249?"

"Good question." Yeron went back to his computer and booted up his program to check his chemical inventory. Letters and numbers labeled each formula. "I have enough to treat two adults. I can mix more in forty-eight hours."

"We'll need it. Joe said to cut the doses to stretch your supply. Can you do that?"

"No." Yeron frowned. "Hoffman's stupidity never ceases to amaze me. The formula will not be effective at reduced doses."

"I figured that. Here's the problem. Mark Adams happens to be a VIP—vice president at Meadowood Hospital. He's threatening everyone with a lawsuit. He knows about CX249, and he's demanding it."

"I heard about Mark Adams." Indeed he had, for Becky had taken him on tour through Meadowood Hospital. Her mother had died there. He remembered gagging on the stink of urine, the bloodstains on the rusty ventilators, and the cockroaches scuttling on the floor. Such filth spoke of sloppy management. "I will not administer a drug to please his whims. Alexis or Shively might sue. When Joe complained about the splints, Alexis quoted the ADA laws and told him to go blow it out his ear."

Steve chuckled. "She might sue, but Shively's more liable to send his thugs after Hoffman. So there you have it. See if you can find a way around this."

Yeron scanned his file for basic histories: Shively Bogart, a twenty-eight-year-old with a prison record, most of it Mob-related. Mob, the humans' word for organized crime. He had learned that much from the news reports. Puncture gashes on his left anterior forearm tested positive for the toxin. Mark Adams, thirty-eight-year-old administrator, non-smoker, non-drinker, with multiple lacerations on his limbs and back. His wound tested positive for staph aureus, but no traces of the toxin. Alexis Carofalo, thirty-five-year-old respiratory therapist, ten-year history of arthritis, and deep gashes on her back, shoulders, and hands. Initial reports indicated Kryszka drool on her shoulder wounds. Her dossier came with a list of medications, mostly painkillers.

"Know what amazes me?" Steve went on with admiration. "Alexis's pain is so severe she needs narcotics to get through her daily activities. Yet she managed to kill one assailant, steal a gun, and run the other off her property. She was trying to protect her sister." He lowered his eyes. "The smoke inhalation caused her sister, Robin, an ugly flare with her asthma. She died on her way here, and we were not able to resuscitate her. I don't want Alexis to find out until you can stabilize her condition."

Yeron took it in while he scooped up syringes, central line kits, and other equipment he might need. "I am sorry to hear about her sister. Alexis sounds like a strong woman and a warrior. She did not deserve Joe's harassment."

"No, she did not." Steve's brown eyes took on a pleading look. "She earned her right to live, but that won't happen without CX249. I hope you make her case a priority."

Yeron nodded. "As you pointed out, Alexis and Shively tested positive. I find it hard to believe Adams avoided contamination."

"Adams used a spiked baseball bat on his assailant, and I've seen the damage that weapon can do." A shadowed frown crossed Steve's freckled face. "He looks like someone used him for a carving board, but we found no markers for the toxin in his blood."

"Very well, then." Yeron gave him what he hoped was an encouraging smile. "If Mark had gotten infected, tissue destruction would have set in by now. I can treat him with antibiotics."

"He won't like it." Steve shook his head. "He already reported one nurse because she had trouble putting in an IV."

Yeron mentally visualized Mark Adams' brain: 20 percent dollar signs, 78 percent meanness, and 2 percent logical thought. Despicable as the man may be, he did not deserve the attempt on his life. "Mark is acting out because he is frightened." He hoped at least part of this was true. "I will try not to upset him."

"Nice thought, but he's already upset. It's having a bad effect on the other patients." Steve waited while Yeron packed his remaining supplies. They headed out toward the elevator. "I've got to ask you a favor." He sounded like a child begging for a favorite toy. "Alexis's arthritis medicines stopped working, and she may have to quit her job. If she survives her injuries, will you accept her into your research program?"

Oh, if only my father were here. He knew how to treat wasting diseases. "That is going to be difficult," he said, avoiding Steve's eyes. "I have not worked with cases like hers. It could take months to develop a formula."

"So the answer's 'no.' How am I supposed to tell her that?"

Yeron sighed, hating the mist of disquiet settling over him. "I said it would be difficult. I never said impossible. I still have to treat her injuries first."

* * * *

At the trauma bay's entrance, two technicians passed them, each pushing a gurney bearing a vinyl body bag. More victims, Yeron surmised. The autopsies would come later. The trauma bay held two patients. The rugged male with the shoulder tattoos had to be Shively. Yeron recognized Mark, having watched him speak on televised conferences. The side doors opened, and two medics wheeled another patient, Alexis, toward the rear. With his kit in hand, Yeron entered.

Hoffman was with Shively. Nurses and technicians wearing isolation gowns, caps, and masks surrounded them. The three technicians near the door skittered sideways at Yeron's approach. The stares and hushed whispers began with his arrival. No one knew, much less cared, that his keen hearing picked up every word they said.

"Here it comes."

"Eigil's cousin."

Yeron stiffened. He turned toward the workers, his eyes narrowing, his brow furrowed. "My family is none of your business. If you have something to do here, glove up. If not, leave."

The three workers scattered out the side door.

"Good for you." Steve patted his shoulder. "Alexis should be cool since you and she already met."

"She may not because our meeting did not go well. I shall examine the two men."

Hoffman poked his head toward Steve and Yeron. "You do that, and make sure everyone gets CX249. Stretch your supply if necessary. Adams needs prophylactic doses."

"I do not recommend CX249 for prophylaxis," Yeron told him.

"Yeron." Hoffman spoke in a patient voice as if he were addressing a dull-witted child. "Adams has deep pockets and a lawyer. A lawsuit would jeopardize our good work. Understand?"

Yeron didn't know how pocket size affected medical treatment, but he understood the ramification of lawsuits. "Yes, I do. The medicine will not work at reduced doses. Suppose Alexis or Shively decides to sue?"

"They don't have the clout Mister Adams does."

With a deep sigh, Yeron proceeded toward Shively's bed. Shively appeared feverish. Perspiration pasted his blond hair to his head. Tributaries of sweat flowed down his ruddy face, huge biceps and the bands of muscle on his chest. Bloody black fluid seeped through the gauze on his left forearm, testifying to the seriousness of his injuries. Despite his pain, Shively managed a grin. It was a ghastly effort, but there.

"Hey, doc." He gave no sign of caring who was listening. "I kicked that creep's ass. He'll be taking a nice long dirt nap, and ... Ow!" The cheer fled from his voice.

With his forceps, Hoffman lifted the gauze off Shively's arm, revealing a crater of black filmy liquid, with grooves and troughs of serrated flesh, worse than Myles's had been. Without CX249, the poison would spread and kill him the way it had Myles. "Doctor Hoffman will start you on an antidote," Yeron told him. "You will need surgery to repair the tears."

"Understood. I'd die before I let that thing touch my wife. We're expecting our first kid."

Thing? Is that what I am to him? "Of course, you would. Is your mate ... wife ... all right?"

"She's shook up, but okay. The docs are keeping her overnight so they can watch the baby." He clenched his teeth, his face a rictus of pain. "Damn ... Alexis is my neighbor. I heard she got cut bad."

"She did, but we are taking ..."

A scream from the neighboring bed cut into Yeron's voice. It came from the fortyish man wearing torn wool trousers and a matching blazer. Someone cut away his right sleeve, exposing deep lacerations and reddened scratches on his arms and shoulders, but none of the dark pus or discoloring he saw with Shively. A nurse slipped a blood pressure cuff on him. "Mister Adams, calm down," she ordered.

"Where's the antidote?" Mark shouted. "I want that treatment *now!* I've got to make a respiratory conference in Houston next weekend."

Mark wants a fight, Yeron concluded. "You are in no condition to travel." He attempted a careful tone that he used with senile patients. "I shall examine those cuts."

"They're not cuts; they're bites. I had a tough fight with that monster."

"I believe you." Yeron approached his bedside. "Your wounds look like cuts, sir."

"Maybe they are, but he drooled on me. Kryszka saliva is poisonous, right?"

"It can be if the attacker ingests ..."

"Let's skip the preamble and start the antidote." Mark spoke in a tone of deepest frost. Yeron felt the chill go out in all directions. He pitied anyone who worked for him.

"Put a sock in it, mister!" Shively glared at him. "You're giving me a headache."

"I have to be on a plane to Houston!" Mark bellowed in a voice filled with rage. "I'm the keynote speaker."

Yeron looked over at Joe Hoffman, who was watching from Shively's bedside. Hoffman looked back at him and winked. This was turning nasty, and Hoffman found it amusing. Where Yeron came from, the healers never allowed such rude behavior. "Settle down, Mister Adams," he said. "I have enough solution for two people. Since Alexis and Shively have active infections, they will get the first available doses. Your laboratory results show infection from Earth microbes, but not the poison we saw with Alexis and Shively, so I will start you on an antibiotic. I can get CX249 for you in forty-eight hours if Doctor Hoffman still feels you need it."

"I don't want to hear about your timetable. I want the anti-dote now. If I run into complications, I'll sue this hospital."

"Shut up!" Shively hollered. "We're wasting too much time bullshitting. Give Alexis my share, Doctor. I'll wait."

"That is generous of you," Yeron told him. "Both of you need the CX249 right away. Mister Adams can wait."

"Obviously, you don't understand, so allow me to enlighten you." Mark's voice reeked with contempt. "I'm raising two children, run three departments at Meadowood Hospital, and I'm healthy as a bull. Alexis will die of her disease, if not her injuries. So let her go in peace."

"A lot of people will miss her, Mark," Steve pointed out.

"This presents a problem, Yeron," Hoffman spoke up, his voice low. "I don't want any backlash from the Mob or disability rights groups. The sickest patients get priority, but Mark's parents have influence with certain judges. Any lawsuit will cause disastrous repercussions for people who could benefit from our research."

"You've got that right," Mark said in a surly voice.

Then Yeron saw his opportunity to use a weapon that worked in every universe. Humans called it blackmail. He considered it a useful way to reason with somebody. "Since you insist on having your way, Mark, I shall tell the Department of Health about your hospital. The ants in the cafeteria, the dirty bathrooms, the way your overworked therapists are forced to omit treatments." His tight-lipped smile widened at the staff's wide-eyed stares and hanging mouths. "The people here look interested."

"I saw the safety violations, too," Steve jumped in with glee. "Tell everyone, Mister Adams, how much the administration pays you to cut spending on equipment and workforce. I bet your Houston contacts would love to know."

"You've got nothing on me. Meadowood's inspections are squeaky clean." Mark's anger was there, but the bluster was gone.

"I can arrange a surprise inspection," Yeron told him. "Unless you quit interfering with our work, I shall send out photographs of the squalid conditions."

"That won't be necessary." Mark's lips puckered a moment,

and then his mouth worked like a guppy. "Go ahead. Give Alexis and Shively the antidote."

"I knew you would understand." Yeron fought the urge to laugh. "The nurses will start you on Vancomycin." After hearing Mark's grunt, he went off to the side with Steve.

"Thank you." The relief in Steve's voice was unmistakable. "I'm glad you shut down Mister I've-Got-to-Go-to-Houston. Would you believe he chased Alexis with that baseball bat?"

"Yes, I would." Yeron gave him a dry smile. "I am glad he did not bring his bat today."

"So am I. If we were on the street, I'd work the man over. Hey…" Steve's pager let out three high-pitched beeps. Yeron stood by while he dialed the number. After he answered, the color on his face faded like clothing washed with harsh chemicals. The smile went next. "Did he get to her children? What about Tyrone?" Silence followed. Steve listened, nodding.

"They got Dee Hobson," he said after hanging up.

"Not Dee!" Sorrow cut through Yeron's heart. Dolores was one of the few people who greeted him with a smile and meant it. "Did the assailant…"

"She died protecting her children. They're in shock. Tyrone shot the killer … his army experience came in handy, but he could not save his wife. Officer Hazlett is bringing them to the hospital." He gave Yeron a solemn look. "Keep quiet about this. Dolores has been a good friend to Alexis."

"Of course, I will." Yeron tried to fight the panic that chased away the self-satisfaction he had over Adams. "After fighting her attackers and a boar like Mark, she may scream when she sees Joe or me."

Steve laid his hand on Yeron's shoulder. "I doubt it. She's hurting so bad she might not care. Take a look for yourself."

"All right." Hugging his kit against his side, Yeron went over to Alexis.

The technicians had cut away her shirt. Yeron lifted the gauze from her right shoulder. The foul-smelling cuts there had turned black as decayed teeth and wept dark, filmy pus. Her back looked as if someone had carved drawings into her skin with a wedge of glass. Blood matted her curly hair, but her face remained unscathed.

Despite her wounds, her widening brown eyes and aquiline face made her look like an angel. *If I were Mark,* he thought, *I would have chased her with gifts instead of a baseball bat.*

"I shall administer the formula now," he said.

"Thank you." Steve retrieved a central venous catheter kit and a bag of CX249 for Shively. "Let Joe handle Shively. His injuries are less complicated."

* * * *

Before Yeron could ask Alexis any questions or explain what he was about to do, harsh weeping assaulted his ears. A beefy woman in a navy scrub dress breezed in through the doors. She waddled toward Alexis and the maze of IV's already covering her. One hand clutched a chain of glass beads while the other dabbed her eyes with a hanky. Her legs, cased in thick stockings, were wide as trunks, but smooth. Blots of rouge flared against her pale cheeks. The woman screamed at everyone in a shrill voice, the way the human prisoners had at Eigil's compound. He tried to find a way to ask the trauma nurses to send her outside, but the words would not come.

"If she's dying, you'd better tell me." The woman's face held a horror-stricken look. She gave no sign of noticing Yeron. "Robin and Alexis are all I have. I have a right to know."

The disquiet that had nagged at Yeron thrust a lead blanket of fear over his shoulders. He had not factored Alexis's mother into his treatment plan.

"Mom." Alexis's voice was a barely audible croak. "I'll be all right."

"Don't give me that." The woman wrung her hands, causing her knuckles to crack and grind.

Yeron's throat tightened at the precious seconds lost because of this woman's histrionics. She needed a sedative, but everyone concentrated on their work. His throat was too dry to speak.

"You've got a toxic poison, and it will take a miracle to get you through this. You'll make it if a priest gives you the sacraments." Alexis's mother burst into a honking sob that Yeron could have done without. "Alexis ... you poor dear..."

"It's time I shut down this circus." Steve looked at Yeron and stepped closer to the bed. "Matilda, go to the waiting room. You're distracting my staff."

"Don't you dare order me around!" The woman whirled on him. "My daughter could be dying."

Alexis surprised them all by finding her voice. "Mom, why don't you go to the chapel and say a Rosary for Robin and me? The doctors have to do something unpleasant. I don't want you to watch."

She turned to her daughter, surprised and hurt. Deeply hurt. Something inside Yeron died at the sight of her wounded eyes. "You're delirious. You don't know what you're saying."

"We haven't got time to debate the issue," Steve said in a firm voice. "My partner needs to start an IV so your daughter can get the antidote."

"She already has three IVs!" The woman's voice rose to high, bugling notes.

"Let's not forget that you work here. If you continue harassing my staff, I'll report you to your supervisor."

Matilda stepped away from the bed. Her glowering eyes warned that she was storing Steve's threat in her mental files. If Alexis died, she'd probably go after the hospital, starting with Steve. Hoffman had feared a lawsuit from Mark, but no one expected problems from Alexis's mother. Alexis's labile blood pressures told him her mother's assessment was accurate. The black, filmy toxin continued to seep from the cuts on her neck and shoulders. She moved her right arm on command, but could not budge her left side, a sign of central nervous system involvement.

Yeron opened a tray containing a hair-thin micro-catheter. He needed her still and quiet so he could thread the catheter through her carotid artery and into the small arteries of her brain. He would then shoot in a drug to open the blood-brain barrier. The CX249 would go in next. While he swabbed the area with Betadine, Alexis's head turned. Her eyes settled on him, not with fright, but kindness.

Any second, she is going to scream, he thought.

"Thank you for talking Mark down." Her intent look made

him fidget. "He's nasty."

Yeron drew back slightly. He had not expected any civility, let alone gratitude. "I am glad I could help," he said in what he hoped was an encouraging voice.

"Will you be able to find a cure for me?"

"I am going to try for better treatment, if not a cure."

"I appreciate it." Her voice softened. "Don't take my mother personally. She's terrified. My sister's here with asthma and it's bad. She might lose both of us."

"You do not know that," Yeron said, threading his catheter.

"I know I'm in big trouble. My left side feels numb. I can't move my leg. Why?"

Because the poison infiltrated your brain, Yeron thought, but he dared not say it aloud. Most Kryszka assailants hobbled and tortured their victims before killing them and this made Alexis's injury unique. The micro-catheter enabled the CX249 to target her brain, neck, and upper shoulders. What then? Will it reverse the neurological effects? What about her brain function? He could not predict the results because he had never used the antidote on the nervous system. Without it, death was imminent.

"I will take your silence as bad news." Alexis spoke in a flat, resigned voice. "I don't care if you came from Mars. You can't work miracles. Steve ..."

Steve, who was eyeballing her monitors and calling out orders to the nurses, bent toward her, ear to her lips.

"Tell my mother I'm sorry and that I love her."

"You can tell her yourself after we operate." Steve smiled, but the confidence left his voice.

Yeron piggybacked the CX249 into the central line. Alexis grimaced but did not flinch.

"Something inside you gave you the strength to fight your attackers," he told her. "Use it now to survive."

"I'll ... try." Then she drifted into unconsciousness.

* * * *

In the operating room, four surgeons and two residents swarmed around Alexis. A dozen hands worked in unison to repair her wounds. Hoffman and Yeron teamed up to remove the glass fragments from her shoulders and back. Some fragments had embedded inches deep into her skin and muscles. Orthopedic surgeon Jack Levy sutured the gashes on her right hand and wrist, then stood back to observe the other procedures.

"Hang a liter of Ringer's and dextrose," Hoffman ordered the nurse beside him. "Get two liters of A Positive, stat. What's her blood pressure?"

"It's 70/40. Pulse 130."

Somewhere, Alexis was bleeding. Yeron probed the skin around her left ear and retrieved two more wedges of glass with his forceps. The blood kept coming, leaving a dark pool on the floor under the table.

"Pressure 60/35," Hoffman's assistant called out.

That was when someone's hand closed over Yeron's.

"You missed something." The spectral hand slid over Yeron's fingers, and chills raced through his body. The voice belonged to his deceased father. "Let me help you."

Teodon nudged Yeron's hand to the base of Alexis's neck, where one jagged piece of glass was embedded next to a major artery. Yeron retrieved it and repaired the nick in the vessel wall. The bleeding stopped. Before Yeron could thank him, Teodon was gone. No one else on the team gave any indication of having seen him.

Squiggly lines spurted across Alexis's monitor, followed by a shrill alarm. Her heart went into ventricular fibrillation, a precursor to cardiac arrest.

"She's going to code!" Hoffman bellowed. A surgeon and two nurses from the team pushed a defibrillator to the table. Hoffman pressed the defibrillator pads across Alexis's chest.

"Everyone, clear!"

The staff stepped away and the jolt of electricity caused Alexis's body to jerk. The tracing on the monitor continued to register ventricular fibrillation ... and then went flat.

"Start CPR."

An assistant proceeded with a cardiac massage. Ditto results.

Yeron knew that CA200 would revive someone faster than traditional methods. Hoffman, who captained the team, would decide whether or not to administer it. Even then, he could not guarantee Alexis's survival.

"Piggyback twenty cc's of CA200," Hoffman called out, "and push an amp of sodium bicarbonate."

The nurse complied, but Alexis's heart refused to stabilize.

Chapter Ten: Alexis on the Operating Room Table

Jackson Hospital's Research Floor, March 5, 1:00 a.m.

"Clear!" Hoffman shouted. Another jolt and Alexis opened her eyes. She drifted from her body and slid down through the table. Light as a piece of paper, she floated up from underneath the table toward the ceiling. She looked down at the top of Hoffman's head when he called for the CA200. The body on the table looked unfamiliar.

I'm checking out now. Okay, where's the tunnel? The lights?

No tunnels or lights beckoned, just a plethora of surgical trays and tired-looking people trying to gain purchase on her heartbeat. One ... not one, but two Kryszka doctors bent over her head. The older Kryszka whispered something to Yeron and helped probe her neck. Strange. No one had said anything to her about Yeron having an assistant. Perhaps Doctor Hoffman had kept this other doctor anonymous for security reasons.

A hole opened above her, and she glimpsed the tunnel. A starry light beckoned from beyond, but an invisible barrier kept her from moving.

"Doctor Hoffman!" she shouted. "Stop what you're doing. I'm going to a better place."

None of the doctors or their assistants looked her way. Why would they? They were trying to revive her corporeal body.

"Clear!" Hoffman repeated.

Alexis drifted downward, trying to think of a way to get their attention.

"Alexis." A man materialized at her side—her father, she noted with surprise. She recognized his black burial suit, his twinkling brown eyes, mischievous smile, and the scar on his chin. He'd regained his salt-and-pepper hair and the muscle tone he'd lost from his cancer treatments.

"Don't interfere. Those men are trying to save your life."

Before she could protest, Robin drifted from behind a curtain, wearing jeans and a sweatshirt. Her wheezing was gone and the fright had left her eyes. She smiled.

"What's Robin doing here?" Alexis turned toward her father.

"I think you already know."

Know what? Memories flashed before her: the lasers blazing across her mother's garden, the trees in flames, and the smoke crawling down her windpipe, Robin's spastic airways starving for air. "I don't understand it. Only one Kryszka works for Jackson Hospital."

"Yeron does not have much experience with your type of injury. I brought Ted ... a friend from the other side to give him a hand."

"Ted? That's an American name."

"You're right, it is. I can't pronounce his given name, so he told me to call him Ted. You fought bravely tonight." He nudged Robin's shoulder and grinned. "Didn't she?"

"She sure did." Robin grinned. "We love you, Alexis."

"I wish I could stay with you. So much has gone wrong...my marriage, my health, and the break-in at Mom's house."

"The last years have been hard, but you must go back. You've got an important job to do." His eyes glistened. "Robin came here to say goodbye."

"Tell Mom I love her and that I'll come for her when it's time," Robin said.

"What are you saying?" Her mind refused to process the truth. Her father gazed at her, his face unrelenting. "If I go back, I'll be alone. I'll become a burden to Mom, unless ... unless Yeron finds a cure for me."

Her father frowned, brows furrowed. "Things will get worse before they get better. If you keep an open mind, he'll find you a cure." He took her into his arms and kissed her on the forehead. "You must go now."

A spiraling black hole opened below Alexis. A vacuum sucked her into the darkness.

Chapter Eleven: Alexis Regains Consciousness

Jackson Hospital's Research Floor: March 5, 10:00 a.m.

Bubbling noises nudged Alexis awake. She lay on her left side inside a private room. At her left, IV pumps fed blood and other fluids into her veins. Her right arm, wrapped with thick gauze, lay propped on two pillows.

Burning like a poison sun flared from her vagina. The sensation of rusty nails twisted in her right arm. Her skin crawled. Her whole left side had fallen asleep. She suspected the burning came from a Foley catheter because of the faint sloshing she heard below her bed. Many of her patients had used one. A bubbling humidifier fed her moist oxygen through nasal prongs. She guessed that the doctors positioned her on the left side since her right had borne the brunt of the lacerations. Thick bandages and an IV port on her neck thwarted most head movements.

"Shit!" The word came through loud and clear. At least she could talk.

Rustling from above her followed. Faint tapping against the ceiling.

"Now what?" A jaw thrust yielded two inches, enough to face the ceiling. Three Mylar bouquets tethered balloon weights floated above her: smiling faces, rainbow butterflies, yellow roses, and two balloons with the Lord's Prayer. The prayer balloons must have come from her mother. Steve's wife, Becky, probably bought the rainbow butterflies. Becky was always buying balloons for patients. The balloons bobbed on long ribbons. Some of them touched the ceiling.

Signatures crowded the yellow rose. She longed for a close-up view of the rose so she could read the names. A lot of people cared about her, more than she expected.

Minutes passed, and the rose balloon drifted down toward her, close enough to read the handwriting. Her coworkers included get-well sentiments. She tried to raise her left hand, but pins and needles sliced through her fingers. The balloon floated back up toward the ceiling. She would have given a week's pay for another close look at the remaining signatures. After a minute, the balloon floated back to her, hovering long enough for her to read the remaining sentiments. She turned her attention toward her side table, hoping someone could move it next to her bed. As if on command, the table rolled toward the bed while the balloon glided back to the ceiling.

"Mind over matter, huh? No, that's not possible." After a brief mental conversation with herself, she tried out an explanation. The doctors installed a mechanism to enable her to move things by thought. No, that didn't make sense. She'd have to wait for her doctors to get an explanation.

She turned her gaze toward her glass doors. For all its technology, Jackson Hospital used manual sliding doors for each patient room. At her door stood a yellow cart. Further ahead, two women, a slender blonde in pink and a husky older woman, chatted in hushed voices at the station just outside her door, their backs toward her. Cindy was the nurse. The husky older woman ... *Dammit, I don't want Mom seeing me like this!*

"Mom!" She kept her voice low. "Mom?"

No answer, not that they heard her. She stared at them, trying to think of a way to get her mother's attention, and then the doors rolled open with grating noises. Her mother's laughter bubbled into her room. She was sipping coffee.

"Mom!" Louder this time.

Still no reply. Her mother laughed at something Cindy said. The Styrofoam cup flew off the counter, spraying steaming coffee on the linoleum floor and her mother's floral dress.

"Shit!" Alexis grimaced. "Mom, are you okay?"

"What's going on here?" Hoffman's voice bugled from the desk. He marched up to the two women, followed by Steve. "I told you the rules. No drinks or food at the station."

Cindy turned toward Hoffman. "Matilda's not on duty."

"Since when do we leave isolation doors open?" Hoffman's eyes glittered. "I don't care whether you're working or visiting. You follow my rules. Consider this a warning."

"Leave Matilda alone, Joe," Steve said in a tired voice. "She's been through enough."

"I understand that, but I can't excuse carelessness with the isolation rooms. Most of these patients are immunocompromised."

"No one meant any harm," Cindy told him.

"Don't let it happen again," Hoffman said in an acid voice. "Let's see if Alexis is awake."

Stopping by the yellow cart, the two doctors donned yellow gowns, gloves, and thick blue masks. Afterwards, Hoffman marched inside her room, Steve behind him.

"I'm awake and alert." Alexis nodded toward the two doctors. "My name's Alexis Carofalo. I'm a respiratory therapist. I'm here because a Kryszka renegade cut and poisoned me. My sister Robin had an asthma attack and my mother's worried about us. Obama's President, and..." She wrinkled her brows at the images of her father swimming through her mind.

Robin and I came to say goodbye.

"Wait a minute. Did Robin die?"

Hoffman jerked his head. He looked over at Steve, and then back at Alexis. "What gave you that idea?"

"I heard you ask for the CA200. Someone tried to defibrillate me and then you gave me CA200. I met my father and Robin. He said they came to say goodbye. They told me to go back, that I had an important job to do." She shook her head, puzzled. "I don't understand it."

"What you said about the CA200 happened," Hoffman said, casting his eyes down. "Your heart stopped beating for a minute. You gave us a scare."

Alexis arched her brows. "Even you, Doctor?"

"You spent most of yesterday on a ventilator. If my patients die, that speaks poorly for me." Hoffman spoke in a calm, sympathetic voice. "I never wanted anything to happen to you."

She looked over at Hoffman, wavering between anger and gratitude for his jump-starting her heart. Already, she missed her father. "Of course you didn't. I am sorry, too, for the way things went with Doctor Stanwood. Is he going to be all right?"

"Don't compare yourself to Myles Stanwood." Hoffman spoke in a strained voice, his eyes watering. "You got the CX249 straight away. Myles was hiking through the woods when he ran afoul of hostile Kryszka. By the time the medics got to him and Medivac'd him here, it was too late to save him."

"The CA200 saved your life," Steve told her. "You had a near-death experience."

"Near-death experience?" She shook her head and rolled her eyes. "Thank you for saving me, I think..." Her chin jerked, and her eyes settled on the two doctors. "What about Robin? She was turning blue right before me. The smoke..."

"Her frail lungs couldn't handle the smoke." Steve's voice saddened. "I'm sorry."

The tears came fast and Alexis was useless to stop them. Hoffman and Steve stood by her bed and watched her.

"Why Robin?" She gazed at the doctors' faces for answers and read sorrow. "Why did I survive, and she didn't?"

"I don't know." Steve drew in a sharp breath.

"Robin was my Jiminy Cricket." Alexis swallowed hard. "She visited every week, rode to my house by bus. If she caught me lifting something heavy, she scolded me. She and my father said they were proud of me."

Steve nodded with agreement. "Of course they are. Everyone here admires you for standing tall against those creeps."

"Your hand did not sustain any ligament damage." Hoffman spoke up in his let's-move-on voice. "Yeron accepted you for a clinical trial. Maybe, one day, you can work without splints."

"From your mouth to God's ears." Alexis tried for a smile but didn't make it. The prospect of a cure didn't mean as much with her sister gone. "Thank you."

"Don't mention it." Hoffman pulled the curtain shut. "I hear the poison affected your left side."

His examination began with auscultation of the lungs, observation of eye movement and facial expression, and memory tests. He tested her reflexes, leg strength, and hand grip.

"Can you feel that?"

"Yes, Doctor, I can."

"What is your pain level?"

"Twenty."

"Lift your right leg."

"Good. How about the left?"

"Sorry, Doctor, my left side went on vacation."

"Physical therapy will end the vacation." Hoffman smiled, but his voice was soft. "You may notice improvement as the CX249 takes effect. In the meantime, I'd like you to see Stanley Klein. He specializes in post-traumatic stress cases."

"Oh, you mean Stan—" *The Man,* she was about to say, but Hoffman's approach wasn't right. Why was he acting so kind? "I'll talk to Doctor Klein, but please don't yell at my mother. The door opened when I was trying to get her attention. She had nothing to do with it."

"Don't worry about it." Steve smiled and patted her shoulder.

"Don't tell me not to worry. I brought that smiley balloon to eye level by just thinking about it. I moved my side table the same way. I'll show you." Alexis turned her eyes toward the balloon, the one with the signatures. She visualized it floating toward her, and it did. She then focused on her side table. The table rolled toward her bed. "See? That's how I opened the doors. I tried to get my mother's attention, but I spooked her."

Hoffman and Steve exchanged glances.

"My mother will be glad to hear about the clinical trial ... hold on a minute." Alexis creased her forehead. "How much does she know about Robin and me?"

"She knows everything." Hoffman bowed his head. "I increased her blood pressure medicines. She's supposed to be home on sick leave, but she won't listen."

Alexis nodded. No surprise there. "She must be upset about the house, too."

"That she is," Hoffman agreed. "She's more worried about you, though, and she let us know it."

"In the emergency room." Alexis took in the doctors' sheepish nods. "She screamed at everyone before I fell asleep. I'm surprised the cops haven't lined up to talk to me. Did they say anything about catching another Kryszka soldier?"

"Whoa, there." Steve chuckled. "One crisis at a time."

"I told the police no visitors," Hoffman told her. "I was a little harsh with your mother just now, so I will apologize and try to convince her to go home."

"I appreciate that, but I still don't understand how I can move things just by thinking about them. At first, I thought you'd installed some mechanism in my bed."

Hoffman snapped his chart shut. "We didn't install any special equipment."

Alexis shrugged. "I figured that. So where did I get this sudden ability? It's not like I woke up and became psychic, right?"

"Doctor Klein can handle this." Hoffman edged toward the door. "We'll talk again later."

Before Alexis could reply, he skittered out to the station. Another shrug and she looked at Steve. "What's with him?"

Steve paced around her room, eyeballing her monitor and IVs. "The CAT scan showed minimal brain damage. Hoffman thought the CX249 might awaken dormant areas of your brain."

"What is that supposed to mean?" The gentle way he spoke inspired Alexis to continue digging for information. "Dee should be here for this discussion. She could handle bad news without getting emotional the way my mother does."

"Dee can't go anywhere." Steve took a seat facing Alexis, hands folded across his lap. His parchment-pale face, shadows peeping under the eyes, made him look eerily like a Kryszka. "An enemy soldier broke into her house and went after her boys. Her husband, Tyrone, got into the fray and shot the killer. The kids are okay, but Dee didn't ... survive."

"Not Dee!" Alexis's head drooped and more tears came to her eyes. "I lost a good friend and a sister. My mother might have a coronary. Now you say I have brain damage and don't give me any bullshit about it being minimal. Either I have it or I don't."

"Alexis ..."

"Dee left behind a husband and two boys, ages six and nine. I don't have anyone, and I'm headed toward SSDI. Doctor Hoffman should have let me go."

"He didn't because he hates losing patients." Steve let out a gusty sigh, his chestnut eyes brightening. "According to your vision, your father said you have an important job to do. So you've got to figure out a way to get on with your life."

"How am I going to do that with arthritis and brain damage? I'm not drinking and drugging as my aunt did." Memories of her aunt's shrill voice and caustic sarcasm made her want to cringe. "She got vicious with Robin because she was too docile to fight back."

Steve nodded solemnly. "Robin told me she was afraid of Susan."

"I don't want to be like my aunt. I don't want to do what she did. I'd rather be dead."

"Unlike your aunt, you have a chance at a cure." Leaning forward, Steve propped his elbows on the bed rail. "The brain damage really was slight. It affected your left side, but the poison would have killed you without a timely antidote. CX249."

"I remember thanking Yeron for fighting Mark for the CX249 doses. The soldier who cut me drooled on me before I poked out her eye." Alexis shivered. "How about defining 'dormant'?"

"We've never used CX249 on the central nervous system, so we don't know what to expect." A long pause followed. "The CX249 may have rewired your brain."

"What does that mean?" Alexis's eyes bulged like saucers. "Will I go berserk like Laurel?"

"No." Steve's voice remained calm, but what color he had drained from his face. "The treatment may have awakened previously inactive areas, endowing you with new abilities. In your case, psychokinesis."

Chapter Twelve: Alexis's New Power

Jackson Hospital's Research Floor, March 5, 12:00 p.m.

Steve looks like he's going to shit his pants, Alexis thought. *He doesn't realize how often I watched the clock for my next Percocet because my hands hurt so much. He never heard my litany of requests: Can someone open this bottle? Can somebody connect this tubing for me? If I can move things with my mind, I won't have to use my hands so much.*

She clung to that thought as she considered the times she had to take unscheduled breaks, leaving Laurel alone in the critical care units. The last time was a capital mistake and, like most bad choices, it snowballed into a huge nightmare: Mayes's asphyxiation, the two alien attackers, and Robin's death. Perhaps Laurel had teamed up with the Kryszka. Alexis promised herself to figure out the why and how after the doctors cut her sedation.

"If I can move things without touching them," she said, watching Steve's facial expression, "I can work around my disability."

"Psychokinesis might make activities of daily living easier." Steve's soothing voice offered her hope. "First, someone has to show you how to master your talent. Otherwise, it can get out of control and things break. Yeron understands psychokinesis better than any human doctor. He taught Becky how to manage her power."

At the mention of Yeron's name, her body tensed. She tried telling herself that clinical trials meant time spent with the respective doctor, but the telling did little to stop the sounds of gunfire flashing through her mind. She gritted her teeth. "If you watched Becky's training sessions, you can show me how to control it."

"It doesn't work that way," Steve told her. "I learned basic steps in managing psychokinesis, but Yeron lived it his whole life."

Alexis sighed. Yeron acted kind, but she kept seeing her Kryszka attacker's drooling mouth full of razor-sharp teeth. She furrowed her brows, contemplating the older Kryszka's presence during her vision. Assisting Yeron with surgery implied a willingness to help. "Is there another Kryszka working here with Yeron?"

"No, he works alone." Steve shook his head with stubborn weariness. "Why are you asking me this? Yeron will move heaven and earth to find a treatment for you. Neither Hoffman, I, nor anyone else knows how to train your psychokinesis. Yeron does."

"Let me ask you something." Alexis averted her eyes, not caring to acknowledge her nightmarish flashbacks. "Did Yeron tell Hoffman my splints were spreading bacteria?"

"No, that was Hoffman going into overkill." A whine crept in with his authority, and Steve sounded worn out and old. The spooked look in his brown eyes reminded her he'd endured his horrors through hostile Kryszka soldiers. "Yeron wants a sterile environment for his patients. He recommended Tyvek biohazard suits, but Administration won't spend the money for them. Yeron may not be able to pronounce contractions or understand slang. That doesn't make him bad." A steely look crept into his eyes. "You've got a chance to overcome your disability. Use it."

Alexis sat quiet, looking at Steve. He and Yeron had insisted she get first dibs on the CX249, under threat of a lawsuit by Mark. *If you keep an open mind, you will realize a cure,* her father had said. Could she put aside the horrors at her mother's house and work with Yeron?

Maybe. She expected to face other monsters—SSDI, hospital administration, and Mark Adams—Meathead Mark—Mark of the baseball bat, Mark who wrote her off as dead. "If Yeron can find a way to cure me and teach me how to use this power, I'll work with him. I don't want him barging into my room though. Tell him to knock, call my name from outside, and wait for me to answer before he enters. If he tries to shake me awake, he's liable to spook me. I appreciate everything he's done thus far, but after what I went through..."

"No problem." Steve smiled like a teacher who had coaxed a difficult answer from a student. "Talk over your feelings about the shooting with Stan."

"Keep Mark away from me. He's so cold-blooded that if you poured boiling hot water down his throat, he'd pee ice cubes."

"Duly noted." The relief was evident in Steve's laugh. He glanced toward the hall. "I think your mother went home. Try to get some sleep. You're going to need a lot of therapy."

After Steve left, Alexis attempted to move her left hand. It slid several inches across her mattress. She tried the same maneuver with her left leg. Ditto results. It was a start. She eased her head against the pillow and drifted to sleep.

Images rose before her eyes. She knelt behind the bushes in her mother's yard, shooting at her assailant. Robin cringed beside her, wheezing, coughing, and screaming. A laser sliced her way, and the tree above her caught fire. She skittered sideways. Her legs tangled together, causing her to spill onto the grass. The Kryszka assailant lunged at her with his eyes rolled back, teeth gaping, and ropy saliva drooling down his chin. She reached into her pocket for the gun. Empty. Screams came and died in her throat; then sirens chorused in the distance. The police arrived too late, and she was going to die.

Chapter Thirteen: "Stan the Man" Counsels Alexis

Jackson Hospital, March 5, 5:00 p.m.

The frightening images fell away, replaced by a liquid supper on a tray beside her bed—gelatin, water ice, chicken broth, and apple juice in sealed plastic cups. She gazed at her hands—the right one swathed in gauze and the left nudging several inches with each attempt at movement. Hardly useful tools for opening such containers. She toyed with the idea of trying her mind power on dinner when her doors slid open.

Her mother ambled into the room, wearing an isolation gown. Alexis's heart sank at the sight of her bloodshot eyes, shadowed features, and set jaw.

"Mom, what are you doing here? Doctor Hoffman wants you home, resting."

"I tried. I've been staying with Fenimore." Her mother's eyes brightened. "I get depressed when I look out the window and see my burned-out house."

"I'm so sorry about that." Alexis's voice broke. "I would have done anything to save Robin. I don't know what else to say, except I'm sorry."

"Honey, it wasn't your fault." Her mother rushed over to her bedside. She cradled Alexis's head in her gloved hands and kissed her on the cheek through her mask. "You stood tall against those monsters. I'm so proud of you."

"I tried so hard to look out for Robin." A tear welled up in Alexis's right eye and ran down her cheek. "I could have dealt with the fire if she had lived."

"I know, honey," her mother said in a gentle voice. "You kept those monsters away from her. I thought I'd lost you, too, but

God has other plans for you."

"Maybe." Alexis attempted another movement with her left hand and winced at the burning pain. "What's this I hear about your blood pressure?"

Her mother lowered her eyes. "I got dizzy and fainted. My blood pressure was one seventy-five over one hundred. Doctor Leicht wanted to check me into the hospital. I said 'no.'"

Goosebumps rose on Alexis's skin. "Why didn't you listen to him? You've got to take care of yourself."

"I can't afford to pamper myself now. Look ..." She pointed an accusing finger at the supper tray and then proceeded to rip open the containers. "How do they expect you to open these lids?"

"I'll take all of it except the broth. Mom ..." Alexis took in her mother's pale, tired features. "You should be home in bed. Ask one of the nurses to help me."

Her mother pointed to the station and wagged her finger. "They're running like chickens." She turned back to Alexis and began spoon-feeding her the water ice. It felt sweet and cool against her parched lips.

"Thanks," Alexis said after she finished. She hesitated, trying to find a lead-in to the topic of her psychokinesis. "I'll be able to feed myself soon. The doctors are working on a better treatment for my hands."

"What kind of treatment?" Her mother arched her fine brows. "Surgery?"

"Well ... first, they're giving me a drug to counteract the poison."

"Doctor Leicht told me about that." Her mother leaned forward, her head tilted. "I can't remember the name."

Alexis studied her mother's red, swollen eyes. She must have been up all night crying. Mentioning her new power might pile on more stress than she could take. "It's called CX249..."

A knock outside interrupted her thoughts. A husky male wearing a brown suit stood outside the glass door. He was reaching for a mask and gown. "Alexis, it's Stanley Klein. May I come in?"

"Stan the Man!" Alexis nodded toward the door. "You are truly the man. Come on in."

"Alexis." Her mother frowned. "He might not appreciate jokes about his name."

"Who said I'm joking?" Her lips quivered, and any trace of a smile that might have materialized was gone. "Two Kryszka came after Robin and me. Robin's gone and so is my good friend, Dee. The doctors told me the poison scrambled my brains. Do I look like I'm laughing?"

Her mother leaned against the wall and sagged. "Oh, my God! Doctor Leicht told me about the poison. What's this about your brain? What happened to you?"

"That's what we're trying to figure out." Stan smiled. "It's better if Alexis and I chat alone. Why don't you go home and get some rest?"

"All right." Her mother's dour look intimated that excluding her from this interview racked up points against Stan. "Alexis, I'll be back tomorrow."

"Thanks, Mom. Now, I mean it. Take care of yourself." Alexis watched her mother's retreating drooped figure.

The doctor turned toward Alexis. "If calling me 'Stan the Man' helps you deal, go ahead and do so. I've been called worse."

"Stan the Man it is. Since when do you work Friday evenings?"

"I work all hours during patient emergencies."

"I guess you can count the attack on me and my sister an emergency.'" Alexis waved him toward the chair by her bed. "Have a seat, and I'll tell you about the shooting and nightmares."

Stan took a seat and spread her chart across his lap. With his bald head and thin-lipped smile, he reminded her of a comic strip character.

"Where do you want me to start? The break-in?"

"We'll get to that. I heard a rumor that you're planning to kill yourself." He spoke in a confiding voice, the kind her coworkers used to reveal someone's firing. "Is this true?"

Alexis opened her mouth to speak, but the words wouldn't come. She stared at Stan, feeling the way she did as a teenager when her father caught her smoking behind the garage. *"What are these doing here?" He smiled when he two-fingered the pack of Marlboros from her side pocket.* Back then, she had no answer, nor did she have one now.

"Who told you that?" she asked when she found her voice. "My mother? Don't listen to her. She can't think straight because she's upset about Robin and me."

"I never spoke to your mother. I got this information from Doctors Leicht and Hoffman."

"They're full of shit. Steve's too close to the situation, and Hoffman loves melodrama." Tingling muttered up Alexis's left arm, but no burning. She shifted sideways. "Both doctors are great medicine men, but they don't know squat about the psyche."

Stan cupped his hand behind his ear. "I hear a rattling drawbridge. It must be your defenses going up."

"Get to the point." What she wanted was peace.

"You're right about your doctors. They don't understand the psyche. They've only worked with Kryszka casualties who watched relatives die because of these monsters—like you, and people coping with serious illnesses—again, like you. Steve's wife went through it, too, and lost her father, a close friend, and a brother. Steve lived through two shoot-outs at the old Kryszka compound. Joe treats the injuries, complicated ones at that. What could they possibly know about the signs of pre-suicidal depression?"

Shit! Alexis gave him a censuring glare. *Why aren't we discussing my nightmares?*

Stan pulled his chair closer to Alexis, elbows resting on her chart. "You have to answer some questions first."

"I'm sure you can't wait to ask them." Alexis mustered as much sarcasm as she could.

The doctor nodded, unfazed by her tone. "I don't subscribe to organized religion, but I believe in a Higher Power. I also believe in responsibility, as I'm sure you do." He lowered his voice. "I'm counseling your coworkers. They're frightened because two of their own died, including Dee, and another, besides yourself, has nasty injuries. You're too intelligent to attempt suicide without making it count, but your coworkers will know."

"Who were the others ...?"

He raised his hand. "Your mother, who's at risk for a coronary, she'll know. No matter how carefully you stage it, she'll figure out what happened."

Alexis couldn't argue with that. She long ago gave up hiding her symptoms from her mother. Her mother could tell how she was feeling by the twitch of her eyelids.

"The surviving Kryszka soldiers—I'm sure there are some—are watching. They'll know, too. Do you want to give them that satisfaction?"

Alexis got to thinking about the two Kryszka soldiers and their weapons, sniffing around the hospital with hidden cameras. She burst out laughing.

Stan shrugged and looked at her with his *I've-heard it-all-before* twinkle in his eyes. "What's so funny?"

"You think Kryszka soldiers are watching me. Do you know something I don't?"

"You'll have to draw your own conclusions about the Kryszka soldiers. The surveillance monitors recorded your description of your near-death experience. You said, 'They told me to go back, that I had an important job to do.' I suggest you contemplate your vision and think about what that job might be. Talk to people."

"Oh, really?" Alexis tried again for the sarcastic approach, but a tear rolled down her left cheek. "Such as who? Dee was a great listener, but guess what, Stan the Man? She's dead. And by gosh, my sister, who could understand more than people gave her credit for, is gone, too. Am I supposed to do this contemplating alone in this hospital bed?"

Another tear slid down her cheek. With her left hand immobile, and her right bandaged, she couldn't stop it.

"Not necessarily." Stan's voice softened. "Speak with the other survivors."

"That's kind of hard when I can't move my left side." Alexis gave a bitter laugh. "Besides, I'm confined to an isolation room. I can't even pick up a phone."

"Sure you can, if you use your psychokinesis," Stan said with a dismissive wave of his hand. "Ask Patient Information to dial the room number for you. You are friendly with the other survivors, aren't you?"

Alexis hesitated, avoiding Stan's eyes. Would Tyrone, Johnny, and Shively make good listeners? Their help had enabled her to squeak through activities of daily living and working at the hospital. When she got right down to it, though, she didn't know them well.

"All but one," she said at last. "I don't know how much good talking to them would do. Unlike me, they went into this healthy, and they've all got children."

"You've got to try," Stan told her. "No one can make the nightmares go away, the dangers less real, or the symptoms less painful. None of this was your fault. If you can accept that, your healing process will start."

"Should I tell these people how it felt to exchange fire with these beings?"

"Talk about your attack, anything, whatever you need to figure out a positive path. Listen to them, and if their stories don't jive, for crying out loud, Alexis, make it look natural."

Stan stood up, chart cradled in his hand. "What do you like best about your job?"

Alexis considered the surface of the question. "Saving lives ... there is that. Before the arthritis got bad, I used to enjoy chatting up my patients and making them laugh. Now, I try to squeak by each day and do the job as best as I can."

In her fantasy world, she'd convinced her patients to stop smoking and made a passel of friends. She had persuaded one middle-aged male to give up cigarettes and befriended an older woman named Alma, who later hired Robin to clean. After the pain got ugly, she concentrated on eking out the workday and sparing a pinch of sympathy. She felt tempted to share the fantasy with the doctor, but Stan would recognize bullshit when he heard it.

"Do yourself a favor, Alexis. Start chatting again. Ask the people you meet how their day went. If something is bothering them and they want to talk, listen. Compassion will make your nightmares less real."

"I'm not treating patients now."

"I'm talking about your caregivers and visitors."

"Yeron too?" Alexis's eyes widened.

"Of course," Stan smiled. "Hearing things from his perspective might be interesting."

Chapter Fourteen: Woehar Punishes Laurel

Kryszka Underground Colony, March 5, 8:00 p.m.

A scraping sound intruded on Laurel's consciousness. She was lying in a metal bed in a Kryszka clinic. Someone had bandaged her arms. She couldn't remember the doctor's name, but her answers brought smiles to his face. He gave her painkillers. As her vision cleared, she realized the bandages were metal straps that tied her chest, hips, and legs. The effects of her pain meds must have worn off because her body ached as if someone had pounded her with a baseball bat. Someone tethered her arms by the wrists to a metal ring above her head. Woehar stood by her table, clad in her navy tunic, rolling a scalpel between her hands.

At the sight of the scalpel, Laurel's eyes bulged. The camaraderie she'd forged with Woehar was gone. More warmth exuded from the surrounding machinery than from Woehar's chiseled features. "You lied to me, animal!" Woehar scolded. "I do not like someone, especially a subspecies like yours, trying to make a fool of me."

"I'm not making a fool of anyone!" Laurel shrunk away from Woehar, as much as the straps would allow.

"Oh, no?" Woehar stuck her face in front of Laurel's, and her features changed. Her cheeks took on a scabrous look, her teeth coated with dried blood, and her hair ebony. A black cape replaced her blue tunic. Her breath smelled like rotten tomatoes, and she was not Woehar. "Seven of my pupils died. You never said your enemies had military experience."

"I told you the truth, Abaddon. I did everything you told

me. My enemies are civilians and most of them disabled."

"My name is not Abaddon," the thing before her shouted. "Have you gone crazy?"

"I'm not crazy. I did everything you told me. You made me hurt those girls and choke that woman. I went along with it because I knew the headaches would come." Laurel's voice broke into a honking sob.

"You only pretend to be crazy." The Woehar-Abaddon thing cradled the scalpel in one palm and jabbed the blunt end against each finger. "One of my instructors contacted me as he lay dying. Alexis, whom you profess to be so sickly, shot him and his pupil at her mother's home. Her mother's neighbor contacted an officer who felled another. Alexis's apartment was empty, but her next-door neighbor, a trained killer, eliminated another. Your nemesis, Dee, died, but her mate shot and killed one. Mark, your former superior, eliminated another and so did your peer worker, John."

"Wait a minute," Laurel cried, overwhelmed by the litany of casualties. The face before her continued to change, one minute Woehar, the next, Abaddon, then back to Woehar again. "Are you and Abaddon working together? Did all your pupils die?"

"I lost seven, but Abaddon has nothing to do with this. In fairness to you, a tough officer killed one of them. I suspect you omitted their military background, hoping my pupils would die. Was that what happened?"

Laurel opened her mouth to scream, but her throat felt like dry cotton. "Alexis's hands are badly deformed. It takes her three times longer than it should to do her work. Most of the time, she asks someone to help her. She has no military experience."

"She has no military experience," Woehar mimicked in a high-pitched voice. "Laurel, she used a gun—Kryszka guns. Her technique was sloppy but effective."

"Tyrone is a church boy who hates violence."

"Church did not prevent him from killing." Woehar propped her hands against Laurel's table. "Your ears must be on your back because people like you only listen after a beating. Beating is a primitive way to discipline someone. I prefer a more sophisticated punishment."

Again, that scraping sound. Woehar went back to rolling the scalpel. The knife jumped from finger to finger and then danced along one side of her hand and down the other. What horrible torture was she planning? Electric shock? Gouging an eye?

Woehar's lips curled into a smirk. "I have plans for your surviving friends. I will tell you more after your operation."

Operation? What operation? Wet warmness flooded her thighs and buttocks as Laurel's bladder let go. The air filled with the faint smell of urine. Woehar's blank eyes never wavered.

"Tell me your plans," Laurel begged, stalling for time. "I didn't know these people could fight. Alexis is dead, right?"

"She is alive and talking." Woehar's voice dripped with sarcasm. "The humans' officers have taken Alexis and her surviving friends to their hospital, but my camera followed them. They will pay, Laurel, they will pay. I expected one or two of my pupils to die, but not seven."

That grin. That was horrible. Worse was the hungry look in her eyes. "How will you make the officers pay?"

"Humans are superstitious and the unknown terrifies them. I will show them the dark side of their moon by making creatures that walk like the dead and kill."

"What does the moon have to do with this?"

"Kryszk, my home planet, has six moons, and during the day, they are dark. According to our legends, horrible things happen on the dark sides of these moons, such as what I plan to show humans. I am using a chemical—vischlausk—that will turn a live human into a mindless zombie. The being looks like a corpse but feeds on human flesh. I am developing hundreds of these specimens. When the time is right, I will unleash them inside your hospital."

She paused and smiled. "Your punishment comes first, though, so I shall proceed with your operation."

Laurel's lips trembled, mostly out of rage. All of this had happened because Alexis squealed about the dead patient. If Alexis had kept her mouth shut, Laurel would have a job and the accident wouldn't have happened. The evil glint in Woehar's eyes and her harsh voice warned that punishment would come hard. This operation ... she didn't like the sound of that. "I know where you could do the most damage at the hospital." She hoped the information would garner a reprieve. "The most vulnerable floor."

"Most vulnerable?" Woehar's lips curled into a malignant grin. "This information could prove useful. We will talk later." She began swabbing Laurel's legs.

"Wait ..." Laurel tried to sit up, but the belts held her fast. "What are you going to do to me?"

Woehar looked at Laurel, favoring her with a mad grin. "In certain cultures, people caught committing a crime forfeit a body part. You are valuable to me alive, but your oversight requires punishment. Do you agree?"

Laurel's sphincter gave way, dropping a huge gooey load in her underpants. The stink of feces overpowered the urine smell. Woehar continued swabbing her feet without so much as a grimace and then started on Laurel's hands.

"There." She regarded Laurel like a job well done. "I shall penalize you for six soldiers since they died needlessly. For each one, you shall lose a body part. I shall help myself to your little fingers, your index toes, and your fifth toes."

Woehar raised her scalpel over Laurel's head, angling for the hands.

Terror, sharp as a tornado filled with needles, blew through Laurel's drug-induced haze. "Wait a minute ... don't I get a second chance? Oh, God, please don't hurt me."

"Next time, think before you give me information."

Woehar's face held a greedy, hungry look. Before a forest fire of terror clouded her mind, Laurel wondered if Woehar had gotten into the vischlausk, too. Would vischlausk affect Kryszka the way Woehar said it did humans? *She killed other humans with that same weapon!* Laurel continued to shriek and cry, but her pleas got lost in the wailing of voices inside her head. She tried to turn away again, but the bands cut off any attempt at movement.

"This will not take long." Woehar's hollow smile sent liquid fear through her veins. "After we finish this dreary lesson, I will show you my laboratory."

Bolts of white-hot agony shot through Laurel's left hand.

Dark red blood jetted from her stump. Hissing followed. The scalpel sliced through meat and joint. Minutes later, her pinky wriggled in Woehar's hand.

"Stop!" she screamed, feet drumming against the table. "I won't let it happen again, only, please don't hurt me anymore."

"Scream all you like." Woehar's frosty eyes surveyed her from her narrowed sockets. "No one will hear you, and no one will care. Not even your humans will miss you."

"Why ... this?"

"So you can feel the pain my pupils did. Besides, I enjoy finger meat."

"Can't you see I'm bleeding to death?"

"Humans do not die easily." Woehar raised the severed finger to her lips and chewed, making horrible chittering sounds. Her eyes filled with bliss. Laurel's surroundings blurred, and then Abaddon was there, sucking blood from the finger with horrible slurping sounds. "This tastes so sweet. Why should I stop?" The Woehar-Abaddon thing moved toward Laurel's left foot.

"Don't!" Laurel jerked her foot, and the metal band dug into the fleshy part of her calf. Gray dots rose before her, but she struggled to stay awake. "You said I was more valuable to you alive. You said..."

Agony like a thousand razor blades sliced through her foot. Woehar-Abaddon helped herself to the index toe. The blood ran out of her wounds in a steady flow. It splashed on Abaddon's cape. He cupped it in his hands and drank. "Wait..." Woehar-Abaddon started as if waking from a dream and she was Woehar. Abaddon was gone. "You are right about the bleeding. I should cauterize."

As if an afterthought, Woehar reached for a tube-like device and fired. The white nova burned through Laurel and then over her stumps and remaining fingers. Smoke drifted up, and the sweet smell got Laurel to thinking about her own human dinners.

"You owe me four more," Woehar said between chews and swallows. "When the blood rushes out in a gush, I do not want to stop. I shall devour your limbs if you continue to provoke me."

She gazed at Laurel, smile in place, with blood and saliva dripping on her tunic. "You, more than any human, should understand why I savor such delicacies."

"All right, you made your point." Laurel was bawling now. She thought about her disciplinary sessions with her girls, understood she was getting the same cruelties she'd inflicted on them. "Your poison will kill me."

"Only vischlausk makes our saliva poisonous. I did not ingest any today, and I am not drooling on you. Besides, I am cutting with instruments."

Woehar loomed over her and Laurel retched at the sight of the gristle on her cheeks, the flecks of pink flesh, the blood trailing from her lips in thin ribbons.

"Your friend Becky can attest to my hunger."

"Becky?" Laurel shook her head. "I don't know anyone named Becky."

"Of course you do. She is the mate of Steve, your lung healer. She watched me consume her friend alive." Another blast of pain, only with the left index toe cut it was like a low primal pain that would not respond to drugs. Woehar moved onto Laurel's right pinky, much the way someone might help themselves to a chicken leg. Laurel squirmed and thrashed against her ties. The stabbing, her nerve endings screaming, screaming ...

The dots rose up before Laurel again. A cloud of gray loomed ahead of her. Laurel went for it, Abaddon prodding from the shadows, followed by her screaming and the stench of raw flesh.

If I survive this, she thought, *I'll make Alexis pay.*

Then there was nothing.

Chapter Fifteen: Alexis's Interview with the Police

Jackson Hospital, March 6, 9:00 a.m.

Another night of troubled sleep passed. The nightmares drummed through Alexis's mind like hoof beats. Stabbing pain in her right arm jarred her awake. Sometime during the night, it had slid off the pillow and flopped onto the mattress. This morning her hand swelled up like a balloon. After she piled two pillows at her side—doing so by levitation—she rested her arm on them. An aide came by with breakfast and more ice. An hour later, knocking sounded at the door.

Two cops entered, Officer Hazlett and the detective who looked like Shirley Temple's twin. Only now, a paler version with labored breathing. Both of them wore gowns and masks.

"Hazlett," Alexis said. "Ah … I mean, Officer Hazlett."

"Hazlett will do." The officer smiled.

"You're the guy who wouldn't let me fall asleep." Alexis shifted her gaze toward the detective. She knew this woman from somewhere but, because the mask covered her face, she couldn't place her. "You came to my house during the fire, but I don't remember your name."

"Julia McMullen. Please call me Julia," the detective said in a pleasant voice. "Your doctors aren't happy about our visit, but they left it up to you. Feel like answering some questions?"

"Sure. Did you find the other Kryszka soldier in my mother's garden?"

"I found his body on a side street not far from your mother's house." Julia laughed and followed it up with a harsh cough.

"You did a great job retooling his face. He must have called for backup before he died." Another fit of coughing. "His backup and I surprised each other. I was faster."

At that, Hazlett chuckled.

Alexis's eyes narrowed. These cops might treat this battle like a tea party, but Alexis, who lost a sister and a friend, wasn't smiling. "Good. He can't hurt anyone else."

"He won't." Hazlett pulled a chair up to her bed while Julia remained standing. "I'm surprised the Kryszka broke into your home. Most assaults happen randomly in deserted areas."

Alexis shrugged. "They saw my sister and me alone in the house and mistook us for an easy meal."

"They went after healthy people, too." Julia's hoarse voice sounded like a longtime pack-a-day smoker. "Mostly people who work at this hospital. The killers planned their route and knew who they wanted to get. That's not the Kryszka's MO. Someone from our town might be giving them names and addresses."

"Do you have any enemies?" Hazlett asked.

Alexis shrugged. "Who doesn't? Morris Klinger, a nurse manager from the ICU, belittles me every chance he gets."

"I'm talking about the kind who threatens bodily harm," Hazlett said. "Morris Klinger is dead. Kryszka soldier."

Alexis's brown eyes widened. "I can't believe that. He's strong as a bull."

"It takes more than brawn to fight those soldiers."

"Shit!" Alex shifted her arm, winced, and then glanced at the clock to see if she was due for pain medicine. She wasn't.

"Has anyone threatened to harm you?" Hazlett persisted like a dog after a bone.

She turned her gaze toward him. "My ex, Mark Adams, ordered the doctors to withhold my medicine because he thought I was going to die. Ten years ago, he went after me with a baseball bat, but you already have that on file." She wrinkled her brows. "Those soldiers put a hurt on Mark, too, so he's not your guy."

"They did," Julia said. "Mister Adams used his baseball bat to defend himself..."

"Julia." Hazlett shook his head and glared at her.

"He killed his assailant with the same bat he used on me." Alexis gazed at the two officers. "What's the big secret?"

Julia gave Hazlett a sharp look. "Mister Adams is entitled to privacy."

"Whatever." Alexis sighed. "Laurel Grant, a coworker, wants me and others here dead. Dee Hobson, our boss, said Laurel looks like someone who'd kill. She begged me to take a day off because she thought Laurel might try to hurt me."

The officers nodded, scribbling notes.

"Thing is, Laurel is too stupid to concoct something like this. I've got one other enemy, Ms. Grese, Director of Human Resources, but she never killed anyone."

Julia burst into another streak of coughing. She drew in a deep breath, and let out a sibilant wheeze. "Jim, we should question the Grese woman. She might point us to a lead." She turned her gaze toward Alexis. "Her partner, Doctor Tynan, is dead too. A neighbor found his remains in his living room the night you were admitted."

Skeletal fingers of terror slithered up Alexis's spine and shoulders. "Who else?"

"Alma Parker and Yvette Johnson. Do you know them?"

Alexis nodded, her breath heaving. "My sister cleaned for Alma and Alma used to watch out for her. Yvette worked the evening shift, and ... my God!" Her voice rose in crescendo with each word. "Are Mark, Shively, and I the only ones who survived these assaults?'

"Two others did," Hazlett said in a bleary voice. "Tyrone Hobson and Johnny Murkowski. You know them?"

Alexis nodded. "Johnny's a work buddy. Tyrone is the only decent security guard here. He's Dee's husband."

"How did you meet Shively?" Julia asked, scribbling fast.

Alexis's left hand moved, seeking the covers. Tingling surged through the limb with every movement. "Shively's my next-door neighbor. He and his wife take my trash out because I can't carry it myself." She raised her hand, sending pins and needles racing down her forearm. "Is Tyrone or Johnny hurt?"

Julia sighed. "After Johnny shot his intruder, something he couldn't describe pushed him down his steps. He busted three ribs and punctured a lung. Tyrone walked away without a scratch."

Alexis gasped. "I'm surprised these soldiers picked on the guys. All of them are tough and healthy."

"All of them share a past with you." Hazlett spoke with a dreadful patience. "These killers don't seem to care about health or gender, but they go after the victim's loved ones."

"I see." Alexis inspected her right arm and then eased it back on the pillows. It was going to take forever to heal. "Any other deaths?"

"Chris Hayes, a security guard," Hazlett said in a sour voice. "Someone found his remains in his car."

No surprise there. Except for Tyrone, those guards are pissants in diapers. Alexis shrugged. "The others and I share a history. That makes me a target, doesn't it?"

"It looks that way." Julia marched over to the door, a woman determined to make her point. "One day, you're a respiratory therapist, minding your own business." She went back toward the window. "The next, two Kryszka soldiers single you out, while their comrades go after your friends." She flung her hands open and faced Alexis. "Why?"

Another sibilant wheeze, louder this time.

In the next second, Alexis visualized Robin sagging against the door, her mouth panting, her body wracked with coughing spasms. Clumps of bloody mucus plopped on her sweatshirt. Robin unconscious, chest heaving. Memories flooded back, and she recalled Julia as a former patient in ICU. Back then, Julia went by the surname McDevitt. She suffered respiratory complications that necessitated a tracheotomy. The stoma had closed long ago, but Alexis visualized the scar underneath Julia's uniform, an angry red testimony of the violations to her body. "Julia, I told you everything I know." Her voice inched notches higher. "Now go to the emergency room, before you have a respiratory arrest the way my sister did. Please. You had no business going to that fire."

"The smoke and fire have been rough," Julia admitted, "but it's my job. Besides, we're talking about you."

"Oh, for crying out loud!" Alexis darted her gaze between the two cops. Either they had gone crazy or she had. "Those renegades killed people I love, including my sister."

"I understand that." Hazlett's voice hardened, stubborn-ness defiant in his brown eyes. "Think hard, Alexis, about the events leading to the break-in. Did you have any arguments with Laurel? Tell me about your last day at work."

"Oh, that." Alexis shifted her right leg, yawned, and glanced at the clock. "Dee asked me to watch Laurel Grant. People die un-der Laurel's care. I took my break and then Laurel called me. She messed up a patient's trach valve and caused them to asphyxiate."

The officers gave her puzzled looks. "I don't understand," Hazlett said. "Aren't the nurses watching their patients?"

"They try to, but they might be in another patient's room changing dressings and other things. With Laurel, she goes into another world. When this happens, she makes mistakes and the therapists working with her have to clean up her messes. This time she put a cap on a woman's tracheostomy tube. She didn't do it right, and the patient couldn't breathe. The patient was still struggling when I got to the room, but Laurel blocked my access to the bedside. I finally elbowed her aside and pulled the cap off the patient's tube. Phlegm came spewing out from her trach, and the patient went into cardiac arrest.

"I reported Laurel, and she got fired. Dee sent me home sick, but she said Laurel might try to hurt me." Alexis exhaled, re-lief flooding her body. At last, she knew the answer. Laurel was in cahoots with her attackers.

Laurel Grant, aka Angel of Death.

Another deep wheeze from the window. Julia lifted her mask and took a drag on her inhaler, much the way Robin did that awful night. "If these killers had a map," Alexis said, trying hard not to watch Julia, "Laura gave them the addresses. Somehow she teamed up with those soldiers and sent them after people she didn't like."

Julia stepped away from the window and slipped the inhal-er back into her pocket. "Other people told us about Laurel. She's wanted for fleeing the scene of an accident, too. Unfortunately, she's missing. We found her car in a ravine, but no body."

Shit! "Then the Kryszka got her too."

"Maybe not." Julia exhaled deeply. "One of the neighbors

complained of a foul stench coming from Laurel's house. When we searched the property, we found human remains in a garbage pail, body parts in her freezer, and a frightened malnourished woman cringing in a closet. None of them looked like Kryszka casualties. We searched the basement. Good thing we did. We found three others chained inside a sump pit, near death from malnutrition."

"It was nasty." Hazlett shook his head. "I'm surprised you didn't hear it on the news."

"I must have slept through the news reports," Alexis told him.

"You didn't miss anything. We put an APB out on Ms. Grant. I'd love to find out what she knows about the Kryszka soldiers."

"She knows plenty. *I knew it!*" Alexis shouted. "Johnny and I tried to warn management about that woman, but no one listened. To them, she was a strong body, capable of eight hours of work. Why didn't ..."

Splintering sounds cut her short. A delta of cracks splayed across the ceiling from the light fixture. The fixture popped loose. The light bulbs exploded, and a crash followed, leaving a smell like burning toast. Somewhere to Alexis's right, the mirror shattered. The overhead light blew apart, but the fragments dropped behind the bed. The tinkling of glass shards punctuated each eruption. Through it all, she screamed.

Horror and understanding replaced what had passed for bravado. "Dammit!" Now the tears were coming, and she fought hard to get control. "Are you guys hurt?"

The two officers edged toward the door, shaking their heads.

"Yeron's new drug gave me some weird psychokinetic ability. I thought it might enable me to work. This is awful."

"Things used to break around Becky ... Doctor Leicht's wife too," Hazlett told her. "Maybe she can show you how to work with your power."

"I'll ask her."

"Let's give her room," Julia said in a faint voice. "Besides, she's right about my being sick. I'm seeing a doctor."

"Right, then. Alexis, we'll get someone in here to clean up the glass."

The hours passed in a haze as two gowned men came in and swept up the glass. No one replaced the mirror or the lights. Night fell and the attending nurses made adjustments to her IVs with the aid of flashlights. One of them walked her balloon bouquets out to the station, mumbling something about doctor's orders. No one explained why or initiated any chitchat. They didn't dare risk upsetting her.

After supper, tentative knocking sounded at her door. Another frightened nurse? "Come in," she said in a weary voice.

Another visitor came in brandishing a flashlight. Despite the dim light, mask, and goggles, Alexis recognized Yeron's scraggly red hair and aquiline features. For a second, she was facing the Kryszka sniper in her mother's garden again. She let out a gasp, and then Yeron removed his goggles, giving her a view of his red eyes. They were not the eyes of a killer. Lonely and sad, those eyes belonged to a gentle soul who wouldn't mind opening water bottles for her. Besides, she was damned curious about his connection with the strange visitor who had helped him during her surgery. She shoved aside her fear and grief and tried for a poker face.

"Hello, Alexis, I am Yeron. Doctor Leicht asked me to see you." His thick accent sounded European to her. "Pardon me for removing my goggles. They are a hindrance in the dark."

Alexis smiled. "I can appreciate that."

"What happened to your room?"

"My psychokinesis wrecked the light fixtures." Alexis smiled again, hoping for a light approach. None of this was his fault. "The present your drug left me."

"Many humans consider psychokinesis a curse," Yeron said in a mild voice. "Do you?"

What do you think? Alexis hesitated, torn between gratitude because this man had helped save her life, anger because his experimental drug had hidden side effects, and the fear of antagonizing him, knowing he could find a cure for her disease.

"If psychokinesis enables me to perform my job without using my hands so much, I'd call it a present. If I continue to have eruptions where things break, I'll consider it a curse."

Barbara Custer

"Steve told me you are a respiratory therapist. When I saw you in uniform, you looked pale and tired. Your job is physically demanding. You could have died. Why are you so anxious to return to work?"

"Bill collectors don't care about your near-death experiences. Jackson Hospital won't hold my job if I'm out longer than twelve weeks. Will my insurance pay for my treatment?"

"That is a good question." Yeron sat to her right, facing her, and regarded her with the intensity of a scientist studying a rare animal. "Steve knows how to negotiate with insurance companies. He will convince yours to pay for the CX249, surgery, and physical therapy. We will write off the psychokinesis training and clinical trial to research. As for your sick leave, given your unique circumstances, your administration might make allowances."

"Ms. Grese won't. She refused to grant additional sick time to a nurse who had cancer. The nurse returned to work while getting chemo. She threw up in patient rooms."

At that, Yeron arched an eyebrow. He acted like the average Joe, not a member of the Monster tribe. His easygoing demeanor encouraged her to volunteer more information. "Some people won't believe I handled that gun. The Good Grips you use for your plasma guns was easy on my hands."

"We factor ergonomics into our products, but they do not compensate for lack of skill. Obviously, this was not your first gunfight."

Images rose before Alexis's eyes: the mobsters breaking into her mother's home, her mother and Robin hiding, Alexis shooting them. She drew in a sharp breath. "It wasn't, but I'd rather not discuss the details. Is that all right?"

"Of course. You seem like a tolerant person. Most victims in your circumstances scream when they see someone like me."

Another look of sorrow in his eyes. She wanted to ask him how his day was, the way Stan advised her, but she was afraid his answer might trigger another psychokinetic eruption. "It helps that you're a guy." She smiled, noting the grin forming at the edges of his mask. "My first attacker was a woman. I never got a good look at the other attacker."

"Well, you survived and saved the life of your neighbor."

"Maybe I saved my neighbor, but I let my sister die. I've got a question about the psychokinesis. I don't want to become like my late aunt, who drank, drugged, and bullied people into financing her habits. I want to continue working as I did before I got arthritis. As it is, I can't open water bottles or hook up oxygen tubing. Will this mind power enable me to do that?"

"Alexis." Yeron's skeletal sigh sounded like wind scattering leaves. Something mixed with the sadness in his eyes ... recognition perhaps, and nostalgia. "The psychokinesis will enable you to lift a tank or push a ventilator. Opening bottles and hooking up tubing will depend on the strength and consistency of your power. I would like to test you so we can find out."

"I can't let you do that." Alexis shivered, terror rushing into her voice. "You could get hurt."

Yeron laughed. "I do not break easily, and I grew up as a psychokinetic. I could lift your bed with you in it if I chose. I doubt yours is that powerful."

"Yeron ..." Her teeth chattered. "Didn't the officers tell you what happened?"

"They told Steve, and he let me know what happened. Pardon me, but your lighting fixtures are ... how you say, shit." With his accent, the last word sounded like "sheet."

Alexis couldn't help giggling. "All right. What do you want me to do?"

"Sit up and face me."

"I can't." Alexis tensed, dreading the pain that came with any touching or lifting. Instead, a force with the sensation of air cushions pushed her upright. Her body turned right, legs sliding over the side until she faced Yeron—all of the movement done by his mind. Except for tingling on her left side, no discomfort troubled her. "Whoa! You are good."

"I told you so." He remained in his chair, feet flat on the floor, eyes on Alexis. "Send me a push, as strong as you've got."

Alexis gazed at Yeron—his milk-pale complexion, his red eyes. He looked like a patient who needed a blood transfusion yesterday. She shook her head. "I dare not."

"Alexis." Yeron's voice remained gentle, no sign of impatience or sarcasm. "People like me can block the push, and I am sitting. Think about why we do unpleasant tests on patients. We want to evaluate their disease. I need to do this so I can evaluate your psychokinesis."

"All right." Alexis thought about Julia and Robin again. She imagined Julia in a hospital bed, taking treatments and a why-didn't-you-come here-sooner scolding from her doctor. She closed her eyes and mustered a violent shove. A force surged through her, building up to the strength of a tidal wave. It slammed Yeron back in his chair, and then shoved him and the chair against the wall. He hollered, and then the tidal wave slammed against an invisible wall.

"Ow!" Sharp pain knifed through her head. She shot a Yeron a look. "Oh, shit! You're hurt. How bad? Didn't I warn you?"

"Only thing wounded is my pride." Yeron rubbed his elbow. "Your power runs strong, but we can train it. We will do the training here or in my lab. Before we begin, I will transfer you to a room that is immune to your power. Doctor Hoffman had built two such rooms. So that you understand, Steve and I feel that leaving helium balloons in your room would be unwise."

"Because you're allergic to helium, right? Helium can be dangerous for humans, too. Didn't Steve explain that to you?"

"It only takes a few inhalations to kill someone like me," Yeron told her. "Becky is half Kryszka, very sensitive to the helium, too. Yet she insists on displaying about fifty balloons or more in her house."

An image rose unbidden in Alexis's mind of Becky hugging a bouquet of balloons against her chest and kissing them. Despite her best efforts at restraint, giggles escaped her lips. "I'm sorry. Steve told me about Becky's fondness for balloons. We laugh about it all the time."

"It is not amusing. Becky was admitted to the hospital after a balloon broke." Yeron stood up and smoothed his gown. "I must go. I will begin training you after your transfer."

After the door closed behind Yeron, Alexis closed her eyes and she was back in the woods. Only it wasn't her mother's garden this time. Shively, Yeron, two other people, and she were trampling through the woods. Everyone wore military uniforms, except Yeron and herself, who had on tunics. Before she could contemplate why, skeletal figures bore down on her, people in soiled rags that might have once been gabardine suits and lace gowns. Weeds sprouted from their necks and cheeks. The eyes were gone on some, leaving behind spongy sockets. Others gazed her way with eyes of glazed silver. One man munched on a human limb.

"Get ready to fire!" Shively hollered.

Alexis and her companions dropped to one knee and battered away at the oncoming figures with plasma guns. The figures shrieked, their cries blasting through her head like shattered glass. Most of their bodies crumbled before her in a grisly rain. The intact forms sprawled on the grass. More kept coming, and Alexis sent projectiles from explosives wired to her arms.

"Nice work, folks." Shively smiled. "Let's stack and burn them."

But the figures didn't stop moving. Their swollen arms, bursting through to the bone, flapped on the grass. Alexis's body broke out in gooseflesh.

"Do not be afraid." Yeron laid his hand on her shoulder. To Alexis's surprise, she didn't recoil the way she usually did when men touched her. "I will help you."

Closer now and the limbs reached through the air. The rancid odor of rot turning to mush in the sun nauseated her. She tried concentrating, using her psychic energy to batter away the figures. Her power didn't work.

Someone grabbed Yeron. Before Alexis could stop them, cold hands seized her by the collar. One silver eye opened its piercing gaze on her.

"Yeron!" she screamed, but her pursuer competed for attention.

The creature opened his mouth, eyes rolled back, revealing two rows of crooked brown teeth set in slimy black gums. It hissed. Its soft, cold hands wrapped around her throat and squeezed. The screams locked inside her, cut off by the pressure on her airway. Her lungs hurt, seeking air, and finding none. The blackness waded in ...

Then Alexis woke up to the cycling of her IVs. Moonlight filtered through the blinds, throwing shadows against the walls behind her bed. In the dark, she concluded that worrying about employment was pointless. Laurel was hiding out there, Laurel wanted her dead, and she had teamed up with a renegade Kryszka to make that happen.

"The hell with work," she said out loud. "I'd better find Laurel and the remaining Kryszka before they get to my mother and me. Okay, Stan the Man, want to know what my mission is, why your Higher Power let me live? He wants me to go after these creeps."

Chapter Sixteen; Woehar Shows Laurel the Zombies

Kryszka Underground Colony, March 7, 9:00 a.m.

"Are you ready to behave?" A harsh voice spoke in Laurel's ear.

Laurel snapped open her eyes. Who was speaking, Woehar or Abaddon? It was Woehar, chittering and smiling. She averted her eyes and stared at the pink circular light on the ceiling. Bad idea. Abaddon's skeletal face was grinning down at her from the light. Her breath hitched.

White hot agony burned through her hands and feet. Her pinky fingers, her index toes, and her pinky toes were gone. Someone had swathed the stumps with gel dressing. She thought of the rapture on Woehar's face as she chewed and swallowed, the crunch her teeth made over Laurel's bones, the blood spattering on the table. Woehar smelled her helplessness and loved it.

"I promise to behave, Abaddon," she said. "May I have something for pain? Please?"

"As humans would tell you, suck it up," *and if you keep whining, I will go for the main course*. The message came through loud and clear without any accent. "For the fifth time, my name is not Abaddon. Get up. We shall go for a walk."

Laurel looked down at her beshitted, bloodstained scrubs. Her clothes stank from the waste satcheled inside them. She wouldn't refuse Woehar's orders. Refusals led to punishment, which Woehar might defer, but never forget.

"May I get washed? At least have a change of clothes?"

"Bodily waste and running water will infect your stumps.

You brought this on yourself, so quit whining." Woehar crooked her finger. "Follow me. I shall show you my laboratories and what I have planned for the humans."

Staying close to Woehar, Laurel forced one foot before the other toward the corridor. The pain was ungodly. She swayed sideways with each tentative step on her heels. No matter how careful she was, she would get an infection. *Damn you, Alexis,* she thought. *Wait until I get my hands on you.*

They proceeded down a steel gray hall that reeked of disinfectant and, underneath, something sickly sweet and decayed sour. Her kitchen used to smell like that after her dinners unless she scrubbed her floors with bleach. Wailing cries echoed from the end of the hall.

A paneled door rolled open. "I store human specimens in my laboratory here. These are street people no one will miss." A ghastly smile traced Woehar's blood-bearded face. "The governor believes I am conducting medical experiments."

"Instead, you're turning your specimens into ghouls." Laurel's voice sounded tinny and distant. *Shut up before you get yourself killed,* Abaddon's voice warned.

"Let us call it 'processing,' for the governor's sake. She does not understand most English, but the word 'ghoul' might attract attention."

Whatever. To argue would cost Laurel more body parts. "All right. Will you send them to Jackson Hospital?"

"Yes ... when they are ready."

At the first set of cubicles, unkempt prisoners lay inside pee-stained clothes, their limbs bruised, and their voices hoarse from screaming. Electrodes attached to each head recorded what Laurel supposed was brain-wave activity.

"I am giving them intense electroshock treatments to destroy their executive functions," Woehar said. "We do not allow the specimens any comfort except the minimal amount of nourishment needed to keep them alive. After the treatments are complete, I shall administer vischlausk to the ventromedial part of the brain, the frontal lobes, and other areas that affect judgment and reasoning. After vischlausk has its effect, the subjects will only be able to act on their basest desires. They will lunge and attack the way creatures do in your picture shows."

"How can you do this without your governor finding out?"

"I work with a healer who delivers medical reports that provide our leader what she wants to see. Governor Quyeba feels so indebted to my father she allows me to do as I wish with the laboratory. She believes I am experimenting on cadavers."

They passed a maze of machinery, then Woehar aimed her tube device at the paneled wall. The panel slid open.

"Walk down the middle of the aisle," she cautioned. "These creatures can reach through the bars."

The occupants let out deep-throated howls, veins standing out on their necks. Gashes streaked their faces in wavy lines, looking to Laurel like *S*'s turned on their sides. She followed Woehar's instructions, keeping an equal distance between the rows of cages, crossing her bandaged hands over her chest. Her feet throbbed and liquid stool leaked down her legs with each shambling step. The rancid odors came to life halfway down her throat, making her gag. The sight of the creatures' yellowed, pointed teeth was awful. Their fingers, tatters of red beef, clawed at the air. Laurel shuddered to think of the damage those fingers might inflict.

"Soon, they will be ready for Phase Three," Woehar told her.

"What then?" Laurel asked in a quivering voice.

"Keep looking."

Further ahead, glass cubicles replaced the barred cages. Creatures with skull-heads, spaghetti-strand hair and skin the consistency of dried leather stamped back and forth in their cubicles. They batted at the doors with fish-belly fingers. The glass quivered but did not break. These once-human things let out dog-like sounds, yipping and howling, their teeth gnashing like rattling keys. Eyes like stones regarded Laurel. The bodies reeked like decaying fish.

Laurel tightened her arms against her chest, hoping to soothe the goosebumps. "Why did you use glass cages?"

"Kryszka glass is like steel."

Good, Laurel thought. *Alexis and those other bitches at*

Jackson will get what they deserve. Yet tears continued streaming down her face. The memories of her severed fingers squirming against Woehar's grip clouded her mind. Her hands and feet had turned into bellowing chunks of agony, and each movement made it worse. The stink from her cauterized stumps and bodily waste competed with the spoiled meat odor wafting off the creatures. On some level, she began to feel sorry she'd been so cruel to her children.

She gave a humorless laugh. "When are these monsters going to Jackson Hospital?"

"Soon. Someone who knows me resides there, so I must take certain precautions first."

"What precautions?"

"We have not finished our tour yet." Woehar waved her hand. The harshness creeping into her voice discouraged further questions. "I have one last thing for you to see."

Another panel opened into a third laboratory, one with recessed cubicles along its walls, each filled with a clear-colored solution. At first glance, they looked like fish tanks. "What's this?" Laurel asked.

Woehar smiled, exposing her bloodstained, pointed teeth, and she wasn't Woehar. She was Abaddon. Those incisors turned his face into a grinning skull. "I harvested eggs and sperm from human donors. You'd be surprised at what you can do with the right DNA and cell structure."

Woehar-Abaddon turned up the lights, allowing Laurel a close-up view of the humanoid infants floating in the liquid. These monstrosities had rows of needle-sharp teeth and madness stamped in their red eyes.

"Draekh and I experimented with embryos." Abaddon's death head's grin widened. "After we fertilized Kryszka sperm and human egg, we added vischlausk. These hybrids will hunger for flesh, too."

"Abaddon ...Woehar." Laurel shuddered. Any question needed careful wording, and always with the name Woehar. "If Alexis and her friends could kill your soldiers, these infant monsters will prove no challenge for them."

"Alexis and her friends are recuperating from serious injuries." Abaddon-Woehar gave her a weird, skeletal grin. "Our poison weakened Alexis's left side. She needed stitches in her right hand and back. She grieves for her beloved sister and a good friend. Another person got vischlausk poisoning in his arm. He will not be able to shoot well. A third is recuperating from broken ribs. Only one of our targets escaped unharmed, but he is grieving, too. Grief and pain medicine distract people. These people are mine for the taking now."

"You found all this out with a camera? How did you sneak a camera in there? That's impossible. Jackson Hospital has surveillance everywhere."

"So? Jackson's version of surveillance is so crude a child could override the sensors. I smuggled my camera to your hospital after my pupils made their attack."

"One camera?" Laurel's curiosity overrode her fear. "How can you get all your information with one camera?"

"Our cameras are not like yours. I planted one the size of a microchip underneath a survivor's skin. Mark Adams." Woehar gave her another skeletal grin. "He was the safest choice because most of the healers and other injured avoid him. They despise him because of his temper and his history with Alexis. I know about that because I would consider it careless not to do my research. Finding Mark alone provided plenty of opportunities to embed the microchip. The microchip can only record conversation and action that occurs in his vicinity, but what I have learned so far has proven vital."

She clicked on a television screen, giving Laurel a view of the activities on Jackson's seventh floor. Laurel didn't recognize anyone except Tyrone, who was chatting with a nurse, and Alexis, who was taking a reaming from Ms. Grese, the personnel director.

"You already used 50 percent of your leave time," Ms. Grese said in a cruel voice. "If you can't come back to work in thirty-five days, your benefits will expire. We cannot hold your job."

"Alexis is going to get canned. I love it!" Laurel shouted with glee. For a second, she forgot about the pain and indignities she suffered. Not longer than that. Neither Abaddon nor Woehar tolerated lapses in judgment and Laurel would do well to remember that. "The person who knows you, whoever he is ... what will happen to him?"

"Yeron," Woehar supplied. "My creations will not harm him because they only want human meat. After I enhance Yeron, he will appreciate our craving for flesh."

"How can you do that?"

"Someone will inject him with vischlausk."

"Yeron, the great doctor." Laurel sneered. "He promised to find cures for our ailments, but only if the patients earn his respect. What a crock of shit."

"He learned his attitude from our father." Woehar's eyes gleamed with amusement. "Two things must happen before we invade Jackson Hospital. First, I will send my beings to a crowded area and test their aggression. Next, I shall appoint three soldiers to capture Yeron. I want competent soldiers because Yeron has a strong military background. Whomever I select must know how to drive human vehicles so they can transport my specimens. After I meet these objectives, I shall move on to Jackson Hospital."

"You thought this out well." Laura had to admire Woehar, despite the throbbing in her hands and feet.

"One day, the earth will be ours," Woehar said. "Infiltrating more cities will be easy once I eliminate the Jackson Hospital survivors. I will need the precise layout of the seventh floor and the best way to get in. The camera will not give me that information, so start talking, Laurel."

Laurel took another gander at those gore-encrusted sharp teeth. Woehar and Abaddon were working together. She promised herself never to get on the wrong side of their food chain in the future. After taking a deep breath, she began.

Chapter Seventeen: Yeron's Office

Jackson Hospital, March 25, 6:00 p.m.

Walking Dead Slaughter Twenty at Trident Mall

The headline, dated March 25, 2010, jumped out at Yeron from his computer screen. The security cameras at the stores captured the massacre in grisly detail. Sore-crusted, skeletal figures descended upon the hapless shoppers exiting the boutiques. Most of the intruders appeared many days dead, but their bodies moved with rhythmic precision, tearing away skin and bone. Gray matter splattered from a woman's head. The creatures scarfed it down with the same greed Eigil and his minions had devoured human flesh with. By the time soldiers arrived to contain the invasion, the figures had strewn battered cars and dead people throughout the parking lot.

Chills inched up Yeron's back, drawing a line across his shoulders. He sat back against his chair, stifling a cry. "People cannot return from the dead."

The figures on the video kept coming until gunfire from police officers felled them. Yeron shook his head at the sight. "This is impossible unless one of my people manufactured a device to make these bodies walk."

Of course they had. Quyeba, a friend of his family, had planned to build another compound so people could escape Eigil. The refugees had remained on Earth since the neighboring planets could not sustain life. If any of Eigil's minions had gone there … of course some had. They were carrying on Eigil's crusade, or had an evil agenda of their own.

He cursed out loud in his own language. After downloading stills from the video, he saved them to a file titled "Trident Mall." He then addressed a group email to Officer Hazlett, Steve, Joe Hoffman, and several department heads, and attached a copy of his file.

"Kryszka renegades may have survived the explosion and plotted the Trident Mall massacre," he typed. "I would urge you to contact the CDC and Homeland Security. Every officer or soldier should be knowledgeable in plasma guns. I would like to transfer Alexis Carofalo and the other research patients to alternate hospitals."

He paused with his fingers over the "send" button. Would the administrators believe his report? How could they guarantee anyone's safety? No one at Jackson Hospital knew how to handle plasma except Steve, his relatives, and Joe Hoffman. The lack of skills with plasma guns had ensured a grisly death for the government agents and soldiers who infiltrated Eigil's compound.

"Alexis defended herself with our weapon," a voice said behind him.

Yeron whirled around in his swivel chair. The speaker appeared as a wraith-like vision, wearing his regulation navy tunic draped over his shoulders. He looked like Teodon, right down to the fine wrinkles in his chin, aquiline nose, and gentle eyes. A rancid odor lingered as the body assumed solid form. He spoke in the same authoritarian voice that had guided Yeron through Alexis's surgery.

Kindness notwithstanding, he was as dead as the assailants in the Army video appeared to be. The line of ice inched up Yeron's shoulders, racing chills along his neck. He felt through his waistband for his gun. No weapon. He had locked it in a drawer since Jackson Hospital banned possession of weapons by medical personnel. His visitor stood by the door, head tilted, his face betraying no sign of madness or hunger that he had seen with the Trident Mall assailants.

Yeron gulped. "What did you say?"

"Alexis defended herself with a plasma gun," his father replied in a quiet voice. "Her poor technique caused a fire. I suggest you show her the proper way to handle our guns."

"Father, why are you here? You are supposed to be..."

"I have unfinished business here, son, and it concerns Eigil's followers."

Yeron swallowed hard again. "This is worse than anyone can imagine," he said after finding his voice. "Laurel Grant's negligence caused a patient's death. Management relieved her of her duties, and the renegades attacked the next day. The police believe this woman is involved."

"Why would they think the two events are related?" the apparition asked.

"Because ..." Yeron hated the way his voice came out sounding dry and dusty. "Most of the victims are people who reported her. The management allowed Laurel to provide patient care here for two years despite everyone's complaints. She went missing, and the police found women starving in her basement. She penned them up like animals, and yet Administration allowed her to treat their sick. Why?"

Eyes on his father, he anticipated a prophecy of doom. Teodon did not have a temperament for lame reassurances.

"Maybe Laurel blackmailed someone in power." Teodon's eyes moved back and forth over Yeron's viewscreen. "If Laurel involved herself with our renegade soldiers, she is acting out of revenge. Teach Alexis and her companions how to use our weapons."

Yeron sighed, shaking his head. He hated conversing with dead people, even if the visitor was his father. "I cannot do that. Alexis and two other survivors have serious injuries. Another is grieving because the soldiers killed his mate ... wife." Another sigh, and then he plowed ahead in a hesitant voice. "Maybe Mark Adams can learn. His injuries are moderate, and he does not live with his mate or children."

His father gazed at him with lifted brows. "You sound uncertain about Mister Adams."

Footsteps. Yeron shot a glance toward the door. At any second, a visitor could barge in and catch him conversing with a ghost. The footsteps receded. Teodon continued looking at him, waiting for his answer.

"Mark shows a blatant disrespect for life. Our supplies of CX249, the drug we use for vischlausk poisoning, had run low. Alexis needed it. Mark did not. He insisted on getting it, and letting Alexis die, since her survival chances were low." Yeron rubbed his arms. "His voice chilled me. I had to blackmail him to get him to behave."

"Not good." Teodon frowned, shaking his head. "Watch him. He may be working with the enemy. These soldiers might send these creatures to your hospital. You have potential warriors, starting with Alexis and the male in the room beside hers."

"No!" Yeron cried. "Their injuries would prohibit them from handling firearms."

"Injuries heal." Teodon looked Yeron in the eye. "Talk to them and see what they have to say. You will make the right decisions."

With that, his father faded from view. Yeron jammed his hands under his legs to suppress their trembling. The rogue soldiers were going to invade the hospital. He knew that. Steve might listen, having survived the explosion at the compound. Convincing Administration posed problems, but Steve might know the best way to communicate with Administration.

With a deep sigh, Yeron deleted his unsent email. He turned off his monitor and headed to the patient ward.

* * * *

Steve was seeing patients in his office. Joe took the day off for a conference. Either man might listen if Yeron approached them at the right moment. He would not believe it himself if he did not see the video.

The front desk was unoccupied. Cindy, the charge nurse, was in Shively's room. She was helping Matilda change a dressing. Yeron started toward the room and hesitated, shaking his head. *Why is Alexis's mother working here? She is supposed to be sick.*

Apparently not. The less he had to do with her, the better. He paged Steve. No answer.

"Cindy." Yeron tapped on the glass door. "Is Doctor Leicht still at his office?"

"No," she replied without looking up. "He had a couple of

consults on another floor. He'll be rounding here soon."

Yeron tiptoed to a charting area to wait. He tried Steve's beeper again without success. Then his gaze settled on the clean utility room. Someone had propped its door open with a wheelchair. Sometimes the storeroom workers used wheelchairs to unload equipment. This time the silver gleam of an IV pole poked above the chair. Beside it, a sheet dangled over the upholstered back. A flurry of movement followed, and Yeron got up to check. The swath of brown curls and gauze on the neck identified the occupant as Alexis Carofalo. The flimsy yellow mask she wore made an inferior barrier against bacteria. The identification on her IV bag confirmed her name.

Alexis gave no sign of noticing him. She sat facing a rack of portable oxygen tanks. Before he could react, a tank drifted up from the rack, floated toward her, and landed inside the holder of the chair.

"Alexis?" he cried when he found his voice. "Who brought you here?"

Alexis whirled around and gasped. Her eyes bulged. "Oh, shit!"

"You could have hurt yourself with that tank," Yeron scolded her. "Leaving your room puts you at risk for an infection."

"I'm going to be all right." Alexis smiled like a parent indulging a temperamental child. "I had to see if my psychokinesis would enable me to work. It will. You saw how I maneuvered that tank. Only now I've gotten a nasty headache."

"I bet you have." Yeron groaned. "Why isn't ..." He shook his head, hating the slur in his contractions. "Cindy or Matilda should be watching you."

"They're busy with other patients. My mother shouldn't be working here at all because I'm family. Tyrone stopped by to chat, so the nurses gave us privacy." Alexis looked up at him, smile intact, unfazed by his unique features, but all that was lost on him. His mind replayed the video. He stole glances over his shoulder toward the exit, expecting the creatures to materialize at any moment.

"I can walk my feet to move the wheelchair now," she went on. "Tyrone wanted to come along, but I told him I had to work this out for myself."

"You were wrong. You have not finished your course of CX249. You may spread an infection to the staff and other patients or get one yourself, thus giving your mother one more reason to worry." Shrillness crept into Yeron's voice. He sounded like a cartoonish version of Matilda, but he couldn't help it. The TV images of the walking dead stormed through his mind like soldiers in pursuit, along with the solemn warning of his ghost father.

"I've been cooped up in that room over three weeks." The friendliness faded, and defensiveness took its place. "Ms. Grese says I've got five weeks left to get better. Five weeks go by fast."

"Five weeks? You cannot put a timetable on your recovery. Your actions may slow your recovery and cause a setback."

"Thank you for sharing." Sarcasm crept in with her defensiveness. "Are you listening? Ms. Grese said I have to be ready to work without restrictions in five weeks, or else I will lose my job and benefits. I had to know if the mental power will enable me to work."

Yeron wasn't sure how to answer. At his compound, most residents enjoyed speedy recoveries. Those who did not were reassigned positions that accommodated their infirmities. Moments of silence passed.

Alexis stared at him with censuring eyes. "Obviously, you never had to worry about money. After you live through problems like mine, you may lecture all you want. Until then, keep your opinions to yourself."

"I beg your pardon." Yeron hated the harshness in his voice, but his mind replayed the screams in the video. "Has money made you stop caring about the welfare of other people?"

He never heard the footsteps. He didn't know they had company until someone's hand latched on his shoulder. "Hey!" Steve cried. "What's going on here?"

Yeron glanced over at Steve and then scanned the desk. Matilda and Cindy huddled behind the medicine cart, looking his way and whispering.

"Alexis experimented with her psychokinesis. She maneuvered herself over here without considering her compromised immune system or that of the other patients."

"I don't care, Yeron. Standing out here and yelling at her is counterproductive. The longer she's out here, the more likely she is to catch some bug."

"You do not understand. Did you hear anything about the Trident Mall?"

"No, and besides, it has nothing to do with Alexis's care. What's going on at Trident? Never mind, I don't want to know." With one hand gripping the IV pole, and the other bracing Alexis's wheelchair, Steve backed her away from the room. "You're not off the hook either, Alexis. I want to know why you pulled this stunt."

"Ms. Grese cut my sick time." Alexis lowered her eyes.

"That explains it." Steve flashed a glowering look at Yeron. "Wait for me. This conversation isn't finished."

Now, he had done it. He had antagonized the one patient who had befriended him. Yeron knew what to expect. Alexis was going to tell every visitor that their fears about the mystery doctor were justified, that he was a creep like the rest of this kind. If not, her mother would. No one on the unit would believe the Army reports. They would think he was reading the tabloid magazines that Alexis kept at her bedside.

He sat in the charting room, folding his elbows on the desk, eyes looking through the glass partition. The two nurses helped Alexis back into bed. Steve and Cindy asked her questions, but they spoke in subdued voices.

The conversation droned on while Cindy came out and got medicines from the cart. On the way back, she pulled an EKG machine into the room. More hushed talking followed. Matilda returned to the desk, facing the room, and darting glares his way. Yeron pulled the papers from his pocket, the ones containing the printouts from his Trident Mall file. The images were vivid, including the grayish brain tissue dribbling from the wound in the victim's head.

Moments later, Matilda went back to her patients. Steve stopped by the charting room and waved his arm for Yeron to follow. They went to Joe's office.

"Thank God Mighty Mouth took the day off." Steve wiped the sweat gleaming on his forehead. He plopped behind the desk and indicated a chair facing him.

Yeron sat, eyes on Steve, the mantle of sadness weighing down his shoulders. "Alexis asked for another doctor."

"She did, but none of us have much experience with CX249 or psychokinesis. As for treating her arthritis ... Alexis needs you. I pointed that out to her."

"Her mistrust will affect how she responds to any treatment."

"If you use delicacy and tact, she may get past it. You cannot expect docility from our injured warriors. They're angry and hungry for payback. Think hard, Yeron, about the way some of us behaved after the explosion at the old compound. Julia fought with Joe all the time. Becky left the hospital against medical advice. The other night, I found Shively and Johnny outside on the patio in thirty-degree weather. Shively with his CX249 IV was smoking in front of Johnny with a chest tube. How they got past the nurses is anyone's guess. I can't scold them like they're children."

"Joe told me that Johnny argues with the nurses, too," Yeron said. "I expected more compliance from Alexis because she acted docile."

"That was before two enemy soldiers tried to kill her. Now, she's desperate. Earlier tonight, she got a visit from Ms. Grese, the vice president of Human Resources. Alexis has used over three weeks of sick time. Because she's taken so much sick time this past year, she's only entitled to eight weeks instead of the usual twelve. So as of tonight, she's got five weeks left. If she can't make it back to work by then, she'll lose her insurance benefits and job. In our world, Yeron, jobs don't come by easily for disabled people. She doesn't have any family except her mother, who's almost old enough to retire. She may qualify for Social Security after six months of no income. She thinks the psychokinesis will enable her to work without restrictions."

Yeron shook his head, trying to make sense of it all. "Does she have friends here?"

Steve nodded. "Most of her coworkers and the nurses like her, but popularity will not impress Ms. Grese. The one person who could help is dead ... Dee Hobson. Doctor Tynan had his human moments, but he's gone, too."

"I am so sorry." Yeron bowed his head. It crossed his mind that his appearance did not frighten Alexis because she had seen much worse. "Would it help if I spoke with Ms. Grese?"

"Write a note explaining why Alexis needs to be out sick." Steve flipped through Hoffman's Rolodex, and then looked up with his bleak and tired eyes. "I know someone who handles discrimination law. Maybe he can help Alexis."

"Alexis cannot accuse Jackson Hospital of discrimination. ADA accommodations or not, she must demonstrate the ability to perform the way her peers do. Her condition has progressed beyond that." Yeron folded his hands in a steeple shape. "If you think your friend can help, ask. I will scan the local hospitals for job openings."

"Do that," Steve said. "Better yet, find a cure or a way to control her symptoms. Alexis knows you're not used to our culture. She agreed to give you another chance. I reminded her you could find a way to treat her arthritis."

"She is still not happy with me."

"That will change if you go easy on her." Desperation slid into Steve's tired voice. The circles under his eyes, the sweat drenching his brown hair, spoke of a lack of sleep. "More than anything else, she wants a day without pain. You can make that happen for her."

Yeron retrieved his folder, the one with the Trident Mall stills. He wanted to share the horrors of the massacre and the warning he received in his vision, but Steve's tense voice discouraged any sensitive sharing. Instead, he laid his file on the desk before Steve.

"If you want to go easy on her, restrict her access to the Internet. You need to see this, Steve."

"All right." Steve opened the folder and read. The pale curves in his cheeks blanched, and with his shadowed eyes, he looked as ghastly as the creatures at the mall.

"This looks pretty damned official." He dumped the folder and its contents, and rooted through the desk, opening and slamming the drawers. He then got up and moved onto the cabinets. "Hoffman keeps plasma guns here somewhere. He stores them for safekeeping. Becky needs protection. She's home alone with Chloe."

Yeron thought of telling him that his father never mentioned Becky or Chloe, but mentioning the vision at all would be going too far. "We must tell Alexis right away."

"Wait." Steve fished a plasma gun from a metal box in the bottom drawer of a cabinet. He stowed it inside his waistband. Yeron stood, watching him. "That's better. You're right about Alexis. If we don't tell her, someone else will. Let me do the talking."

"I owe her an apology."

"You do, but wait until tomorrow. What she needs now is rest."

"She will not rest well if those creatures break into the hospital."

"That's true." Steve patted his weapon. "Administration will hate spending money on extra security. People here better look out."

* * * *

Yeron headed back to his two-room apartment across the hall from the research unit. After a dinner of sushi and raw vegetables, he watched a televised replay of the Trident Mall slaughters. He hoped to see something to explain how the dead could walk, but he found no answers.

By now, Steve had gone home and sought comfort from Becky. Yeron gazed at his phone, tempted to call Becky, but he dared not. He already did enough damage with Alexis. He thought about the Jackson workers who planned outings with their friends, a ball game, or dinner at a local restaurant. Some took extended trips to other states, or "abroad," as Steve called it. Yeron deemed such activities impossible.

The prospect of lost income and worsening disability must have terrified Alexis, enough for her to put aside any revulsion at his looks. She needed a cure for her arthritis, and find it he would. He'd scoured the hospitals for jobs compatible with Alexis's skills. No positions. Tomorrow, he promised himself to work on a better drug for Alexis, beginning with pain control.

Tonight, the Trident Mall held his attention. Before the explosion, Eigil's troopers chose their victims at random. Now they planned their foray, and they executed the move well. Why did they wait three years after the explosion before resurfacing? Why invade the Philadelphia area? Why go after Alexis? The traditional news channels did not offer any clues. He had gotten his video after hacking a confidential army file. It was easy, since the software he devised enabled him to find a back door to his choice of agencies. This device enabled him to access the files without passwords or other security procedures.

How many renegades were out there? Did they salvage part of the compound? What about the second colony his father mentioned? Yeron typed two names into his laptop: Quyeba and Zoltar. They were family friends until years before, when they had moved to "someplace safe." These speculations circled in his mind, circling the way Eigil and his soldiers circled their victims before a feed.

Chapter Eighteen: Yeron's Apology

Jackson Hospital's Research Floor, March 26, 9:00 a.m.

At the nurses' station the next morning, Yeron sighted Steve at Alexis's bedside, listening to her breath sounds and hacking cough. Two bouquets of Mylar balloons pressed against her glass wall, glaring at him. Someone must have brought them to her during the night. This was going to make his apology difficult. With sagging shoulders, he went over to the charting area to wait for Steve.

Steve emerged from her room, his face bland. "Alexis spiked a fever. Her chest X-ray showed left lobe pneumonia. I ordered Levaquin and Albuterol."

Yeron sighed and covered his eyes. "She contracted it when she left the room."

"Last night's ride didn't help, but the hours she spent outside a burning house in unseasonably cold weather caught up with her."

Yeron nodded, but disquiet gnawed at him. "The stress is affecting her, too."

"You've got that right. I checked out the ADA law. No lawyer can help her because Ms. Grese has no legal obligation." The deepening crevices around Steve's eyes whispered rumors of another sleepless night. "Her pneumonia is mild. She may continue her other therapies."

"My search for positions did not go well," Yeron admitted.

Steve let out a groan. "I expected that."

"Expected what?" Hoffman's voice boomed behind them. He slapped a stack of sheets onto the desk beside Yeron. "You damn well better expect the worst. I've got photographs and a report on Trident Mall from a reliable source. Read for yourselves."

Yeron did not need to read. The grisly photographs of blood and gore on each page told him everything. "Steve and I already know."

"Where did you get your information?" Hoffman asked.

"Does it matter?" Steve asked in a strained voice. "Trident Mall is twenty miles from here. Some renegades survived when Eigil's compound exploded, and this latest massacre's got their name all over it. If I'm right, these people know that Alexis, Shively, and the other wounded are here, and they're working their way to our hospital. Are we adding more security?"

"Administration said they were hiring more officers." Hoffman sneered with derision. "I find that hard to believe, so I'm installing biometric locks for this ward."

A glimpse up close and personal revealed a bulge in Hoffman's jacket. Yeron would bet his position at the hospital that Hoffman was carrying a plasma gun.

"I've got my protection." Steve patted his side. "I won't trust some Rent-a-Cop."

"So you've been filching from my drawers," Hoffman said with a dry smile.

"Steve wants to protect his family." Yeron touched his waistband where he kept his gun. "If you want to report us, I cannot stop you."

"Administration can go to hell." Hoffman's voice oozed contempt. "Do me a favor. Keep a closer rein on your patients. Alexis took another ride outside her room last night."

"Matilda gave me a browbeating about it." Steve let out another groan. "I spoke with Alexis."

"Some good that did." Oh, how Yeron hated Hoffman's sarcastic tone. "A night shift nurse caught her rooting through the utility room after you two left. Have you considered restraints?"

"No!" Yeron and Steve shouted in unison. Yeron wanted to explain that using restraints sounded too much like something Eigil would do, but the right words would not come. Hoffman's mouth was like a blustery wind in March, and no one could fight him.

"Alexis panicked because Ms. Grese threatened to fire her," Steve told Hoffman. "She's got five weeks to become fully functional for her job."

"Oh really?" An edge crept into Hoffman's voice, his eyes glittering. "Isn't Alexis entitled to twelve?"

"Under normal circumstances, yes." Steve lowered his voice. "Alexis used up much of her leave during prior illnesses. Unless she's back on the job in five weeks, her income and her health benefits will go. Ms. Grese wants blood."

"Don't worry about Ms. Grese. I'll handle her."

Yeron gaped at Hoffman, his eyes bulging. He had not expected sympathy from Hoffman, much less help. "How do you plan on doing that?"

"I'll hit her where she lives. If Alexis loses her benefits, I'll treat her *pro bono* and write the hospital cost off to research. Jack and Stan indicated they would do pro bono. Are you two with me?"

"Definitely." Yeron let out a sigh of relief.

"Amen." Steve grinned. "Alexis will be glad to hear this."

"No problem." Hoffman nodded with a self-satisfied smile Yeron did not like. "You can stop Alexis's isolation precautions, but keep her on the CX249 another week. Her labs still show traces of the poison."

Yeron watched Hoffman's retreating figure. "Since when did he care? He did not want Alexis to work on his floor."

Steve shrugged. "Joe and Ms. Grese were once married. Things got ugly between them, and Joe will use anything he can to aggravate her, including free medical care. Whatever his intentions are, Alexis will benefit." He nodded toward Alexis's room. "Hoffman's with her now. After he's finished, you can go in and apologize."

Yeron listened to the interaction from where he sat. Any second, he expected shouting, tearful weeping, or other signs of heated interaction, but the voices remained steady. Toward the end of the exchange, Alexis said, "Thank you." Hoffman exited her room, smirk tucked into place, and moved onto his next patient.

Yeron went in next, fighting the chills wreaking his body at the sight of those balloons. He estimated about twenty. The mask hid his Kryszka teeth, but would not protect him from leaking helium. Alexis sat in a chair, with her head down and side toward Yeron. Her leftovers from breakfast sat on the radiator, but she gave no sign of caring. She seemed more interested in her *Weekly World Reporter* and its article titled "Human hatches from an egg." Her vital signs were normal, except for her temperature. A sheet draped over her shoulders and the bandages on her back. She was smiling.

"Alexis." Yeron mustered a soft voice he might use on a frightened, elderly patient. He did not dare upset her with the balloons decorating her room. He counted thirty of them.

"Yeron." The smile dropped off of Alexis's face. The helium balloons jiggled against the glass, grinning at him as if to say, *that's right, Yeron, you don't belong here.*

I do not like you either, Yeron thought, *so the feeling is mutual.*

"I should have stayed in bed," Alexis continued after a silence seeming long as death. "Now I've got pneumonia. This was my fault."

Yeron remained by the door. He was ready to bolt if her emotions caused a balloon to break. He was convinced that any attempt to apologize would go sour.

"It's too bad you never dealt with the likes of Ms. Grese." Alexis's skeptic tone implied she was not ready to trust him. "When she said five weeks, she means five. If I call out sick one extra day, my job and benefits are history." She looked him in the eye. "For the record, I don't enjoy harming patients. Laurel Grant is the captain of that ship."

The jiggling of the balloons intensified. They swelled and deflated, and slapped at the wall. Yeron jammed his hands into his pockets to conceal his quivering. He did not understand how ships related to this conversation, but he wished he had donned his helium-proof mask. The agitation among the balloons warned that one of them would pop any second.

"I was trying to find a way to work around my disability. Can you understand that?"

"Of course," Yeron was eager to diffuse the tension. "I should not have scolded you. I came here to apologize."

"I realized you're not used to our ways. Maybe I should cut Doctor Hoffman some slack, too. He bawled me out for roaming—no surprise there—but then he assured me no one would charge me for treatment if I lose my benefits."

"That is correct." Yeron glanced at the balloons again, still huddling against the doorway. "I will be glad to help, but I cannot work near those balloons."

Alexis shrugged. "Can't you wear a special mask to filter helium?"

"Yes, but the helium mask does not hide my teeth. Most females scream when they see my face."

"Your teeth didn't bother me last night. Just make sure I'm awake before you come into my room." Alexis tilted her head, eyes pleading as if to say, *please do not get mad at me.* "Steve told me your renegades broke into the Trident Mall and killed twenty people. All the sterility in the world won't help if I'm dead. Am I right?"

Yeron nodded. "Go on."

"I went back to the utility room to look for something I could use as a weapon. My leg is getting strong enough to work the chair, and I moved my IV with my thoughts. My mother caught me this time. I told her I'd stay in bed if she'd give me my balloons. She managed to get back the ones people had given me. Someone else picked up a bunch from the auditorium after a party. They'll protect me against your rogue soldiers."

"Not necessarily." Then the words came out before Yeron could stop them. "The people who did the killing were not soldiers."

"I see." Alexis spoke with a flat tone. Yeron was not sure if her depression caused that or, more likely, shock. "The *Weekly World Reporter* claims your scientists are making zombies. Are they right?"

Yeron glanced at the pile of *Weekly Worlds* on her side table. "Why would you believe anything you read in a tabloid?"

"You said helium wouldn't help me, and Steve's face had an oh-God look when we talked. *Weekly World Reporter* published several articles on the zombies. Maybe they're clones made by your scientists, the kind immune to helium. Am I right?"

Yeron pursed his lips. He was heading into another gray area, the one labeled Too Much Information. He thought about his mother and the way his father shielded her from bad news. Had his mother known the truth about Woehar, she might still be alive. *Is that so?* The balloons grinned at him. *You don't know as much as you think you do, buddy.*

"I think I should get my helium mask."

"You do that. When you come back, I want you to level with me. Tell me what's really in that report. I'd like to hear my prognosis too."

So much for Steve's wonderful bedside manner. Yeron hurried to his suite for the helium mask. He slapped it on and tightened the corners to make a seal over his mouth and nose. Its treated mesh covering would filter out the deadly helium. Back in Alexis's room again, he shot a defiant glance at the balloons at her headboard. *I dare you to try to poison me now.* The balloons stared back at him with their mocking grins.

A shadow of fear crossed Alexis's face and then vanished, much like birds flying through a window. "Are you ready to talk?"

When Yeron nodded in the affirmative, she continued. "Suppose I go for intense physical therapy. Will I be ready to work in five weeks? Can you find a cure for the arthritis?"

Fear of the balloons forgotten, Yeron concentrated on Alexis, trying to think of a tactful approach. Lecturing and lying did not work. What she needed was the truth.

"I can contain your symptoms and help you to become functional. I cannot guarantee this will happen in five weeks."

"That's what I thought." Alexis remained calm, but her eyes were like those of a trapped animal that had mustered its courage in a final attempt at survival. "Do you have any reports on this forthcoming invasion?"

"Yes." Without comment, Yeron handed her the documents.

Alexis studied the reports, her face turning whiter as the seconds passed. "This is worse than anything *Weekly World Reporter* published. I've got to tell Shively and Tyrone. Shively has friends ... people who can provide protection, and Tyrone's got army experience."

"If you believe your friends can offer a solution, please call them."

"I've told Stan—Doctor Klein—how much I tried to protect Robin and how I worry about my mother. He asked me when I was going to start taking care of myself. I can protect myself with a good weapon. Otherwise, I'm dead meat. Where are the police? Where's ..."

"Easy, Alexis." Helium-proof mask or not, Yeron hated the rustling of those balloons. "Doctor Hoffman is working on security measures now. This floor has fail-safe alarms." Oh, how lame that sounded. Anyone competent in Kryszka technology could neutralize those devices.

"Do you honestly think our alarms could stop someone from your compound?"

Yeron had to shake his head no.

She coughed up mucus into a tissue. She opened it, peeked at the sample, and then discarded the tissue. "A plasma gun would enable me to protect myself because of its ergonomic handle. The gunfight I mentioned involved two thugs who were after my father. They pulled a gun on my mother and sister. I took them down, though they were armed." She spoke in a conversational voice as if she was describing a workday. "Ms. Grese frightens me because she can put me on the street with a flick of her pen. Guns and helium balloons won't protect me from Ms. Grese. I hope you can concoct a working medicine for me soon."

"Before I can try new drugs, you must finish the CX249. You must be free of infection, and your incisions healed." Yeron spoke in a measured voice, trying for a reassuring approach. "You have many friends here. You will get through this fine."

"From your mouth to God's ears. If your treatment or the psychokinesis enables me to perform patient care, another hospital may hire me. The sooner I start my therapy, the better I can protect myself and go back to work."

"A private practice might hire you." Yeron allowed himself to smile. "I am surprised my appearance does not frighten you the way it does other people."

"Let me tell you something." The fear faded from Alexis's voice, and sympathy took its place. "Most of the folks here can't look beyond their noses. They judge the person's appearance but not their actions. You want frightening? Look at Meathead—I mean Mark Adams. You saw how he tried to get me bumped off and it wasn't the first time."

"Bump off? How?" Yeron thought about the way Eigil used to poke people's rectums with sharp objects, but Alexis was speaking in an allegorical sense. She was offering her brand of acceptance. Confused as he felt, he could accept that.

"I'm talking about when he ordered Doctor Hoffman to withhold the CX249. I heard every word he said. Now *that* frightened me." She lifted her right leg, revealing a jagged scar on her calf. "In case you wondered, I got this from Meathead's baseball bat." She gave him a weak smile. "Your appearance had an unsettling effect at first, but when you reasoned with Mark, you reminded me of Doctor Phil."

"So Mark is your monster." He smiled at her nod. "Still, I am surprised my face does not scare you. How would you react if we met alone outside the hospital?"

"I'd mistake you for a sickly person like I did when I met you at work." Alexis coughed up another mucus sample, peeked, and then tossed it into the trash. "Okay, maybe I was scared until I saw your eyes. Unlike my attackers and Mark, you've got the eyes of someone who'd gladly open a bottle for me if I asked—but you look sad. I should realize other people have problems, especially you because of the language and cultural barriers. Most times, I can only think about getting through the pain."

"Alexis, you almost died."

"That's right, I did." Alexis nodded understanding. "Sometime during surgery, I had an out-of-body experience. I saw my father, but he said I wasn't ready to die yet. The other doctors called what I had a near-death experience. Is this making sense?"

Yeron averted his eyes, not caring to admit that he, too, had met up with a deceased person. Most people did not want to ask about his day, let alone his visions. "Of course. It makes more sense than you realize."

"Does it? I saw another Kryszka assisting you during the surgery." Alexis's face scrunched in a puzzled frown. "My father said he came from the other side to help you. He called him Ted because he couldn't pronounce his real name. It was strange, seeing this other person."

"I am the only Kryszka working here."

"I know." Alexis furrowed her brows. "So what was this

stranger doing in the operating room?"

"Alexis, why are you dwelling on this? Such visions can distort reality."

"Not this one." Stubbornness edged into Alexis's voice. "I saw the flat line, and Hoffman giving me the CA200. Ted moved your hand around my neck." Her breath came out in pants, her tone rising. "Did he come back to warn us about the hostile soldiers? I'm surprised no one else saw him."

Yeron lowered his eyes. Steve had advised him not to bring his personal business to the bedside, least of all the visions he had of his father. *Alexis, it happened only in your imagination,* he opened his mouth to say. *Now let us proceed with a treatment plan. I do not have time to listen to such nonsense.*

The words did not come. It sounded too much like a scolding Ms. Grese or Mark might deliver. "He had unfinished business," he said after a pause.

Another cough. Spit. Peek. Alexis then turned her pain-filled eyes toward Yeron. "Obviously his business involves me, but my parents never mentioned Kryszka friends. Does this man know me from somewhere?"

Yeron gazed at Alexis, not knowing what to make of her willingness to ask questions and listen. He tried to summon the dignity to tell her to let it go, but he could not. No, that was not it. What he needed was a friend.

"I don't mean to pry." Alexis's voice softened. "It's not every day that people return from the dead to help with an operation. If you don't want to talk about it, I'll shut up."

Yeron stood back, stunned into silence. It was the first time an Earth stranger asked him about anything personal. "The man you saw was my late father," he said when he found his voice. "He came back to warn me about the renegade Kryszka."

Chapter Nineteen: Alexis Gets to Know Yeron

Jackson Hospital's Research Floor, March 26, 11:00 a.m.

This is getting deep, Alexis thought. *The man must be scared out of his wits. Do I want to hear the whole story?*

Then again, Yeron helped save her life. Stan the Man theorized that listening to people's problems would relieve her nightmares. She hoped he was right because some of them were doozies. He assured her that despite her misfortunes, she'd meet people with worse problems.

So far, all of her visitors enjoyed great lives except her mother and Tyrone, who were grieving. Now, here was Yeron, who was having a year's worth of horrible days. What could she say to someone who saw ghosts?

"When my mother and I talk, she serves coffee." She indicated the remains of her breakfast, still on the radiator. "Someone left me extra milk, and it's cold. I know processed drinks are bad for you, but milk should be okay. Help yourself."

"Milk agrees with me, but beverages will not make this go away." Yeron sagged into the chair by her bed, cradling his chart, and looked at Alexis. "I appreciate your kindness."

So comfort food won't help the distressed Kryszka. Alexis contemplated a different approach, but Yeron made the next move.

"Most underground people were friendly, but the 10 percent who ruled the compound hated humans and tried to destroy them. The victims did not die easy deaths." Yeron hung his head and looked at his chart. "Earth people remember this when they meet me. Even you found my features unsettling."

"Ouch." For a moment, Alexis forgot about her injuries.

She forgot about Ms. Grese's warnings. She forgot about everything except the sad ruby eyes, fiery red orbs burned in albino skin. "That was because I had a flashback. When that soldier shot at me, it was like my hair had caught fire. I was so afraid of burning up alive...or worse. I see my attacker every night in my dreams. I never counted on asthma killing Robin."

"It is the things you do not worry about that turn bad," Yeron said. "Your assailant may be the soldier who killed my father. Eigil made life miserable for my parents."

"I'm sorry to hear that. You only get one mother and one father." Alexis gazed in awe at Yeron, wondering how he kept it together. "Steve told me your father was a brilliant doctor."

"He was. My father loved to teach, and we were close. You were bleeding, and I could not find the source. He came up behind me, placed his hand over mine, and guided me to a glass fragment next to one of your major blood vessels."

"I saw what he did." Shudders wreaked Alexis's body. The thought of a ghost assisting with her surgery was awesome. "What happened was a miracle."

Yeron shrugged. "My father said he had unfinished business. None of this makes sense. Where I come from, people do not acknowledge belief in the supernatural."

"Maybe when my heart stopped beating, a gateway opened between life and death, enabling your father's spirit to visit. My family taught me to believe in spirits. The church services I go to allude to the hereafter. Going to church might help you understand this."

"I doubt it. No one taught me religion and these ghost visions violate nature as I know it. I avoid large crowds of people." A bleak, shadowed expression crossed his face. "Whether I go to a church, a restaurant, or work, people look at me and see a killer."

"Yeron, you were a victim, too, but a lot of people don't get that." Alexis studied Yeron, moved by his pain. "One rotten apple spoils them all."

"We never grew apples on the compound," Yeron told her.

"It means one person's bad behavior gives his group a bad name. Take Mark. He makes managers look bad. Many of my coworkers used to work at Meadowood Hospital until he started terrorizing his staff."

"I know." A glint settled in Yeron's eyes. "I agree with your assessment of him. He tears up magazines when he thinks no one is looking. He is ripping something now. Listen."

Alexis listened, and someone was tearing paper down the hall. She realized she'd heard it for some time. "You're right. At first, I thought it was the paper shredder."

Yeron shook his head. "Mark rips newspapers and magazines with his bare hands. Steve and I caught him. We found the scraps under his bed."

"His bed, huh? So Meathead has resorted to tearing paper." Alexis burst into gales of laughter. The mirth started her coughing again, yielding another sample from her mucus factory. "Meathead's gone bonkers. Crazy and mean."

Yeron sighed. "I wish I could find this amusing, but your peers act mean, too, and they are not crazy. They remember Eigil when they meet me."

"Oh." Alexis's laughter stopped. She told herself Yeron's sharp teeth frightened people, but that explanation didn't wash. If an oral surgeon shaped his teeth to human perfection, his body would spell one hundred percent Public Enemy Number One. All the same, his sad eyes spoke of a gentleman who deserved kindness after years of brutality in a police colony.

"I didn't mean to be insensitive. You've lost both parents, and you haven't found many sympathetic ears. When Stan the Man—Doctor Klein—said I'd meet people worse off than me, he wasn't joking."

"Our problems are what they are." Yeron's ruby eyes measured her with the curious look of a cat. "I should not bring mine to your bedside, let alone discuss my visions. You have enough of your heartaches. Perhaps humor is a wise approach."

"It depends on the ...." The rattling started again. Another brutal cough jarred her back incisions. "The circumstances. Let me ask you this. If you could use contractions and slang, would this help you interact better?"

"It might. When Joe first hired me, Steve and Becky taught me remedial English. Most things I learn fast, but no one understands me when I try to use contractions. I never learned your idioms because the patients demanded our attention."

"I owe you for persuading Mark to let me have the medicine." Alexis furrowed her brows, measuring each word. The throbbing from her incisions slowed any attempt at thinking. "I can teach you slang. It shouldn't be hard. Your IQ must be over two hundred."

"I am not familiar with your IQ tests, but I thank you for your compliment. I appreciate your gratitude, too, but you are in too much pain. With those flashbacks ..."

"I'll have those, no matter what I do." Alexis shrugged. "If I help you with your language barrier, that part of me may heal. Stan the Man said as much."

"You mean Doctor Klein," Yeron said, puzzled.

"Doctor Klein reminds me of a baseball hitter nicknamed Stan the Man. Like Stan, he catches on to people fast." She eased back and looked up at Yeron. "You and the other doctors agreed to treat me without charge if my insurance expires. Will you let me do this for you?"

Yeron gazed at her in stunned surprise. Alexis had to wonder if any stranger had ever done favors for him.

He drew in a deep breath. "If you lose your insurance, your government will pay me. I will consider lessons when you are feeling better. You must allow me to do something for you."

Alexis lifted her brows. *Well, Yeron, how about convincing Ms. Grese to extend my sick leave? Or waving a magic wand to make those creatures disappear? Something bad is headed our way, and your dad came back from the dead to warn us.* "Zombies—or whatever they are—can't think. The surviving soldiers who lead them here can. If you teach me Kryszka, I'll understand what they're saying."

"You want to learn Kryszka?" Yeron leaned back, his red eyes wide as golf balls, and dropped his chart. He retrieved his chart, then looked back at Alexis. "No one ever asked to learn my language. Why you, Alexis?"

Her back stung as if a swarm of bees had attacked her, but Alexis held her gaze steady. "I want to know why they killed Dee and Robin. Why Jackson Hospital? Why not New York or Los Angeles? They can't speak English, so it would behoove me to learn the language.

"My father worked for an underworld figure named Charlie. He made it his business to become fluent in other languages to sniff out trouble." She shifted and winced. "During his chemotherapy, he cursed at the nurses in five different languages: German, Italian, Spanish, Russian, and of course English."

Yeron threw his head back and laughed. The laughter was subdued behind his mask, but there, with musical notes.

Yeron, you should laugh more often. Then women would find you attractive. "If nothing else, I can get a job as a translator."

"Do not worry about it." Yeron let out another stream of giggles. "I shall speak with your other doctors. If they do not object, you can teach me slang, and I will teach you Kryszka. Now, you look pale. Get some sleep."

"All right. I need one favor." Alexis watched his eyes, intent and listening. "If you see your dad again, could you tell him I said thanks? Without his help, I wouldn't be here."

"No, you would not. So yes, if I see him, I will give him your message." He touched her shoulder. "Thank you for listening to me."

Alexis nodded and curled up on her side. Something nasty was headed their way all right. The pain was brutal. Throbbing invaded every nerve ending in her back. The burning sensation in her right hand brought tears to her eyes. The paper-shredding from Mark's room made everything worse. He kept it up through lunchtime. Pretty soon, she'd scream. It was time for a chat with Meathead. Maybe if he heard about Trident Mall, he'd cut it out. The doctors could bitch all they wanted. She needed something that would work as a weapon.

She glanced at the desk. Deserted. Cindy was working with another patient. With a grimace, Alexis stood up, favoring her bad leg, and plopped into the chair. The impact induced a fresh bolt of stabbing pain. Moments later, while she leaned forward, the throbbing subsided. A sheet flapped over her thighs. The pump with her CX249 unplugged and moved up behind her chair. She managed each movement with levitation. She smiled. *Damn girl, you're good.*

Another glance down the hall. No one. Pushing the chair with her feet, and the IV with her mind, she exited her room and headed past Shively's room. Shively nodded at her with a wink. Alexis smiled at him, holding a finger to her lips.

Her chest rattled and ached. She should have stayed in bed but, dammit, she needed protection. Surely she'd find scissors in a utility room. She worked her way around the L-shaped hall to her former room and, next to it, Mark's room, two doors from the back elevator. The IV pump rolled behind her, the glass bottle of CX249 tapping against the pole.

Mark's curtain was drawn, but an open slit at the right corner gave her a clear view of his bathroom. He stood by his sink. Her plans for searching for weapons faded into the background.

Why is Meathead wearing a diaper?

Broken fragments of memories stormed her mind: Mark raising his hand, Mark brandishing his bat, Mark throwing her onto a sofa. *Sofa? When did that happen?*

She didn't know, but Mark was facing the drapes. If he turned his head left, he'd see her. It was best if she got the hell back to her room, but moving her chair and IV now would create enough noise to attract his notice.

Also, a perverse curiosity about the diaper nagged at her.

She backed up and darted a glance toward the station. No one at the desk, but the jangling from her bottle had gotten oh, so loud. She moved forward again, trying to summon the courage to call Mark's name. Instead, she froze at the sight of him standing in his bathroom, fingering his diaper. One look to his left and she was in deep trouble. A voice inside her whispered, *don't worry, honey, Meathead can't tell your IV from the rest of the ICU sounds.*

He peeled away his diaper, revealing thick bandages on his hips and thighs. Someone had shaved the hair around his penis. Hysterical giggles bubbled up inside, forcing Alexis to clap her hand against her mouth. The movement stung, but Mark catching her watching would be worse.

Now she had to cough. She burrowed her mouth inside her sheet, making faint chuffing sounds. When she thought of how brutal Mark could be with his fists and bat, especially on his sofa, her blood ran cold.

She peered into his room again and picked out more details. The pile of paper scraps on his floor. The faint smell of urine. The pee stains on his mattress. She guessed his set-to with the Kryszka renegades had gifted him with kidney damage. His wanger was growing stiff and erect. He was massaging it with a gentle stroking motion.

I don't need to see him jerking off, she thought. *I wonder if Yeron does that.*

Of course, he does, the phantom voice inside her whispered. *He has a wanger like Mark's.* Her mind visualized her holding it, stroking it, feeling its texture, and then a hot feeling surged through her, causing her cheeks to flush. Soft moaning from Mark jarred her to reality.

I can't look. Alexis buried her head in her sheet. Her heart thudded in her ears, and in her mind, Mark was throwing her onto the sofa. Other images appeared: Mark ripping at her clothes, a smack across her face ... and then her mind shut down. The images sent chills through her body. *I can't think about it. Don't want to.*

Alexis snuck a peek, but Mark made no sign of moving. He stood by the sink, wiping himself with the diaper, a dreamy expression on his face. *Come on, Meathead, shut the damn door.* She had lost all interest in her quest for weapons.

A flick of her mind might close the curtain, but any resulting noise increased the chances of Mark catching her. Perhaps he was too engrossed in his playtime to notice. Her mind nudged at the wheeled carriers that held the drape. They did not budge. Such a delicate operation required fine-tuning of her psychokinesis. *Shit!*

In that instant, Mark looked up. For a second, it seemed, his eyes locked with hers. *Please, God, distract him. Please! I'm sorry I snooped, I'm sorry for thinking wrong thoughts.*

An agonizing pause followed. Sweat plastered her gown to her body. Droplets of perspiration rolled down her face and chest. Her back incisions ached terribly. Leaving her room was a capital mistake. Any second, she'd pass out. That would draw Mark's attention for sure. God help her if that happened.

Then Mark spoke, and his voice came from outside the bathroom. His footsteps crunched over the paper shreds. He was circling his room, cell phone against his ear. "What's up, Mom ... I'm okay ... really, I am..."

She'd never heard it ring. He must have set it on vibrate. *You've got your distraction,* the phantom voice whispered. *Go back to your room. Now!*

Maneuvering her feet, she guided her chair away from Mark's room and pushed the pole with her mind. It was amazing that her talent worked, given her pain level—she'd rate hers a twenty. She proceeded down the hall back to her room.

Her mother stood by the desk, watching. She had on her nurse's uniform and fanny pack, her face getting redder by the nanosecond. "Alexis, what are you doing out here?"

"I should ask you why you're working here. Jackson Hospital has a policy about people working the same floors where family members are getting care."

"I think too much when I'm home, and besides, two nurses on this floor quit. So my boss made an exception to that policy and had me transferred here. We're talking about you. Haven't you caught enough hell for leaving your room?"

"I was looking for Cindy to get me pain medicine."

"I can get you pain medicine. Go back to your room. This will take a few minutes."

Alexis wheeled herself back to her bed. Moments later, her mother came in hauling a medicine cart. "You're not due for more pain medicine yet, but I can make you comfortable."

She plugged in the IV. Arm braced across Alexis's shoulders, her mother helped her into bed. "Your department's hurting for staff, too. Ms. Grese called in agency help."

Alexis sighed. "I'm not surprised. They lost two therapists and two others are still recuperating from injuries."

"Since the shootings, people are staying with relatives out of town." Her mother fluffed up her pillows and placed a cold, damp cloth on her forehead. "What were you doing in the hall?"

"Mark's been shredding paper, and I can hear it even with the doors closed. It gets on my nerves, especially with the pain. I was going to tell him to stop."

"Did you?" Her mother's voice softened.

Alexis shook her head, swallowing hard. "I couldn't."

"That man spooks everyone," her mother said in a sad voice. "Doctor Hoffman might discharge him tomorrow. I wish I could put my hand on your head and make this go away."

Weapons would make some of it disappear, preferably a plasma gun that's easy on the hands. Alexis assessed her surroundings ... the IV machine, a walker left by Physical Therapy. No knives or scissors. Since her initial chat with Stan, the doctors banned all sharp instruments from her room.

Then she regarded her mother: wrinkles around her lips and eyes, seventy pounds overweight. She carried much of her girth in muscle from lifting patients.

"Maybe you can help." Alexis leaned back and looked at her mother. "Have you noticed how antsy the doctors are lately?"

"That's because you never listen to them," her mother said, smiling.

Alexis shook her head. "The doctors are frightened. Steve and Yeron told me why and, frankly, Mom, I'm scared, too."

"I see." Her mother canted her head to the left, giving Alexis an oblique look. "Did they find something else wrong with you?"

"No." Alexis tried for a calm tone, aiming for the fine line between making her mother understand and upsetting her. "Yeron pulled a report off an army website. It says the people who put me and others in the hospital are planning another visit."

"Yeron shouldn't be frightening you. He's brought nothing but trouble here."

"Mom, why are you blaming Yeron? Just answer me this? Did Hoffman add security?"

"Yes," her mother replied with a sigh. "He sealed the back elevator, but he never said why. He installed biometric locks for this ward and the dressing room. You need your user ID and two pass codes, or you hope your fingerprint works on the scanner."

"Fifteen of those locks won't stop the soldiers." As Alexis spoke, blatant terror radiated from her mother's widened hazel eyes. "Did Shively already tell you?"

"I can't discuss my other patients with you." Her mother's face went red, then pale. "Don't worry. I'm sure Administration knows people who can handle such crises."

"Yes, and the check is in the mail." Alexis heaved a ponderous sigh. That came out damned tactless.

"Doctors Leicht and Hoffman have guns that spray fire." Her mother huddled against her cart, her face white in the dimly lit room.

"You've heard rumors about this, haven't you?" Alexis noted her mother's quivery lips and darting eyes. She dropped her gaze toward Yeron's file. "Those people are clever. If they want to get in here, they'll find a way. They got into our house, remember? Do me a favor. Go to my condo and get my Beretta. Ask Fenimore to show you how to use it."

Her mother's eyes bulged. "You expect me to carry a gun?"

Alexis nodded. "Everyone who works up here should carry one."

"Alexis, I can't." Terror bled into her mother's voice. "I've never fired a gun."

"Look inside my yellow folder." Alexis pointed toward the chair. "It's got Yeron's report on Trident Mall. Then you can decide if a gun is necessary."

Her mother snatched up the file like a drowning sailor grabbing a life preserver. Alexis waited for her reaction. Moments later, Matilda dropped the folder. She began to babble as if the report contained a switch that had turned her on, like a radio.

"My God, what will happen to us? I don't think Fenimore ..." The reassuring nurse and mother vanished, and a woman terrified for her life stared at Alexis. "I should go."

With that, she bolted, leaving behind her cart.

Alexis shifted to her left and dabbed her face with the cloth. That was brutal, but it was better than lying. Soon her mother was going to pack heat. That concluded, she closed her eyes. She had slid into a light doze when the ring of her cell phone jolted her awake.

Pushing her button to raise the head of her bed, she reached for the phone with calculated movements. Each move demanded precision because the tingling and stiffness in her hand caused her to drop things.

"Alexis," Shively's hoarse voice whispered. "How did your trip go?"

"I came back here feeling like a piece of shit on a rainy day. I was looking for sharp scissors but came up empty-handed. Is this about Trident Mall?"

"Damned straight. Watch what you tell your mother. She can't handle it."

"Maybe she can, Shively. Her friend Fenimore knows guns, being a hunter. Maybe he can protect her or teach her how to fire a gun."

"That's two more 'maybes' than I like."

"My mother's skittishness won't stop the rogue Kryszka. I don't care how many soldiers guard the hospital."

"You've got that right. Charlie became their dinner, and everyone in my organization wants to make this go away. My boss asked me to recruit people who know the renegades' weakness. I've talked with Tyrone and Mark. Johnny's being sprung this week, and he wants in on this, too. We're meeting next Sunday night, around seven. Sixth-floor conference room. You interested?"

"Next Sunday?" Alexis thought a moment. "That's Easter."

"Like these creatures give a shit!"

"They don't." Alexis ran her gauze-clad hands through her hair. Despite the dry shampoo, the strands felt oily. She grimaced. Thoughts about her father and how he begged her to avoid the criminal underworld singed through her mind. "We'll need weapons and body armor, I'm thinking. How much do these things cost?"

"Don't worry about the money. My guys will take care of it. Are you in or not?"

Another flashback, this time of Robin's gasping lips and the evil in her attacker's eyes. "In." Alexis shuddered. "Easter might work. Half the crew takes the day off, and the others wish they could. I should be done with the CX249 by then. I'm using a walker for short distances. Count me in, but we'll have to get past watchdog nurses and two electronic locks."

"Let me handle the locks. Use your mind trick to distract the nurses."

Alexis laughed. "I guess you couldn't help noticing, huh?"

"Nope." Shively's chuckle came through loud and clear. "Tyrone will keep Yeron busy. Mark and I will figure out the locks. You find some work for the nurses."

After they hung up, Alexis eased her head against the pillow again. After convincing herself that she and Shively's underworld friends were fighting the same enemy, she let the darkness wash over her. This time she slept without any nightmares.

Chapter Twenty: Meeting of the Survivors

Jackson's Sixth Floor Conference Room, April 4, 7:00 p.m.

While Mark tore up his periodicals, Alexis spent the next week waking her tired muscles, receiving counseling, and starting Kryszka lessons. She struggled through the alphabet and greetings with repetition and practice. Contractions were difficult for Yeron, but he soaked up every idiom she fed him. Not a sneer or frown crossed his lips at her bungled pronunciations.

When she wasn't doing those things, she listened to her mother's fiscal report on Robin's estate. Her mother, stabilized with blood pressure medicines, worked twelve-hour shifts and returned from her breaks with treats for Alexis. Though work was therapeutic, it put her mother in the path of would-be invaders. Alexis concentrated hard on her lessons and muscle retraining and let Mark worry about his own problems, paper-shredding included.

Hoffman, Steve, and Yeron took off on April 4. Easter Sunday. Cindy and Matilda fielded questions from staff resident doctors. For Alexis, the hours dragged, despite a visit from her coworkers and Tyrone. After they left, she flicked through the TV channels. Nothing worth watching. The hours marched on and, at six, Cindy took her dinner break, leaving Alexis's mother to run the floor. Her mother remained at the station to finish her paperwork. Doctor Hoffman had left a dozen folders on the desk beside her. She shifted her gaze between her charting and the TV monitors, pausing to reach for a folder.

Shit. Why did her mother have to pull duty? Didn't someone need a bedpan? Apparently not. Alexis's nerves were tauter than piano wires. At six thirty, Shively poked his head through his door and motioned toward the exit. The three patients in the A cubicles were asleep. Alexis contemplated setting off a fire alarm to distract her mother, but fire alarms locked the elevators. She was nowhere ready to try stairs. She had to engage her mother's cooperation and do it gently. *Shit!* Gritting her teeth, she pressed her call bell.

At the sound of her buzzer, her mother marched to the room. "What's wrong? Are you in pain again?"

"No, but I'd like to take a walk. The more I walk, the stronger my leg will get. I'll need to run if those dead-looking beings swarm through here." Her mother winced, but Alexis pressed on. "Don't worry; I'm okay. Doesn't one of your other patients need you?"

"I finished my dressing changes an hour ago. Everyone's fine. Let's keep it that way." Her mother spoke firmly, but a muscle in her neck twitched.

"Mom, we can't ignore that army document." Alexis kept her voice quiet, noting her mother's pallor. "Did you think about what I said? About the—"

"Yes. Fenimore's teaching me." Her mother heaved an exasperated sigh. Her face flushed. "He made me buy a Glock. Are you satisfied?"

"Almost." Alexis shot a glance toward Shively. He waved his hand. "Shively and I need to talk. Maybe we can come up with a solution."

"Solution for what?" Her mother asked between clenched teeth. "Let me guess, Johnny's involved."

Alexis nodded. "Johnny's meeting with us downstairs."

"Both of you need a pass to leave the floor. I'll get one for you tomorrow when Doctor Leicht's on duty."

"I've got to see Johnny tonight. I'm not going far. Shively and Tyrone will be with me."

"No, and no!!" Stark terror bled through her mother's features. "Regardless of what happened at Trident, my job is the same as it always was. To keep my patients safe."

Her mother's set jaw and narrowed eyes warned she wasn't budging on this one. Alexis's gaze turned toward the file folders. She was preparing to create a distraction.

"Safety is important," she humored her mother. "I'm sorry I gave you a hard time."

She knotted her brows and gave those files a shove and a twist, moving them with her thoughts. One folder slid off the pile. Two more. The remaining files dive-bombed to the floor. Papers spilled out of the folder pockets.

"My God!" Her mother's cheeks flamed. She let out a cry of helplessness and scurried after the runaway papers. "Doctor Hoffman's going to be furious. I hate this. I hate this!"

"So do I, Mom." Alexis got to her feet. Hands curled around her walker's cushioned grip, she exited her room. Shively joined her at the nurses' desk. So far, each step was steady with her walker for balance.

Mark came up to her left, his cold blue eyes on her. Her muscles tightened, fearing another blow from his baseball bat. It had served him well against Kryszka invaders and errant wives. Her gaze went to his hands, and she let out a deep breath. No bat, just a plastic container with ballistics gel and other items he'd need to bypass the locks. Either way, she didn't like him so close to her one bit. She gave Shively a pleading look.

"Mark, go on ahead." Shively stepped up beside her. "Take your time, Alexis. I've got you covered. You've gotten Matilda plenty busy."

"Thank you," she said under her breath. Then louder: "I can't believe I did that to my mother."

"The renegade soldiers will do worse." His voice softened, offering a reprieve. "Unless you make a plan."

Mark waited at the exit, wearing his perpetual frown. He tripped the lock and propped the door open with his elbow for the others to pass. The trio continued down the hall, past doctors' offices and laboratories. The walk was longer than any Alexis had taken in Physical Therapy. The tingling started on her left leg, but she managed to ignore it until they reached the dressing area. Her hands throbbed, her left foot wobbled. Shively grabbed her shoulders with his good arm, steadying her.

Bins filled with yellow cloth gowns sat to their right. The shelves above them held thick isolation masks and other gear. Another steel door ahead made more work for Mark and Shively. After they overrode the biometric mechanism, the door slid open with creaking sounds. Tyrone waited by the elevators.

"Hey, Tyrone, give Alexis a hand," Shively hollered. "She's getting shaky."

"I'm all right." Alexis smiled, grateful for Tyrone's husky arm around her shoulder. "Has Steve or Doctor Phil made an appearance?"

"Doctor Phil?" Tyrone laughed. "Is that what you call Yeron? Both doctors have been back since five. I started a lively discussion between them."

In the conference room, flowers, balloons, and two baskets filled with chocolate eggs and marshmallow Peeps greeted her from the table. Johnny sat by the table, gazing at a photograph. It was of his wife and two children. He had on dungarees and a sweatshirt. The chest tube was long gone, but he kept favoring his side. Before his attack, he had a deep tan. Now, he looked pallid. His wire-rimmed glasses remained intact.

"The walking wounded!" He grinned. "Who did you bribe to let you down here, Alexis?"

Alexis laughed. "No one, but I created busywork for my mother. Obviously, you've read about Trident Mall."

Johnny nodded. "Sit."

Tyrone plopped into a chair at Johnny's left, while Alexis went for the chair next to Tyrone. Mark claimed one opposite Alexis, facing Tyrone. He swapped his frown for a crooked smile that didn't touch his eyes.

Shively stood kitty-corner to Johnny and his companions, his shrewd eyes measuring everyone. "We all know why we're here, right?"

A silence followed. Tyrone fingered his wedding ring. Johnny looked down at his photo, now folded in his hands. Despite their somber looks, Alexis found herself staring at Mark and shivering. He gave her the creeps and she badly wanted ... no, needed to get away from him. The idea of telling these guys about his special baseball bat popped into her mind. Perhaps she'd tell them what she saw him do in his room. Revealing both incidents would make her sound whiny though, and worse, could result in payback from Mark. After thinking about it some more, she decided on a different approach.

"Mister Adams might need a reminder," she said, focusing on recent events. "He tried to make Hoffman withhold my medicine."

"I heard something about that." Tyrone's voice was low, but his dark eyes flashed fury. "How come?"

"Hoffman only had enough CX249 for two people. Mark didn't have the toxin, but he wanted my share of the medicine because he thought I was going to die anyway." Alexis took perverse pleasure in watching Mark squirm. "That's how come."

"Mark." Tyrone gave him a reproachful look. "That was a low thing to do."

"Not for him, it wasn't." Johnny cackled, holding his side. "Don't you guys know he and Laurel Grant are lovers?"

Alexis exploded with laughter. "I heard a rumor she's having his baby."

Tyrone guffawed and held his nose. "Then he caught a disease from her."

Mark's face went deep red and purple. The tendons on his neck bulged. His fists clenched. "Stupid jerks! I was entitled to that drug. Johnny's mad because I cut costs at Meadowood and made him quit. He wasn't man enough to handle the workload."

"Enough!" Shively's loud voice cut through the laughter. "We'll work as a team. That means keeping guns at the bedside. Mark, you owe everyone, especially Alexis, an apology."

"I don't owe any apologies." Mark folded his arms across his chest, eyes on Shively. "Alexis bad-mouthed me to everyone. She made me out to be the devil."

"Because you are a devil," Alexis said, looking at him. Another shiver. His eyes had a chilling, reptilian look that made her feel like a mouse staring into the eyes of a cobra.

"Alexis, you're not helping." Shively spoke in the tone of a referee addressing two fighting players. "We need all the people we can get. Mark, show everyone you're the bigger person. Apologize."

"I am the bigger person." Mark's voice dripped with sarcasm. "I'm six feet tall."

"Let's go outside." Using his healthy arm, Shively yanked Mark by the elbow. He walked him out to the hall.

Alexis regarded Tyrone and Johnny, weighing them as allies against Mark. "Including Mark was a capital mistake. That man is dangerous."

"Tell me about it," Johnny said. "I worked for the bastard."

"Don't worry." Tyrone patted her arm. "Bastards like him won't last. They never do."

Moments later, Shively marched a flushed Mark back into the room. He shoved Mark into his chair. "Apologize."

"Alexis, I never wanted anything to happen to you." Mark's voice was contrite, but there was no mistaking the hatred in his eyes, the redness on his face, or the throbbing vein in his neck. "I panicked. I'm sorry. That goes for you, too, Johnny and Tyrone."

That man shits out of both ends, Alexis thought. "It's done, Mark. Let's try to stay alive. Shively, how do we go about doing that?"

"Someone I know owns a safe house near Trident Mall. If things get ugly here, he'll let us use it. Homeland Security's sending officers to patrol the hospital grounds and stores across the street, but the Kryszka will find ways to get in here. So we better start carrying."

Reaching into a briefcase by his feet, he pulled out Glocks. He handed them out to Johnny, Tyrone, and Mark. His eyes measured Alexis, and then he nodded. "I've got something better for you."

"She can't handle firearms," Mark piped up. "Her hands are useless."

"Don't dare tell me what I can do." Alexis mustered a flippant voice, but the memories of Mark's bat loomed large in her mind. The skin on her arms pulled into gooseflesh.

Shively's voice hardened. "Enough, guys. I mean it."

Tyrone nudged Alexis's shoulder. "Don't let him get to you."

"Tyrone." Shively pointed toward the windowsill. "Give

Alexis the basket with the pink ribbon. It's got her stuff."

"Easter candy?" Alexis grinned. "Did you lace it with poison?"

"Nope." Tyrone set the basket on her lap. "One of your coworkers took up a collection for you and Johnny. Shively's buddies slipped in an extra something."

Alexis dug underneath the eggs and chicks, past Reese's Peanut Butter Cups and an envelope. A peek inside it revealed cash. Further on, her fingertips brushed cold metal, and she felt the shape of a plasma gun in the basket. It looked like the same one she'd used on her Kryszka attacker. She lifted it out with levitation, not yet ready to trust her hands.

"Shively, you clever dog!" She laughed. "Where did your friends get this?"

"It's a secret." Shively's eyes gleamed. "That should be easier to use."

"Definitely. Tell your friends I said thanks."

Mark gave her another withering look, but Alexis held her smile.

"We should all learn to use plasma," Shively went on. "Alexis, show us how it works."

"I don't know how." Alexis looked over her gun, noting the foreign symbols on it under the light. "This one has three buttons, so I pushed them all. Although I killed my attackers, I set my mom's property on fire. Maybe Yeron could show us how these work. He's teaching me the language. If the renegades come around, I'll understand what they're saying."

"So that's the gibberish I hear from your room." Shively chuckled.

"The hell with the language," Johnny said. "I want those bastards to take a long dirt nap."

"Yeron's out." Mark's voice chilled like ice. Alexis felt the cold go out in all directions. "I don't trust the man."

"I do." Alexis looked over at Mark. "He helped save my life."

"He's a great doctor," Tyrone conceded, "but he won't want to be bothered teaching us his language or guns. He's aloof."

"He's not aloof around me," Alexis said. "He's been patient with me trying to learn his language."

"Whoa!" Johnny cackled. "Got the hots for him, do you?"

"No!" Intense heat flushed through Alexis's cheeks. "It's just that he's …"

"Look how red she is." Shively snorted.

"Yeron knows how the native Kryszka feel and think, and how to work the weapons."

"You've got a point there." Shively nodded, laughing. "The language would come in handy, too, but we don't have time to learn."

"What if Yeron doesn't want to be bothered?" Johnny asked.

Alexis's eyes shifted toward the door. She thought she heard footsteps. "He watched the video. He might consider teaching us if I ask him real …"

The door banged open, hitting an empty chair. Yeron stood facing the group, all seventy-seven inches of his wiry build filling the doorway. He had traded his helium-proof mask for a thick green one, but the green did not hide his red frizzy hair or eyes. *Dammit, what's he doing in the sixth-floor conference room? Why isn't he with Steve?*

"Your conversation carried all the way to the elevator." He hurried over to Alexis, frowning. "I left Matilda strict orders not to allow you outside your room. She was too busy rearranging her papers to watch you. No one pays attention."

"Oh, shit." Alexis glanced over at her companions. Shively yawned. Johnny pulled the neck of his sweatshirt over his chin, snickering. Tyrone lowered his head with a sheepish grin, while Mark favored her with a glowering expression.

"My coworkers took up a collection for Johnny and me." She patted the basket on her lap. "I needed to get out and visit."

"A person's got a right to their comforts," Tyrone added.

"Don't worry, doc, Alexis listens to every word you say," Johnny spoke up from his shirt. "She wants to get into your pants."

"Why does Alexis want to wear my pants?" Yeron gave him a puzzled stare.

Alexis lowered her head, the redness spreading up her cheeks. *This is not the time for Johnny's stupid jokes.*

"She wants to get it on with you."

"Johnny, stop." Tyrone smacked his shoulder and burst into raucous laughter. "We can't take you anywhere."

"No one is going anywhere, Tyrone," Yeron said without emotion. "Johnny's ribs will take another month to heal. Alexis and Shively need extensive physical therapy. Mark is the only healthy person here. So why *are* you here, Mark?"

"I was invited, unlike you." Mark's harsh voice reeked with contempt. "Shively, I'll call you later."

"See you, Mark." Shively ambled over toward Alexis's chair. "Here, I'll carry your basket. Maybe Tyrone can walk you back to your room."

"No, Shively, I brought a wheelchair. I will take her back." Yeron shook his head, exasperated. "Alexis, I suspect you did not come here to chat."

Alexis gave a deep sigh, forearms hugging her basket. "Doctor Klein said I should interact with people. I told you that, right?"

Silence. The wheels creaked along the linoleum. The elevators slid open, waiting for Alexis and Yeron. At the entrance to the ward, Yeron swiped his ID card and entered two passwords. He then rolled her past the sliding doors into the research unit and back to her room.

"Johnny was teasing you." Alexis lifted her gaze toward Yeron. "My work buddies were trying to be supportive."

Yeron traded his thick mask for the clear one. He didn't say a word.

Chapter Twenty-One: Yeron Confronts Alexis

Jackson's Research Floor, April 4, 9:00 p.m.

Dammit. She didn't want to antagonize the man who offered a freedom-from-disability ticket. "Okay, because of what happened at Trident Mall, my friends and I made plans. Please don't yell at my mother. She knows about Trident Mall, and she's terrified. Sometimes she drops things … like folders."

"Of course, you did nothing to cause her accident." Yeron turned toward her, holding his gaze steady.

Alexis gave him an innocent look, determined to keep the discussion low key. "I didn't get within ten feet of her desk."

"No, you simply used your push." Her eyes widening, Alexis sat agape while Yeron wriggled his hand inside the basket, digging through the foil candy. He withdrew her gun, flashing a mischievous grin. "Does this look like chocolate? You do not lie well."

That man needs a life. No wonder Johnny teases me about him. "So you think I'm a lousy liar." She gave him a stern glare. "Didn't your father tell you it's rude to go through people's belongings without permission?"

"Yes, he did." His smiled broadened. "He called such behavior disrespectful, but I overheard you and your friends discussing firearms. When someone investigates a security breach, privacy does not matter. Your hospital forbids possession of firearms. How should I handle this?"

He had her there. Unlawful possession of firearms could land her in jail. How much did Hazlett and his officers know about Trident Mall? She wasn't sure, and she would do well to appeal to his practicality. "I was trying to protect myself."

No comment. Yeron gazed down the barrel of the cylinder and studied the symbols circling the hand grip.

"If we lived on a Kryszka compound, would you allow me to keep the gun?"

"The average Kryszka citizen carries a gun as you would your keys or wallet, but we are not in a Kryszka compound." A puzzled look crossed his red eyes. "You have just started to recover from injuries caused by monsters who want you and your family dead. You require heavy painkillers and, yet, you are riding off this floor so you can acquire firearms. Joe Hoffman installed new locks and Administration is hiring extra security. Homeland Security will supply officers as well. Allow them to protect you."

"Protect me? Come on, Doctor Phil, get real." In the next instant, Alexis clapped her hand over her mouth. "Hey, I'm sorry. You remind me of Doctor Phil. I mean no disrespect."

"What does 'getting real' mean?" Yeron asked.

"We should face reality, such as the lousy capabilities of our security officers. We call them Rent-a-Cops. Last year, when I got sick, one of them demanded to know why I parked illegally. So, I coughed up blood in front of him. The guy went white and fainted. Would you trust your life with someone like that?"

"No, I would not. Your Administration hates spending money for efficient officers."

"Given your technology and despite our army soldiers, Eigil's troopers can get in here if they try. Right or wrong?"

"Right." Yeron heaved a sigh.

"My father would want me to carry a gun. Stanley Klein encouraged me to start taking care of myself. That means carrying a plasma gun to protect myself."

"So your father would expect you to carry a gun." Yeron paced around the room, darting glances toward the door and out the window. "What about your mother?"

Damn! Why did he have to mention my mother? "She'd get upset, but she'd hate losing a second daughter more. Please don't tell her about this. You can't because you're like a priest listening to me in a confessional."

"So, I was a television celebrity before, and now I am a priest." Yeron sagged into a chair beside Alexis and let out a steady stream of giggles. "Which one am I, Alexis?"

At the sound of his laugh, Alexis found herself chuckling. "Maybe both. Knowing what you do about our security officers, will you let me keep the gun?"

Yeron sat, tracing and retracing his forefinger across the symbols on the hand grip. "No. This weapon is worthless. Its chamber has three shots left. Your friends do not know plasma."

He stood up and rooted under his side waistband. He withdrew another plasma gun and placed it on her lap. This one had four buttons, blue, red, yellow, and green, much like the kind Steve had described. "This one is fully loaded. If you agree to abstain from future field trips, I will teach you how to use it." He smiled again. "Without causing fires."

Alexis looked up at Yeron, her mouth an open 'O' of surprise.

"Do not look so shocked. I saw photographs of your mother's house and her garden. You did your best, considering your circumstances. I should not tease you."

Alexis shrugged. "It's all right. I'm just surprised you knew. So what's this blue button?"

"The blue rays cause temporary muscle paralysis and unconsciousness. You press the blue button and then hit the green to execute your shot. The blue ray will take down your assailant without harm. The blue works well for someone you might later want to interrogate. You can free a hostage and then take the assailant into custody while the hostage sleeps off the effect." Yeron tucked the gun back into his waistband. "After you learn the proper way to use this gun, you may keep it. I have many more in my suite."

Yeron came loaded for bear, Alexis thought. "Thank you, Doctor Phil ... I mean Yeron."

"You may call me Doctor Phil. He is an intelligent man."

"All right, Doctor Phil. How will you teach me? I'm surprised no one caught you on the monitors."

"I kept my back toward the monitors when I brought you to your room. You, Alexis, must learn subtlety if you want to survive. No more unsupervised trips. If those creatures break in on another floor, and you are alone, I cannot help you."

"I'll stay ... I promise."

"I am testing a formula—248AR—for rheumatoid arthritis in rats. If these tests yield no surprises, I will start you on it in about a week. You can take your treatment at my suite and get your lessons."

"I'll behave." Alexis leaned forward, looking at him. Under other circumstances, they might have become good work buddies. "Shively, Johnny, and Tyrone want to learn how to use these guns."

"I will be glad to teach them, but I will not work with Mark." Yeron straightened up, eyes on Alexis. "You overheard the conversation between him and Doctor Hoffman about your CX249. How will you feel about fighting alongside a man who had no regard for your survival?"

"Not good." Alexis straightened up and dragged a set of trembling fingers through her curls. Yeron's intent gaze made her squirm. "The others and I think he's a meathead, but Shively said we need him."

"Shively does not think well."

Alexis leaned sideways and winced. Her muscles tensed at the prospect of fighting alongside Mark, given his behavior in the bathroom and his affinity for violence. She could blame the CX249 incident on the heat of the moment, but attacking someone with a nail-studded bat, and on a couch, spoke of sheer brutality.

"Shively's got a lot of street smarts, enough to control Meathead." She traced her right fingers along her leg scar. "I certainly hope so. If Trident Mall is any indication, we need all the fighters we can get."

"Then maybe you should get real, as you say." Yeron's voice saddened. "Did you know your Meathead turned Meadowood Hospital's respiratory department into a pigsty?"

Alexis nodded. "Meathead and I were married when he became manager at Meadowood. His personality changed after that. He complained about his staff and called them lazy bums."

"He ruined that hospital." Anger seeped into Yeron's voice, and his fiery eyes flashed with fury. "Becky's mother—Florence—

died there. Becky used to find her lying in urine, riddled with bed sores. Mark cut his staff down to one respiratory therapist per shift for each wing. That created a workload of forty treatments or more per therapist. If there was an emergency, Florence did not get her treatments. No one had time to bathe or toilet her."

"That sounds like Mark." She looked down at her scar, a hideous reminder of Mark's temper. "I told you how I got this scar. He didn't use any bat. He used one studded with nails, the same weapon he used to fight his attacker."

"Steve told me about that," Yeron said in a doleful voice. "Mark was cruel to his patients, too. He allowed them to develop weeping bed sores and drown in their secretions. I saw the sordid conditions when Becky took me on a tour of the hospital."

"My God, Yeron!" Alexis stared at him, overwhelmed by the enormity of it all. "Why didn't Florence—or whatever her name was—go to another hospital?"

"I never understood why. Mark started cutbacks by not re-placing people who quit their positions. He put a freeze on capital equipment. His lips smile, but his eyes never do."

Alexis nodded. "Mark smiled at me that way before he hit me. He gets high off of meanness. He tried to kill me that night, but I kicked him where it hurt the most and ran."

Yeron took in what she said with a solemn look. "Then you see how dangerous he can be. Why would you agree to fight along-side a man who assaulted you?"

Alexis gazed at her crooked hands and contemplated what had provoked Mark's assault. Robin's asthma attack had started the fight. No, that wasn't it. Sending Robin to Jackson Hospital instead of Meadowood had made Mark furious. Angry enough to kill. Something else happened, something unfathomable, linger-ing in a dim recess of her mind. Whatever it was, Robin should have gone to *his* hospital.

"I don't ... really." The images of Robin's final asthma at-tack rolled through her mind, leading to what ifs. What if Mark had been present when the Kryszka attacked? She could picture Mark beating her senseless and leaving her body for the renegade while he ran.

"Oh, my God, we can't have Mark on board," she cried. "No, no, no ..."

The psychokinetic force stirred inside her, causing the balloons to rustle again. It was all she could do to keep it in check.

"You can control it, Alexis." Yeron's soft voice gentled her. "Try the deep-breathing."

Alexis took three deep breaths. A fourth, just in case. The force edged into the nether regions of her mind. "I can't believe I loved a man like Meathead."

"Maybe you like to see the good in people. My mother was like that. She went to her death believing Woehar could not kill."

"Maybe she was right. Woehar helped you and the others escape, didn't she?"

"She did." Yeron's lips curved into a bitter smile. "Before that, she shot and killed our mother. Woehar and Eigil were lovers, and she did everything he asked, including holding Becky prisoner for forty-eight hours. She made Becky watch the slaughter of a good friend."

"She wouldn't..." Of course, she did. Sadness loomed huge in his eyes. The anger she had felt toward Mark couldn't compare. The shoot-out with the Kryszka soldier couldn't touch it. Laurel's actions with her hostages were abominable but, at the bottom of it all, lower than anything she could think of, was *matricide,* the grisly killing of someone who'd raised you.

She furrowed her eyebrows, trying to think of a sensitive answer. "Steve said Woehar proved her remorse by helping you get out alive. Maybe Mark will soften up the way she did."

"Woehar did not act out of remorse." His smile faded, and weariness replaced it. "She realized things were going bad and she wanted to get out alive. Her reasons no longer matter since she is dead. Mark's behavior does. He may try to hurt you again."

"Tyrone and Johnny agreed to stand by me," Alexis said. "Shively, too. If anyone can control Mark, he can."

"Shively cannot control someone else." Yeron gave her a sad look. "Your friends mean well, but they underestimate Mark. I am coming on this mission with you and your companions."

Alexis's eyes widened. "I can't let you fight my battles. Your patients need you."

"This is my battle, too, and my people started it. I know their weaknesses better than anyone here. I can set up a makeshift laboratory and send Joe the formulas he needs through the networks. If your friends want, I will teach them about plasma guns and the Kryszka language, but..." His face hardened. "I will not work with Mark."

"Shively will teach Mark what he learns."

"That is between Shively and Mark. I will not let you not go through this alone."

I know why, Alexis thought. *Your visits with Stevarino got mighty painful because you want a family of your own. Your technology forgot to invent treatment for loneliness. It's there in your eyes, clear as glass.*

"I'd feel better if you came along," she admitted.

"I am glad to help. Hopefully, my arthritis protocol will help you. Continue to exercise your psychokinesis, but try not to practice on patient files." Kneeling down, Yeron retrieved her laptop from her cabinet. He plugged its charger into the wall.

Alexis bit back a laugh, trying hard to resist the urge to tease, but she couldn't help herself. "You must love going through my things. Are you having fun yet?"

"I might if I find something interesting." Yeron grinned. "I have to see my other patients. I will order something to help you relax. When I come back tomorrow, I will give you another Kryszka lesson."

Alexis hobbled to the bed. She flopped onto the mattress and eased herself onto her left side.

Yeron headed toward the door, then he turned, facing Alexis. "You invented an interesting name for me. I shall invent one for you."

Alexis giggled. "What might that be?"

Yeron smiled. "Steel Rose seems fitting. You are delicate as a flower, but you have a will of steel."

Chapter Twenty-Two: Alexis's Doctors in Conference

Jackson's Seventh Floor Conference room, April 6, 8:00 a.m.

"This has to stop." Hoffman's steel-blue eyes measured Yeron. He sat facing Yeron, white-sleeved arms folded across the table. His set jaw and thin-lipped frown discouraged argument.

Yeron was sitting in the seventh-floor conference room when Hoffman delivered his warning. Hoffman called a summary meeting with Jack Levy, Stanley Klein, and Steve Leicht.

"Joe, let's cut to the chase." Steve, seated to Yeron's right, stifled a yawn. "Chloe kept Becky and me up all night."

Yeron gave Steve a sad look. He would have gladly foregone a night's sleep for a child of his own, for a family.

"This morning, I found a gun stashed in Shively's closet," Hoffman continued, ignoring Steve. "After I grilled him, he admitted that someone told him and his friends—Alexis, Johnny, and Tyrone—about the Trident Mall disaster."

"Mark knows, too," Levy piped up. "Your surveillance cameras caught him tripping the locks."

"Mark, then. Mark, of all people." Hoffman's face reddened. His lips puckered as if he were fighting the urge to vomit. "One of them told the nursing staff. Cindy and Matilda jump when they hear the slightest noise. When they're not seeing patients, they're whispering among themselves. Where did these people get their information?"

Yeron studied the other doctors, trying to interpret their body language. Steve massaged his forehead. Stanley Klein sat expressionless, listening. Jack Levy, Alexis's orthopedic surgeon, flipped through Alexis's chart and stole glances at his watch. Alexis and her friends had their pipelines to the truth, but Yeron could not find the words to explain this. Anything he said would make an unfavorable impression.

"Joe, get a grip," Stanley said in a bleary voice. "Shively's street buddies must have told him, and he shared the information with the other survivors."

"I cannot speak for the others," Yeron said, "but Steve and I told Alexis. We thought she would handle the news better if she heard it from us."

"You thought wrong." Hoffman's frown deepened. "If you tell Alexis something, you might as well broadcast it on the *Channel 6 News*. Now, no one can concentrate on their work. For Pete's sake, don't give her any firearms."

"Joe, stop this." Steve pursed his lips and stared at him. "Let Alexis and her friends do what they need to survive."

"You don't give firearms to a patient, dammit!"

"Since when?" Steve asked in a quiet voice. "During Detective McMullen's recent stay here, she kept a gun at her bedside."

"It figures." Hoffman snorted. "You treat patient care like the Wild West. I won't allow *my* patients to have firearms."

"Have you taken extra security measures?" Stanley asked.

"What kind of a fool do you take me for? At my orders, maintenance sealed the back elevator with tungsten steel and installed two biometric locks with different access codes."

"That won't stop the Kryszka soldiers." Steve gave him a contemptuous scowl. "Your fancy locks didn't prevent Alexis and her friends from leaving."

Hoffman glared at him. "I'm working on hiring better officers, too."

Yeron started. "Working on" in Hoffman-speak, meant he was having trouble finding competent officers. No doubt Administration refused to pay the extra salary needed.

"Speaking of hiring, where did our patients get the money for these weapons?" Levy swept his gaze among the others, settling on Yeron. "Mark's got money, but the others are on leave with little or no pay."

"What do you think?" Steve chuckled. "They borrowed the cash, or maybe Shively's street friends supplied the weapons."

His answer elicited titters from Stanley and Levy but drew another deep frown from Hoffman. "So, we're trying to decide if it's okay to send a frail woman like Alexis to fight among the ranks of mobsters. Have we gone crazy?"

Yeron shook his head. Hoffman's reddening face reminded him of a rocket engine getting ready to explode. "Joe, Shively is the only mobster among them."

"Yeron, Joe has a point." Stanley looked his way. "Johnny, Tyrone, and Shively have supportive families. Alexis has no one, except a mother with a nervous breakdown waiting to happen."

"Where does Mark Adams fit into this?" Levy wanted to know.

"Do we care?" Steve shrugged. "He beats up women and runs a pigsty of a hospital."

"We'd better care if he's around Alexis." Hoffman heaved a ponderous sigh. "His loose-cannon tactics will guarantee her death."

"They will unless Alexis learns to protect herself." Yeron tossed his current paperwork toward Hoffman. "These are updated reports on the Trident Mall casualties. More people are turning up dead. The renegades will come here next. I do not care how people get their weapons. They are fighting a common enemy."

"Forget it." Hoffman gave him a dismissive wave of his hand. "Alexis performed brilliantly, fending off her attackers. I wouldn't take that from her for all the blue-chip stocks in the world. Back then, she had motivation—a loving sister, a close friend, and a secure job. All of that went bye-bye."

Yeron sighed again. In his own way, Hoffman cared about Alexis. Perhaps he admired her. Grateful as he felt, he was not going to compromise his principles to cater to the whims of a man with the disposition of a schoolyard bully.

"Alexis told me her Higher Power spared her so she could go after the scoundrels who killed her sister." Stanley directed his gaze toward Levy. "Can she?"

"We'd better consult the Department of Wishful Thinking." Levy's eyes surveyed the others. "She might squeak by with a .22

pistol. Better yet, if we have any available, the plasma gun. In any case, her poor endurance and coordination present serious drawbacks. What about her psychokinetic power?"

"Her mind-over-matter might work if she incorporates it with the plasma." Stanley smiled. "Alexis reports fewer nightmares and flashbacks since you started working with her, Yeron. My concern is that, if things get ugly, no one will look out for her, and that's bad. She's fragile as it is."

"My point exactly." Hoffman swept his gaze over each person. "Working this floor was the best therapy for Matilda and Alexis. Matilda's presence reminds Alexis that she still has someone who loves her. If anything happens to either one ..."

The others nodded their agreement.

"Matilda's toughening up," Steve said. "I think she's carrying something more lethal than nursing supplies in her fanny pack. However, her health problems will prohibit endurance for prolonged fighting."

"Alexis has an endurance problem, too." Yeron lowered his eyes. He hated admitting any disadvantage, for Alexis was a good fighter. "Steel Rose needs supportive friends, and I will not let her go through this alone."

"Steel Rose?" Levy chuckled. "Does she let you call her that?"

"Of course, she does. She smiles when I do so."

"I don't find this amusing," Hoffman said in a firm voice. "Whether we like it or not, Mark's temper will precipitate her death. I sent him home before Easter, but he keeps turning up here like an infection. I recommend we transfer her to a hospital across the country. We could correspond ..."

"I do not want that," Yeron cut in. "What I mean is, transferring Alexis is a bad idea."

"He's right," Steve said in a flat voice. "She has friends here. If those renegades want to get her, they'll find her wherever she goes. Maybe she's stronger than we think. Let's not forget that her dad belonged to the Mob."

"I don't care." Hoffman's eyes smoked with fury. "She cannot ..."

"Wait a minute." Stanley's gaze settled on Yeron. "You obviously think Alexis can learn to defend herself. What kind of support do you think she'll need?"

That sounded like a land mine. Any answer he gave would violate some unwritten law. "My answer does not matter. You accused me of indiscretion. I have limited contact with humans, and Alexis never spoke to me until after her attack."

The others exchanged knowing looks and nodded among themselves.

"That's why I'm asking," Stanley told him. "My mother used to say that new eyes see clear. Can Alexis learn to handle a gun? How?"

Yeron sat in his chair and thought hard about his talks with Alexis. The others sat facing him and watched him. "We have to consider her loneliness and health problems. I have seen loneliness kill my people. When I caught Alexis plotting with her friends, she had determination in her eyes, a strength of purpose. She seemed stronger."

"I should fire Matilda for not watching her," Hoffman said. "Bad enough she food-stained my reports when she dropped those files."

"Alexis caused the mishap with your folders," Yeron told him. "She used her push to distract her mother. That is how badly she wants to fight. Unfortunately, Mark's presence presents a serious liability, so I shall join her."

A series of gasps escaped the others.

"Oh no, you're not," Hoffman said. "Jackson Hospital paid good money ..."

"No one's money will make this go away," Yeron said. "People from my world started it, and I know, better than anyone, how they think. Our research is vital, but your alarms are primitive by Kryszka standards. The administration will not ante up the money for competent security. Alexis reported Laurel, who happens to be a serial killer. She killed two Kryszka soldiers, so their friends will come after her. If you send her across town, these people will find her, and she will not have friends to protect her. You do not want that, do you?"

Hoffman's lips puckered as if he had swallowed a chicken bone. "No, Yeron, I don't want that at all."

"No one's sending your Steel Rose anywhere." Steve smiled and patted Yeron's shoulder. "Maybe more people love Alexis than we think."

"She hasn't got endurance." Levy's protest sounded like a decree of a weak king. "Even you, Yeron, pointed that out."

"I can increase her strength training exercises," Yeron said. "I will fine-tune her mental powers and teach her how to use a plasma gun."

"That's all good," Stanley conceded, "but, Yeron, I must repeat, Alexis is fragile. She hasn't told us her whole story, and I suspect the missing pages are ugly."

Hoffman's face turned crimson. His eyes bulged. Any second, smoke would drift from his flared nostrils. "Jackson Hospital paid six million ..."

"Joe," Steve said, "Alexis needs to learn plasma guns so she can live. Maybe Yeron can teach her techniques that don't involve her hands. I know, because those soldiers once put me in the hospital with their mind control maneuvers."

"Dear God!" Levy let out a deep breath. "If her psychokinesis is as strong as everyone says, maybe it could save her life."

"All right, *all right!*" Hoffman's face was turning purple. "Personally, I would like to strangle Ms. Grese. She hates spending money for decent officers. I'll go along with your cockamamie scheme, but you will obey my Commandments, Yeron. Are you listening?"

"Listening," Yeron agreed.

Hoffman stood up and glared at everyone.

"First Commandment: Thou shalt not include Alexis's mother in your plans. She can't take the stress. If something goes wrong, lie. Got it?"

Yeron nodded. "Alexis does not want to upset her mother."

"Second: Thou shalt not involve other hospital personnel. Leave the nurses out of it."

"The Bible according to Joe Hoffman." Steve giggled.

Yeron glared at Steve, wondering how he could laugh. He did not find anything about Hoffman the least bit amusing.

"Third ..." Hoffman plunged ahead, eager to have his say.

"Thou shalt not allow teaching to interfere with patient care. Keep thy patients' treatment current, along with any new cases."

Yeron nodded. He counted himself fortunate to get by on four hours of sleep a night.

"Fourth: Thou shalt put Alexis's safety first. Stan's missing pages probably involve Mark, so keep him away from her. If any harm comes to Alexis, I will hold thee responsible."

This brought a groan from the other doctors. Yeron grimaced at the lead weight of responsibility cloaking his shoulders. The other doctors understood that, sometimes, things went wrong. Hoffman did not. He was eager to dole out blame, with Yeron being his chief recipient.

"Fifth commandment," Hoffman droned on in his authoritative voice. More groans escaped the others, but he gave no sign of caring. "Thou shalt not get personal with Alexis. Alexis grew up in a strict, religious family. Thou art required to keep a professional distance."

"Are we finished now?" Levy asked. "I was expected in the OR a half hour ago."

"That about covers it." The gleam in Hoffman's eyes said he scored a power play. He headed to the door, his way of ending the meeting.

"Alexis would say that man shits out of both ends," Yeron said.

"So she's teaching you our idioms." Steve laughed. "Joe's scared, Yeron. He made a strong point about Mark."

"He is wrong about Alexis. She does not talk about religion."

"That doesn't mean she's not thinking about it," Steve said. "Be patient with her. She's taken a battering by Mark and grieved over her sister. Now she may lose her job."

"I know how to practice patience. Better yet, I shall talk with Shively about Mark."

* * * *

Eyes focused and jaw set, Yeron headed to Shively's room. Every so often, security officers passed him. They were the Rent-a-Cops that Alexis described. Paper tigers. Useless in a crisis.

Shively was sitting at the edge of his bed. He was talking on his cell phone, hand clenched on the receiver. At Yeron's approach, he hung up and sighed. "Now what?"

"Why did you involve Mark?"

"Okay, the man's got issues. So what? Everyone has issues."

"That man hates working with all of us."

"So?" Shively's eyes narrowed. "You're the bright one in the group. What do you suggest?"

"Do not involve him. He is a dangerous man."

"I was afraid you'd say that." Shively raised his arms up and let them drop on his lap. "Don't worry. I know how to control Mark."

"What do you...?" Yeron's voice trailed off as chills shuddered through him and his hair stood on the nape of his neck. "Did you blackmail him?"

"I call it 'friendly persuasion.'" Shively gave him a wintry smile. "Trident Mall looked bad, and word on the street has it that they're coming our way. So I need disposable fighters, and everyone else, you included, is too valuable to waste. Besides, Mark knows how to use a gun. Mark's got a secret, and he'll work with us if he wants to keep it quiet."

"What secret?"

"Mark's an adult baby."

"He acts like a baby," Yeron said.

"I'm not talking about his temper. He's got an itch."

A child molester, Yeron thought, his chills deepening. "I do not want to hear any more. As humans say, do not ask or tell."

"Don't ask, don't tell," Shively corrected him. "We don't ask Mark about his business because his answer might put us in a bad spot. If his secret gets out, we lose the trump card we hold over him."

"Mark and Alexis have a long history, worse than you know. Pushing Mark may, how you say, fire back on Alexis."

"You mean, backfire." Shively's lips pulled back into a crooked grin. "Don't worry about Alexis. I've got special plans for Mark."

"What kind of..." Yeron hitched his breath. "Don't ask, don't tell." His contractions still came out slurred.

"You're catching on. Good." Shively smiled again, but it looked like a ghastly effort. "Teach us what we need to know and do what you want with Alexis. Just leave it out of our mission."

"Don't ask, don't tell," Yeron tried enunciating the words, slurring his contractions. He left the room shivering. He was thinking about the bloody gore on the Trident Mall stills and the sound of teeth tearing at the human flesh.

Chapter Twenty-Three: Break-in at the Research Floor

Jackson Hospital's Seventh Floor, April 16, 8:00 p.m.

For Yeron, the next week passed in a blur of medications, patient rounds, weapons training, and Kryszka lessons for Alexis. For a human, Alexis learned fast, though she became impatient with herself. Her pronunciation was garbled, but this would improve with practice. He wasn't so sure about the gun practice.

Each session, Alexis, Shively, Tyrone, and Johnny filed in, joking and chatting. The worst of the injuries had healed, and everyone was eager to learn. Then Yeron set up his dummy and got out the training weapons. The men's shots left scorch marks on the wheelchair and dummy. At the sight and sound of the simulated gunfire, Alexis fell into stony silence. Her eyes became like glass, vacant and blank when she picked up her gun and aimed. One shot streaked the wheelchair. Another scorched the wall behind the dummy.

Once, Yeron placed his hand over hers and guided her, drawing wisecracks from the fellows. Alexis did not laugh. She stiffened. She said nothing, except "thank you" when he fashioned a cushioned grip for her gun. None of his efforts improved her technique. Yeron expected coordination problems, but he hoped her psychokinesis would compensate. Instead, her face turned the color of parchment every time she picked up the gun. Her spooked eyes left a sick feeling in his stomach.

About a week after he received his Commandments, Yeron reviewed Stanley's notes, Alexis's CAT scans, and other test results. Perhaps the brain damage was worse than he thought.

The poison had infiltrated the right side of the brain, leaving a mild weakness in her left leg. The tingling and numbness had resolved, and the damage did not affect her vision or executive functions. Her IQ scored at 140. Her fingers remained crooked from her arthritis, necessitating help with cutting her food. Otherwise, her push compensated for the weakness in her fingers. According to Jack Levy, physical therapy and psychokinetic training could give her a normal life.

At the sound of footsteps, Yeron closed her file. He headed out to the hall to check.

A woman from Environmental Services was hauling a supply cart toward the patient ward. It was Gloria, who cleaned the offices during the night shift. Up until now, she had avoided the research floor after Yeron's warning about the dangers of spreading infection to the patients. He had developed robotic equipment to handle such chores. Tonight, Gloria wheeled her cart into the ward. The Gloria he knew walked with a marked limp, but this female's gait was normal. That and her blatant disregard for infection control got his attention.

"Gloria!" He hurried toward the unit. "Where are you going?"

Gloria did not answer. She continued walking, fingers curled around the cart handle, past the nurses' station toward Alexis's room. There she paused, and the sliding door opened.

"Get away from there!" Yeron reached for his gun. *"Now!"*

The mop clattered to the floor. The woman turned toward him, clutching her scarf and face mask ... and she was not Gloria. Gloria had a mocha complexion and copper hair. The pale skin and fiery hair belonging to this woman was unmistakably Kryszka. So was the push she used to open Alexis's door. She gave him one look and then tore through the exit doors. He worked up a mental thrust, ready to stop her until an earsplitting scream from Alexis broke his concentration.

Intruder forgotten, Yeron sprinted to her room. He forgot to knock before entering. He forgot Hoffman's Five Commandments. He forgot the balloons and their lethal gas. He forgot everything except her safety. Alexis sat up, screaming at the top of her lungs.

"Alexis." He tried to keep his voice gentle. "I am here. What happened?"

"She's back. The creep who tried to kill me."

"Alexis." Yeron nudged one foot before the other, aware of

her balloons rustling. "You had a nightmare."

"I know what I saw." Alexis looked up at him, tears streaming down her face. "She wore a housekeeper's uniform, but she had the red hair and hungry look in her eyes, just like my assailant did at the house."

"What house? You killed your assailants."

"Then she's a relative. She wants to kill me, and I can't stop her."

"I can." Yeron took another step toward the bed and considered Hoffman's Commandment about professional distance. *The hell with his nonsense,* he decided. He sat at the edge of her bed and folded Alexis into his arms. Her body quivered against his but, as the moments ticked by, the shaking stopped.

"I will not let anything happen to you," he added, determined to honor that particular Commandment, "but I need your help." He eased her against the pillows.

"How?" Her glassy eyes met his. "I can't handle a gun. Mark said so."

"Mark again." Yeron sighed with exasperation. "Damn Shively for involving him. Why do you listen to a man who tried to kill you?"

"My coordination is bad. You must notice that."

"I can work on your coordination. Something else is bothering you, but now I must report this intruder." He straightened up and edged toward the door. "I will order you a sedative and post an officer by your bed."

"Who was this intruder?"

"I am not sure ... did not get a close look. We shall talk in the morning. I can help you, but only if you are honest with me."

Alexis nodded. "All right."

* * * *

In his suite, Yeron flopped before his computer and stared at his phone. He started to page Security, stopped in mid-dial, and then proceeded to check his army database.

"You have feelings for that woman, son. She cares about you, too. She confides in you more than she does her human friends. You and she might have something good."

Yeron whirled around and started. His late father stood facing him, palms at his side, lips curved into a gentle smile.

"Father..." *You are supposed to be dead,* he was about to say. He drew in a sharp breath. "Alexis is my *patient,*" he said out loud. "Humans frown on romantic dalliances between patients and their healers."

"You must notice the way her friends tease her, son."

"I have, Father, but ..." Yeron glanced toward the door, fearing that any passersby would think him crazy if they overhead him talking. Maybe he was; but dead or not, the man was his father. "Her mother fears losing Alexis, and she despises people like me."

Rattling impinged on his thoughts. His printer spit out another document reporting sightings of nonhuman creatures around Trident Mall. Another trail of bodies, dead and battered.

"You see that, Father?" He jabbed his thumb toward the printouts. "This is why most humans dislike me. They associate me with the monsters that did this."

"Alexis considers you her hero and admiration can lead to stronger emotions."

"Alexis is afraid to be with any man, let alone someone like me."

"She did not protest when you comforted her. Whether people approve or not, you and she have to deal with this."

I do not have time, Yeron thought, but he wondered if he and Alexis could become friends. He might ask her to the movies after she no longer needed his care. He looked over at his father to say this, but he was gone. Yeron found himself staring at the file cabinets.

With a deep sigh, he paged Gloria Hanson and made his call to Security. Security paged Gloria, too. Three pages and fifteen minutes later, still no call back from Gloria. When his phone rang, it was Joe. He opened with a string of curses.

"Joe, what happened?" he asked in a tense voice.

"Come down to the basement, Yeron. Now!"

Yeron glanced at his document. "Where at in the basement?"

"Outside the morgue. Wear full isolation gear. Someone went after Gloria and dumped her remains in our basement. So much for Ms. Grese's brilliant security."

Chapter Twenty-Four: Murder in the Basement

Jackson Hospital's Basement April 16, 9:00 p.m.

In the basement, crime scene tape cordoned off the rear section of the main corridor. Behind it, bloodstained sneakers and Gloria Hansen's gutted torso lay in puddles of blood. Gaping sores cratered her flesh. Both hands and one arm were gone. Her face stared with one vacuous eye. A matted socket with bloody gore replaced the other. Her death had not come easy.

Hazlett and another officer deposited samples into evidence bags. A third snapped photographs. Steve, Hoffman, and two security guards stood outside the crime scene, eyes on the officers. Hoffman cursed the guards out loud.

"This is a disgrace!" He wagged his finger at the two guards. "Lousy bastards, where were you when this happened? At the cafeteria having coffee?"

One of the guards, a short man with a crew cut, folded his arms across his chest, eyes glaring. "No one called us with any problems."

"You're supposed to check." Hoffman's eyes roved over the others. "Who could have done this?"

"A Kryszka dressed in Gloria's clothes," Yeron volunteered. "She—the killer—tried to harm Alexis, too. She got away before I could stop her."

"This has Laurel's name on it." Steve shook his head. "All this trouble started after we canned her."

"I doubt it," Yeron told him. "The woman is a rogue soldier who survived the explosion. Alexis got a good look at her face."

"She did?" Hazlett regarded him with wary eyes. "Then I

have questions for Alexis."

"Not now." Yeron fixed his eyes on Hazlett. "I gave her a sedative. She has had enough excitement."

"Damn straight," Hoffman agreed in his blustery voice. "You can talk with her in the morning. Call me when your medical examiner is ready to do the autopsy."

Yeron looked over at the officers. "Who shall notify Gloria's family?"

"I will," Hazlett said in a small voice. "This is going to hit the papers."

Steve shrugged. "People should know the truth."

"Maybe you should shut up." Hoffman jerked his finger toward the officers. "Make your calls, take your photographs, whatever you've got to do. I'll be at my office."

* * * *

The next morning, Yeron forced one leaden foot before the other toward Alexis's room. How should he approach Alexis? His mother died because his father had spared him the ugly details of Woehar's behavior. It would not do to lie.

The thought circled in Yeron's head, circling the way a renegade might his victim. Without thinking, he strolled into Alexis's room. She jumped upright in bed, and, at any second, she would scream. Instead, she gazed at him, her eyes wide as saucers.

"I should have knocked." He backed toward the door. "I am sorry."

"You startled me." The wide-eyed look faded, and she giggled. "Since you're a nice guy, I'll forgive you. I feel safe around you."

Nice guy? Safe? His eyes swept her from head to toe. "Thank you."

"Now, if you were a woman, I'd scream bloody murder. Most of the monsters in my life were women, except Mark, and you look nothing like him. The bitch who tried to get at me last night was the worst."

"She was a monster." Yeron took a seat by Alexis's bed, keeping his voice low. "That is why we must talk."

"You look terrified." Alexis sat up facing him, moving without the struggle he had seen during her admission. Her left leg lagged behind the rest of her, but outpatient therapy would resolve that. "Let me guess. The real Gloria is either missing or dead and in pieces."

He sighed. "Who told you this?"

"I'm making a logical deduction. In my dad's business, if people don't turn up, someone eliminated them."

Yeron hesitated, fearful of upsetting her again. She deserved the facts but needed a delicate and tactful approach.

"I don't know Gloria well, but she's worked here over twenty years, and she kept the bathrooms spotless. So, cough it up, Yeron. Is she missing or dead and in pieces?"

"Dead and in pieces." So much for delicacy and tact. "Joe and Steve are speaking with Hazlett and the medical examiner. Someone cut Gloria with a serrated knife, the kind we used at my compound. They amputated her legs and hands. Our security men did not intervene because they considered break time more important than Gloria's life."

"Oh, Jesus!" Alexis whispered.

"Joe recommended that I transfer you to another hospital, but I can better monitor the effect of the 248AR here. Sending you away will not guarantee your safety. We need backup security here. Your familiarity with this floor makes you an ideal candidate, but you continue to have trouble learning the plasma gun. It would help if you paid attention."

"I'm trying." The muscles of her lips quivered, her voice pained. "I wish Dee was here. She was a great friend. Johnny and the other guys are cool, but I can't tell them things."

"What things?"

Alexis lowered her voice to a whisper. "After you first told me about Trident Mall, I snuck out of my room to look for scissors, something I could use as a weapon. Then I got this crazy idea about asking Mark why he tears paper."

Yeron gasped. "Steel Rose, you should have avoided him."

"Yes, I should have, but his curtain was partially open. I saw the papers on his floor. He had a diaper, and he was ... he was ..." Her face turned scarlet.

"Masturbating?" Yeron kept his voice low.

Alexis nodded. "I started having these flashes ... memory

fragments having to do with his house. That's crazy. The thing with the bat happened years ago."

"Did you talk to Stan about this?"

"I did. He said I needed to go easy on myself."

"He is right," Yeron agreed. "Spying on Mark is not the way to do it."

Alexis sighed. "Tell me about it. Mark called me terrible names when we congregated in Johnny's room. He gave me chills and the flashbacks are getting worse. When I pick up the gun, my hands freeze. I keep seeing his beady eyes. Sometimes I relive the attack in my mother's yard. Mostly, it's like Mark's chasing me with his bat. What's wrong with me?"

"Perhaps there is more to your history with Mark."

Alexis shrugged. "If there is, I don't know about it. Stan told me to remember why my Higher Power—his word for God—gave me a second chance. He prescribed Xanax, but that made me sleepy. I tried thinking about my mother's safety, but that didn't work when I picked up the fake gun. I said a Rosary, but the fear comes back during lessons. I watched a comedy flick. Laughter didn't help either." Alexis shook her head. "I'm not strong as you think. Could you convince Shively not to include Mark? Please?"

"I already tried." His heart ached at the sight of her spooked expression. "Shively does not want to lose any of us. Whether we like it or not, we need Mark for, ah, insurance."

"Oh, great." Alexis rolled her eyes. "What do you mean by insurance?"

As a sacrifice to save the rest of us, Yeron thought. Could Alexis process this in her fragile state? He doubted it.

"All I know is that we need him."

"If my father were alive, he'd find a solution. So would Dee, but she's gone, too. Do you have any ideas?"

"Maybe." Yeron gazed at Alexis, reflecting on the moments before his compound exploded. Becky had broken down in tears. She calmed herself after a scolding by Teodon, but her hardy Kryszka constitution enabled her to withstand his stern approach. Alexis could not handle any scolding. She was fragile, like the humans in his father's laboratory. They would have gone mad unless he hypnotized them into forgetting. Without a modified version of hypnosis, Alexis might, too. He had never introduced his technique to the Earth doctors. Dare he try it now?

With those painful memories festering in her brain, Alexis might give up and die.

"If my father were here, he would have an answer," he told her. "Since the people we love have died, we must work with what we have."

"How do you propose we do that?"

Yeron drew in a deep breath. "When my father and I rescued the humans from Eigil, we hypnotized them into forgetting their tortures. Without hypnosis, those memories would have driven them insane."

"I can imagine." Alexis nodded in agreement. "Stan the Man and other shrinks hypnotize their patients, too."

"Unlike your healers, we use chemicals for this treatment. The drug enables your brain to suppress an unpleasant memory or your fear of it. This will stop your flashbacks."

"Will it make me forget Robin?" Alexis recoiled and, again, that terrified look settled into her eyes. "I want to remember the good things in my life."

"You will never forget Robin, but you may remember unpleasant events you had suppressed."

Alexis shivered. "What you're proposing sounds dangerous."

"Any procedure can harm you if it is not done right. Eigil makes your terrorists seem like angels. His prisoners spent days on his webbed rope, burning from the chemicals, watching the guards cut their fellow prisoners, and wondering if they would be next. Trauma like that destroys people, but our hypnosis saved them. I believe this treatment will help you."

"These chemicals ... do they contain carcinogens?"

Carcinogens! Yeron sighed. He had not factored in humans' fear of cancer. "Alexis, you said I was nice, and that I made you feel safe. If you like me that much, you must ..."

"Let's get one thing straight." Alexis let out a sigh of exasperation. "Don't buy into any crap Johnny tells you about me. He loves to hear himself talk."

"Johnny is not part of this. Do you trust me as a person?"

"I would trust you with my life. You wouldn't hurt anyone ... at least not on purpose. Could you test your chemical on rats first? Like you did with the 248AR?"

"A proper observation takes months, and I only tested the 248AR two weeks. We do not have two weeks. Every other technique you tried failed. I want to help you heal. Repressing those flashbacks can make that happen."

"I appreciate what you're trying to do. Let's talk this over with Steve and Doctor Hoffman. Okay?"

"No one can know, including the nurses." Yeron shook his head, amazed at the reasonable way she stated her concerns. This woman believed in him, and he wanted to keep her trust. "When you told your mother about Trident Mall, she went ballistic. She told the other nurses, and now no one can concentrate on their work. Joe found out, and he is furious with me. He will never listen to my ideas."

"Oh, dear, I'm sorry." Alexis lowered her eyes, the contriteness evident in her voice. "I told my mother so she could find a way to protect herself and me. Frankly, I'm surprised that Hoffman allowed the lessons. My pain is gone, thanks to the 248AR, but my hands are deformed and puffy. Cindy and my mother take turns cutting my chicken for me."

"Alexis." Pain went through his heart like an arrow. If only he could lay his hands on her forehead and heal her like the aliens did in her *Weekly World* stories. It would take multiple complicated surgeries to repair her misshapen fingers. "I am doing everything I can to help you."

"I know that." Her voice softened. "I appreciate it. I just want to know why Hoffman allowed you to give me lessons."

"Joe read the Trident Mall report, and he fears our hospital will be the next target. Despite his concerns, it took an hour-long meeting with me, Stan, Steve, and Jack to convince him. I never mentioned the hypnosis. By offering it to you without consulting the other doctors, I have violated the Five Commandments."

"Five Commandments?" Alexis arched her brows. "There are ten, Doctor Phil, but they have nothing to do with this."

"I am not talking about the ones Moses received on a stone

tablet. During our meeting, Joe gave me five commandments. I broke his fifth one by hugging you and prescribing an untested treatment. Comforting a patient with a hug was acceptable at the compound. People consider it inappropriate here."

"That's bullshit. What's wrong with Hoffman?"

"Ask him. He said, 'Thou shalt keep a professional distance.'"

"Professional distance?" Alexis exploded with laughter. "Hoffman delivering the Sermon on the ..." She let loose more gales of laughter, and proceeded to imitate Hoffman's deep voice. "Thou shalt keep a professional distance ..." More snorts of laughter.

"You can't be serious," she said after she collected herself.

"I am one hundred percent serious." Yeron smiled, glad to see he had made her laugh. "He makes many laws I do not understand. What shall I do now?"

"Well, with the Ten Commandments, you confess your sins to a priest. He gives you a penance, usually a prayer ritual. Since you confessed to me, I'll think of a penance for you." Another gleeful burst of hilarity.

"Oh?" A grin played on Yeron's thin lips. He bent toward her, and as he did, her rose scent teased at his senses. "What might that be?"

"Your hypnosis—or whatever you call it. Will it really make my flashbacks stop?"

Yeron nodded. "You cannot tell Steve or anyone else. Steve is protective of you and may not understand."

"What you say here, what you do here, when you leave here, leave it stay here," Alexis said with good cheer. "Let's go for it. Are you giving me pills?"

"No, I shall give you an intramuscular injection. I have given it enough times that I memorized the formula. It will take no time to prepare."

* * * *

Yeron ushered Alexis to his suite for the injection. Having her relive painful history in a room full of helium balloons would invite disaster. She walked ahead of him to the reclining chair with a slight limp.

"You sure know how to give a needle." She smiled at him after he administered his formula. "The first-year residents don't know what they're doing."

"Thank you. I had a lot of practice."

"What happens next? Do I have visions? Will I get sleepy?"

"You will become drowsy and fall into a twilight sleep. You will hear things I tell you, and be able to answer, but you may not recall what we say after the effects of the drug subside."

"Is this conscious sedation?"

"Not really. With this treatment, I can influence your thoughts. You may relive unpleasant experiences. The images you see will frighten you, but nothing in this room can harm you."

Yeron waited five minutes. Ten minutes. The formula took twenty minutes to have its full effect. Alexis sat there, staring at him, and then yawned. "I think I'll take a nap."

She eased the reclining chair to a thirty-degree angle, and her eyes closed. Yeron watched her until her breathing became deep and regular.

"Alexis." He addressed her in a calm voice. "Sit up and open your eyes."

Alexis's eyes flickered open. She cranked the recliner to an upright position.

"Let us go back to the night I found a gun in your candy basket. Tell me what you felt when I caught you."

"Embarrassed," Alexis said. "I'm annoyed that you went through my basket, but I don't want to upset you. You might tell the police, so I'd better be cool."

"Did I tell the police?"

"No, you were laughing. You said the gun was useless."

"That is right." Yeron nodded, pleased that his chemical had the desired effect. "Now, you shall relive the night of the attack, before the renegade broke into your mother's home. What are you doing?"

"Robin and I are in the living room watching a movie. She's taking a treatment for her asthma, and ... uh, oh, I hear footsteps."

"Where at?"

"On the roof of the house. Laurel's trying to scare us because I reported her to the boss. She knows my mother's address."

"What will you do about it?"

"Robin's terrified, so I'm going to my mom's bedroom with a screwdriver. There she is, outside the window, and ... oh, no!" Alexis's voice rose to a high-pitched squeal. "She's Kryszka!"

"Who is? The intruder?"

"Oh, my God, she wants to kill me!" Alexis groaned and squirmed. Her rose scent faded, wiped away by the sweat pouring down her face. "She's throwing me onto the bed, and the glass ... oh, God, how it hurts!

"I've got to find my screwdriver before the glass cuts me to shreds. There it is. Good, I stabbed her in the eye. She's jumping off me and drops her gun. I've got it, and ... checking on Robin. She's petrified, but that woman's after us. My hands are cut bad, but I have to make her stop. This gun should work. I'll push all the buttons. Good, I got her, and ... oh, shit, I set the hallway on fire. Where's Robin? Where'd she go?"

Tears ran down her face. Her voice rose and fell as she described the shoot-out in the garden, Robin's wheezing, and the way she tried to administer a breathing treatment. Badly hurt as she was, she was determined to save her sister. Any moment, her cries would attract attention. He had to get her out of this memory fast.

"I'm bleeding everywhere. Am I going to die?"

"No, you shall go to a hospital, and I shall heal you. We shall make this nothing more than a bad memory."

Alexis did not answer. Her chest heaved and fell. He still had to address her fear of Mark.

"It is only a bad memory. Learn from it and leave it in the past." Her heaving slowed. Her moaning stopped, and her breathing became less labored. Yeron nodded, preparing her for the Mark memories. "Imagine yourself floating."

"I'm floating." A weak smile surfaced on her lips.

"We must go back to a time when you were married to Mark. Specifically, the night Robin had a severe asthma attack. Tell me what happened after you brought Robin to the hospital."

"Robin was with Mark and me when her asthma flared up. I asked the medics to bring her to Jackson Hospital because it's clean. Their equipment is newer than what Meadowood Hospital has. I wanted the best for Robin because she was sick enough to need a ventilator."

Yeron watched her face for signs of agitation. So far, none. "Does Mark agree with your assessment?"

"Well ... not exactly. He gets real quiet. The Jackson doctors are great with Robin though. They tell me to go home and rest. That's when Mark starts screaming at me."

"What does he say?"

"He accuses me of bad-mouthing his hospital, and ow!" Alexis's hand went up to her cheek. "Why is he hurting me? Why won't he let me leave? Mark, stop ... let me be. Oh, no, he's dragging me to the sofa!"

The sofa? Yeron's red eyes widened. *Steel Rose never said anything about a sofa.*

"No, Mark, don't do this. Not tonight."

Her legs thrashed and kicked. Her hands slapped against the cushioned arms of the chair. "Stop it, Mark, you're hurting me!" More thrashing. The chair jiggled. Perhaps her push was doing it. *Sofa ... she never mentioned anything about a sofa. What did Mark do to her?*

"Don't do this, Mark. No, no, no!" Alexis's body stiffened. Her face became a rictus of pain. She clamped her legs together. Her eyelids fluttered. She fought the drug, trying to pull herself out of the hellish pool of horror in which she found herself. "I can't do this, no, I can't do this."

Yeron hesitated. More than anything else, he longed to yank her out of that nightmare and wall her away in safety, but the renegades would find her wherever he took her. "Do not fight the drug," he shouted. "Let it work. Mark did something terrible to you, something besides the bat. You have to retrieve that memory so you can fight and survive."

"I don't want to remember."

"The knowledge will enable you to handle what is coming." He kept his eye on her, prepared to give another injection. The eyelid fluttering stopped. Alexis's breathing deepened.

"Go back to that night and tell me what Mark is doing to you," he said.

She answered with a spate of weeping. "He ... he ... Mark,

you're hurting me. Stop!" Moments passed. Alexis wept, her chest heaving.

"Where is Mark now?" Yeron asked.

"In the shower." Her faint voice cracked. "Where's my bathrobe? I've got to get cleaned up. I'm bleeding ... I've got to get out of here."

More writhing in the chair. Yeron stood beside her and watched, not daring to interfere.

"I've got to hurry," she mumbled. "Oh, damn ... he's got his baseball bat—it's the one with the nails."

"Can you escape?" asked Yeron.

"Yes—I've got my car keys and—oh, no, he's got me by the leg. I'm on the ..." Alexis's scream rose like a siren. Sweat dripped down her face in rivulets. "He's going to kill me!" Heavy breathing again. "I kicked him in the balls. Got to get away." Alexis sat up and wrapped a sheet around her scarred leg. "I'm getting out of here."

"Alexis, this was not your fault." Yeron laid his hand on her shoulder. "Let it go."

Alexis flopped in the chair, panting.

"You will get away from him and work many years at Jackson Hospital. One day, you will love again and what happened will become nothing more than an ugly memory. You will remember everything he did to you, learn from it, and move on to the present."

"I will move on to the present," Alexis said in a timid voice.

It never failed to amaze Yeron how pliable humans became under the drug. Someone could program Alexis to kill with impunity, hence his reluctance to share the formula with the doctors. "You will rest for a few hours. When you wake, you will remember everything that happened. The next time you pick up a firearm, you will leave these unpleasant memories in the past. When you meet someone, you shall approach them with an open mind."

"I will leave it all in the past," Alexis said.

She eased back against the cushions, head tilted sideways, her sleep uneasy. He called the nurses' station to let them know her whereabouts. Another call to Stanley. He could help her deal with the rape. After his calls, he sat watching Alexis and got to thinking about the old compound. Some Kryszka used hypnosis to manipulate humans into sex. Yeron could not imagine doing that to Alexis, given the horrible things Mark did to her. His heart ached at the thought of her going through life alone. She deserved happiness, wherever and with whomever she could find it.

* * * *

The next afternoon, amidst a hallway crowded with officers, Yeron led Alexis, Shively, Tyrone, and Johnny to his suite for his lesson. Alexis kept stride with them, her eyes twinkling as she chatted with them.

Target practice began. The men left scorch marks on the dummy as they had been doing. Now came Alexis's turn. Yeron watched her, his breath held, hoping his formula would work. She stepped up to the yellow line and brandished the gun as if she had handled one all her life. She fired with the precision of a soldier, streaking the dummy's face brown. Try as Yeron might to navigate the manikin in a zigzag line, Alexis made her mark. Behind her, the three men clapped their hands and whistled.

"Whoa!" Johnny shouted with glee. "Yeron, give her a kiss. Show her how proud you are."

"Johnny, stop!" Alexis whirled around, dropping the gun. She bent over to retrieve it. Too fast. Her left leg buckled, and she pitched to the left. Yeron moved in and caught her by the shoulders. Arm braced around her, he walked her to a chair.

"Aw, ain't that sweet!" Tyrone clapped his hands.

"Look how red she's getting." Shively shook his head, laughing.

"Boys, we had enough for today," Yeron said. "I will start you on positioning tomorrow." He looked down at Alexis. "Are you all right?"

Alexis nodded, her face pink.

"You must not allow anyone to distract you, including jokesters like Johnny."

"I know." The blush inched up her cheeks. "Guess I'd better learn to shoot from a lying position since my balance is still poor."

"Your balance is much better, but I shall increase the weights for your leg exercises. You should learn other positions because you might have to shoot from behind a tree, rock, or undercover. I would like to train you to handle a gun with your push."

"Sounds good." Alexis grinned. "No flashbacks, not even any involving Mark. Stan tells me Mark's behavior wasn't my fault. Sometimes I believe him."

"None of Mark's behavior was your fault. You said no, and he refused to listen."

"You've got that right. Thank you for giving me that drug. You should market it."

"I wish I could, but it can be dangerous if the wrong people get it."

"I suppose so. Do you think I can protect myself now?"

"I think ..." Yeron gazed at Alexis, weighing her health issues, but also her assets: her aim, her friends, and her psychokinetic powers. He then slipped a loaded plasma gun in her hands. "I shall include you for backup security."

Chapter Twenty-Five: Woehar's Plans for Jackson Hospital

Woehar's Underground Laboratory, April 9, 10:00 a.m.

"Wake up, sleepy one."

Laurel's eyes snapped open, and she met Woehar's gaze. Pain burned through her hands and her feet. Woehar towered over her, her shadows long against the grid floor. Worse was anticipating Woehar's sadism up close and personal. Try as she might to suppress it, a groan escaped Laurel's lips.

Woehar's red eyes glittered, but her voice softened. "You really think I work with Abaddon."

Laurel did not answer. "Yes" would provoke Woehar into another fit of rage. "No" might incite accusations of lying. In either case, a disastrous punishment would follow. "I'm not imagining Abaddon," she said in an empty voice. "I saw you and him together."

"Maybe you did." Woehar nodded with a smile. "I think I can use Abaddon to our advantage. Do not worry. You redeemed yourself. The information you gave me about Jackson's back elevator proved invaluable."

"In what way?" Laurel regarded Woehar with wary eyes. One wrong word and the monster inside Woehar would rear its gruesome head.

Woehar burst into laughter. "The humans made getting in too easy. Someone used flimsy locks on the back doors. I got in through the basement and checked the service elevator. My plasma cut through the humans' tungsten nicely. I went back to the basement and disguised myself as a worker so that I could check the front entrance to your floor. The guards did not cause any trouble. Only one was there, talking on the phone. He said his partner went to someone named John."

"John?" Laurel allowed a giggle. "He probably used the toilet."

"Whatever he did, those men were distracted. Those locks you mentioned are so simple the lowly humans got past them." Woehar laughed again. "I saw your archenemy."

"Alexis?" Laurel started and then winced at the jolt of pain. "I can't believe you got past those nurses. They notice everything."

"They mistook me for a cleaning woman named Gloria. I met the real Gloria in the basement and asked her for directions. She started to scream, but I quieted her. I wore her uniform when I went to your floor." Woehar let out another laugh sounding like rattling bones. "I deposited my leftovers in the basement."

"I know Gloria." Laurel sniffed. "I should have included that witch on my list. She wrinkled her nose every time I got too close, told me I stank. She thinks the horses don't shit on her side of the road."

"Horses?" Woehar canted her head, her eyes curious. "How do horses affect Gloria?"

"They don't. It's a figure of speech." Laurel gritted her teeth, anticipating a spate of fury for using slang. "Gloria would have been an easy kill for your pupils. She hates firearms. I overheard her saying so to people."

"Gloria was easy. Alexis would have been easy, too, but my dear brother guarded her like a prize. It was sickening." She spat blood on the ground. "He hugged her as if they were lovers. He attracts weak women the way our father did."

"I beg your pardon." Laurel kept her tone light. Though Woehar's approach was friendly, the shine in her ruby eyes warned that any goodwill was fleeting. "Miss Bitch loves the taste of Communion wafers. She'd never let someone like Yeron touch her."

"Communion ...what?" Woehar gave her a questioning look. "What kind of wafers?"

"Some humans like religion and Alexis thrives on it. She attends a service where a man wearing a robe gives out wafers. They represent the body of her God. It never made sense. My parents liked Communion wafers, too, and they did terrible things to me." Laurel sighed, trying to think of a way to explain without using slang. "Alexis won't socialize with human men. She's been afraid of men since her former husband beat up on her."

"I know about her past." Woehar's sardonic smile reminded Laurel of a grinning corpse. "The man was Mark Adams. He beat her with a stick covered with pointed nails, the same weapon he used to kill my pupil. Mark thinks he is intelligent, but he has filthy habits."

Laurel gazed at Woehar with bleary, uncomprehending eyes.

"Why are you so surprised? I told you I research my enemy." Woehar's intent stare made Laurel squirm. "Learn to research someone. If Alexis does not like you, she will not tell you where she goes. Do you know for sure if she avoids men?"

Laurel shuddered. She'd made another bad call. "I suppose not," she admitted in a small voice. "I don't know where she goes when she leaves the hospital."

"Exactly." Woehar gave her an indulgent smile, much like a teacher praising a student who had come up with the answer to a difficult math problem. "Alexis did not protest when Yeron hugged her. They make up play names for each other. He is teaching her Kryszka and how to use our weapons. When he is not with other patients, he is at her bedside. If she has not mated with him yet, she will soon."

"What?" For the moment, Laurel forgot her pain. She sat up, realizing now she was no longer tied to the table. She wasn't lying on a table. Someone had laid her on a cushioned bed. "You found that out with one tiny microchip?"

"You would be amazed at what our microchips can hold. As I told you earlier, I dressed as a healer and implanted my microchip into Mark after someone brought him to their clinic. The healers there were too busy to notice. Three Earth men are teaching Mark how to use our plasma. Yeron and Alexis avoid Mark, but these Earth men teach Mark everything they learn."

Dark tumors of rage engulfed Laurel's heart. That damned

bitch managed to charm every man she met. Now she was using Kryszka to garner sympathy. "Alexis is scared of her own shadow. I bet she hasn't slept right since her attack. She might stand up to someone once. After that, she freezes. I've seen her do it."

"Yeron knows how to help her overcome any fear," Woehar told her.

"I'll bet he does if she allows him. She won't fool with some-one like Yeron. It's against her religion."

"Are you sure?" Woehar smiled a crooked grin. "Many humans lean on religion until it becomes inconvenient. Her father worked with organized crime. He may have taught her his version of religion."

"Whew!" Laurel had to admit she was impressed. "If your people can interpret the human psyche and spy from where we are, why is Eigil dead?"

"Eigil ingested an overdose of vischlausk. It induces our craving for blood, but in excess doses, it can cause impaired judg-ment. He began feeding on high profile people—people whose disappearances attracted attention. If he had used discretion, the humans would have left us alone. I allowed the humans to destroy him because he had become so sloppy. Draekh is my lover now. He enjoys human meat, but he does not do stupid things." Woehar turned toward a panel and typed in some symbols. "He is prepar-ing a solution for your next treatment."

Another treatment? The words brought images of sliced fingers and gushing blood to Laurel's mind. This time, Woehar was going for the main course. "Please don't hurt me," she begged in a trembling voice. "I've been helping you, haven't I?"

"Relax." Woehar patted her shoulder. "This is your reward for helping me with Jackson Hospital. Draekh is going to augment your muscles."

"My muscles?"

Woehar smiled. "It will be painful initially. You will need a series of injections. I think the results will please you. Frankly, I am surprised that none of your people tried to help you."

"They didn't lift a finger, Woehar. They were afraid my so-called bad hygiene would give them an infection." Laurel averted her eyes, cringing at the shame that washed over her. "Bastards, all of them. I would love to chain them in my basement. Those bastards hated me because I blackmailed someone into letting me work at their hospital."

"You blackmailed someone?" A tinge of admiration crept into Woehar's voice. "I would love to hear about this sometime. You deserve something good for giving me such important information. I know now how to go about destroying Jackson Hospital."

"You do?" Laurel stared at Woehar with bulging eyes. "What about Alexis?"

"After one of my soldiers injects Yeron with vischlausk, we shall see how he behaves toward Alexis."

"I love it." Laurel folded her hands together and smiled. "What a fitting punishment for the Ice Princess. I'm glad you punished Gloria, too."

"Be quiet. We have a visitor." Woehar held a finger to her lips. The door slid open behind her. An android marched in, wheeling a tray on a stand. He set the tray before Laurel and then left.

Laurel gave Woehar a wide-eyed look. "I didn't think you cooked anything."

"My android cooked the meat for you," Woehar told her. "Very soon, you will be able to enjoy your meat raw."

Pain forgotten, Laurel shivered at the ecstasy rushing through her. She could not remember when she'd last eaten human meat. She sampled the first morsel. Its sweetness slid down her throat, warming her stomach. It reminded her of the way she invented reasons to punish her girls. "How much did Gloria beg before you let her have it?"

"She cried for a man named Jesus, but she did not fight or beg for mercy. No one came to help her. As you say, she loves her Communion wafers."

"The pliable ones are the easiest kind. My girls used to argue with me, but I broke them after the first week." As she scarfed down her food, Laurel's questions about the forthcoming treatment faded into the dim recesses of her mind. She got to wondering when Abaddon had last spoken with her. His Voice had lain dormant with all the pain medicine on board. More would be coming with this treatment. "How does Draekh plan to augment my muscles?"

"Draekh will give you a series of injections to alter your DNA."

Laurel's eyelids grew heavy. Woehar wasn't making sense. Maybe she'd ask her more about the treatments after she got some shut-eye. "Before I nod off, what are you going to do at Jackson? How will you get your specimens there?"

"On buses. They are easy to navigate, and I assigned three soldiers to drive them. Once there, they will send my specimens in through the back elevator and more through the emergency room. Others will visit the stores near your hospital and perhaps feed there, too. The humans will have their officers, too, but I shall send enough specimens to overwhelm them and more." Woehar let out a harsh laugh.

"Good. I hope Hoffman and Leicht become dinner."

"They will, especially Doctor Leicht. If he survives our visit at the hospital and later goes to his house, he will find his child and his mate dead."

"I love it." Laurel chortled, but her voice sounded tinny and distant. It was like talking through a pane of glass. "I've always wanted to kill that bastard." She wolfed down the last morsel and rolled over onto her side. Moments later, darkness enveloped her.

* * * *

When Laurel woke, the sensation of hot coals burned her lower back, accompanying the stinging in her hands and feet. This was supposed to be a reward, but it sure felt like punishment.

"Come with me, sleepy one." Woehar crooked her finger.

"Aw, lemme sleep." Somewhere in her world of dope and cluttered dreams, she managed to sit up and grimace at the stabbing pain. "I'm tired."

"Punishment does not sleep." Woehar rolled her tongue across her teeth, catching the bloodstains and saliva. "I want you to see what I prepared for Jackson Hospital."

"Mmmmph."

"Including Alexis, the one who gave you so much trouble."

At that, Laurel pulled herself upright, trying hard to ignore the pain. Teeth clenched, she swung her legs over the side of the cushions. The room spun. She braced herself against the mattress.

"I knew that would motivate you." Woehar laughed. "Follow me."

Laurel staggered after Woehar down the hall, past the door into the specimen laboratory. During her last visit to the laboratory, the prisoners were writhing in agony from the IV vischlausk. The IVs were delivering this poison to some, but others staggered, batting their hands at the glass. Blood bearded their faces, with gargoyle scars, razor-sharp teeth, and yellow eyes visible between the gore. One man gnawed on a human bone coated with gristle.

"Hungry." The creature growled out the word.

"Watch." Woehar indicated a panel in the wall behind the creatures.

The panel opened, and someone shoved a milk-pale woman through the aperture. Her tattered clothes made her look older, but her smooth skin and dark hair said she was in her twenties. Woehar must have captured her from the street.

The creatures gave no sign of caring about her age or where she lived. Three of them fell on her and tore into her flesh. The woman flailed at them, screaming as one creature tore a chunk out of her right leg, while the other bit into her arm. Arterial blood jetted, pelting the floor with splashes of blood. The third ripped into her gut. The mobile prisoners lapped up the blood, shoving each other like pigs fighting over a trough.

Laurel imaged replacing that woman with Alexis or another shithead from the hospital. Pain forgotten, she shivered at the ecstasy surging through her being, an orgasm as she had never known. The Power was waking up from a long sleep. The shivering came from anticipating the thrill of the kill. Woehar was bringing punishment to a creative level.

"I thought you were tired." Woehar smiled.

"When is this visit going to happen? How soon?"

"As soon as I have at least two hundred specimens. I want to send about thirty to the mall, another ten to the emergency room, and seventy or more to the seventh floor. A few shall visit Steve and his mate and others will go into the woods surrounding our compound. I estimate about four to six of your weeks. When it happens, we shall show Jackson Hospital and its communities the dark side of their moon."

"Dark side?" Laurel yawned. "What does that mean?"

"I am referring to the dark moons that surround my home planet, Kryszk. Your moon is white, of course."

Laurel nodded. "As long as Alexis gets what she deserves."

"She will become Yeron's first meal after my officer injects the vischlausk. Three of my soldiers shall accompany these creatures to Jackson Hospital, and one of them will administer the drug. No one will be able to help Alexis or Yeron. The doctors and officers will concentrate on treating the casualties and staying alive. No one will care for their patients or each other."

"Finally." Laurel grinned at the thought of the creatures mauling Doctor Leicht. "Everyone at that hospital will get what's coming to them."

"Not just the hospital. I am going after the officers and other people who destroyed Eigil's compound. They need to pay for what they did." Laurel gave her another toothy smile. "I shall escort you back to bed now. By the time the party begins, you will feel much better."

Chapter Twenty-Six: Visitors Arrive

The Grounds outside Jackson Hospital, May 27, 7:00 p.m.

Though the 248AR had banished the aches and stiffness, the hamburger and fries Alexis had for supper stuck in her throat with each swallow. Her cuts had healed, leaving behind unsightly deformities that made movements awkward, but doable. She was heading into her fifth week as "auxiliary" security for Hoffman. After the fiasco with Gloria Hanson, he'd take any backup he could get. Alexis masqueraded as a patient, wearing a hospital gown over her sweatshirt and workout slacks and, underneath her shirt, a ballistic vest.

At her window, she gazed at the purple flowers sprouting on the trees lining the stores across Jonasville Street. The flowers reminded her of the kind at funerals. The sun blazed in the sky, a ball of fire with menacing brightness. At the Food Fair supermarket across the street, people pulled into the lot, eager to take advantage of the Memorial Day sales. Armed officers paced the street and courtyards, but the activity did nothing to still her apprehension. Perhaps Yeron's hypnosis was losing effect. The flashbacks would come next.

A distraction. That's what she needed. She grabbed a pen and scrapbook from the side table, tore off a sheet of paper, and started sketching. Before arthritis maimed her fingers, she used to doodle. Her cartoonish creations elicited chuckles from other people, but drawing got her mind off her problems. It still did. Thoughts about the zombies and the renegade Kryszka receded into the background as she penned in the nose and eyes. Wavy, coarse hair came next, followed by Yeron's angular features. She concentrated on the slant in his eyes, the sadness, and his high cheekbones. When she finished, her sketch looked like a caricature of Dracula.

"Alexis." She smiled to herself. "Some people climb the mountains. Some people paint them. You're not fit to do either."

She balled the paper and tossed it in the trash. Tossing by hand felt better than using her thoughts. She grabbed another page and tried again with a tight-lipped grin. The slant of his eyes, his smile, and his wavy hair made Yeron look like Bozo, the clown. Another gift for the trash can. A third presented a feminine-looking being wearing a tunic. Ditto trash can material.

Dammit, why am I mooning over this man? We come from different worlds, and besides, he's my doctor. Still, Yeron was one of the few people who coaxed a laugh out of her and one of the fewer men who could touch her without making her cringe. If he were human, he'd be cute.

Dammit, he is cute, and no qualification about it, a voice whispered in her subconscious. *Let's tell it like it is. If he wasn't your doctor ...*

Boowooooop! Boowooop! Boowoop! The alarm sliced into her daydream with serrated edges.

"Code one hundred!" a voice boomed over the intercom. "Code one hundred!"

"Oh, no!" Alexis's pen dropped. She covered her eyes. "Oh, no!"

Code one hundred meant a disaster. It could be a gas leak, terrorist attack, or any event that resulted in multiple victims and casualties. Most trauma admissions came from the stores across the road: construction workers, people backing out of parking spaces without looking, or wayward toddlers.

A glance out the window told her what happened. A chartered bus smashed through the Food Fair's side window. A nearby tree canted against the bus. Two more buses came up Jonasville Street. They smacked into the rear of the first and swerved sideways, colliding with oncoming cars and blocking traffic. Amidst the crumbling metal and blaring horns, gawking bystanders pointed at the buses and screamed.

People exited the bus, most of them limping and shambling. This drew more screams from the bystanders. Most of them raced into the stores.

"Holy shit!" Alexis quivered like a wire. "This is worse than I expected."

She yanked open her drawer, retrieved her gun, and slipped it into her waistband. The quivering subsided. "Get hold of yourself," she scolded herself. "Yeron taught you how to use plasma guns. You've got him and Shively in your corner."

Guns won't mean squat if you can't move right, the phantom voice jeered.

I can move fine, thank you very much, she thought back at it. She walked without any limp when she wore her brace. With Yeron's latest treatment, her arthritis remained quiet. She moved more slowly than her companions, but her shots fired true during practice. Yeron taught her how to compensate for the slowness with her mind, and he schooled her well. By golly, she couldn't paint or climb a mountain, but she could defend herself.

Running was for cowards.

Shively, another guard, paced around his room, wearing a johnny over his ballistic vest and jeans. Alexis would have given anything for thick jeans, but she couldn't manage the metal buttons. At night, while he and Alexis were asleep, Tyrone stood watch. Mark staked out in his old room by the elevator, and he relieved them for meals and family visits. Johnny returned to the orthopedic floor as another spotter. These people afforded better protection than any Rent-a-Cop service Jackson Hospital offered. Yeron, a regular Doctor Phil with firearms, was examining his cancer patients in the A cubicles. Even her mother, who worked the floor today, carried heat in her fanny pack. So far, all bases were covered.

Mark continued shredding his magazines, sometimes long after midnight. During her nighttime visits to the john, Alexis heard him weeping into his pillow. She never asked him what was wrong. Offering concern was a prelude to forgiveness, and she could never forgive him for the rape. Her leg scar testified to his capability for violence.

The cancer patients, weakened by their disease, had nothing to offer except prayer.

When you're dealing with monsters, Dee would have said, *God is your best friend.*

The doors to her room slid open. Steve and Hoffman shuffled in, clad in soiled scrubs. Closer up, their bodies exuded the stink of rotting tomatoes. Her stomach churned at their acrid smell and the sight of the grayish goo streaking their short-sleeved shirts.

Her heart hammered in her chest. No one dared to show up on Hoffman's floor without showering unless it was a dire emergency. Today the pallor and oh-God look on Hoffman's face spoke of a man who'd gotten shot in a vital organ. Steve's freckles stood out like raised dots on his bleached face.

Where was Hoffman's I-am-God 101 demeanor, the self-proclaimed king who laid down his Commandments for Yeron? Where did Steve's *we'll-get-through-this* smile go? Gone, silenced by the unspeakable.

"Alexis, Steve and I will be unavailable," Hoffman told her. "We're telling patients and visitors that a bus was involved in a multi-vehicle accident. The medics are setting up a triage across the street." He glanced over his shoulder and continued, his voice dipping. "A Kryszka soldier was driving the bus. That part we're keeping quiet."

"Oh, yeah?" Alexis gazed at his darting eyes. "I saw the whole thing go down. It looked to me like the bus driver smashed into the store on purpose. People will make similar assumptions if they look out the window."

"Most accidents involve casualties and rubble." Hoffman's voice cracked on the last two words. "That's what I'll say if ..."

"She's right," Steve said. "It looks awful."

"Of course, it does." Hoffman lowered his eyes. "Alexis, Homeland Security sent us officers ..." He shook his head, trying to find his Authority voice. It didn't happen.

"We know what happened." Steve sighed. "Joe and I have to bring the injured here."

Alexis drew in a deep breath. "Are there zombies on those

buses?"

Hoffman let out a long, skeletal sigh. "The officers have confined the problem to the stores. Nothing can get past that steel on the back elevator."

Alexis's jaw tightened. Her mouth twisted. How she hated his attempt at sugarcoating. "Are. There. Zombies. On. Those. Buses."

A long silence followed and then Hoffman nodded. "These buses carry at least fifty-five passengers each, and they were packed. It would sound lame for me to say I'm sorry."

Alexis wrapped her pink-sleeved arms around her shoulders, trying to still the shivers.

"Yeron taught you how to use plasma." Steve shifted his gaze toward Hoffman and then back to Alexis. "Shively's got street smarts. Do whatever he and Yeron tell you."

"I will." She swallowed hard. "How's my mother dealing with all this?"

"As well as can be expected." Hoffman's pointed gaze made her fidget. "She found out Yeron's nickname for you."

"Dammit!" Alexis cried. "Who told her?"

"Does it matter?" Hoffman shrugged. "It got her mind off of Trident Mall."

"I bet both of you got an earful." Alexis buried her head in her hands.

"She informed everyone in no uncertain terms that you're a delicate child," Steve said in a gentle voice. "She spends most of her break time on the phone. I'm guessing it's with Everett Fenimore since he taught her how to use a gun."

"She trusts Fenimore. Her trust and his skill with hunting make him an ideal teacher."

"I suppose it does. You can get through this, too, if you stay strong."

"I will do the best I can." Alexis gave him a weak smile.

"Steve, we should go." Hoffman started toward the door. "You coming?"

"In a second." Steve fixed his gaze on Alexis. "Do you have any questions?"

"Just a favor." Alexis's voice clicked from her chattering

teeth. "Be careful."

* * * *

After the doctors left, Alexis turned her gaze toward the prayer beads her mother had left on her night table. God may be her best friend, but He was not going to handle the plasma for her. Still, she was glad to have all the reinforcements she could get, including the Rosary and her ballistic vest. Shively had gotten the vests for her and the others from his Mob friends.

She retrieved a mint-green bathrobe from the closet and slipped it around herself. Her mother had given it to her last Christmas, never suspecting she might one day wear it to a brawl with zombies. It took away the chills.

She reached for her Rosary and got to thinking about her father's saying about atheists and foxholes. She didn't expect to meet any atheists today.

"Let's try the Sorrowful Mysteries," she said aloud. "It doesn't get worse than this."

The prayers rolled off her tongue with urgency. She offered the first Mystery for her mother's protection against evil Kryszka. She dedicated the second for the stamina to survive the hospital invasion. It was going to happen. She knew this as well as she had come to know the sick feeling in her gut.

"Third Mystery: The Crowning of Thorns. Our father..." *The way the Kryszka soldier crowned me with ground glass.* Her steady voice drowned out the wailing sirens and horns, and her anxiety subsided. She offered the fourth for Robin and Dee. She tendered the fifth for Yeron since so many people castigated him without taking time to know him. Clicking footsteps outside her room punctuated her Hail Holy Queen.

Before Alexis could respond, Ms. Grese barged into her room, her face crimson. Her blue eyes flashed with anger. She wore a navy business suit and matching pumps, dressed as if she were going to a funeral. Her coiffed blonde hair, leather briefcase, ruby earrings, and spiked heels made her look dignified enough to appear before the president.

"Alexis Carofalo, I'm giving you fair warning," she said in a harsh voice.

"Not now," Alexis shouted, close to panic again. "Whatever your problem is, this is a bad time."

Ms. Grese walked over to the window and slammed her briefcase onto the heater. After withdrawing a thick wad of papers, she marched to the bed. "Then you'd better make it good. Look at what I've gotten on my desk." She waved the papers in Alexis's face like someone scolding a puppy for piddling on the floor. Alexis made out a list of signed names on the front page. "Cindy wrote a petition, begging me to hold your position. See it? See it?"

Ms. Grese rattled her papers. In the next instant, Alexis saw a trace of the monster in those cold blue eyes.

"Get out of my face!" she screamed. "Doctor Hoffman doesn't want you here."

"Well, isn't that too bad?" Ms. Grese's voice reeked with contempt. "Your letter caused a lot of trouble."

Alexis stood up, braced her arm against the bedside table and looked Ms. Grese in the eye. "I didn't ask Cindy to write that letter, but I'm glad to know people care about me. It's late. Shouldn't you go home?"

"Not tonight." Ms. Grese heaved a disgusted sigh. "No one can leave during a disaster like this."

"It's worse than you think." Alexis watched Ms. Grese's narrowing eyes. "You'd be safer if you had stayed in your office."

"I've heard enough nonsense out of you, young lady..."

"Quit badgering her!" Yeron tore into her room, jabbing an accusing finger at Ms. Grese. Alexis gaped at him, startled, never hearing his footsteps. "Leave now, before I call Security."

Alexis found herself suppressing a grin. *You go, Doctor Phil.*

"My, aren't we protective?" Ms. Grese jeered with mock wonder. "Okay, I will make this short. Your five weeks of sick leave ended long ago, and you're nowhere ready to work. The petition is denied, and your job is terminated."

"How can you tell? Were you looking through her file?" asked Yeron. "Rest assured, I shall report you for violating her privacy."

"I would worry more about how she's going to pay your fees," Ms. Grese countered. "I apologize for my intrusion, but

Alexis needs to know so she can apply for COBRA."

"Then get ready for a stiff fine or jail time." Alexis hoped to make her squirm. "You violated HIPAA."

"Why you ..."

Shattering glass. Plodding footsteps. IV poles crashed to the floor. Glass shards tinkled, punctuated by low-pitched groaning from the rear elevator, the exit Hoffman had claimed to seal.

"Dear God, help us." Alexis reached for her gun.

"What are you doing? Guns are forbidden on this floor, and ... Oh, my God!" Ms. Grese cupped her hands over her mouth. Her authoritarian demeanor vanished, replaced by horror-stricken pallor. "Where are the officers?"

"You think our visitors give a shit?" Alexis scuttled toward the door, feeling vulnerable. The vest didn't protect her face or hands, but the intruders wouldn't care about that either. She shoved Ms. Grese ahead of her, pushing with her mind, Yeron beside her.

"Run!" she hollered.

As the creatures poured through the ward, a stench crawled down her throat, the stink of things many days dead. Moaning drowned out the sound of Ms. Grese's cries, a continual chant of "hungry."

Skeletal figures in tattered rags skirted around Mark, who fired at any who got too close. Their tendons flashed gray against cold cobwebs of rib and knuckle. The flesh that quivered through widened skin tears had the sheen of rotting meat. The skin resembled cracked leather. Weeds sprouted on some of the figures' necks and hair, the way they did in her nightmares. They made their way to the desk, where two nurses sat. The two women jumped up, both screaming. One of them opened fire with a Glock.

The armed woman was her mother.

"Oh, my God!" Alexis gasped.

Yeron nudged her shoulder, keeping his hand cradled around his weapon. "Follow my lead," he said.

Chapter Twenty-Seven: Woehar's Army Attacks

Jackson Hospital's Seventh Floor, May 27, 9:00 p.m.

People with rotted skin, hair matted with blood and dirt, swarmed the desk. Her mother hopped up on top and continued shooting. Her bullets cut craters into skulls, dropping the ones closest to the desk, but more kept coming. Cindy climbed onto a windowsill and made her way to the cabinets. Shively darted from his room to Alexis's right, while Yeron stayed to her left. Ms. Grese stumbled in front of them, letting out bloodcurdling shrieks. Her pumps skated on the spilled IV fluid, causing her to land on her backside. The intruders closed in on her, chittering away, their voices gravelly from damaged vocal cords.

Extending his right arm in an arc, Yeron sprayed flame and dropped six figures. Alexis did the same, but her movements felt pathetically slow. Yeron cut through five creatures in the amount of time it took Alexis to fell three. The creatures scattered away from her and descended upon Ms. Grese. They tore into her legs, tearing off flaps of skin. Flashes of light raced across the room. Shards of glass flew as the advancing figures battered the doors to the cubicles. Screams dying in her throat, Alexis scrambled toward cubicles A1, A2, and A3.

Another tangle of grisly heads, legs, and arms streamed from the elevator. Shively charged ahead and pumped lead into the creatures with his machine gun. Their bodies exploded in a geyser of bone fragments and skin. Unseen hands landed on Alexis, bone and rotting flesh digging into her shoulders. She gave a twisting push that sent her assailants, two of them, flying. They rattled against a wall with a sickening crunch, splitting their heads and limbs into fragments. Foul-smelling lice and maggots spewed in a grotesque streak down the plaster.

More creatures approaching skirted around Yeron. He felled the ones passing by him. More kept coming. The air thickened with the stench of death.

Alexis shoved back toward the nurses' desk, using her psychic force field as a shield, and picked them off, head by head. Her mother climbed up onto the cabinets beside Cindy, one hand gripping a pipe and the other brandishing her gun. Her aim held steady. Her shots fired true, and then the blasting stopped, replaced by clicking.

"Alexis!" she cried.

The panic in her mother's cry spurred Alexis into action. Dammit, she wasn't losing another family member. No. No. No. She chased four figures that were climbing onto the desk after her mother. "I'm your worst nightmare," she hollered, blasting fire at them. The creatures dropped, charred black, bugs spilling from the cracks in their skin. "Mom! Move back against the wall."

Her mother did not need to be told twice.

More figures with gargoyle faces hopped onto the desk, angling for the cabinets. "Nightmare!" She picked them off with each attempt to ascend the cabinet. "Nightmare."

"Way to go, girl." Shively peppered shots at the creatures coming up behind her.

Mark was ... where was Mark? What happened to Jackson Hospital's so-called officers? Before Alexis could ponder an answer, skeletal hands grabbed her shoulders. She batted them away with her mind. Yeron materialized at her elbow, slipped her a fresh gun, and then ... he disappeared. Her balloons bobbed out of her room, snagging the creatures' arms. That didn't slow their relentless hunger. Shively moved with a panther's speed with his machine gun. He must have carried a near-endless supply of ammunition. The muscles in her left leg ached, slowing her pace, but her relentless fire thinned the gruesome crowd around the desk. Six more wasted figures plowed out the back elevator. Blasts from her plasma brought down all of them. Searing pain burned into her leg but she kept going. Where the hell was Mark?

Clinking jarred her gaze toward her right. Two creatures laid hands on Mark, eyes rolled back and teeth gaping. His gun lay on the floor inches from his feet.

"Help me!" he screamed.

Alexis aimed her weapon and hesitated. The things were all over Mark, ripping open his coveralls. She couldn't destroy them without harming him. Immobilizing was better. Yeron had explained that the blue button immobilized victim and assailant, thus giving her an opportunity to pull the victim free. She took aim, and blue rays encircled the three figures. They tottered on their feet and dropped. Her gun went into her waistband. After two steps toward Mark, her left leg wobbled. She lurched toward him in a sidestroke motion. Along the way, she leaned against the wall and shot two more monstrosities plodding her way. The move cost her stinging in her back, caused by the ballistics vest rubbing against her barely healed scars. She made another stop several steps further to throw up. The stench was unbearable. Closer. She sank to her knees and landed in a jellylike material. She screamed.

"Alexis, what the fuck are you doing?" Shively hollered.

"I'm pulling those things off Mark." Chest heaving, she shot off the heads of the figures holding Mark. Another group exploded from the elevator. Leaning sideways, Alexis fired and took down three. Shively finished off the ones she missed. The stink coming off everyone's clothes was awful. She had to find Yeron, preferably before the government agents showed up to quarantine the hospital.

"Alexis." Shively touched her shoulder. "Did Mark get bitten?"

"I don't know. I couldn't eliminate those things without hitting him, so I subdued the three of them with the tranquilizer. I've never seen him so terrified." She turned her head and vomited again. "Sorry."

"No need to be. Someone should check out both of you."

Alexis sighed. "Hoffman's busy, and I don't see Yeron anywhere. I'm afraid those monsters got him."

"Maybe he saw more trouble and tried to head it off."

"Someone got to him, Shively. I'm going to look for him."

"What do you mean, look for him? You can hardly walk."

"I'll find a way if I have to crawl. I'm getting sick of watching people I care about die." She fought back the threatening tears, not caring to cry in front of Shively or her mother, and turned her eyes toward the cabinets. The two nurses cringed against the wall, hugging each other. "Cindy! Mom!" Her voice cracked. "Come down. It's all right ... at least for the moment."

"This place is abominable." Her mother burst into tears. "If any more of those things come around, I'm out of bullets."

"Take Mark's gun." She kicked the weapon away from Mark's feet. "Over here." She then met her mother's gaze and attempted a tone she might use for a traumatized patient. "Mark might be hurt. Can you and Cindy check him out? I have to find Yeron."

"You're in no condition to go traipsing around the building." Her mother frowned. "Page Doctor Leicht. See if he can examine you."

"I'll talk to Steve after I know Yeron is okay," Alexis told her.

"One of us should call Doctor Hoffman, too," Cindy said.

"Go ahead." Alexis tightened her brace. Her left leg trembled, but she stood without swaying. "I'm looking for Yeron. My mother and I are alive because of Yeron, so I owe him that."

"Alexis." Shively softened his voice. "You think any kidnapper would take him through this mess? He probably didn't get past the main elevators."

Alexis swallowed hard, her throat slate dry. "They could take him out through the dressing room. We've got showers and plenty of clean gowns there."

"I'll find him. Stay put, in case we get more visitors."

"Shively, I'll handle the visitors." Her mother tucked Mark's gun inside her fanny pack. "Cindy can look after Mark. Take Alexis with you and find some help."

"Thanks, Mom." Alexis breathed a sigh of relief. She patted her brace. "I can walk now."

"Are you fucking crazy?" Shively shot her a harsh look. "No one's taught you reconnaissance."

"I can learn." Alexis met his gaze without flinching. "I know my way around this hospital."

"I said no, Alexis. You look like shit." His clenched jaw discouraged argument.

"So does everyone else here. My gut instinct tells me that Yeron's hurt." She heaved a deep sigh. "To make you happy, I'll help my mother with Mark and the visitors. Take Cindy with you. She'll know how to treat any injury."

"Fuck!" Shively wiped the sweat from his forehead. "I want a medic who knows how to shoot. Come along, but keep your mouth shut."

* * * *

Alexis crept down a corridor, with Shively behind her. They made their way past the doctors' offices on the left and to their right, laboratories with caged mice and other equipment. At the corner, something yellow streaked to her right.

"Get down!" Shively yanked Alexis by the robe. Alexis's leg buckled, but she splayed her elbows, breaking her fall. Another flash of yellow. At Shively's prompting, she crept behind a stretcher.

Someone in green scrubs and glasses whipped around a corner, brandishing a plasma gun. His uniform made him look like a Jackson employee, but his albino complexion and fiery hunger-maddened eyes said he was a Kryszka soldier. Shively aimed at him from behind the stretcher, but his shot went wide. The assailant blasted again, streaking fire inches from Shively's head. Breathing hard, Alexis summoned her energy and telegraphed a psychic punch toward the shooter's wrist. The gun dropped. The intruder started, and Shively squeezed off another shot. The attacker's face exploded in a wash of blood.

"Damn!" His breath came fast. "That was close. Where are the officers? Didn't your hospital hire any security?"

"You mean the Rent-a-Cops? We've got those." Alexis sniffed. "Ms. Grese must have sent them on their break before she came in to fire me."

"Fucking assholes! What kind of outfit is this?"

"The kind that fires people for taking sick leave." Alexis gazed at the soiled remains of her clothes. "Yeron and I played

God with Ms. Grese's life. She barged into my room, and I told her to scram before things went bad. She didn't listen. We shoved her out to the hall, right into the mouths of those things."

"So what? I heard everything that went down between you. You gave that bitch ample warning. She didn't listen. This is a war; everyone pulls their weight." He shrugged. "That creep is dead."

"Good." Alexis doglegged out to the hall again, but Shively pulled her back and shook his head no.

"Wait," he said in a low voice. "He may have brought backup."

He disappeared behind a corner. Alexis knelt, arms leaning against the stretcher, and her breath rasping. At the angle in which she knelt, the vest rubbed against her skin, digging wedges in her back. What was he doing, prospecting for gold?

"Alexis," he called moments later. "Come here."

Alexis came, limping past the fallen Kryszka into the dressing area. Another Kryszka lay prone near a rack of pressurized suits. His head and face looked like burnt charcoal. The shredded remnants of her balloons snagged around his calf with their ribbons. Further back, Shively stood holding a cloth in his hand. Along the way, Alexis caught a glimpse of herself in the mirror. Her mint-green bathroom and pink shirtsleeves had turned yellow, bloody, and black. Maggots and flecks of gray flesh had embedded in its folds. The stench coming from her was awful. Worse, maroon tufts of fascia streaked the sides of Shively's overalls. She started to gag again.

"Cut that out and look at this." Shively held up his cloth. "This is important."

He opened his cloth, revealing a filled syringe. Its contents looked like beef soup.

"Yeron uses those syringes for my 248AR, but my medicine is colorless," she told him. "I can tell no one used it. Once you open those caps, you can't reseal them. It's a safety precaution."

"So what is this stuff?"

"Yeron could tell you." Alexis shifted her gaze toward the prone figure. "Any chance of that soldier regaining consciousness?"

"Nope. I fried him."

"Then I'm getting a shower." Alexis half shambled, half walked toward the pressurized suits. "I can't go outside like this."

"Not yet. I want to find the creep who left the syringe." Shively went over to the wall phone, lifted the receiver, and slammed it. "Fuck, the phones don't work."

Alexis patted her pockets. Empty. "Regular cell phones don't work on this floor, but the red emergency phones might. We have only one up here at the nurses' station." She grimaced. "Welcome to Jackson Hospital."

She retraced her steps to the canvas bin. "I need a change of clothes, but those big suits are too heavy. Maybe they've got lighter..."

"Wait, wait, wait!" Shively darted ahead of her to the bin. "That bin might be booby-trapped. Let me check it out first."

He put his ear up against the clothing and shrugged. He then grabbed a mop hanging overhead, poked it inside the bin, and lifted out a laundry bag. A stack of gowns came next, and then he hollered, "Son of a bitch! Someone dumped Yeron in here."

"Are you sure?" Alexis approached the bin, propped her elbows on its rim, and peered downward.

Yeron lay on his side, knees bent and curled against his chest. His hospital scrubs were stained crimson and gray. One arm folded across his chest. The other propped up against the side, as if he were waving goodbye. The fiery tumor of panic reared its head inside her. Someone had drugged him, maybe killed him.

Chapter Twenty-Eight: Ruins of the Seventh Floor

Jackson Hospital, May 27, 11:00 p.m.

"Yeron?" Her voice trembled. "Can you hear me?"

No answer.

"Yeron?" Louder this time, and more urgent. "Open your eyes."

With shaky fingers, Alexis stretched her hand down into the bin. She placed it over his mouth. Air blew against her fingers. She moved her hand further down and felt the rise and fall of his chest. He was alive but unconscious. How badly was he hurt and could she help him?

"Alexis!" Shively nudged her in the side. "Stop that."

"I'm trying to see if he's breathing. He is."

"You don't put your hand over his mouth, for crying out loud." Shively shook his head, exasperated. "He might bite."

At that, Alexis burst into harsh laughter that sounded like screaming.

"Alexis." Shively mustered patience into his voice. "Pull yourself together. You know full well that someone in his condition might bite or become combative."

Alexis straightened up on her knees and regarded Shively. "Yeron is a gentle person. He would never hurt me."

Shively threw up his hands and dropped them by his side. "I don't give a damn if you love the guy. He might not act so gentle if someone poisoned him."

"As you can see, he's in no condition to attack or bite." Alexis touched Yeron's throat. His skin felt warm, but no palpable pulse. She pried open his eyelids. The eyes were red, with birdshot pupils, smaller than she remembered. Then she decided to try his native language. "Yeron, it's me. Alexis. Please talk to me."

Shively sighed. "What kind of gibberish are you speaking now?"

"Kryszka. Sometimes it helps to approach a patient in their native language." She shone Shively's flashlight over Yeron, assessing him for treatable injuries and then started. What was she doing? She didn't know squat about the Kryszka body. "It's not safe to move him. He might have broken something. We've got to get hold of Steve. He'll know what to do."

"With no phone out here?"

Alexis furrowed her brows, eyes on Yeron. "You'll have to use the emergency phone at the nurses' station. Cindy or my mother can show you how it works."

"Yeah, and maybe I should believe in the tooth fairy. Sit tight until I get back."

* * * *

Shively returned, wheeling a chair loaded with a blood pressure machine, pulse oximeter, and a walkie-talkie radio. "Your mother told me to bring these," he told Alexis. "She said you'd know what to do with them."

"I'm not a nurse. She is."

"Yeah ... well, she's busy taking care of Mark. The other nurse ... Cindy... is too shook up to do anything."

"All right." Alexis made a wry face. "I'm unemployed, but my license says I can provide treatment."

"Go for it." Shively handed her the radio. "I'll nose around and find out who left that syringe."

Alexis punched in two buttons and got the emergency room. A woman's voice answered. "This is emergency trauma, can you hold?"

"No, I can't. The seventh floor is a shambles, people are..."

"You'll have to wait. We have a disaster down here."

"Well, guess what? The so-called passengers from your bus accident trashed the seventh floor. In case you're wondering, I'm Alexis Carofalo, a patient. Doctor Hoffman's key man, Yeron, is lying here in a bin unconscious. "

A low gasp followed. "Oh, my God! *Doctor Hoffman!*"

Shouting erupted in the background. Alexis knelt by the bin, peered down at Yeron and waited.

"Alexis, what's going on?" Hoffman's voice crackled in her ear.

"Those monsters, like the ones from Trident Mall, came in through the service elevator."

"They couldn't have. Nothing can get through that steel."

"Someone forgot to tell them that. Shively found a dead Kryszka soldier, busted balloons, and a syringe. Short version—Shively and I are okay. So are your two nurses. Mark may be hurt. My mother's checking him now. I don't know about your patients. Yeron's hurt real bad. He's unconscious, and he has no palpable pulse."

"The circulatory system on Kryszka work differently than ours. I'll talk you through an assessment, but first, I need to speak with Shively. Shower and put on gloves before you touch Yeron."

"All right." Alexis looked up and realized she was alone. She raised her voice. "Shively? Hoffman wants to talk to you."

"Alexis, you talk loud enough to wake the dead." Shively came running from behind a wall post. "Bring it down a few notches. I found another soldier by the exit. He's unconscious but breathing. I fried him. What does Hoffman want?"

"He didn't say." Alexis handed him the radio. She picked up a clean gown and shuffled to a shower stall.

The soiled robe and gown went into a laundry bag. Ditto for her pink shirt and pants. She stripped her military vest and allowed the steamy hot water to wash away the grime. Using a brush laden with disinfectant, she dug away crud from under her fingernails and wiped her vest off as best she could. She worked the soap through and around her leg brace. So far, no scratches, just fresh bruises minted on her arms, and one on her right knee. After a quick wipe with a towel, she donned her vest again and doubled up two fresh gowns over it. She put on gloves and hobbled back toward the bin.

"Hoffman has instructions for you." Shively handed her the radio. "He's sending officers up here. I'm going back to check on

Cindy and Matilda."

Alexis nodded. She understood without being told that more of those things might assault the survivors.

"Shively told me you held your own," Hoffman said with admiration in his voice. "Yeron did right, teaching you to use the plasma gun. Now he needs your help, so I need you to focus."

"All right." Alexis fought to control the quivering in her voice. "He looks bad, Doctor. He's got regular respirations, but no palpable pulse. His pupils are tiny. He does not respond to any verbal stimuli. I'm afraid he's going to die."

"You're not a doctor, so you can't make that call." Hoffman spoke without rancor. "The Kryszka has his palpable pulse under the rib cage. Certain drugs can cause his pupils to contract. In most ways, you approach an unconscious Kryszka as you would a human. What's the first thing you do when you find somebody unconscious?"

"I make sure he has a patent airway."

"Exactly. Yeron might have trouble breathing, being cramped in that bin. Get him out of there. Then you can assess him."

"What if he injured his neck?"

"Any injury won't matter if he can't breathe." Hoffman's voice tensed. "Get him out. Use whatever means you've got."

"Hold on." Alexis sized up Yeron's crumbled form. He was over six feet tall, and about 170 pounds. She had never levitated a person before. "Yeron, you've got to help me out here." Then she directed her psychic energy the way he'd taught her

The bin tipped and dropped, socking Yeron's left shoulder against the floor. Alexis focused on easing Yeron out of the bin. At first, the bin came with him. She braced her feet against the upper rims, holding the bin in place. A corkscrew of pain twisted up her left leg. She ignored that, too. Yeron's body slid forward, head and shoulders first. Her head throbbed by the time he came out as far as his knees.

After pausing to massage her temples, she balled up a clean gown and wedged it under his head and neck.

With a sigh of relief, she pressed the "hold and speak" button on the radio again. "I've got him out—at least close enough for government work. What's next?"

"Keep the government out of this," Hoffman roared in her ear. "How does Yeron look to you now?"

"Still unconscious, no pulse, but he's breathing at a rate of eighteen."

"Open his shirt, and feel below his left rib cage. You should find a pulse there."

"Hold on." Alexis pulled up Yeron's isolation gown and his white shirt. His T-shirt came next. She palpated along his gut until she felt a strong, steady throbbing below his left rib cage. "Doctor, we've got a pulse. It's in the seventies and regular."

"Very good. A regular blood pressure cuff won't work on Yeron, but you can tape your oximeter probe below his ribs to get his oxygen saturation. Look for saturations above 92 percent."

"He's 95 percent," Alexis told him after completing that chore.

"Fine. Turn Yeron on his side to the recovery position. Leave him that way until Steve or I can take a look at him. Watch his vital signs. If anything changes, call me. Any questions?"

"How much damage did those things do in the Emergency Room?"

"None. Two officers, Steve, and I disposed of the ones that made it across the street. They left the Jonasville Street stores in shambles."

"The seventh floor is a disaster, too."

"I heard. Rest assured, you and the other survivors will be compensated for your ordeal."

"That is comforting to hear since Ms. Grese fired me before the invasion." *And sweet little me fed her to those monsters. How's that, dear Doctor?*

"She had some nerve. The officers she hired are worthless."

Alexis nodded but kept her voice neutral. "They're hiding, aren't they?"

"They ran, Alexis. Plain and simple. Shively didn't see any trace of them."

"Chickenshits!" Alexis shouted, and then she clamped her hand over her mouth. "Sorry about the language."

"That's what they are," Hoffman agreed without hesitation. "Call me if anything changes with Yeron."

* * * *

People in blue isolation suits and masks swarmed the shower area, among them Steve and Hoffman. Hoffman knelt beside Yeron while Cindy ushered Alexis to a wheelchair.

"Okay, folks, listen up." Steve spoke with his boardroom voice. "The police are bringing in a SERT team to have a look. What's going on in the ward now?"

"Later." Shively nodded toward Alexis. "Alexis has had it."

"*I* saw it happen," Alexis snapped, close to tears. She cringed at the sight of Hoffman wrapping a modified cuff around Yeron's chest. "So let her rip."

"Four more of those things came up through the elevator," Shively said. "Matilda shot them and then she slid on the gore. She's complaining of chest pain. Cindy hid in the bathroom with Mark. That was why they couldn't help with Yeron."

"My mother out there alone ... my God, her heart!" Alexis cupped her hands against her mouth, her lips trembling. "God knows what the stress did to her blood pressure. I shouldn't have left her alone."

"I examined Matilda," Steve told her. "Her EKG was fine. I suspect she cracked a rib when she fell. She's hurting, but she looks exhausted more than anything. Mark should have helped more."

"He tried." Alexis turned her eyes back toward Yeron. Hoffman called out something to two nurses. One of them wheeled her mother into the hall and parked her besides Alexis. Her mother looked pale and haggard, but everyone had a right to feel exhausted. Alexis's eyes turned toward Yeron again. The other nurse draped a blanket over him. His eyes remained closed. "Two creatures got him. I shot the creatures and Mark with the sedative before they could consume him."

"Yikes!" Steve gave her a sad look. He rested one hand on the handle of her wheelchair. "Alexis, I've got to examine you, too. I'm taking you to another room."

"Oh, no, you're not," Alexis said. "More of those things might show."

"We've got regular soldiers on the premises now, and no one's sighted any more of those visitors. I'm moving you to another floor under an assumed name."

Alexis glanced toward Yeron. He showed no sign of regaining consciousness. "I don't care about the soldiers. I'm not going anywhere until I know Yeron's okay."

"Alexis," Steve said. He looked like a beaten old man. His eyes were red from lack of sleep. "I had an hour-long argument with Becky this morning about why I didn't want her going in to work. Becky knows guns, but our babysitter doesn't. Good thing she stayed home. A couple of those things broke into our home. Plus we lost power, along with everyone else." He gave Alexis a pleading look. "You're not going to give me a hard time, are you?"

"I can't leave Yeron alone." Alexis's voice cracked with unshed tears. "He taught me how to fight, and that's why my mother and I are alive. I'll take that examination, but let's do it around Yeron. Okay?"

Her mind whirled with mostly gratitude for his lessons on the plasma gun and some other feeling that she didn't dare describe. She'd lost her sister and her best friend, and she couldn't bear to lose anyone else.

"It's a pisser for any soldier to see his buddy hurt," Shively said. Of course, that was her other feeling. Case closed.

"Let her stay, Doctor Leicht." Her mother laid a gentle hand on her arm. "Yeron gave her a fresh gun so she could shoot the things coming after Cindy and me. He stayed by her side the whole time and may have gotten himself seriously hurt because of this. You can examine her here as you did me."

"I can't." Steve's sigh was the cry of a beaten man, someone who'd seen more horror in his life than what he wanted. "Matilda ... Shively, Alexis takes an experimental drug. We don't know how the exposure to the bacteria will affect her. I need to examine her privately." Steve shifted his gaze toward Alexis. "Don't compare Yeron to Robin or Dee. They had respiratory problems, and neither knew how to protect themselves. Yeron needs a friend like you, but he would not want you to forego medical treatment."

"No, Doctor Phil would tell me to get real." Alexis tried to work up a grin, but couldn't. She took a seat in the proffered chair. "I'll let you take me only because that's what Yeron would want."

"Hoffman," Steve hollered. "I'm taking Alexis to the rehab unit."

"Make sure someone takes blood cultures," Hoffman called after him.

Steve wheeled her into the main elevators and pressed four, the floor for rehab, where people relearn the activities of daily living. Along the halls and in front of the exits and elevators, men in fatigues stood with guns at the ready, eyes intent, and ears listening. The sight of all those soldiers did not ease her trembling.

"What's this about you losing power?" she asked after a pause.

"Everyone did on my block. Our visitors have caused nasty accidents that wrecked telephone poles and transformers, so a lot of people are without electricity tonight."

"No wonder the hospital phones wouldn't work. Hoffman has been great with all this. He's changed."

"I'm glad you've seen his good side. He catches the shit when it hits the fan."

The elevator doors opened, and he wheeled her past a solarium decorated with plants. They went past a gym to the patient rooms. Except for the soldiers manning the exits and a stray officer pacing the halls, no violence marked the floor.

"Why are we going to the rehab floor?" Alexis asked.

"Administration needed rooms and the Rehabilitation Unit had them. You are Jane Doe number twenty-five. Shively, Johnny, Mark, your mother, and Yeron are staying overnight for observation under the Doe name. Cindy will provide what care you need." He wheeled her into a room three times the size of her seventh floor room. "You can stay until you and Shively make other arrangements."

Alexis's lips quivered. The room came with a leather reclining chair, wide bed, and chest of drawers, but she would give anything for a hug from her mother and a home-cooked meal. She thought about the last time she and Johnny had laughed over *Weekly World Reporter*. The feeling about Yeron gnawed at her, but she refused to analyze it. Doing so might necessitate a terrifying reappraisal of her upbringing.

"When will that happen?" she asked between clenched teeth.

"I don't know." Steve's words rumbled forth like a dirge. "I expect the government officers to quarantine this hospital. The police will debrief you and your buddies in the morning."

"I'll give them an earful. What about my mother? What are you doing about her rib?"

"Until I confirm it with an X-ray, nothing but analgesics. All the patient lifting she's done built up her muscles and will splint her chest. Her blood pressure is high, but not enough to cause symptoms. Mostly, she's exhausted from forcing her sixty-year-old body to do things it's never done. She'll feel better after a good night's sleep.

"Try to get some rest. We haven't heard the last from the renegades. Yeron and Shively will give you more detailed training."

"Steve, we don't know if Yeron is all right."

"His vital signs are stable," Steve assured her. "Joe didn't find anything out of the ordinary with his blood tests. I think if we're patient, he'll come around on his own."

"I don't do patience well." Alexis regarded him with mournful eyes. "The last few months didn't give me that luxury."

"The last months have been difficult," Steve allowed, "but you made new friends, acquired new skills, and a remission. Can you try optimism? Yeron comes from hardy stock."

"Maybe." Alexis tried for a smile. "Yeron must be hardy. He never sleeps."

"Oh, he does. He gets four hours a night." Steve gave Alexis a somber look. "By the way, I heard you and Shively found a syringe."

Alexis shrugged. "Yeron uses those syringes for my treatment because he doesn't trust the hospital brand. I never saw this chemical, whatever it is. Did anyone send it to the lab?"

"They did, and the lab couldn't come up with answers. Joe thinks that syringe contains something poisonous. I guess we'll find out soon. Whatever goes down with Yeron, Alexis, you'll have to stay strong. I'm not comfortable with Mark being on your team."

Neither am I, Alexis longed to tell him, *but right now I'm too tired for any history lessons on Mark or psychoanalysis of my feelings for Yeron.*

"Neither am I." She shrugged. "Shively has his reasons for involving him."

"Mark didn't lift a finger to help you or Shively. Shively, Tyrone, and Johnny will look out for you, and Yeron made it clear he'll stand by you. Stay close to those fellows, and you'll get through this alive."

Alexis nodded, trying to brush back the fresh tears coming to her eyes. The mention of Yeron's name was an arrow through her heart. "You expect more trouble, right? How many areas got hit?"

"A lot." Steve jammed his thumb against his palm each time he roll-called the hits. "Johnnie's floor received visitors. The worst casualties happened in the cafeteria, where people had to run around the tables to get to an exit. Becky shot up a few visitors tonight. The rest went to four other homes in the area. The police hauled out a lot of body bags, especially from the stores across the street."

"The boys and I will find the people behind this." Alexis rubbed her arms, shivering. "I want this all to be over."

"I hope you find the compound that sent these things came. Whoever sent them might make a return visit. If they do, we're in for a nasty summer."

Knocking sounded at the door. "I'm here to take Alexis's vital signs," Cindy said.

"Good. While you're at it, get blood cultures." Steve straightened up and touched Alexis's shoulder. "Be careful."

Chapter Twenty-Nine: Yeron Regains Consciousness

Jackson Hospital's Fourth Floor, May 28, 12:00 a.m.

Yeron woke up in a patient room with a start. Someone had wrapped a blood pressure cuff around his chest and hooked a telemetry monitor to his rib cage. Nasal prongs fed him oxygen and a pulse oximeter probe taped below his sternum gave out a normal oxygen reading. He felt all right, except for a headache and an ache in his left shoulder. Why was he in bed?

With a nudge of his mind, he turned on the light, or at least he tried. Darkness continued to surround him. He pressed the "light" button on his call bell and checked his limbs for bruises. There was one the size of a frying pan on his left upper arm. Otherwise, no cuts or injuries marred his pale skin. He flexed his limbs. No trouble there. No chest pain or shortness of breath either, but something caused him to lose his push, at least temporarily. Why was he wearing a hospital gown? Those flimsy gowns made him feel naked. He never understood why humans insisted on wearing them. His father used to give his patients thick tunics with long sleeves to preserve their dignity.

"I should be at work in my laboratory." That concluded, he ripped away the nasal prongs and oximeter probe. The cardiac leads and blood pressure cuff went next. He got to his feet, took two steps, then stumbled. A wave of dizziness washed over him. His legs wobbled like cooked vegetables. He placed one hand against the wall and steadied himself. The room reeled around him, and he sank into a chair.

How did he get up here? Just minutes ago, he was in Alex-

240

is's room, scolding Ms. Grese for disturbing her—or was it hours? Whenever it happened, Ms. Grese yelled loud enough for the entire floor to hear. It must have been mortifying for Alexis and the people who overheard it. He remembered shouting at Ms. Grese, and then ...what?

Steve burst into his room, his eyes wide with alarm, with Hoffman at his side. "Yeron," he shouted. "Why did you pull your leads off? You gave us a scare."

"I am not sick," Yeron said. "I want to report Ms. Grese for breaching HIPAA. Why am I here?"

"You've been unconscious for several hours," Hoffman told him. "Steve, let's get him back to bed."

"I am not going back to any bed. Are you not listening? Ms. Grese violated Alexis's privacy. The poor girl lost her job."

"That's right, she did." Steve nodded with agreement. "What happened after your argument with Ms. Grese?"

"I ordered her to leave the room." Yeron shook his head. Either these men were crazy, or he was. "I shall not allow Ms. Grese to upset my patients. I was going to report her, but you seem determined to confine me to bed."

"Ms. Grese isn't your problem anymore." Hoffman wiped his bloodshot eyes. His pallid face and circles around the eyes spoke of sheer exhaustion.

Joe could rest if he needed to, but Yeron had work to do. "Ms. Grese is the biggest problem. If you need blood samples, get them, and let me get on with my work."

"Assuming we have a business," Hoffman said.

"Joe, he doesn't remember." Steve wiped the sweat from his forehead. "Yeron, all hell broke loose after your debate with Ms. Grese."

"Hold on a minute." Hoffman cast Steve a withering look. "Can you tell me where you are, Yeron? At a restaurant? At the movies?"

"Spare me." Yeron gave a dismissive wave of his hand. "My name is Yeron, and I was born in the Kryszka compound underneath Philadelphia. Obama is your president. Some of the renegade soldiers survived the 2007 explosion, and they found a way to alter the human body. These specimens, or zombies if you will, terrorized the mall shoppers across the street. I stayed with our patients while you examined the casualties in the emergency room. I started Alexis on a clinical trial with 248AR. Are you satisfied?"

"No." Hoffman glanced toward the door. "You didn't say what happened after Grese's visit."

"We expected the zombies to invade the hospital," Steve reminded him. "Five of them broke into Emergency and more through the cafeteria and orthopedic floor. Johnny and Tyrone did damage control, but fifty or more tore through our research floor. They broke in through the back elevator. According to one autopsy, these bodies are live people with severe brain dysfunction. They came in on buses, and the drivers—the rogue soldiers—tried to kidnap you. Shively overpowered the soldiers. He and Alexis found you in a clothes bin by the showers."

Yeron shook his head, puzzled. "I do not remember any of it."

Hoffman shrugged. "As I said, you've been unconscious. I thought someone drugged you, but your blood work doesn't show any traces of poison."

"Not all Kryszka chemicals show on a blood test."

"So you think someone drugged you." Reaching through his lab coat, Hoffman retrieved a plastic bag containing a syringe half filled with brownish fluid. "Ever see anything like this?"

Yeron looked at the syringe, and then the spinning hit him again. He never used any such chemical, not even when he lived with his father. Then it came to him. His father had found a syringe like it among Woehar's belongings. He tested it on rats.

"Yes. We call it vischlausk. It incited my father's laboratory animals to attack." He shivered from the chills cresting his shoulders. "Eigil and his soldiers ingested the solution before they went hunting. Vischlausk induces a craving for fresh blood and makes the Kryszka's saliva poisonous."

He rubbed his arms. "Did someone inject me?"

"No one injected you," Steve assured him. "The lab technician attempted an analysis, but he could not figure out what it was. We found the remains of Alexis's balloons tangled around a trooper's legs. The heat from the shooting must have caused them to break, and the helium poisoned him. Good thing. That renegade was going to inoculate you."

Yeron let out a chuckle. "How ironic. The balloons I hated so much saved me." He laughed again. "What happened to the officers guarding our floor?"

"Those Rent-a-Cops ran." Anger crept into Hoffman's voice.

"They ran?" Yeron echoed feebly. He could not imagine anything like that happening in his compound. "What about the nurses?"

"Cindy's shook up, and Matilda's exhausted but otherwise okay," Steve said. "Shively's talking with the SERT tactical team. Those creatures got Mark, but Alexis fried them. Right now, he's out cold because she sedated him with her plasma gun. Alexis sustained some bruises, but she's all right. She drove us both crazy asking about you. She's afraid you're going to die like her sister and friend." He grinned. "She has a thing for you."

At that, Hoffman let out a groan.

"She was cool," Steve went on, ignoring Hoffman. "She hauled you out of that cart with her psychokinesis. If you think I'm joking, you can watch it on tape." Reaching into his pocket, he handed Yeron three crumpled papers. "I found these in her wastebasket. She was drawing pictures of you. You should ask her out."

Another groan from Hoffman, louder this time. "That's enough."

Yeron glanced through the drawings. Crude, but unmistakably him. How did she manage to pull him from the box? He had never expected her to go through so much trouble to help him. "She is truly my Steel Rose. Where is she?"

"Two rooms to your left, down the hall." Steve laughed. "Let her sleep. She used up energy she didn't have tonight. She and her mother are lucky you and Shively covered them."

"Cindy told me about the rescue," Hoffman said. "Make sure Shively and Alexis get anything they need. Those two were brilliant. I'm not sure about Mark."

Steve grimaced and shrugged. "He shot the zombies coming near his room."

"What about my other patients!" Yeron shouted as a horrible understanding dawned. "What about Ms. Grese? Did they get out alive?"

"Ms. Grese became dinner." Steve's brown eyes shifted between Yeron and Hoffman. "I hope her autopsy shows a natural cause of death. On camera, it looks like you and Alexis shoved her at the monsters. Shit happens, but Administration can get nasty."

"Administration can go to hell." Hoffman frowned. "I'll make sure the autopsy shows something to bypass questions ... if there's enough of her left."

A sick feeling crept into Yeron's stomach. "You have not answered my question about those patients."

Steve sighed and looked at Doctor Hoffman. Hoffman looked back and said nothing. "Their passing happened quickly. I'm sorry."

"Those people trusted me to cure them. What should I tell their families?"

"Nothing," Steve said. "This wasn't your fault."

"What about Becky and Chloe?"

"Becky's dealing with a power outage, like most of the people on our street. She disposed of two of those things when they broke into our home. Chloe slept through the whole thing."

"I was hoping to send Alexis, her companions, and you to a government safe house." Hoffman took a long, pained breath. "There is too much red tape. Shively informed me that his street buddies set up a cabin in an area not far from Easton. Do you know anything about that, Yeron?"

Yeron nodded. "Alexis and I will need all the plasma guns we collected from the old compound."

Hoffman gave him a solemn nod. "Talk to Shively. I suspect he's worked out that detail with his buddies. Get me the address so that I can send you Alexis's medicines and other supplies. For now, though, don't dare leave that bed until the sedative or whatever that soldier shot you with wears off. The SERT team has questions for everyone."

"I will stay," Yeron humored Hoffman. "Please let me know if anything changes with Alexis or Shively."

Steve and Hoffman left, whispering among themselves. Their wide, haunted eyes spoke of devastation greater than his. Casualties aside, they faced issues of livelihoods, lawsuits, medical licenses, and the likelihood of Jackson Hospital suspending operations. When their footsteps faded out of earshot, he sat on the edge of his bed and dangled his legs over the side. Someone—a patient perhaps—had hooked a cane over his closet doorknob. He got up, slipped on a robe, and reached for the cane. If he went slow, used the cane and held onto the wall railing, he could walk without swaying, despite the buzzing in his head. Moving one foot before the other, he worked his way toward Alexis's room.

Low-pitched groaning straightened him to attention.

"Alexis!" Yeron tapped her door. "May I come in?"

The moaning stopped. Dragging footsteps followed. Yeron cracked the door. The light was on. Clad in a hospital gown, Alexis elbowed her way along the wall toward a reclining chair.

"Please do. I feel like I got hit by a truck. I've got bruises on my shoulders, but the rest ..." She looked down at her feet, then jerked her head in his direction. "Yeron! I thought you were ... never mind. Are you all right?"

With that, she lurched toward him, hands flailing, and folded him into a tight hug. The impact caused Yeron's knees to buckle, and the two of them tumbled to the floor in a tangle of arms and legs. His cane clattered by the chair.

"Geez, that went well." She giggled. "That sedative Hoffman gave me is making me act weird. Are you hurt?"

"Not at all. I feel strange myself from whatever the renegades used to quiet me." He smiled. "You look exhausted. Let me help you back to bed."

Yeron sat up. He tried using his push again, this time on Alexis. She did not budge. Most Kryszka sedatives rendered the push useless for hours at a time. He had seen it at the compound. In her twisted position, Alexis looked uncomfortable. She was not moving anywhere unless he resorted to prosaic methods such as physical lifting.

He struggled to his feet. So far, no problems. Alexis made it to her knees without assistance. He grabbed her by the armpits and hauled her the rest of the way upright. "Guide right," he said.

They moved in slow steps to the bed. Yeron concentrated on holding her steady. He forgot about the reclining chair. Big mistake. His foot snagged against the leg, and he stumbled. Alexis's left leg wobbled. Another wave of dizziness shot through him, causing him to pitch and yaw. Several steps further, he plopped across the bed, with Alexis sprawling beside him.

"We made it," Alexis said, laughing again. "Obviously, no one taught you how to transfer patients. You should have used your mind-over-matter."

"Yes, I should have, but apparently whatever my assailants used on me defused my power temporarily." He pushed himself upright, gauging the chair's distance from the bed. The sedative did not allow clear thought, but he estimated six or seven steps to the chair. Too far to get there safely. The cane was out of reach. "Where is your call bell?"

"Under here." Alexis sat up and patted her pillow. "Steve or Joe probably saw us fall on the monitors. They'll come and help us. Um, maybe not. They've got bigger problems, like the SERT officers breathing down their necks."

"Their problems are complicated, Alexis. Nothing can replace the people who died tonight. Steve told me about the patients on my cancer protocol."

"I know. I saw it happen." Marked sadness swept across her face. "There were so many of those things, and they were hungry. Shively covered my back after you got kidnapped." Her eyes glistened with tears when she described her difficulty finding his pulse. "Steve said they want to move us as soon as possible because of the breach of security. What security? Hoffman said the officers who were supposed watch our floor put their tail between their legs and ran."

"They did, and worse, Mark left you, Shively, and your mother of all people to do most of the fighting. Mark is turning into a major liability."

"Shively insisted on bringing him on board."

"I know." Yeron lowered his voice. "I do not remember the fighting. Joe and Steve said you lifted me from the bin and that you and Shively shot a renegade who was after me. You did well,

Steel Rose."

"Shively did the shooting. I distracted the renegade with my mind trick. Getting you out of that bin was the worst—170 pounds is a lot to pull, even with mind power. I never did thank you for saving my life, so it was the least I could do."

Yeron smiled. The deep set of her eyes, her rose perfume, and her fine features teased at the corners of his mind. She wore nothing under her flimsy gown, and the threadbare cotton outlined her curvy hips and legs. Heat was building in his groin, followed by the beginnings of an erection. Under better circumstances, he would ask her out, and more. "I weigh 200, and I stand six feet five. You would be surprised at what you can do under duress. Becky's psychokinetic powers enabled her to throw a man who weighed over two hundred-fifty pounds. You thanked me by staying with me until the doctors came. I wish I could remember the details."

"Your memory will return when you're ready to accept it."

"Is that right? Where did you get your degree in psychiatry?" A smile played on Yeron's lips. He wanted an evening with her without a doubt but under happier circumstances.

"I've heard it on the talk shows. When something awful happens, your mind blocks it to protect you from the pain. I know because I did that after Mark raped me. Maybe Stan the Man can help you remember."

"Stan cannot help me because the chemical my assailant used caused the amnesia. He cannot bring back the dead either."

"I realize that." Alexis crooked her elbow against the mattress and looked into his eyes. "You've tried so hard to gain people's trust, and this massacre shit-canned any progress you made. Will you be allowed to practice here?"

"Not for a while. We will have to use Shively's cabin, but Joe assured me he would get us any medical supplies we need."

"Shively told me about the cabin, but he never said anything about supplies." Her eyes brightened. "Where is he? What about my mother and Johnny?"

"They are sleeping somewhere down the hall. You can talk to them in the morning."

"You saved my life and my mother's." The apprehension on

her face eased, and she gazed at Yeron with admiration. "Those things came after me first. You told me to follow your lead, and we mowed them down. We owe you our lives."

"You are alive because you listened to me." Yeron saw something else in her eyes besides admiration. Her floral scent exuding from thick brown curls toyed with his nostrils. He imagined himself running his fingers through her hair.

"I wish we could talk all night, but we need some sleep. One of us should stay in bed while the other sleeps in the chair. You take the bed. I'll sleep in the chair."

He shook his head and half-smiled. "That is not safe. You could fall and hurt yourself. You should have stayed in bed."

"Oh yeah? I suppose Hoffman told you to stay in bed. You didn't, and you broke one of his famous commandments in the process." She pointed one index finger at him and rubbed her other index finger across it, and giggled. "Shame on you. Go straight to Hoffman's shit list. Do not pass go, do not stop at any hotels." Her giggles built in crescendo to bellows of laughter. "I can't kick you out of bed after what those soldiers did to you. Besides, I sleep better sitting up."

Yeron was having too much fun to let her go yet. "How will you get to the chair? We agreed walking in your current condition was not safe."

"Where did you get this 'we' stuff?" Another gust of laughter. "It's easy. I'll push myself to my feet, then hop on my good leg to the chair." With that, Alexis grabbed Yeron's shoulders and pushed upward, her hair brushing his cheek.

Too much. The smell of her perfume, the soft curls caressing his face, the curves of her body were too much. Her gown rode up her back, exposing her nakedness below her hips. He pulled her down and onto his lap, Alexis facing him. Why plan an outing when he could enjoy her here? Hands cradling her shoulders, he folded her into his arms and kissed her. It was a slow, lingering kiss. Alexis responded by leaning into him and kissing back, buttocks exposed, with her arms curled around his shoulders.

Who am I, her intent eyes asked him. *Who are you? What are we together?*

Then she pulled away, her mouth a widened circle of surprise, her hands yanking down her gown. "Oh, my God! What are we doing?"

"We kissed." Yeron gave her a lingering smile.

"I don't believe I did that."

"I do." This was turning comical, and he enjoyed a welcome relief from a horrible night. "Steve showed me the pictures you drew of me. They need a lot of work."

"That was the first time ... look, I was frightened, and I needed something to distract me."

Yeron gave her a wide smile. "I distract you?"

"Yes ... I mean, no, I mean ... dammit, we shouldn't have this conversation!" Her voice wavered, and her cheeks flamed red. "Look, we're both saying and doing inappropriate things because of the mind-altering drugs running through our systems."

"Inappropriate, are we?" Yeron laughed, and he got to wondering when he had last felt any joy. "Perhaps we are speaking the truth. Most sedatives facilitate honesty."

"I..." Alexis shook her head as if struggling to find the words.

"You realized you had feelings for me when you found me unconscious."

"As a friend, yes."

"Steve believes it is stronger than friendship and I agree." He laid his hands on her shoulders. "Whatever your feelings are, we can take this slow. I would never force you to do anything you do not want."

"But I do want ... never mind, I give up. God help me." Alexis stared at him, lips trembling, then nodded. "After Mark, I avoided men. I thought I could never love again ... and yet I have strong feelings for you. What am I supposed to do? No one ever told me how ... how..."

"How people like me express love?" Yeron stroked her thick chestnut ringlets. "It would not be wise for us to tongue-kiss. Other than that..." He lifted her off his lap and eased her into bed, and then climbed in beside her. It was a cozy fit. He cupped his hands over her breasts.

"We shouldn't," Alexis protested, but her eyes were naked with raw emotion. Her nipples stood hard and erect against his fingers. After snapping out the light, he pulled her close for a more intense kiss.

Alexis leaned in for his kiss and wrapped her arms around him. He took one hand and cupped it over his erect penis. Probing southward, he felt sticky wetness between her legs. Her gown slid off and moments later, his followed. Keeping his hands away from her bruised shoulders, he guided her legs so that she straddled him. White heat blazed like fire from her loins. Her embarrassment was gone, leaving behind raw desire. He moved with her with a gentle rocking motion.

She went into orgasm at once, moaning and splaying her hands across his shoulders. The two of them rocked together with long, slow strokes, rider and ridden. Her thick curls tossed with each movement. He inhaled her floral scent, savored the feel of her smooth skin. Sliding inside her was like sinking into a romantic dream.

Moments later, she began to jerk her hips harder and faster and cried out as she climaxed again. He exploded inside her and groaned with pleasure.

She rolled over to his right side and gazed at him with rapt eyes. "I'm so glad you're coming with me."

"I would never let you go alone." Yeron traced his finger along her cheeks. No signs of terror or repulsion in her eyes, only genuine passion. "I may have forgotten tonight's invasion, but not the way I feel about you."

"I want to see where we go with this, but I can't let you be my doctor anymore. I'll work with Doctor Hoffman. Underneath his bluster, he's got a good heart." Alexis's smile was visible in the gloom; her voice radiated cheer. "You can police him and make sure he's treating me right. Maybe you can write your Commandments."

At that, Yeron had to laugh. "I might do that. I wish I could keep you safe and give you a normal life."

"I think I can keep myself safe. Normal is just a setting on your dryer. I don't want normal, Yeron. I want happiness."

"I can do happiness." Yeron pulled her close again. Alexis turned on her left side and draped her right leg over his thigh. "I am not going anywhere, Steel Rose."

There was no answer. Alexis nestled against his chest, asleep. Yeron slid his right arm around her while, with his left hand, he felt her pulse. It was rapid but steady and strong, and this was good because he expected more trouble from the renegades and their monstrous creations. He did not discover love only to have the renegades snatch it from him. In the morning, he would speak with Hoffman about intensive exercises to improve her endurance for running. Perhaps weight training. Whatever it took to keep her alive. If that meant him giving up his life to protect her, he would leave this world a happy man.

* * * *

Hideous memories rose unbidden before Yeron. He was scolding Ms. Grese for disturbing Alexis. The scuffing of shoes, groaning, and rustling clothes announced the break-in of the vischlausk-poisoned beings. These emaciated creatures smelled like rotting meat. Cobwebs of bone peeked through tears in their desiccated flesh. Their red, cratered sores wept green pus and a coppery odor. They were coming at Alexis when his plasma gun blasted them. Alexis's movements were slow, but her shots fired true. Shively disintegrated the ones coming to their left with a machine gun.

Mark remained in his corner, shooting the invaders approaching him. He made no move to help Alexis or anyone else. Sore-crusted, skeletal hands descended on Alexis's shoulders. The creature was about to tear into her. Instead, she thrust it against the wall with her mind. Her ammunition was low. Yeron handed her another gun, and then the blue rays engulfed him. He reached out toward her, but blackness swallowed him. He was falling, falling...

Chapter Thirty: Arguments in Alexis's Room

Booming voices from outside jarred Alexis awake. She shifted in Yeron's arms and snuggled against his chest. If she ignored the voices, they'd go away. Then she and Yeron could continue from where they left off last night. If she had her way, she and Yeron would fly to an island where the dead stayed dead, and people minded their own business. She fell into a light doze, capturing the remnants of a romantic dream.

It didn't last. Mark burst into the room, screaming, followed by Tyrone and Johnny. All of them had on dungarees and bathrobes.

"What's this?" Mark gave a high-pitched bellow, his face livid. "You call yourself a doctor? What are you two doing, you stinking lowlifes?"

Alexis struggled to a sitting position, wrapping a sheet around her, her eyes heavy with sleep. "Get lost, Meathead. Yeron and I have had enough of your crap."

"Look at what you did to me!" Mark thrust out his forearms in front of her, showing two red streaks. "You shot me with your damned plasma gun."

"Awww!" Johnny nudged Tyrone and the two of them, in unison, continued. "One, two, three: aw-w-w!"

Alexis sighed. The last thing she needed was shit from Mark and for the others to goad him. Mark's narrowed eyes held a mean look, the kind she'd seen with the baseball bat and the sofa. No one understood Mark's capability for violence except Yeron.

Learn from it and leave it in the past, a voice whispered

from her subconscious.

"It's not funny." Mark shook his fist. "What kind of idiots are you?"

"Just plain old idiots, Markipoo." Johnny's voice dripped with sarcasm.

"It's okay, Johnny," Alexis said, giggling. "He can't help that he's a meathead."

Movement rustled behind her. Yeron sat up and wrapped a sheet around his shoulders. He cradled his arm around her. "Alexis," he whispered, "do not provoke him."

"He can't hurt me." She sniffed. "I'll throw him across the room like I did those creatures yesterday."

"I'm real terrified." A crooked smile spread across Mark's face, but the indignation remained in his eyes. "Here's a news flash. I saw you push Ms. Grese at those monsters. Yeron, you had no business giving that incompetent a gun. Doctors do not have steamy sex with their patients."

Yeron hugged Alexis against him, eyes on Mark. "Are you finished?"

"Nope. I'm reporting both of you to the police and your head administrator."

"You bastard!" Alexis's lips tightened. "Put an egg in your shoe and beat it."

"Oh no," Mark said in a sing-song voice. "I'm not going anywhere."

"Obviously, you know nothing about plasma guns, so allow me to explain." Yeron's body trembled as he spoke. Alexis reached for his hand. "Two creatures were about to consume you. Alexis could not destroy them without hurting you, so she sprayed a chemical which sedated all of you. It did not harm you and allowed her to pull you free. It was the only way she could save you. Ms. Grese could not run because she wore high heels."

"You'd say anything to cover for Alexis because you're after her like a dog in heat."

Dog in heat ... like Mark was when he jerked off into his diaper. At that, Alexis let out a bray of laughter. "It's none of your business," she managed between snorts. "You took ten years of my life away, diaper boy."

That drew peals of mirth from the others, including Yeron.

"What did you call me?" Mark raised his fist, advancing toward her.

The laughter stopped. Before Alexis could work up her mind power, Tyrone yanked him away from the bed. "Hey, man, you don't want to do this," he warned Mark.

Mark shook himself free and glared at Alexis. "Come on, what did you call me?"

"Diaper boy." Alexis looked him in the eye without flinching.

"You'd better watch what you call me." Mark spoke with false bravado, but his eyes danced in their sockets. He was a childish version of Adolph Hitler. Something made him miserable, and he loved to share his wealth. If he wasn't so nasty, she'd feel sorry for him.

"Mister Adams, make your report." Yeron loosened his arm and turned toward Mark. "I will tell the police you tried to blackmail Hoffman into withholding Alexis's medicine. Your laws call it 'extortion.' Shively, Steve, and Joe heard the conversation. Perhaps JCAHO shall inspect your hospital, too. You insist on your laws, so let us do this the proper way."

Mark's face turned purple. He looked ready to explode. Tears trickled down his cheeks. "You son of a bitch!" His voice cracked. "You've got nothing on me."

More voices outside, followed by pounding on the door. Shively barged in, clad in a plaid bathrobe, along with Alexis's mother and Cindy. "Okay, everyone," he commanded in his mob-boss voice. "Let's take this down from a level ten to a level two."

"Mark started it," Alexis said. "He's got his diaper in a twist."

That brought titters from Johnny and Tyrone.

"Mark wants to report us to Administration," Yeron told him.

"Wha-a-at?" Shively shook his head, massaging his left arm, the same one where he'd gotten bit. "Mark, what's wrong with you?"

"Everyone insists on sticking up for Alexis, that's what." Mark gave a disgusted sigh. "That pea brain has no business handling guns."

"You'd better shut up about my daughter." Her mother's eyes flashed with indignation. "You and I are alive because of her."

"Mom, thanks." Alexis's heart burst with gratitude at seeing her mother up and walking. She looked pale, but steady. "I couldn't have done it without Shively and Yeron."

"I don't care who did what." Shively glared at everyone, still rubbing his arm. "If we keep up this yelling, everyone will wind up in body bags."

"Shively, I'm sorry." Alexis's eyes settled on Shively. "What happened to you?"

"I pulled a muscle. Shit happens." Shively shrugged. "Pretty soon, we're heading out to the cabin. We've got no power out there, so some of my men are moving generators there. You'd all better quit whining and prepare for more trouble."

Alexis slid sideways, laid her hands on Yeron's shoulder and stood. Her left leg wobbled. "My brace is shot, so I need a new one. I'm not complaining; I'm stating a fact."

Her leg buckled. If she tilted any further, she'd fall. Yeron jackknifed to his feet so quickly that his sheet slipped, exposing his shoulders. Alexis grabbed his elbow and leaned on him as he walked her to a chair.

"Joe will get you another brace, honey," he whispered. "In time, you will not need one."

"From your mouth to God's ears."

"Look at them, the lovebirds," Mark's voice oozed contempt. "In case you're wondering, Matilda, your precious daughter and Yeron slept together like guinea pigs."

"Mark!" Alexis swung on him, her face reddening.

Yeron lowered his eyes, trying to hide a smile.

"Alexis!" Her mother sent her a disbelieving look. She gasped. "My God, both of you are wearing sheets. How could you?"

Alexis drew in a deep breath. She had every intention of telling her mother about Yeron, but not now ... not in front of an audience and not with her and Yeron half-naked. Her face flushed. "Mom, I'm sorry you're finding out this way..."

"You're sorry because I found out?"

"Well ... yeah." Alexis tried for her therapist's voice, the kind she used on frightened, sickly patients. "I wanted to tell you privately, but privacy doesn't seem to be an option. Yeron and I worked together several months, and ... things happened. In all the ugliness that went down, I found something beautiful. I want to see where this takes us."

"Oh, my God!" Matilda wrung her hands and paced.

"Don't worry, Momsy." Johnny grinned. "Yeron's got her back."

"It's not that simple." Tears trickled from her mother's terrified eyes. "He comes from a different world, and he's her doctor. Doctors don't sleep with their patients, and this could cost him his position here."

"Matilda, Yeron's the least of our problems," Cindy spoke up. "Especially with those monsters chasing people."

"It will catch up with him down the road," Alexis's mother said in a sour voice.

"Mom, chill." Alexis kept trying for a gentle approach. "Yeron's not my doctor anymore. I fired him before we got intimate."

"Liar, liar, pants on fire!" Mark smacked his fist against the palm of the opposite hand with a rhythmic sound. "Hanging on a telephone..."

"Mark, stop it." Alexis's mother clasped her hands, her voice weepy. "I don't want everyone to find out about this."

"That's too bad." Mark kept smacking his fist, his smirk tucked in place. "The hell with all of you. I'm heading downstairs to Administration."

"No one's going anywhere." Hoffman's voice boomed from the doorway. His laboratory coat and the stethoscope dangling around his neck contrasted with the plasma gun poking from under his belt. "Ms. Grese suffered a heart attack. Her blood ... what we were able to test ... showed elevated cardiac enzymes. Furthermore, Jackson Hospital has no policies on proper decorum during a massacre."

"There, Meathead, you see?" Alexis smiled. "Mom, don't listen to Mark. Yeron supplied me with fresh ammunition when those creatures came after us."

"I saw that." Matilda kept wringing her hands. "I don't

know what to think."

"Just a minute, folks." Hoffman stepped up to Alexis and performed a cursory examination. "You're spiking a temperature. You should have stayed in bed. I'm not letting anyone out of here without squeaky clean blood tests."

"We're not going anywhere, Doctor Hoffman." Alexis weighed Hoffman as a potential ally. Stern demeanor notwithstanding, he came through when people were in trouble. "Yeron and I feel it's best if you became my primary doctor."

"Is that right?" Hoffman shifted his gaze between her and Yeron. "Who's going to manage your psychokinesis therapy and 248AR treatments? I can't and neither can Steve. Yeron knows those specialties best."

Shit! Her mother blanched several shades paler. Perhaps pain from the cracked rib caused it. More likely, she couldn't take finding her daughter in bed with Doctor Yeron.

"Joe, I can handle her psychokinesis and 248AR." Yeron shrugged. "Can you order her a new leg brace?"

"Leg brace?" Hoffman arched his brows. "I could, but that's not going to solve your problems. From outside, it sounded like everyone wanted to kill each other."

"We went through hell," Cindy said in a shaky voice. "Mark can't take it."

"Tell me something I don't know." Hoffman swept everyone with a censuring glare. "We've got fifteen dead, a bunch of expensive equipment demolished, the hospital on lock-down and a research protocol shot to hell. The Department of Public Health has placed us under quarantine because those creatures happened to be live humans. Reporting this person or that person will only muddy the waters."

"Don't worry, Doc." Shively grinned. "Who we see here, what we hear here, when we leave here, leave it stay here."

"Right." Hoffman's frown and narrowed eyes warned that he was not impressed. "Mark, you especially should keep quiet. Otherwise, you run the risk of your colleagues finding out about your habits."

Mark's jabbed his fists into his robe pockets. His face blanched. "But ..."

"Mark." Shively yanked him by the arm toward the door. "Let's go to my room. We have to talk."

Alexis breathed a sigh of relief when the door closed behind them. "Thank you, Doctor."

Hoffman's glare settled on Yeron and then Alexis. "The next time you two have a tryst, go to a hotel." He turned on his heel and banged the door behind him.

"Those were live people I killed?" Matilda's mouth became an open 'O' of horror. She waved her quivering hand toward the bed.

"None of this is right." With that, she stormed out, giving the door another slam.

"Your mom's going to need time," Cindy said, edging toward the door. "She kept waking up last night with nightmares. I'd better see if she's okay."

"That did not go well." The sadness returned to Yeron's eyes, big black waves of it. "I am on your mother's shit list."

"She's mad because I'm still your patient." Alexis laid her hand over his. "Any doctor can lose his license for dating a patient, and she's more worried about that than she is about your DNA. She hates it when I call any doctor by his first name."

"I can see that," Yeron said, his voice saddening. "I will never understand people."

"Sometimes I can't understand people either. I think my mother will come around, but not Mark. Maybe you can use your special treatment on him as you did with me."

"For the treatment to work, Mark has to consent to the injection. He will never do that."

"That's true." Alexis stood up again and shambled toward Yeron. "However anyone feels, it's my life, and I want to spend it with you."

"Steel Rose..." Yeron folded her into his arms. "Whatever happens, I will never let you go through anything alone. I cannot promise you peace, but I can give you love."

He kissed her, a slow long lingering kiss. Alexis kissed him back, contemplating the romantic sunsets to come.

Chapter Thirty-One: Laurel's Awakening

Woehar's Underground Laboratory, May 28, 9:00 p.m.

The burning came and went, depending on the painkillers flowing through Laurel's bloodstream. She lay on her air mattress, eyes on the domed ceiling lights, and contemplated her mother's civil moments, like the time she brought Laurel and her sisters to the shore. While her sisters made sand castles, Laurel gazed at the piling in the ocean. During the day, while they feasted on hot dogs and soda, the waves covered the top of the piling. After sunset, after her mother bagged the leftovers and the moon cast its first slivers upon the sand, the tide went out, and the piling stood above the waves, its face like a gargoyle with jagged teeth.

The burning was the piling, and the tide was the painkillers. Right now, the tide was way out and agony, like rusty nails, twisted through her hands and feet. Long stretches without painkillers meant Woehar was having a bad day. Worse, the huge pink ceiling light turned into a skeletal face with blood red grin, ruby eyes and a crooked nose. Abaddon's features. Ghost voices whispered from the light, but Abaddon's was the loudest. *Prepare for some bloodletting,* he ordered.

Footsteps from the hall invaded her observations. Laurel could tell it was Woehar by the sound of her cleats. Light, clicking steps meant a good mood. Loud, clonking steps warned trouble was coming. Woehar was stomping to the door.

The panel slid open, revealing her gloomy face. Her red eyes smoked with fury.

"Whatever's wrong, I told you everything I know," Laurel

plowed ahead.

"Yes ... well, none of it worked." Woehar's eyes blazed. The wrath was there, but no hunger, at least not yet. "I sent over two hundred humanoids to your clinic and surrounding area. They destroyed the stores, part of your clinic—hospital, and killed over thirty people. I did not count the injured. No one who matters died."

"What about Alexis?"

Woehar burst into raucous laughter. In the bright light, her glittering teeth drooled saliva. Drooling meant bloodlust and the brunt of it would come down on Laurel. "Yeron taught her how to use plasma, and she destroyed my specimens. When her legs gave out, she killed from the floor. When she could not shoot, she fought with her push." Woehar sighed. "The plasma gun and push have turned our invalid into a warrior."

"I find that hard to believe." The idea that Alexis could handle Kryszka guns had repercussions Laurel couldn't face. It was like Yeron had given her keys to the White House. "What's the push?"

"It means whatever chemical Yeron administered gave her the ability to move things ... and people with her mind the way Kryszka do. I did not realize this until too late. Mark was not with Alexis during her training, and the microchip only records activity near Mark."

Laurel gulped. This was worse than she expected. "What about the vischlausk ... the stuff that could make your brother violent?"

"I sent three soldiers over to inoculate Yeron. They sedated him, but Alexis and Shively interfered before they could inject the vischlausk. Shively killed my officers and confiscated the vischlausk. Alexis nursed her beloved to consciousness. Yeron, Alexis, and their friends are alive, and their dignitaries have walled them away like prizes."

Black tumors of rage bloomed inside Laurel, making her forget her fear of Woehar. "That bitch gets away with everything."

Woehar smiled. "Not everything. She lost her position with the hospital."

"Yeah, right. I bet people are offering her handouts."

Woehar nodded. "They are, especially my brother. He is so much like our father. Both of them admired the human ... how you say, spirit." The anger returned, but she directed it at her family. "Yeron deserves to die because he betrayed our people when he taught Alexis and her friends our weapons."

"Alexis would never let someone like Yeron near her."

"She has, Laurel, she has. The microchip recorded Mark chastising Yeron and Alexis. He caught them in bed, naked."

"Either Yeron brainwashed Alexis," Laurel said, "or that bitch fell down a well of shit and came up with diamonds. Both of them wrecked our operation."

"Maybe not." Woehar gave her a malignant grin. "Maybe they just think they did."

"They did. You just said Alexis and her buddies destroyed your specimens and officers."

"No, just the ones I sent." Woehar's eyes measured Laurel. "I have more, but I have to think. Be quiet."

Laurel turned her eyes toward the domed light. Abaddon's face nodded and smiled. *That's right, Laurel. Deflect her attention away from you.*

"I understand. You're planning a punishment." Laurel gave Woehar a savage grin. "Like I did with my children. When you're ready, I'll help you get Alexis."

"I can best hurt Alexis through the people she loves. When I get done with her, she will wish she had never been born."

"Good. Then I'll roast her." Sheer ecstasy surged through Laurel at the thought of cooking Alexis over a slow fire. Her wiry build, though wasted around the arms, offered delectable muscle. She rolled her tongue across her lips. "When do we begin?"

"I intend to use Abaddon to my advantage after I turn you. Draekh will give you a final treatment tonight. If it has the desired effect, we shall administer it to all our specimens. By the time Alexis and her companions leave their clinic, my augmented specimens will be ready."

"What do you mean by ...?"

"Be still." Woehar held a finger to her lips. "We have a visitor."

A tall, older woman dressed in glittering navy entered, her robe whispering with each soft footstep. Laurel had to admire Woehar's sensitive Kryszka ears.

The pink light illuminated the visitor's metal-plated tunic. The older Kryszka's eyes seethed with hate directed toward Woehar. She let loose a spate of gibberish. Woehar gave it back, and the shouting went up to a level ten. Laurel cupped her hand over her mouth, fighting hard not to laugh. Woehar had gotten into big trouble.

After the senior Kryszka had her say, she stormed out to the hall. The panel closed, but Woehar continued screaming in her native tongue.

"What's wrong?" Laurel asked.

"Quyeba found my other specimens." Woehar stomped around Laurel's table. "She said I am like Eigil and that I am no longer welcome here. She wishes I was dead."

Laurel gasped. "Did she say that?"

"Are you listening?" Woehar grabbed a bed rail and shook it. "She thinks Yeron is dead, and during her tirade, she said, 'Yeron should be living here. Sometimes the wrong people die.'"

"Oh, shit!" Laurel sat up, rubbing her eyes. A million thoughts swam through her head: How would she get pain medicine? What about Woehar's partner, Drake, or whatever she called him? Underneath it all, the question that had haunted her since her arrival at the compound hammered through her brain—what if Woehar's anger incited her bloodlust, and Laurel wound up on the short end of her food chain?

"I'll take you to my house," she offered.

"Your house?" Woehar's voice came out brusque, her narrowed eyes saying, *bad call, you idiot!* "Your officers use primitive techniques, but they are shrewd. By now, they have searched your car and your house and associated you with me. Surely Alexis suspects and shared her suspicions with these officers."

"Alexis again," Laurel said between her gritted teeth. "That girl should die."

"Destroying her will not be easy." She tilted her head, regarding Laurel. "Do not worry. I anticipated this. I cloned my specimens before sending them above ground."

Laurel gasped. "You what?"

"You heard me. My androids have erected another building adjoining this one—one large enough to support my equipment and specimens."

"Another building?" Laurel looked at Woehar. "Quyeba will be furious."

"Only if she finds out. I shall not allow that to happen. Anyone who enters this laboratory without my knowledge will die." Woehar grinned, showing her bloodstained teeth. "That is why I decided to turn you."

As if on cue, the panel opened again, and another Kryszka, a male, entered. At seven feet tall, he wore a silver metallic gown that flowed to his ankles. His birdshot pupils sent chills through her body. He'd check his first-do-no-harm rule in the nearest receptacle when he got hungry. He walked over to Woehar, gave her a long smooch, then set his eyes on Laurel.

His fingers cradled a hypodermic needle. The doctor turned toward Woehar and asked, "Are you sure about this? Too many drugs can damage the specimen."

He spoke in English, but his thick accent made it sound like, *too many drocks can demmege the specimen.*

He looked at Laurel and smiled. *If you're smart,* his smile said, *you won't ask for details.* It said it loud and clear without any accent.

Laurel backed off on further questions, but she bit back a scream when the doctor plunged the needle into her forearm. Seconds later, the darkness washed over her.

* * * *

"Wake up," Abaddon's voice crooned. "We shall go for a walk."

Laurel's eyes fluttered. She swallowed hard and paid for it with a burning sensation in her throat. She rolled her tongue against her teeth. All of them sharp and pointy. Her pain was gone, and a primal hunger took its place. Fantasies of blood drinking and tearing flesh danced through her mind. She looked at her hands, what remained of her dirt-crusted fingers. Her nails had sharpened into talons.

She hopped to her feet. The sudden movement jarred the stumps on her toes, causing them to burn as if on fire. The name Alexis came to mind, someone who deserved punishment, but she couldn't remember why. Over the last three years, she had been edging out over some mental abyss, walking on a bridge that narrowed with each step. On the day that she lost her job, the bridge thinned out into a tightrope. Sometime during her stay with Woehar, the tightrope snapped, and now a red haze swam around her.

"I'm so hungry I could eat a bear," she said through the red cloud.

Abaddon's distant cackle sounded as if it came through a gauzy blanket. "That does not surprise me. Follow me."

Her gait shambling, Laurel followed a blurry form in the red haze. Paneled doors slid open, and she descended through the haze into a room the size of a football field. She stood before rows of metal tables with human specimens. Their cries echoed distantly, but laced with hunger. Hungry or not, she knew that this visit would end in fun. Her mouth salivated.

The figure nudged her to the foremost table. Tatters of a woman's shirt swam through the reddish mist. One sleeve hiked over the prisoner's elbow, revealing tracks along her forearm. The dirt crusting her hair and forehead made her look old, but the smooth skin around her eyes said she was in her early thirties.

Long ropy strands of saliva drooled from Laurel's mouth at the sight.

Get her, Abaddon's voice whispered. *This is your time to relax. Think of this woman as dinner, and this laboratory as your restaurant.*

Another three steps. The prisoner wheezed high-pitched notes with each intake of air. At an earlier time, before her mutation and descent into madness, Laurel would have recognized her as an asthma patient. *I can't do this,* she thought, one clawed hand clenching at her snarly hair. *This girl needs treatment—maybe Drake, or whatever Woehar called him, might have asthma medicine.*

Asthma medicine? Abaddon's laughter rang in her ears.

You're hungry, Laurel. Feed your bloodlust.

At her approach, the prisoner let out plaintive cries. "Please help me," she begged, sobbing. "I can't breathe."

She coughed. A fine trickle of blood oozed from the left corner of her mouth. Perhaps the woman recognized Laurel as her former caregiver. More likely, she was desperate. Laurel continued worrying her hair, wondering how she could harm a patient. The filmy figure watched her, nodding and smiling.

Stabbing pain knifed through Laurel's head. The pain and the trickle of blood jarred Laurel's primal hunger, and the thirst came on her with a burning force. *That's right,* the ghost voice whispered. *Give in to it. There's no fighting it.*

"Of course," she said, smiling. "I'll be glad to help you."

The woman heaved a sigh of relief. Like most people, she interpreted Laurel's gentle voice as a sign of good intentions. The girls who'd lived with Laurel and knew her best knew that a soft voice meant forthcoming death.

Laurel grabbed the woman's arm as if to lift her off the table. She wrapped her arms around the shoulders and bit into the woman's wrist. The relief on the woman's face turned to terror. She shrieked, but her cries excited Laurel more. After savoring the sweet gush of blood, Laurel moved on to the muscle. As she swallowed each morsel, Abaddon rubbed her back.

"Draekh implanted a mixture of vischlausk and DNA from Kryszka and our animals," he said. *"Woehar and I shall make several clones of you. Then we will see how long Alexis and her people last."*

Laurel nodded and continued feeding. Somewhere above ground, a dog howled.

About the Author

Barbara Custer lives near Philadelphia, Pennsylvania, where she works full time as a respiratory therapist. When she's not working with her patients, she's enjoying a fright flick or working on horror and science fiction tales. Her short stories have appeared in numerous small press magazines. She's published *Night to Dawn* magazine since 2004.

Other books by Barbara include *Twilight Healer* and *City of Brotherly Death*. She's also coauthored *Alien Worlds* and *Starship Invasions* with Tom Johnson. She enjoys bringing her medical background to the printed page, and then blending it with supernatural horror. She maintains a presence on Facebook, Linked-in, Twitter, and The Writers Coffeehouse forum. Look for the photos with the Mylar balloons, and you'll find her.

To contact Barbara, e-mail her at barbara-custer@hotmail.com. Visit her at:

http://www.bloodredshadow.com

http://www.facebook.com/barbara.custer

http://www.linkedin.com/pub/barbaracuster/10/aa9/bba

About the Artists:

Dawné Dominique:

Artist Dawné Dominique is a best-selling, multi-published author and an award winning professional book cover artist. With over sixteen years' experience, she devotes her time between creating cover art for numerous publishers and Indie authors, while trying to write the next paranormal/fantasy bestseller.

Being an author herself, she knows how important cover art is to an author. She has humbly accepted many awards and honorable mentions, but she's quick to attribute her success to the diverse authors she represents. Without them none of those accolades would be possible.

An accomplished oil painter and sketch artist, she has dabbled in all mediums of art.

She loves what she does and every covers is a challenge to exemplify an author's deepest desire to see their words depicted into art.

http://www.dusktildawndesigns.com/

Teresa Tunaley:

Originating from the UK but residing in the Canary Islands for the last 10 years, freelance artist Teresa Tunaley devotes time to her love of art and painting. For more than 30 years she has been doodling with pencils and dabbling with watercolors. More recently she has been painting traditionally in oil and creating large canvasses full of color and life. Sometimes she uses a more modern technique using software such as Photoshop, Corel Draw and Paint Shop Pro to produce her creations for online publications.

During her art career, she has produced countless illustrations, book covers and paintings. Along with published stories and poetry, she can be credited with award winning cover art and illustrations for author stories. Her work can be seen online and in print across the UK, US, Canada and Europe.

In May 2011, she opened a new Exhibition in Puerto del Santiago (Tenerife, Spain) entitled Tutto per la vita (All for the life). She has over 30 works on show and is hoping to be selected to participate in the Capitals annual Art Festival. Should she win, there will be invitations to exhibit her work in a whirlwind trip across Spain and Italy.

Touching and spectacular "has been the inauguration; Tutto Per la vita" Some thirty of their works appeared, giving you a journey to Spain, Africa, America, Japan and Thailandia. The work was intense with feeling, in full color and textures, where figures, landscapes and moments will leave the visitor with a memory of a magical trip."

Jose Francisco Morales

Comisario de la Exposicion (Tenerife)

http://www.artesigloxxi.org

I like to think that I am very versatile in my choice of subject matter - my new surroundings provide the inspiration for me to paint on a daily basis and the fact that others may enjoy my work gives me the confidence to continue.

Website: www.artstopper.com

www.ingramcontent.com/pod-product-compliance
Lightning Source LLC
Chambersburg PA
CBHW021521240626
47154CB00002B/725